"How I love this funny, smart, full of heart novel about the 'I Do' coming before the 'I love you.' Lauren Lipton is one of my new favorite authors!"

—Melissa Senate, author of *See Jane Date* and *Questions to Ask Before Marrying*

"Stylishly written, closely observed, and compulsively readable, MATING RITUALS OF THE NORTH AMERICAN WASP is an absolute treat. It's *The Undomestic Goddess* meets *The Gold Coast* with fantastic results."

—Alison Pace, author of *City Dog*

PRAISE FOR *IT'S ABOUT YOUR HUSBAND*

"Striking a balance between silly and serious, this tale... will resonate with readers everywhere."

—Emily Giffin, *New York Times* bestselling author of *Baby Proof* and *Love the One You're With*

"Wickedly funny, yet deeply poignant, this book marks the debut of a sparkling new voice. Lipton writes with wit, intelligence, and, most of all, heart."

—Carol Goodman, author of *The Lake of Dead Languages* and *The Ghost*

"Light-hearted and full of laughs... a fast-paced read... Lipton is an exciting new fictional voice."

—ArmchairInterviews.com

more...

"A humorous starting-over novel, *It's About Your Husband* is chick lit with a twist... Lipton is a new voice, from whom readers will want more."

—BookLoons.com

"Chock-full of delightful characters... will keep you entertained all the way to the surprise twist at the end... a lively, fun read that only gets better as the story progresses."

—FreshFiction.com

"What makes *It's About Your Husband* such an excellent read is not the plot so much as Lipton's ability to capture the flavor of New York, the foibles of her characters, and the metamorphosis of a delightful heroine... We look forward to what Lauren Lipton has in store for us next."

—BookReporter.com

MATING RITUALS OF THE NORTH AMERICAN WASP

LAUREN LIPTON

NEW YORK BOSTON

5 Spot
Hachette Book Group
237 Park Avenue
New York, NY 10017

Visit our Web site at www.5-spot.com.

5 Spot is an imprint of Grand Central Publishing.
The 5 Spot name and logo are trademarks of Hachette Book Group, Inc.

Printed in the United States of America

First Edition: May 2009
10 9 8 7 6 5 4 3 2 1

Library of Congress Cataloging-in-Publication Data

Lipton, Lauren, 1966-
Mating rituals of the North American WASP / Lauren Lipton.—1st ed.
p. cm.
ISBN 978-0-446-19797-7
1. Mate selection—Fiction. 2. Marriage—Fiction. I. Title.
PS3612.I68M38 2009
813'.6—dc22

2008031353

To my father, Lew Lipton
Who taught me how to catch lightning in a bottle

ACKNOWLEDGMENTS

I am fortunate to have a gracious and serene agent, Laura Langlie, and an incisive editor, Selina McLemore. Thank you to Caryn Karmatz-Rudy, Elly Weisenberg, Miriam Parker, Latoya Smith, Melanie Moss, Tareth Mitch, Sona Vogel, Rick Willett, Claire Brown, and Allene Shimomura at Grand Central Publishing, and to Tooraj Kavoussi of TK Public Relations. Melanie Murray, thank you for believing in this book.

Miriam Komar and Sarah Sheppard spent a year helping me shape my story and characters and pushing me to do better. I am indebted to them and to Carol Goodman, an exceptional teacher and writer. I'm grateful for the support of Davyne Verstandig, director of the Litchfield County Writers Project.

Thank you to the many who gave generously of their time and expertise, including freelance television cameraman Pete Stendel, Connecticut divorce lawyer Steven H. Levy, Esq., and Napa Valley wine and port expert Paul Wagner. Lee Lipton, MA, PA-C, provided medical information. Mary Clare Bland, of East Side Tae Kwon Do in New York City, gave me a crash course in small business ownership. Tom Herman (Yale '68) and Marilyn Lytle Herman took me to the Game.

Litchfield, Connecticut, contractor Ben Buck explained how to apply roofing tar. Tedd Rosenstein, my Las Vegas bureau chief, described the Brooklyn Bridge at New York

New York in painstaking detail. Thank you also to Reverend David Rockness, pastor of the First Congregational Church of Litchfield; docent Rosemary Sant Andrea of the Bellamy-Ferriday House; car expert Jonathan Welsh; and Stephanie Chang. I assume full responsibility for any mistakes or omissions in, or embellishments to, the information these sources provided.

The Silas Sedgwick House is modeled on a real mansion in Litchfield County. Russell Barton gave me a tour of his exquisite home and let me take extensive photographs.

Girls-in-the-know Melissa C. Morris and Sandra Waugh saw to it that the Sedgwicks served the proper appetizers, drank the proper liquor, and attended the proper church.

The poet and hedge fund manager Lee Slonimsky not only advised me on Luke's investments but wrote Luke's beautiful sonnets and verse fragments (with the exception of the limerick, for which I take full blame). Lee, thank you. I couldn't have done it without you.

And without David and James, there would be no poetry in my life. I love you both.

MATING RITUALS
OF THE NORTH AMERICAN
WASP

ONE

Early Fall, September

Something wasn't right, and she knew it before opening her eyes.

She'd been having the oddest dream about a man she was sure she'd never met in her waking life, though in the dream he was as familiar as an old friend. A man she would not be able to recall later, beyond that his presence had buoyed her with happiness. A man she only understood wasn't Brock and was in fact someone Brock should never know about. And though she knew the correct thing to do was to go home to Brock at once and apologize for all of it—the argument, the way she'd left things, and now *this*—she couldn't bring herself to break the spell. She and the dream-man were laughing and talking, about what she wouldn't recall, either, as bells rang and cheers erupted in bursts, and smiling dream-people stood back to watch them in the manner of wedding guests ringing the floor for the first dance. Then, just as she and the man were about to embrace, Peggy Adams had a moment of clarity. *Something isn't right,* she thought in her dream, and with that, it all dissolved.

This was one of the many side effects of Peggy's chronic anxiety: Traveling made her jumpy, and she could not get comfortable in a strange bed. Not even in a luxury hotel. She'd try to laugh it off—*Hello, housekeeping? There's a pea under my mattress*—and go to sleep. But the pillow would be too plump or the fitted sheet would come untucked, revealing an expanse of bare mattress inches from her face. The rest of the night she'd alternate between imagining exactly what might be on that mattress, thinking wistfully of her own bed, and chastising herself. When had she become afraid of everything? Why couldn't she snap out of it?

But this particular out-of-kilter feeling went beyond the dream and beyond Peggy's sense that her world was closing in and it was her own fault. It went beyond her concern that her friends were leaving her behind, moving ahead with their lives while she remained in the same place. It certainly went beyond being in not-her-bed. The past two mornings, Peggy had awoken not to the distant growl of Manhattan traffic on Ninth Avenue or, depending on the day, the splash of Brock shaving in their apartment bathroom, but to the gusty air conditioner in a room at the New York New York hotel in Las Vegas, with Bex Sabes-Cohen—her best friend, business partner, and fellow bachelorette-weekend guest—rustling sleepily in the other double bed and a view of a reproduction Chrysler building out their window. It had caught her off guard Friday and Saturday, but it was Sunday, she'd be flying home later today, and with her everyday life within an afternoon's reach, the foreignness of the hotel room, her remaining hours of contrived gaiety in Las Vegas, even her fight with Brock, seemed perfectly manageable.

Still, Peggy wasn't ready to face any of it. She burrowed into the unyielding pillow, suspecting she hadn't slept nearly enough. Her eyes seemed glued shut, and she wondered, *Makeup?* Had she somehow not washed her face? She ran her left index finger across her lashes. They were gummy and stiff. When she moved her other hand under the covers, the clasp of her watch caught on the knit fabric of her cocktail dress.

Watch? Usually, Peggy set it on the bathroom counter before brushing and flossing. Why couldn't she remember brushing and flossing? Could she have forgotten to, just as she'd forgotten to remove her makeup, her watch, and...this was curious. Was she really wearing her dress?

She opened her eyes. The curtains were open, and blue white sunlight shrieked in through the window. She shut her eyes, but not before registering that she *was* still wearing the low-backed black jersey number she'd chosen for the weekend's climactic evening of dinner and drinks and blackjack with Bex and their other former college roommates.

What in the world was going on?

Peggy did remember having faced a wardrobe dilemma. Las Vegas had turned out to be a city of tourists wearing baggy T-shirts and shorts. Bex had already pointed out that the other bachelorettes weren't much chicer. Jobs, relationships, and circumstance had flung their four New York University friends thousands of miles from the city and out into the wide world of sneakers and sweatpants and logos on everything. For the past two days, Andrea, the guest of honor, had lived in a white tracksuit with "Bride-to-Be" appliquéd across her backside.

Peggy had had her dress over her head and been about to shimmy it down over her hips when she'd heard Bex come out of the bathroom.

"Do I look like an alien from Planet Overkill?" Peggy had asked through the layers of fabric. When no response came, she slithered the dress all the way on, letting it brush silkily around her calves.

Bex was wearing a camisole, black pants so snug that a thong would have left lines, and one skyscraper-heeled, pointy-toed, patent-leather boot. She laughed. "You're asking the wrong girl."

Peggy adored Bex for her brash self-assurance, her unflagging trust in her own choices.

Unfortunately, Peggy did not share these characteristics.

"I'll wear jeans." She started to back out of the dress.

"No, you don't. You're going to be festive this weekend if it kills us both. . . ." Bex had gotten a look at Peggy's face. She stopped tussling with her other boot. "I know, sweetie. Fights—they're miserable."

Peggy let the dress fall back around her and dropped onto the bed. "Thirteen months, Bex."

"I know," Bex said.

"Andrea meets Jordan, they go to dinner, they move in together, and poof—engaged." She held up her palms, mimicking a scale. "Andie: thirteen months. Me: seven years."

Bex nodded. "I know."

"And I shouldn't have yelled at Brock. I never yell at him. I don't nag; I don't push; I give him space. How long am I supposed to wait?"

"I don't know. I would have left him already."

"I'm not leaving him."

"I know," said Bex.

Peggy had registered the disapproval in her best friend's posture and slipped on her shoes. Shoes that she now suspected—

Her heart began to pound. She kicked the bedclothes off her feet.

She was still wearing them.

As for Bex, what had become of her? Bex, along with her bed and the Chrysler building outside their window, had disappeared. How was that possible? The only bed in the room now was Peggy's.

But Peggy wasn't the only one in it.

It took multiple tries to work through this last piece of

information. Man. A man. A man in bed. In her bed. No, on her bed. He lay on his back on top of the coverlet, in a rumpled shirt and a diagonally striped tie, in slacks, socks, and burnished dress shoes that looked as if they'd been polished and repolished for the past twenty years. He had blond lashes and a peaceful face. His chest rose and fell gently. He could have been a sleeping boy, except for the red gold stubble on his cheeks.

She had never seen him in her life.

She scrambled to her feet, one high heel leaving a small, three-cornered tear in the hotel sheet, and stood swaying next to her bed—which, of course, couldn't really be hers. She'd already forgotten the dream; her imagination was busy doing what it did best: spinning ghastly scenarios. He'd slipped her a drug, and they'd had wild, condom-free sex all night. He'd won her trust by dressing like a nice, traditional gentleman, gotten her drunk, and persuaded her to empty out her bank account. Or what about that urban legend where the traveler wakes up in a hotel room with a kidney missing?

The man mumbled and stirred.

Who is this person? Peggy tried to force down her rising panic, the choking, suffocating sensation that signaled she was especially anxious. She tapped him on the arm. "Excuse me." Her voice was barely audible, a twig scratch on a pane of glass.

The man didn't move. "Excuse me," she croaked louder, and tapped him again, then jiggled his arm. Nothing happened. *I'm practically middle-aged,* Peggy thought. She hadn't done anything like this in her twenties, when it might have been excusable. She was thirty-four and mortified.

She tottered into the bathroom, hoping despite all odds to find Bex washing her face. There was no Bex, only Peggy's own reflection: chin-length hair falling in dirty blond strings across a forehead already traversed with worry lines like her mother's; dark circles and the first signs of crow's-feet. Yet even as Peggy was bemoaning her appearance, she registered the leather Dopp kit on the otherwise empty counter, and the full impact of the situation hit her.

She'd passed out in a strange man's room.

Her next thought was, *My purse!*

She half expected not to find it, but it was there, on a table with a scattered stack of papers, two smudgy champagne glasses, and a bottle nose-down in a bucket of melted ice. The man's jacket was draped neatly across the back of a chair. Peggy swooped up her bag and wrenched it open. Wallet and credit cards—check. The photo of her and Brock at the Sports Emmys—check. Cash—not as much as she remembered, but a few bills, and the card to her own hotel room.

A blast of electronic music shrilled. Peggy jumped and tripped over her feet to the door, fumbled with the safety latch, and stumbled out into the hall, holding the door ajar with her elbow. She reached into her purse for her phone and flipped it open. Mercifully, the music stopped.

"Bex?" Peggy whispered. "Are you okay?"

"Where are you? Brunch, remember?"

Peggy was flooded with relief at the sound of her friend's voice. She glanced back into the room. All she could see was the lower eighteen inches of the man's legs. He didn't appear to have woken up. She shut the door carefully. "I'll be right there," Peggy said into the phone, steering herself toward the elevator.

"Are you bringing your future husband?"

Peggy made herself walk slower—the corridor was spinning. "What?"

"You told us you were engaged. You were skipping around with that WASPy guy, calling him 'my future husband.' The two of you were all over each other. We couldn't figure out what had gotten into you, Peggy. You wouldn't let us take you upstairs. We finally left you at the roulette table. Did you actually go to his room?"

Peggy pressed "Down," and an elevator opened as if it had been waiting. There was a family inside—a mother and father and two children, all bright-eyed and fresh and well rested. "I guess so. I'm coming to ours now."

"We're not there. Hilary and I packed and checked out for you. Meet us in the lobby and we'll go straight to brunch."

The children were staring at her. The parents were pointedly trying not to. Peggy wished she could vanish. "I have to change my dress," she whispered.

"No time, sweets. We've all got planes to catch. Meet us downstairs. We'll wait for you."

"Thanks, Bex. I owe you."

"You'll pay me later," Bex said. "I expect a full report of last night."

"All right, then, what about hepatitis?" Peggy worried aloud once the plane was in the air and pointing east. She was in the window seat, and she lowered the shade against the sun. Every women's magazine cautionary tale she'd ever read, every casual-sex exposé about the dangers of letting one's guard down for an instant, was coming back to her in a dizzying rush. She shook out a small white pill from a vial in her purse.

Bex tilted back her seat and twirled her black-coffee curls into a chignon, which she secured with a pen from her handbag. "Come on, Neurotic Nelly, open your shade or we won't see the Grand Canyon. And don't take that. There's nothing to be afraid of. The pilot knows how to fly the plane. And if you take the Ativan, you'll pass out, and I'll be lonely for the rest of the flight."

"Then you take one, too."

"No thanks." Bex pried Peggy's fingers from the vial. "From here on out, my body is a temple. No alcohol, no late nights, no stress. Only organic foods, yoga, and Josh giving me shots in my ass. Sexy, right? Put that pill back in here."

Peggy dropped it in. "Bex, do you think I've caught hepatitis? Or worse?" She was making herself breathless.

"That guy was so conservative, he looked like a 1962 Brooks Brothers ad." Bex clenched her teeth and finished in a mock upper-class drawl, "No one like that could possibly be diseased."

"That's not true and you know it."

"And no one has sex and then puts his conservative pants, shirt, tie, socks, and shoes back on before passing out. Therefore, you don't have to worry about whether you had safe sex, because you didn't have sex." Bex capped the pill vial and returned it to Peggy's purse. "If I were you, I'd feel kind of cheated."

Nauseated. That's how Peggy felt. "If you knew anything, you'd tell me, right?"

"Only you know what happened. It's back there in your subconscious. Concentrate." Bex opened the in-flight magazine.

The plane vibrated. Peggy's heart jolted. She looked past Bex into the aisle, at the passengers chatting or sleeping, the flight attendants doling out drinks and bags of pretzels. Just a little turbulence. She made herself loosen her death grip on the armrests.

Bex set down the magazine. "Did you get his name and number?"

"Why would I want his name and number?"

"He was cute. Did you give him yours?"

"I thought you were going to be quiet." Of course Peggy hadn't given out her phone number. *Then again,* she realized with dismay, *how would I know?*

"Think back to the last thing you remember." Bex rustled the magazine so Peggy would see she was reading.

Peggy had gone with Bex to Andrea's room. There were margaritas from room service. She'd had one, possibly two. Jen, with whom Peggy had bonded over a mutual love of Wallace Stevens during their freshman honors poetry seminar, had raised a glass: "Okay, let's go around the room. When did you know he was going to pop the—" She'd looked at Peggy and winced. "Yikes, Peggy, sorry." To shake off the weight of the bachelorettes' pity, Peggy had busied herself gathering trash and going down the hall for ice, reciting to herself a stanza from "Thirteen Ways of Looking at a Blackbird."

A man and a woman
are one.
A man, a woman and a blackbird
are one.

When she returned, Andrea was describing her wedding. It would be in Hawaii—just the bride and groom and their families. The other bachelorettes clamored to hear about the dress, the food, the flowers. Peggy had poured herself another drink, reminded herself to be happy for Andrea.

They'd had steaks and martinis and hit the casino. Peggy, by then considerably more cheerful, had played roulette with Bex, jumping up and down and hollering, "Come on, rent money!" At some point, holding yet another martini, she'd lost her grip and seen her drink on the floor. She was, inexplicably, on the floor, too.

"Are you all right?" The man had rushed over to her. He'd taken her hand and pulled her gently to her feet. She'd stood, leaning against him.

Peggy tapped Bex's magazine. "Why was I calling him my future husband?"

"You know," Bex said. "Because of the tiara."

It was frightening. Peggy rarely had more than a glass of wine with dinner and never in her life had gotten so drunk that she'd blacked out. What subconscious, self-destructive impulse had taken over?

"Andie gave us tiaras at dinner. Remember?"

Oh, right. Peggy did, thankfully, remember: The bride-to-be had presented them all with gag veils—froths of tulle attached to shiny rhinestone tiaras. Peggy had loved hers and worn it into the casino. "What happened to it?" She hadn't seen it that morning in the man's room.

"You must have lost it. Anyway, you told Brooks Brothers you were a bride, and all you needed was a groom."

"I wouldn't say that!" It was too hot on this plane. Peggy reached up to the air blower above her seat, but it was already on. "I respect Brock far too much. *Don't* say a word about you-know-what," she added—she'd just given her friend the perfect opportunity to mention Florida. Considering the way Peggy had acted last night, she was in no mood to hear Bex, whom she loved with all her heart, dig up a two-year-old mistake Brock had promised over and over not to make again. Bex's disdain for Brock never failed to hurt Peggy's feelings.

"Well, I think it's great that you broke out of your comfort zone," Bex said cheerfully. "You should do it more often. And if you did sleep with Mr. WASP, you can just call it payback."

"Shut up, Rebecca. I mean it."

"Let's change the subject." Bex took a cardigan out of her bag. Peggy couldn't understand how Bex could be cold when it was stifling in here. "How are Max and Madeleine?"

"Remember Dad's little cough that wouldn't go away? He went to see some guy in the RV park. A retired veterinarian." Peggy rubbed her temples. "He told Mom it was cheaper than paying a real doctor. What if it's serious? Those two make me crazy."

"They're cool—free spirits. All right, work. Think Padma accidentally burned down the store this weekend? Speaking of catastrophes, how much do you think the Evil Empire will raise our rent? I was sure we'd hit the jackpot in Vegas and our troubles would be over."

Peggy had been struggling all weekend not to fret about the inevitable increase in their store's rent. It was the exact opposite of Bex's way of coping—Bex liked to attack worries head-on. "Ugh, don't remind me," Peggy said.

Bex immediately upended her frown back to a smile. "Don't beat yourself up over last night. You had a fight with Brock, and you were acting out. Understandably, I might add."

"I gave him an ultimatum. I said if we weren't engaged in a year, I'd leave him," Peggy mumbled.

"Maybe that's a good thing," Bex said. "To show him you mean business."

"He knows I'd never follow through. And to top that stupid move with last night's stupid move—"

"Sweetie, stop. All that happened was you drank too much and had fun with a man and didn't make it back to our hotel room. Nothing bad. You'll go home, and your life will be exactly as it was before. And if you do follow through on that ultimatum, my offer stands."

"I'll keep that in mind," Peggy said. Bex, who still lived

in the apartment she and Peggy had shared in their twenties, was always telling Peggy she could move back in anytime. Peggy was usually offended at the suggestion, but she had to think now that it might come in handy.

"Here, eat." Bex poked at Peggy's bag of minipretzels. "And ask what's going on with me for a change. It's been Brock, Brock, Brock, all weekend."

Peggy opened the pretzels, ashamed of herself. "You're right. I'm so sorry. When's your appointment with Dr....?"

"Kaplan. Guess what *New York* magazine calls him? The King Midas of fertility—everything he touches turns to gold."

"So when are you going? Josh will be there, too, right?"

"Tomorrow morning. It'll just be me. Josh will be in court." Bex's husband was a lawyer with the Legal Aid Society.

"I'll go with you." Peggy was glad for the chance to turn the tables and help Bex. "For moral support. You're always taking care of me. I'll call in Padma to open up the store."

"Some other time." Bex helped herself to one of Peggy's pretzels. "He's just going to explain the protocol he's picked for me. The real fun begins later: hormones and blood tests and more hormones and blood tests."

"And then what happens?"

"Then they retrieve my eggs. That's what they call it, 'retrieval.' Like the eggs are lost in there. Then they fertilize them in a petri dish or something, see if any of them take, put those in me, and it's *Next stop, Babyville*. I mean, if it works."

Peggy studied her best friend's profile, the stubborn set of her chin. She ached for Bex whenever a customer came into the store with a baby, whenever one of their friends blithely announced another pregnancy. When she and Bex walked together on the Upper West Side, its sidewalks clogged with young families, Peggy tried to run interference. As if stepping between Bex and a stroller could shield her friend from the fecundity that mocked from every corner. "It will work," Peggy said. "It has to."

"Says the woman who's sure a thief stole her kidney."

Peggy laughed for the first time all day. "Then let me do the worrying, so you don't need to. I'm excellent at it." She took Bex's hand. "Let that be my job."

It was nearly eleven when the taxi driver hoisted Peggy's suitcase out of the trunk with a grunt and thudded it onto the sidewalk. "Thanks, sorry," she said, and overtipped him.

She stood in the middle of Fifty-ninth Street in last night's dress and heels. She pressed her left leg against her suitcase, claiming it, and looked up at the glass-and-granite facade of her building, trying to spot the dark windows of her and Brock's apartment on the twentieth floor; and then at the cab speeding off into the late-September night. A part of her wanted to chase after the taxi and have the driver take her . . . where, she didn't know. She reminded herself of what Bex had said: "Life will be exactly as it was before." Of course it would. Nothing had happened.

In the elevator, she searched her purse for her keys. Before she'd stormed off to the airport, she was pretty sure Brock had said he was going to Chicago. Wait, Cleveland. Bengals at Browns. His return flight wouldn't get in until past midnight. If you were going to be a sports cameraman's girlfriend, you had to accept that he'd be away most weeks, from Thursday or Friday through late Sunday night. It had come to seem normal to Peggy. She spent her weekends minding the shop anyway and often came home drained from hours of bright-eyed girl chatter, with nothing to talk about beyond the typical store happenings—a European tourist who'd bought one of every soap, lotion, and shower gel on the shelves; a customer who'd tried to return an empty jar of body scrub. Tonight, Peggy was downright glad of Brock's absence. For starters, she wouldn't have to explain why she'd flown across the country in a little black dress badly camouflaged with an airport gift shop T-shirt that said "Sin City."

She stepped out of her shoes at last and dragged the suitcase through the dark living room into her and Brock's bedroom. A bath. That's what she needed to wash away last night once and for all.

In the tub, Peggy channeled the instructor of a meditation course she'd once taken. She imagined Birch—that had been the woman's name—in the lotus position with one of the different-colored stick-on *bindis* she'd change to coordinate with her tank tops, saying, *If a negative thought enters your mind, observe it impartially, and let it go.*

It was time to let Las Vegas go. Peggy was home, where she was comfortable and knew her place in the world. Tomorrow at the shop she had two deliveries coming in and was planning to redo the windows and balance the books. A busy day, but she could do these tasks in her sleep. She'd just spent the weekend with her oldest and most beloved friends. Tomorrow morning, she'd apologize to Brock for her outburst. The truth was, they had been getting along far better than during the rocky period after Florida. Maybe that's why Peggy had been so shaken this morning: She'd barely escaped pulling the rug out from under herself, upsetting the stability she'd worked so hard to create.

She slid deeper into the tub, tipping her head back into the lavender-scented bubbles. She concentrated on relaxing.

"Hey!" The front door slammed. "What's for dinner?"

It was Brock's voice, she knew it as well as her own, but

still she shrieked. There were heavy footsteps, and Brock appeared.

"Sheesh!" He had his keys in one hand and a colossal bouquet in the other. "Kidding. I ate already."

"You scared me!" Peggy's hands were shaking. "I thought you weren't back until late."

"I caught an earlier flight." He held out the bouquet. "For you."

So *he* was apologizing. Peggy reached out both hands to take the flowers—each bloodred rose the size of a child's fist. She braced her arms on the edge of the tub. After Florida, Brock had sent bouquets just like this to the store—one a day for twenty-three days, until Peggy had relented and let him move back into the apartment.

"They're beautiful," she told him now.

Brock Clovis was black-haired, blue-eyed, a former high school football star with the shoulders to prove it. People on the street often mistook him for someone famous. When he smiled, a dimple deepened in his chin. "How do they smell?" Brock bent to nuzzle his face in the roses.

"Careful, thorns." Peggy waited for him to apologize so she could, too. Marriage was overrated. She and Brock were in a committed relationship. What did she need a piece of paper for?

"Huh." Brock lifted his head. "They don't smell like anything."

Peggy drew her knees to her chest. "Could you please put them in a vase for me while I get out of the tub?" The bubbles were starting to dissolve, reminding her of a dream she had occasionally where she'd be in Grand Central, confused about which train to take, and she'd realize her clothes were slowly falling off....

A wisp of something, perhaps a déjà vu, drifted into her

brain. A vague memory of laughing with a friend while lights sparkled all around.

"Hang on a sec," Brock said. The wisp drifted back out. "There's one thing. It's kind of serious." Rarely emotional, he had the faintest tremble in his voice.

Peggy shivered in the no-longer-hot water. She wasn't irrational enough to imagine he knew how she'd woken up this morning, but something was clearly bothering him. Had he had another slipup? That's what he'd called it last time: a slipup. Wouldn't that be ironic, she and he both in the same twenty-four hours. "Brock—" she began.

"Close your eyes."

"Something very odd happened this weekend."

"Close 'em."

Peggy bit down on the inside of her cheek and closed her eyes.

"Open."

She opened her eyes.

Brock was holding out a small blue box with a white satin ribbon.

"Open it, Pegs," he said as Peggy sat in the tub, fingertips wrinkling, wet hair plastered to her face, the last of the bubbles melting away.

TWO

"A promise ring?" Bex yelled. The string of bells on the shop door jingled as it shut behind her. "Brock gave you a *promise ring*? What is this, seventh grade? Hi, Padma," she added to the only other person in the shop, their new, nineteen-year-old salesgirl, as if "seventh grade" had reminded Bex of her presence.

"It's an engaged-to-be-engaged ring. It's pretty, see?" Peggy was behind the counter, unpacking a case of Gaia Apothecary's Vision Body Splash, with extracts of hibiscus and ylang-ylang, reconciling the contents of the carton against a purchase order in her accounts binder. She held up her left hand to show Bex the ring, a spray of small diamonds set to resemble a flower and leaves. It glinted in the late morning light.

"He couldn't give you the real deal?"

Peggy had known this was coming. "This is a major breakthrough for Brock. You know how afraid he is of commitment."

Bex rolled her eyes. "I realize he'd be shocked to hear this, but at a certain point men do grow up. Let me guess. He gave you that line about not wanting to turn into his dad."

"How was your appointment?" Peggy didn't need to hear Bex say anything else discouraging.

"It went well. Actually, I can't stay long." Bex took a

square of paper from her pocket. "Would you believe it's a prescription for—"

The phone rang. "I'll get it!" Padma shouted unnecessarily—the phone was three feet away—and picked up. "ACME Cleaning Supply." Pause. "We sell specialty soaps and lotions, uh-huh.... Um, Columbus Avenue, between, uh, Eighty-first and Eighty-second." Peggy made a mental note to coach Padma on her phone manner. "Today's Monday, right? Till eight.... Okay, yeah, bye."

"—birth control pills?" Bex went on, seemingly oblivious to the interruption. She walked through the store as she talked, neatening shelves, straightening sample bottles so their labels faced forward. "Kaplan says I'm supposed to take them for a few weeks before the hormone injections to 'quiet my ovaries.' All I can think of is my ovaries rampaging around in there like hyperactive schoolkids— Oh, no!" She interrupted herself, pointing out the front window. "Black and White Books is going out of business!"

Black and White Books was an Upper West Side institution, a large, cluttered store across the street from ACME Cleaning Supply. Both Peggy and Bex hated to hear of any shop failing.

"I can't believe it." Bex shook her head sadly. "I've been buying books there since I was six."

The phone rang. Peggy picked up before Padma could.

"My darling. You've been ignoring me. I call and call." Peggy recognized the voice of Mark, the sales representative for Promised Land, a line of biblical-themed products. His flirtatious greeting was a giveaway that he was about to try to wheedle her into placing a bigger wholesale order than she'd already committed to. Bex was better at dealing with the line reps; you had to talk fast or they wouldn't let you off the phone. Yes, Peggy agreed with Mark; Promised Land's frankincense-and-myrrh shampoo *was* flying off the shelves, but—

Mark cut her off. Peggy let her attention roam around the familiar room. The store was a tiny, narrow rectangle, with windows at the front, a tin ceiling, and a trompe l'oeil cloud mural Peggy and Bex had painted on the back wall. It had taken them twelve years to build their little business, including two working at Bex's parents' store, Sabes Shoes, after college before landing a small-business loan for a place of their own. Peggy was proud of the shop and of herself for gambling on it in the first place. She'd been a different, braver person back then. *The real me,* she liked to think. *She's still in there somewhere.*

Bex waved good-bye. The door jingled shut behind her. Mark was still talking. "Tell you what," Peggy jumped in. "I'll have Bex call you." She hung up.

Padma was wandering among the displays, dabbing herself with essential oil. "Who was that?"

"A sales rep. If you get one of those calls, give it to Bex. She's the only one who can rein them in." Peggy wished Bex had stayed a little longer; she would have liked to hear the rest of what Dr. Kaplan had said. She decided to stop over at Bex's place after work.

"Got it." Padma reached her arm up and over to scratch her own back. There was a small tattoo on the side of her neck that said "IH." Padma had explained this was so she got a friendly message when she looked in the mirror: HI. "Can I run out for coffee? I was up till, like, four."

"Get me a cup, too, and I'll treat." Peggy took a twenty from the register.

Padma dashed for the door. "Someone dropped off an envelope for you guys yesterday," she called over her shoulder.

The envelope was from Empire Property Management.

The new lease would be inside. Peggy wasn't ready to open it without Bex around for moral support, although if Bex did get pregnant, Peggy would have to shoulder more of these burdens on her own. *When* Bex got pregnant, Peggy corrected herself. She wished she could figure out a way to solve the coming rent crisis on her own.

She put away the unopened envelope and returned to the Gaia Apothecary purchase order, then gave up and studied her pre-engagement ring. All right—a vague promise wasn't what she'd hoped was in that Tiffany box. What she'd really wanted to do last night was shake Brock and yell, *Just get on with it! Everyone's already having babies!* How long would it be before Bex, too, abandoned Peggy for her new role and new friends—mommy friends with whom she'd have everything in common?

No, Peggy decided. Better to think positive: A real proposal couldn't be far off. She tested phrases in her head: *Mrs. Patricia Adams Clovis. Brock and Peggy Clovis. Mr. and Mrs. Brock Clovis.* She could use this waiting time to at long last get Bex to see Brock's good side, to think of him as a friend in his own right, the way Peggy loved Bex's lawyer husband, Josh. Bex could certainly stand to be more tolerant of Brock's marriage fears, since Bex had her own odd notions about relationships. She'd been with Josh eight years, ever since he'd moved in down the hall from the apartment Bex and Peggy had shared and had come over with a letter for Bex that had accidentally ended up in his mailbox. But after five happy years of marriage, Bex and Josh still lived in their separate apartments. Bex called it the best of both worlds—she and Josh could be together when they wanted and alone when they needed. But once, Josh had confided in Peggy, "I think she likes to believe she has an escape route."

The bells tinkled, and in a flash the room was overflowing with the orthodontic smiles and tossing hair and high-pitched shrieking of a horde of teenage girls cutting class. One was preoccupied with a text message on her pink phone and nearly upended a table of organic soaps. "Watch *out*, Courtney!" a second girl screeched from behind her Chanel sunglasses.

"Stop it!" squealed a third.

"Devon, cut it *out*!" yelled a fourth.

Peggy was thinking she'd have to say something, but just then the bells heralded the return of Padma, who stepped briskly into the maelstrom. "Hold this." She handed a teen a coffee cup. The girl took it, surprised. Padma held a patchouli-passion-fruit candle high above her head, a retail Statue of Liberty. "Get this. A couple of nights ago I lit one of these just before a guy came to my apartment to study, and now he's, like, my boyfriend. The wax melts into massage oil!"

"No way!" The girls started to grab for candles.

Padma caught Peggy's eye and grinned, just as the phone began to ring. Peggy nodded—*Don't stop doing what you're doing*—and reached for the handset.

"I'm looking for Peggy Adams," said the man on the line.

The teenager Courtney placed her candle on the counter. Peggy clutched the phone in one hand and started to ring up the purchase. "This is Peggy," she spoke into the receiver.

"This is Luke."

Another sales rep. Peggy held the receiver against her shoulder. "Enjoy your candle." She gave the girl her receipt.

"Are you there?" the man asked.

The girl with the Chanel sunglasses put three candles on the counter.

"You're calling from where?" Peggy understood the man on the phone was just doing his job, but really, there were too many reps asking for their money. There was a new chain of stores in the Midwest, Bath, that was having success by showcasing hundreds of bath-and-body lines in huge, airy spaces, but Peggy and Bex had to make do with keeping their shop small and praying the rent stayed low enough to keep them in business.

"I'm from New Nineveh. But we—"

"The thing is, we already carry a biblical line that's doing well for us."

The Chanel girl waved an American Express card from chipped-burgundy-polished fingertips. "I'd like each of these candles gift-wrapped individually."

Courtney clutched the girl's arm. "They're presents? For who?"

"For me. I like opening presents."

"I want *mine* wrapped!" Courtney shrilled.

"I think it would be best if you called back and spoke with my partner," Peggy said into the phone.

"This is important," the man said. "You and I, we met in Las Vegas. You passed out in my room."

Peggy felt her heart stop beating.

The Chanel girl drummed her fingers. "Hello, gift-wrap?"

"Why are you calling?" Peggy was untethered, careening between disbelief and alarm; anxiety wrapped itself around her chest.

"I live in Connecticut. We should meet."

"You live in Connecticut?" This was a practical joke. Or a mistake. Or a scam. It had to be. How could a person she'd met nearly all the way across the country possibly end up residing one state away? She didn't bother hiding the disbelief in her voice. "Then what were you doing in Vegas? Isn't that a little far from home?"

His voice was aggravatingly calm. "I could ask the same of you."

"It was my first time there. I'm not a Vegas person, believe me."

"Rest assured, neither am I. Now, can you meet me? For coffee, maybe."

"I can't meet you. I'm..." She ducked her head and whispered, "Involved with someone."

"It didn't seem that way Saturday night."

This couldn't be happening. "I'm engaged. To be engaged. I'll be getting married probably in a year or two." Nor was she sure why she felt the need to explain herself, especially with a trumped-up story. Brock had put no time frame on their pre-betrothal. "I have a promise ring," she finished lamely. "I can't have coffee with you."

"You can't get married," the caller said.

"Oh, really?" She didn't need this. Not from Bex and not from some stranger she'd...*No, don't think about it.* She turned to face the wall, away from the prying eyes of her customers and Padma. "Brock and I love each other, and when people love each other, they get married. I can get married, and I will get married."

"I'm afraid you're wrong," he answered. "You're already married. To me."

THREE

Luke!" Abigail was calling. "Luke!"

Luke Sedgwick awoke with a start at the unexpected noise. He must have dozed off. The events of the weekend, topped off by this morning's uncomfortable phone call, had left him with a deep weariness a good night's sleep would go a long way toward curing. Now sleep wasn't in the cards tonight, either.

"Luke!"

He consulted his watch: It was Monday, one twenty-two in the afternoon. He'd been unconscious only a few minutes. He slid his glasses onto his forehead and rubbed his eyes. If only he *had* been asleep for the past fifty-two hours. There would have been no trip to Las Vegas, no Family Asset Management Conference, no unfortunate dalliance.

He tried again to recall what had happened Saturday night—after the point where he'd drunk so many Scotches that he'd forgotten he was Luke Silas Sedgwick IV of the Connecticut Sedgwicks. The Connecticut Sedgwicks who, with the possible exception of Luke's black-sheep uncle Bink, would never have gotten into such a mess. Luke thought back and came up with the same unsatisfactory snippets: An intoxicating fragrance. A black dress. An attraction so intense, it had seemed preordained. A piercing disappointment at finding himself alone in the morning. Beyond that, impenetrable nothingness.

He shouldn't have let Tom Ver Planck talk him into attending that conference. "It's an opportunity. Don't waste it," his friend had said. Ver Planck, whose name and business reputation garnered him a hundred such unsolicited invitations a year, had been offered an all-expenses-paid trip by the conference organizers. "If anyone asks, just pretend you're one of my associates." Ver Planck had practically shoved the first-class plane ticket into Luke's hand. "And have some fun. You and Nicki called it quits, right? You're a free agent."

"Luke!" his great-aunt continued to call.

Still, Ver Planck had been right; Luke had picked up some useful investing advice. And despite his weariness, he had actually written a little today. A small miracle.

He contemplated a jagged sheet of plaster about to fall from the ceiling of his third-floor study, then reread the paper in front of him:

They're all so frail, these sunveined southern winds
vanishing the day dark northern chill begins;
Bright leaves imitate flowers, but soon descend
to frost-barbed, tattered ruin...

These were the first lines he'd composed in ages, arriving out of nowhere this morning as soon as he'd hung up the phone, and not that bad, though "imitate" was all wrong and threw off the meter. "Bright leaves suggest flowers" worked better.

Luke returned to his computer screen, where columns of numbers taunted him. He thought he should turn on a light; the day was already fading. Summer was over, and any of its lingering pleasures—a long afternoon, a last, unexpected blackberry from the bush by the south fence—were understood by Luke, as by all native New Englanders, to be temporal.

Another thing Luke knew was that it was hard to be alone in a two-hundred-plus-year-old New England house, even with only one other person living in it. It wasn't the presence of ghosts—though Abigail insisted there were many—it was that the musty old mausoleum couldn't keep quiet. Luke tracked the progress of Abigail Agatha Sarah Sedgwick as she ascended the front staircase: a sharp creak from the third step from the bottom, which had been making that same noise for as far back as he could remember. Then a rhythmic trembling as the staircase strained to support all five feet and ninety pounds of its owner. Luke was nearly twice Abby's weight and over a foot taller, and when he walked, the house would vibrate with each footstep, its six-on-six paned windows rattling in their rotting casements. The Silas Sedgwick House—erected twenty years after the Revolutionary War by Silas Ebenezer Sedgwick, farmer, merchant, and patriot, and built grander and larger by his descendants; for over two centuries the pride of New Nineveh, Connecticut—threatened to come crashing down around the only two remaining Sedgwicks: Abigail and Luke, Silas's great-great-great-grandson.

Any day now, Luke thought. When he was having a particularly bad time in the market, which so far in his new career of Sedgwick family financial manager was the rule rather than the exception, he would cheer himself with fantasies of the house's demise. In his current favorite, Abigail's beloved black cat, Quibble, in a rare daytime foray out from under Abby's bed, leaped onto the mantel in the grand parlor, setting off a chain of events ending with the cat still perched calmly on the intact fireplace surrounded by three stories of rubble.

"Luke!" The scratched crystal doorknob rasped, the double doors squeaked open, and his great-aunt stepped into what had once been the Sedgwick ballroom and was now Luke's study. Abigail's faded brown eyes were fierce. Her white hair stood out from her scalp. "It's that Riga woman." She stomped one foot. "Come with me."

"What's she done now?" Luke decided to interpret Abigail's appearance as a sign that it was time to quit for the afternoon. He closed out his positions and shut down the computer. He stretched his legs, which felt easily as old as the house.

Abigail led him down the new staircase—as the family still called the back steps, rebuilt after the fire of 1827—to the first floor. She skirted the grand parlor and led him down another hallway, past the east addition, circa 1850 and now closed off and cobwebby, and onto one of the Sedgwick House's three porches: the screened-in one called Charity's Porch, after the long-deceased ancestor for whom it had been built. Charity's Porch faced out onto the garden, which extended back three acres to Market Road. It was toward that far end of the garden that Abigail pointed a spindly finger.

"There. Plain as day."

Luke squinted toward the road at the new structure that had sprung up. It appeared to be a small, covered, open-sided farm stand. Its yellow, virgin wood had not yet been battered by one of New Nineveh's legendary nor'easters. "Go get your sweater and we'll have a look," he said, thinking of Abby's bark-colored gardening sweater, which hung on a hook in the mudroom, its pockets always filled with crumpled Kleenex, and was older than he was.

"I don't need a sweater."

Luke tried to argue that it was getting cool outside. Abigail insisted she wasn't cold, and inevitably won, and it wasn't until some time later that the two were walking over the uneven stone path, Luke moving aside overgrown bushes of crispy brown roses, until they reached the structure and went around to the front, which faced the traffic on Market. A neatly hand-lettered sign read: "Fall Color, $1.50 Per Branch." The stand was otherwise empty; the autumn leaves wouldn't be at their peak until at least Columbus Day.

"It's the spitting image of our flower stand," Abigail said. "If I weren't a Sedgwick, I'd march right over to Lowie's office. If I had stolen Ernestine Riga's idea, instead of the other way around, *she* would prosecute to the full extent of the law."

"Now, now..." Luke put his hand on her arm.

"Don't you 'now, now' me, young man."

"It's called capitalism, Abby." *And I'm hardly young,* he added silently, though currently he wasn't convinced he'd learned anything in his forty-one years. He, unlike Abigail, did need to talk to Lowell Mayhew, and right away. He wanted this mess over with. The sooner the better. Thankfully, it seemed Peggy Adams did as well, though if Luke were the sort to let his emotions rule him, he might have admitted to the smallest pang of disappointment that she'd been so quick to agree.

Abby turned her back on the flower stand. "In that case, I'll beat Ernestine at her own game. Anyone can see the quality of our trees. Before Bink sold off the pumpkin patch, we had the most marvelous pumpkins, too. Perhaps we should grow pumpkins on our twenty acres, Luke."

Pumpkins. That would cover the property tax for sure. "I'm off, Abigail. I've got to run to Seymour's and do some errands and tie up some loose ends. I'll be home tonight, but very late."

"Loose ends, my foot."

You have no idea, he wanted to say.

"Seeing that Pappas girl is more like it. Why are you still courting her when you should be out finding a wife? A wife with proper manners and a proper name?"

Luke felt slightly ill at the word *wife*.

"There's nothing wrong with 'Nicole.' It's a perfectly fine name." He was aware this wasn't the half of his currently off-again (but no doubt after tonight, if history was a reliable predictor, on-again) girlfriend's name to which his great-aunt was referring. Abigail wanted Luke to pair off with a nice girl from a nice old New England family with a nice old New England pedigree; a woman worthy of providing an heir to the obsolete Sedgwick legacy and the no-longer-existent Sedgwick fortune. Luke had never pointed out that Abby's plans for him ran counter to her own youthful romantic past. He knew how she would respond: that he was the last Sedgwick, and a man. That he had a duty to the family.

Nicki was neither wholesome nor pedigreed, precisely what he found most appealing about her. That, and her aversion to marriage, which matched, if not surpassed, his own. *You don't need to worry about Nicki. She doesn't believe in marriage any more than I do,* he generally told Abigail. *And in case you hadn't noticed, nice old New England families are virtually extinct.*

Both statements were true. Yet here Luke was in a position he'd never considered: not only married, but married to a stranger.

"I'm not seeing Nicole tonight; I'm playing poker," he lied, not in the mood to be scolded. "You'll be okay. Don't forget to leave on the hall light in case you get up in the night. And put your cell phone near your bed. If you can't reach me, call the Fiorentinos, and Annette or Angelo will help you."

Abigail drew her mouth into a frown. "Leaving lights on wastes money. And if I need to talk, I'll talk to Quibble. I don't like that cellular geegaw. I don't trust a phone without a cord."

Though he wouldn't admit it to Abigail, Luke shared her innate suspicion of any technology not around since he was a child. He tolerated his computer and cell phone only because he couldn't do his job without them. "I put Annette's number on your nightstand. It's right there, so you can't miss it."

She wore the same keen expression she had when he was sixteen and home from school for the summer and Ernestine Riga had told her a nighttime vandal had been running amok through town, knocking over flower boxes and throwing eggs at shop windows. Abigail had repeated the story to Luke after his parents had sent him to mow her lawn. "I sure will be sorry for the culprit's family once Officer Wharton catches him. They'll be terribly ashamed," she'd said mildly, and pinned Luke with that look. The vandal never struck again.

When she looked at him that way now, it was hard to believe what anyone could tell after spending ten minutes in her company, and as he had been told by the best gerontologists in Connecticut. At ninety-one, his headstrong Yankee great-aunt was losing her marbles. It was why Luke had quit his job at Hartford Mutual, why he'd taken his friend Ver Planck's advice and committed to two years of hands-on management of the Sedgwicks' pitiful assets—to "grow," as Ver Planck had phrased it, what was left of the family money, in order to afford the medical care his great-aunt would soon need. It was why Luke had given up his apartment and moved into the Sedgwick House, so he could keep an eye on her. For now, Abby's doctors had deemed her competent, but as she slipped further into dementia, someday soon she'd need more care than Luke alone could provide. And that cost money. More than he could have possibly brought in at Hartford Mutual.

You have to take risks to reap rewards, Ver Planck always said. *You can't be risk-averse, Sedgwick.*

"Remember I told you they're building a new assisted living development in Torrington? If we sold this place, you could afford your own condo and people to do your cleaning and check in on you twice a day," Luke told Abby, by rote.

Her answer, too, was predictable: "The Silas Sedgwick House shall never be sold, Luke. Ever."

Seymour's Hardware had always been New Nineveh's only such store until last year—when the area's first minimall had sprung up a mile out of town. Pilgrim Plaza had a pristine black parking lot, an entrance right off Route 202, and an outpost of a national home supplies chain that sold the same products as Seymour's at lower prices. This afternoon, Seymour's was empty except for a few diehard locals who all had known Luke since he was in diapers, and loved nothing more than to remind him of it. To Luke's surprise—not because he didn't run into someone familiar each time he stepped outside Abby's house, but because this time it was to his advantage—Lowell Mayhew was standing by a display of leaf blowers.

"Nice to see you. How's your great-aunt?" asked the lawyer.

"Same as always. Nice to see you, too." Luke shook Mayhew's hand. He hesitated. "I need a word with you. Can you see me in your office tomorrow? It's urgent."

"What's going on?"

Luke saw Emily Hinkley, president of the New Nineveh Ladies' Auxiliary, incline her head in his direction from over by the pruning shears. He lowered his voice. "I'd prefer to come to your office."

"Just call Geri and she'll make an appointment."

Luke thanked Mayhew and exchanged passing nods with Wesley Buckle, an old family friend who, as the recently appointed head of the town zoning commission, had been the most enthusiastic champion of the Pilgrim Plaza project. Luke wondered why Buckle wasn't at the new home supplies store; perhaps old habits died hard. Luke headed to the back of the room. He should get more candles. And kerosene. Winter wasn't what it used to be, but it was on its way, and there was no excuse for being unprepared.

Mayhew followed. "Luke." His grin had faded. "You should talk to your great-aunt about her will. I can't say much, you understand, but she's made significant changes I suspect you would agree are ill-advised."

Luke dared not hope. Abby's long-standing will had made it clear that the Sedgwick House was to go to him—along with ironclad legal provisions preventing him, and any theoretical descendants, from ever selling it. The thought of being saddled with this burden for all eternity had kept Luke awake too many nights of his adult life. "Meaning what—she's not leaving the house to me?"

Mayhew scratched his pink forehead under his gray hat.

"Hallelujah!" Luke exclaimed, a rare show of excitement. He pulled a twenty-pound sack of ice melt off a low shelf and led Mayhew to the front of the store. He couldn't imagine what his great-aunt had in mind. For years, he'd been trying to get her to donate the mansion to the New Nineveh Historical Society to turn into a museum. "So who gets the albatross? I know you can't tell me."

"Just talk to her."

"What makes you think she'd listen to me any more than she'd listen to you?"

Mayhew scratched his chin. "Try."

Not a chance, Luke thought, suddenly lighter than air despite his troubles. "Will do," he said, and went to get the kerosene.

This absolutely, positively, couldn't be happening. Peggy clenched the wheel of her rented Chevrolet and peered through the slanting rain for a sign that she hadn't lost her way literally, even if it appeared she had done so metaphorically. Outside was nothing but wet trees. Connecticut was leafy and luxuriant—a five-thousand-square-mile Central Park—a fact Peggy would have appreciated more in other circumstances.

Her phone was still out on the front seat from her call minutes ago from Bex. Against her better judgment, Peggy reached for it and dialed her parents. Someone ought to know where she was.

"Virginia?" Madeleine Adams shouted over a bad connection; Peggy had already discovered the cell service out here was spotty. "Why are you driving to Virginia? Max, slow down!" The last command was clearly for Peggy's father; it seemed they, too, were on the road.

"Not Virginia, Mom, *New Nineveh,*" Peggy repeated. "In Connecticut—"

"Max!" Her mother interrupted, again to her father. "You'll kill us! Stay in the lane, please, honey!"

Peggy had forgotten what it was like to be in a car with her mother. Madeleine's nervousness was starting to rub off on her from all the way across the country.

"What were you saying, Peggy? Are you all right? Is everything okay?"

"Never mind, Mom. I'm fine."

Peggy hung up just in time to spot the road sign she was looking for—NEW NINEVEH, POP. 3,200, SETTLED 1719—and make her seventh wrong turn of the morning, this time a right onto Church Street, which she quickly realized was leading her straight out of town. By the side of the road, an orange backhoe had paused in the rain, its predatory jaws poised midbite over the roof of an aged barn that sagged under the weight of its years and the vines growing across it.

Peggy's whole body crackled with anxiety. If only she hadn't drunk so much coffee. All that caffeine had done nothing to calm her; nor had ninety minutes on the interstate and the last half hour of twisting, two-lane highways; nor had the crackly call from a numb-sounding Bex. Peggy hadn't had the courage to tell her friend the real reason she was skipping work today, claiming food poisoning instead. "Well, this will *really* make you sick," Bex had responded.

Peggy doubled back on Church, past the tall-steepled, white-clapboard building for which the street must have been named and huge old Colonial and Victorian houses she would have swooned over had she not been so preoccupied. She hadn't driven a car for two years, and she was twenty minutes late for her meeting. There it was: Number 3, a converted two-story brick house, also old. She parked the car. Bex, Brock—she'd not told them she was driving to Connecticut. For all Brock knew, she was at the store as usual. Peggy couldn't shake the worry that this all might be an elaborate ruse to lure her up to the country, kidnap her, and sell her into white slavery.

She could see the aftermath already—a lurid story about her mysterious disappearance on the front page of the *New York Post:* WAYWARD WIFE GOES AWOL. Poor Brock would learn of Peggy's Vegas marriage from some reporter, and it would kill her mother, and... *Enough, Peggy.* There was no need for feverish imaginings. Her current reality was weird enough.

"Goodness, you're soaked. Care to warm up a bit?" The receptionist at the front desk of the Law Offices of Lowell C.

Mayhew set down the muffin she was eating and rose from her chair as Peggy came in.

"Thank you, that's all right." Peggy pushed against the inside of the door, which was still open a crack. "I'm Peggy—"

"I know, dear. May I assume of the New Nineveh Adamses? And here I thought you'd all died out. It's warped."

Peggy was shamefaced. The receptionist was right: This situation with Luke was nothing short of twisted.

The woman came around the desk. "Silly old thing always warps in the rain." She shut the door with a bang.

Peggy flinched. She didn't know which had unnerved her more, yesterday's bomb from Luke Sedgwick or this morning's from Bex: When the store's lease expired next May, their rent wasn't just going up, it was doubling.

"Before you go on in, may I say..." The woman picked up Peggy's left hand and studied her ring. "It's wonderful news. Miss Abigail must be over the moon!" Before Peggy could ask what was wonderful or who was Abigail, the woman was bustling her into a cluttered, wainscoted office—"Here she is!"—and its two occupants were standing, the older man clasping her cold, damp hand in his warm, pink one. The receptionist bustled out.

"Lowell Mayhew." The lawyer appeared to be blushing a little. "And you've met Luke."

Peggy shook Luke Sedgwick's hand as briefly as she could. He mumbled, "Nice to see you," though she was pointedly avoiding his eyes. He wore threadbare khaki pants and green rain boots and, as best as she could tell without lifting her gaze north of his knees, was long-legged and lanky. She recalled, suddenly, the way he'd looked asleep on the hotel bed in Vegas. Had at any point his legs been entwined with hers?

She said to Mayhew, “I’d like to get started.”

The lawyer gestured at a chair. She went toward it, nearly tripping over Luke Sedgwick. He had returned to the other chair, stretching out his legs casually, as if he were in someone’s living room enjoying a hot toddy.

Peggy sat up straight and crossed her ankles. She looked across at Mayhew. “How long will this take?”

The lawyer aligned his blotter with the edge of his scratched, wooden desk. “About an hour. We know you have to get back to the city.”

“I meant the annulment.”

She was probably coming off as rude, but she didn’t care. A brisk Manhattan efficiency was sweeping in to replace the foggy disbelief that had gripped her since yesterday morning, when this stranger now sitting next to her, who claimed to have no recollection of their night, either, had informed her they’d legally bound themselves together till death did them part. It occurred to Peggy that the service could well have been performed by an Elvis impersonator, something she imagined would be funny in a romantic comedy—which this certainly wasn’t.

“I want to see the photo,” she said. “He told me there was a photo.”

Mayhew slid a folder across his desk. Inside was a Nevada marriage license with her signature, Patricia Ann Adams, and his, Luke Silas Sedgwick. A heart-shaped cardboard frame stamped with “The Little White Wedding Chapel” held a picture of Peggy in her black dress, with a tousled-haired man—she snuck a sidelong glance at Luke Sedgwick’s strawberry blond head—inebriated smirks on both their faces, arms wrapped around each other, the rhinestones on her bachelorette-party tiara winking in the camera’s flash. She waited for a bolt of recognition. None came.

Mayhew almost seemed sorry for her. "Shall we get started?"

Annulments were rare in Connecticut, he explained, granted only in a handful of special circumstances. The difference between an annulment and a divorce was that a divorce was a decree from the court that the marriage was over. "After an annulment, however, it's as if the marriage never happened."

"That's what I want." Peggy addressed Mayhew, still not looking directly at the man next to her, who hadn't spoken a word. This was *his* lawyer. She didn't see why she had to do all the talking.

Mayhew rolled a fountain pen between his palms. "The process takes a little over ninety days. But the court will only grant the annulment if it finds the circumstances behind your marriage warrant it."

"He got me drunk to the point of blacking out and dragged me to a wedding chapel. Isn't that enough?"

Luke spoke. It was about time. "I didn't drag you anywhere. My guess is you dragged me. And, forgive me, but you seemed to be doing a fine job of getting yourself drunk."

He might have made an effort to dress up for this meeting, Peggy thought. His sweater was so thin at the elbows that the pink of the button-down shirt underneath peeked through. Peggy knew for a fact he owned at least one suit.

"Let's stay focused." Mayhew pointed his pen at each of them. "Ms. Adams, I assume you're not already married? If so, this marriage with Luke would be void ab initio—void at its inception, an automatic annulment."

Peggy was unexpectedly furious at Brock. He should have married her years ago. Then none of this would have happened. She was immediately ashamed. This was her fault, not Brock's. She dreaded telling him the trouble she'd gotten into.

It was a topic she had no idea how to broach. She'd have to tell Bex, too. If nothing else, she'd want Josh to look over the legal documents.

"If the two of you failed to, ahem, consummate the marriage, we can also use that," Mayhew said.

"We passed out with our clothes on!" Peggy sprang forward in her chair, nearly slipping off the edge. Bex had been right all along. Nothing had happened! Absolutely nothing! "Luke? Tell him nothing happened."

At last, she looked Luke in the face.

He had a longish nose and ruddy cheeks, as though he'd just come inside from the cold, and thin, tortoiseshell-framed glasses. His shaggy hair needed cutting, but it gave him an appealing, boyish rumpled quality. *Brock is a hundred times more handsome,* Peggy corrected herself fiercely. *He doesn't dress like some aging J.Crew poster child, either.*

But the air in the office was at once steamy, and she was conscious of it, and of an animated-sounding discussion in the front room.

"If that's what you want to say, I'll back you up," Luke answered as the noise of women's voices came up outside the office door.

"Failure to consummate it is," Mayhew said.

The door opened.

"She's right in there!" chirped the front-desk woman, who escorted in a very small, very wet, very old lady in a yellow rain slicker.

Mayhew was clearly surprised, but he stood up and extended his hand. "Miss Abigail. To what do we owe this pleasure?"

The lady's rain hat was patched with duct tape. Rain pooled under her rusty galoshes. "Lowie, is it true? My great-nephew has taken a wife?"

Luke's jaw tensed as he, too, got to his feet. "What are you doing here?" He sounded as if he were trying hard not to raise his voice.

"Why, meeting your bride. And this is she? Well, well." The lady came up to cup Peggy's chin in one hand. "The proper question, young man, is why was it necessary for me to hear about this just now, over the telephone, from Geri? How long have you been married, Luke? Where did you two meet? How have I never heard of this young lady?"

To his credit, Luke remained in control. "You *told* her, Geri?"

"Gosh, I figured she knew! I called to say congratulations." Geri's round face drooped. "Did I spoil a surprise?"

"Welcome to the family, dear," the old lady told Peggy. "I'm sorry Luke seems to have forgotten his manners. I am Abigail Agatha Sarah Sedgwick, and I understand you are of the New Nineveh Adamses? You do plan to have children, I presume?"

Peggy tried to dislodge her chin from the old woman's iron grip. "Um, I—"

Luke was still speaking to Geri. "Why do you think Peggy and I are here today?"

"Naturally, to update your paperwork. We always advise newlyweds to come in and—"

Peggy pried Miss Abigail's hand away. "That's not it." She looked from Miss Abigail to Geri and back again. "We're getting an annulment."

Miss Abigail stepped back as if she'd been slapped.

Luke glared at Peggy. He tried to take his great-aunt's arm. "Abby, have a seat."

Miss Abigail yanked her arm away and remained standing. "We're New Nineveh's oldest family, Luke, and our survival is at stake. You're the only hope. It's your responsibility as the last surviving Sedgwick to provide an heir."

"Lowell, please put the paperwork through as we've agreed," Luke said quietly.

"Lowie, kindly explain to my great-nephew. We do not get divorced. When a Sedgwick marries, a Sedgwick stays married. We must set a good, moral example. And this young lady is of the New Nineveh Adamses! I didn't know there were any left."

Luke's hands were in fists. He stuck them in his pockets. "Abby, our family has no power anymore. We don't need to set examples. It's a brave new world out there. And technically this isn't a divorce, it's an annulment."

Miss Abigail gasped and fanned herself with her rain hat.

"Forgive me," Luke said evenly, "but when will it occur to you that the only person left who cares about the Sedgwick legacy is you?"

His words were eclipsed by Geri's shriek.

Abigail Agatha Sarah Sedgwick was collapsing. In slow motion her knees buckled, her eyes fluttered shut, and she pitched forward onto the well-worn carpet of the Law Offices of Lowell C. Mayhew.

Peggy had read every page of a three-year-old copy of *AARP* magazine and was considering moving on to *Field & Stream* when a man in scrubs strode into the emergency room waiting area. Luke, who had been absorbed in the sea-foam green walls for the past ninety minutes, stood up. Peggy did the same.

Luke looked at her. "You don't need to be here." He sounded about as pleased at her company as she was at his.

"I don't have a choice." Somehow she had ended up in the ambulance with Luke and Miss Abigail, and now she was stranded fifteen miles from New Nineveh in this hospital in

Torrington, Connecticut, a place she'd never heard of. What if Brock were calling the store, looking for her? It was two o'clock; she'd been out of communication half the day. She'd forgotten her phone on the front seat of the Chevy on Church Street. If she ever got back to the car, she'd no doubt find the window smashed and the phone gone.

The doctor motioned Luke down a long corridor. Peggy followed; Luke was her only link to the outside world. After a few steps, the doctor said, "Luke Sedgwick, right? Tim Stancil. Your parents were on my paper route. How are they?"

"Dead. How's my great-aunt?"

"Sorry, man."

"Thanks. How's my great-aunt?"

Dr. Stancil didn't appear affected by Luke's unfriendliness. "We'll need to do a few follow-ups to be sure, but the neurologist will fill you in." They had arrived at the room. Luke's great-aunt lay asleep in bed, her legs two sticks under the thin blanket. An IV protruded from a knotty blue vein in one crooked hand.

A doctor with ballpoint-pen marks on the pocket of his white coat stepped forward. "Your grandmother has had a transient ischemic attack, a brief cessation in blood flow to a region of the brain."

Peggy had half a mind to explain that Miss Abigail wasn't Luke's grandmother and to ask the neurologist to please speak in English.

"A stroke?" Luke asked.

"A sort of practice stroke, if you'll pardon the expression. TIA presents with strokelike symptoms—vertigo, partial numbness, weakness, and so on—but the symptoms resolve within minutes. In a real stroke, the effects can be permanent."

Abigail's eyes snapped open, alert in her thin, wizened face. "I'm fine. It was the shock. Nothing more."

Luke knelt beside her. "How are you?" He spoke softly, holding his palm against her forehead as if she were an ill child. "Are you dizzy, or numb?"

"I'm ready to go home." Miss Abigail's voice was reedy but firm. "Gentlemen, if you'll excuse me so I may get dressed…"

The neurologist said to Luke, "We'll need to keep her for a day or two. We consider TIA a warning signal. About a third of patients who've had one will eventually have a larger stroke."

"How eventually?"

"It might be days or months, but likely within a year. She'll need to curtail any strenuous activities that might put stress on her heart—stair climbing, lifting heavy objects, and so forth."

Miss Abigail was annoyed, Peggy could tell, that the doctor was talking not to her, but to Luke. The old woman addressed the neurologist: "I'd like to speak with my nephew in private."

When the doctors moved on, Miss Abigail pressed a button to raise herself to a sitting position. "Pull the curtain."

"I'll wait in the hall." Peggy started to leave.

Miss Abigail rattled her IV. "Nonsense. Luke, pull the curtain, please"

Luke drew the privacy curtain, enclosing the three of them in a bubble of turquoise vinyl.

"When did you two get married?" Miss Abigail said.

"Last week," Luke mumbled.

Peggy waited for him to add an explanation. "It was kind of a whirlwind courtship," she said, when it became clear he didn't plan on volunteering anything else. "You know how that is. You get caught up in the moment and all of a sudden you're married." She tittered agitatedly.

Miss Abigail looked Peggy up and down.

Peggy's mind raced, anticipating the barrage of questions to which, she knew, her own parents would subject her. No one said a word. Rattled, she blurted, "It was love at first sight. Like in the movies? We saw each other across a crowded room, our eyes locked, and we *knew*." Blushing at the lie, she looked over at Luke, signaling that it was now time for him to flesh out the story, but he appeared absorbed by an invisible spot on the hospital floor.

Miss Abigail cleared her throat. "I see."

Peggy waited; now the questions would begin. When they didn't, she continued, desperate to fill the silence, "So I guess, then, you might be wondering why we're getting an annulment. I mean, *I'd* wonder, if I were you." She glanced again at Luke, but his impassive expression made it clear she was on her own. "All right," she stammered. "I think the easiest way to explain it is to say that sometimes, what seems right in a romantic moment doesn't pan out in the cold light of day." She was blathering, mixing metaphors. "I mean, as one example, there's the simple matter of where we would live. I have a small business in New York I can't possibly leave behind. And Luke, well, he simply adores Connecticut—" She stopped, distracted by a barely detectable flash of alarm on Luke's face. "S-so, you see," she concluded, "for this and many other reasons we think it best to go our separate ways."

Miss Abigail stayed silent for a moment, and then said, "You heard the doctor. I don't have a lot of time left."

"You don't know that," Luke interjected. "It's only a third of patients—"

"Don't give me that claptrap, young man. I'm ninety-one years old. I've lived a long life with no regrets. Until this morning. Now I must go to my grave knowing I let the last living Sedgwick get divorced."

"It's an annulment." There was nothing in Luke's voice to indicate he was upset, but his hands were in fists again.

Peggy squirmed. "I'm happy to wait in the hall now, really."

The elderly woman fixed her with the most piercing look Peggy had ever witnessed; the fact that Miss Abigail had started to cough violently only made its immobilizing power more impressive. Luke offered his great-aunt a cup of water from the bedside carafe, but she snubbed him. "This concerns you, too, young lady," she said when the coughing had subsided. "Luke, you've been after me for years to sell my home. I've been after you for years to find a suitable wife. Now you've got one, a descendant of a fine old family."

"Actually, I'm not related to—"

The rest of Peggy's response was lost in a fresh round of coughing from Miss Abigail. The poor woman didn't sound good. Did these doctors know what they were doing? The caliber of medical talent here couldn't be what it was in Manhattan. On the monitors behind the bed, lines of light traveled steadily up and down, up and down.

"You have a wife. I'd like you to keep her." Miss Abigail had again recovered. "I'm offering you two the house. Stay married, and I'll sign it over to you both. You'll of course move in right away, Peggy, and then the two of you may take control of the house after a year, assuming I don't die first."

"Abby, you're not going to die. And I have no interest in that house. I've said so a hundred times."

"Yes, but this time I've made a decision. When I deed it to you, you may sell it, if you must, and move me into one of those infernal rest homes. The balance of the money would go to the two of you, naturally." She eyed Peggy. "May I presume you've seen my charming home?"

Peggy said nothing.

Miss Abigail clucked her tongue. "What has happened to your manners, Luke?"

"Sell the house? What happened to 'Only Sedgwicks shall live under the Sedwick roof'?"

"I've changed my mind. As I'm certain you and Peggy will once she's moved in."

"Abby, this is absurd. Neither of us wants to stay married. I'm sure Peggy will back me up."

Lowell Mayhew's pink face appeared around the curtain. "Miss Abigail? Pardon the intrusion. I came to check on you. You gave us quite a scare."

"It's no intrusion, Lowie, I'm fine. Come in." Miss Abigail pulled the blanket up to her chin. "I'd like to change my will."

Mayhew raised a bushy eyebrow at Luke and asked in a low voice, "Did you talk to her?" Luke shook his head.

If Miss Abigail had overheard, she didn't let on. "Luke? Peggy? Do we have an understanding?"

"I'm afraid not," Luke declared. "Peggy?"

The monitor light made its endless hills and valleys. Hills and valleys. Hills and valleys. Peggy felt hypnotized. *Bex will be in the hospital eventually,* she thought, out of nowhere. *If the fertility treatments work, I'll be visiting her in the maternity ward.* She wouldn't acknowledge her next thought: *Unless something goes wrong.*

"Peggy?"

"Right, yes," Peggy said. "I'm sorry, Miss Abigail. I agree with Luke."

Peggy was so glad Mayhew had offered to drive her back to New Nineveh, she barely worried whether he might be a serial killer disguised as a kindly country lawyer. She was so happy to be in her rented Chevy—which hadn't been broken into after all—she forgot to fret about skidding in a residual puddle and flying off the interstate into a ditch. The rain had ended, and as she drove out of town, she sang aloud to the radio.

But by the time she'd gone thirty miles, she was again apprehensive over whether Luke's batty great-aunt would really be okay. That fall onto Mayhew's floor had looked serious, and she had to have been delirious in the hospital, making that offer. Did the old lady really think she could keep two people together by dangling some quaint country cottage in front of them like a carrot on a stick?

"I'm Crazy Carl Kirkendall, Connecticut's Carpet King. And if you need floor covering, we'll treat you like royalty!" a man shouted out of the radio. Peggy shut it off so she could think.

Maybe it's not a cottage. The Sedgwicks were the oldest family in New Nineveh, Miss Abigail had said. Families like that had money. And cottages didn't have names like the Silas Sedgwick House.

New Nineveh certainly had its share of mammoth old homes—the kind New Yorkers called "antiques," spent a fortune on, and used as weekend places. If Miss Abigail's house was one of the fancy ones, it might fetch two, or three, or four million dollars—half of which, after she'd split the proceeds with Luke, would handily cover the increased rent on the shop. What if the house was worth five, eight, ten million? She and Bex could hire more sales help, redecorate, open a second store on the East Side or downtown. They could get better medical insurance that would cover Bex's fertility treatments and some sorely needed therapy for Peggy.

It was outrageous. Why was she thinking this way? She turned the radio back on and forced herself to sing along until she crossed the Henry Hudson Bridge into Manhattan and the thoughts of easy money crept back in. *Stop it, Peggy.* She couldn't imagine what, even drunk, she had seen in Luke Sedgwick. He wasn't her type. Brock was a confident man's man, not some sullen or unkempt preppy. She shelved her twisted fantasy, thankful she'd have to see Luke only once more—in court in about three months for a final hearing on the annulment. The idea of this whole mess being over by December or January pleased her to the point that, she thought, pulling into the car rental place, settling the bill, and walking down Broadway toward home, she might just confess her mistake to Brock tonight and get it over with. It was six-thirty; Brock would be back from the gym. She could cook him dinner and break it to him gently.

Brock was in their bedroom, packing. "Last-minute gig," he greeted her, putting a rolled-up T-shirt into his travel duffel. "A guy in L.A. needs some fast B-roll for a surf documentary. Going to JFK ASAP."

The barrage of abbreviations hurt Peggy's brain. "But you don't shoot surfing footage."

"Ha! I do now." Brock pumped his fist in the air victoriously.

Peggy crossed her arms over her chest. "But I was going to make chicken piccata." *Beautiful. Now you're a whiny housewife. In every way but the "wife" part.* How was it a stranger could marry her after a few hours when her own boyfriend couldn't make up his mind after nearly a decade? Against her better judgment, she muttered, "I don't understand why we can't just get engaged."

"Hey." Brock play-punched her on the shoulder. "Hang in there." He added a pair of swim trunks to his duffel. "You know I don't want to end up having a midlife crisis and trading you in for a newer model."

"Then don't. You're not your father." How many times had she heard this excuse?

"Plus," Brock said, "there's the money thing."

This was new. Brock wasn't one to lie awake at night mentally counting pennies. "Money thing?"

"Weddings are expensive, Pegs. And you know I want the best for us. Why do you think I'm working like a dog?"

It was the first time Brock had mentioned an actual, concrete wedding.

She wanted to be sure she'd heard him correctly. "You're working this hard to pay for our wedding?" she repeated, trying to contain her hope and excitement.

"Sure." Brock hoisted the duffel onto his shoulder and started toward the apartment door. "I'll be in California till Thursday, and then to Denver for the Broncs game. See you in a week."

And that's when she knew what she was going to do.

Peggy threw her arms around Brock's neck and kissed him.

"What was that for?" Brock staggered backward, clearly as surprised as she was at her enthusiastic good-bye.

She hugged him as hard as she could. "You don't have to worry. Go on your trip. I'll take care of everything. And wear sunscreen!" she added, unable to resist, as he disappeared into the elevator.

"I still don't get why you couldn't come to SoNo tonight. I hate this house. Your great-aunt looks at me like I'm some dead thing the cat brought in."

"Abby's in the hospital." Luke preferred the privacy of Nicole's place in South Norwalk as well. On the rare occasions she did visit the Sedgwick House, he tended, ungentlemanly as it was, to usher her quickly up to his bedroom. Tonight's conversation would take place in a more decorous location. Luke could have done without the painted Sedgwick ancestors judging him from the den walls, but the den still beat the library, which was presided over by a life-size portrait of Silas Ebenezer Sedgwick that never failed to look disapproving. "Nicki, I need to talk to you."

That got Nicole's attention. There was very little serious discussion in their relationship, exactly how they both liked it.

"If you truly want to get back together, there's something you should know."

Luke chose his words carefully as he told Nicki of his mistake in Las Vegas. He didn't have the energy for an argument, and Nicole was mythic when she was angry. Years ago, early in their relationship, Luke would get distracted by the way her green eyes seemed to darken into black and her fiery hair flashed around her face like a modern-day Medusa. He'd quickly learned to keep her away from any object she might hurl at his head.

Instead of raging at him, she stood, stretched, jutting her hipbones forward, and rearranged herself on her chair: legs extended, back slightly arched. "So you're getting it annulled for sure?"

That Nicki's pose was utterly calculated made it no less mesmerizing. A rush of heat came into Luke's groin. "It's as good as over already."

The phone—fifty years old if it was a day—rang. "The hospital," Luke said apologetically, and reached over to answer it.

"It's Peggy," said the voice on the end of the line. "Peggy Adams. I called information for your number."

Nicki yawned and got back up. "What's there to eat?" She headed out, Luke assumed, to the kitchen.

"This isn't a good time," he told Peggy. "Is there something I can help you with?"

"Actually," she said, "I have a way you and I can help each other."

FOUR

Fall Color, October

Peggy's acupuncturist, Jonah, thought she was in denial. Peggy knew because he had asked, in a studiously detached way, "Is it possible you might be in denial?"

"If anything, I'm taking charge of my own destiny." Peggy grimaced as Jonah slid a needle into her wrist. The needles were the width of hairs; she could hardly feel them, but the idea of them bothered her. Nor was she sure how much the acupuncture was helping. She felt calmer and more grounded this week, having made her deal with Luke, than she had after three months of Jonah's needles and herbs.

Jon-Keith, Peggy's colorist, went bug-eyed when she told him. "You're doing this behind Brock's back?" He had a bandanna tied around his head, and diamond earrings, and he resembled a pirate who'd wandered into midtown. "Won't he notice you've moved to Connecticut? And while you're gone, who'll mind the store?"

Peggy spoke to his reflection in the salon mirror. "Here's what's so brilliant. I won't be moving to Connecticut. Luke's great-aunt wanted me to, but I told her I couldn't give up the shop completely, at least not right way. So we compromised. I'll live in the city during the week as usual. Then on weekends, when Brock is working anyway, I'll go to New Nineveh and pretend to be happily married to Luke. Brock won't have any idea. In one year I'll be able to shore up my business, with plenty of money left over for a big wedding. Then Bex won't have to worry about money, and Brock won't have to worry about proposing." She'd say the money was an inheritance from a long-lost relative. It was the only shaky part of the plan. Given her family's utter lack of wealth, she couldn't imagine anybody believing that some fourth cousin twice removed had left her a truckload of cash. But Brock wasn't one to get bogged down in details. With luck, he'd be too thrilled to ask questions.

"Oh, okay." Jon-Keith began to section off Peggy's hair with plastic clips. "So you'll spend a year screwing this Luke What-You-Said-His-Name-Is, and then marry Brock. Dare you wear white?"

"It isn't like that." The arrangement she'd worked out with Luke was all business. With Luke's great-aunt restricted from stair climbing except to get to her own second-floor bedchamber, Peggy would have a private room on the third floor, entirely separate from Luke's, and Miss Abigail would be none the wiser. There would be no sleeping together. That was a given. Peggy knew Luke Sedgwick had no more interest in her than she had in him. Once he'd finally agreed to her terms, he'd done so emotionlessly.

"Even if we wanted to, we couldn't," Peggy explained to Jon-Keith. "Otherwise we can't get an annulment when it's all over."

Nor was Bex as enthusiastic over Peggy's save-the-store scheme as Peggy would have liked.

"You're insane," Bex's disembodied voice barked out from the intercom at the entrance to her and Josh's building. "I mean, you're insane generally, but scared-of-everything insane, not throw-all-caution-to-the-wind insane." Peggy shifted the six-pack of beer she was carrying and waited for

Bex to wrap up the lecture. "Nobody does this," Bex continued. "*I* wouldn't do this, and I'd do a lot more than you would." The interior doors buzzed open, and Peggy scaled the five flights of stairs and found Bex, furiously gnawing a half-eaten slice of pizza, and Josh, holding a sheaf of legal documents, standing together out in the building corridor at the open doorway to Josh's apartment.

Peggy handed the beer to Josh. "Your fee." She looked at Bex. "So much for the organic food, then?"

"I can't help it. The Pill makes me starving all the time. I'm not even pregnant and I'm turning into a whale." Bex sank her teeth into her pizza and continued with her mouth full, "You should be anxious. You don't even know the man! Why aren't you anxious? Josh, tell her she should be anxious."

"No way." Bex's husband bent to retrieve a piece of pepperoni on the floor. "I'm Switzerland over here."

"Let's go inside." Peggy stepped between her friends to enter the apartment. Wasn't Bex always pushing her to break out of her comfort zone? Peggy felt no anxiety whatsoever about what was happening. No anxiety—like a normal person. She felt insulated, as if enjoying a madcap play in which the spunky heroine, Peggy Adams, was preparing to drive up to Connecticut tomorrow to start her brand-new double life. Or a stirring drama at the end of which brave Peggy would save her business, help her beloved best friend, and end up married to the real man she loved. The only hard part would be making sure Miss Abigail thought she and Luke were truly mad for each other, like real newlyweds, making a go of their marriage instead of just biding time to win their prize. That would be no small feat.

"The terms of the deal look fine." Josh hugged Peggy and gave her the papers. "I also had a guy I know in Connecticut look it over, and he says it's pretty straightforward stuff. Turns out this lawyer, Andy, has a cousin who went to Yale with your new weekend hubby. Says Sedgwick's an okay guy."

Bex plopped down on Josh's scratchy plaid couch. "I'm working weekends so you can go live with an okay guy."

"An okay guy who's sitting on a gold mine," Josh said. "Andy checked into the value of the house. Based on its last tax assessment, it's worth about three million."

"Three million dollars!" Bex bounced on the sofa.

Peggy wasn't surprised. She had done her own due diligence. She'd researched Sedgwick genealogy on the Internet. The family dated back to *Mayflower* times. Silas Ebenezer, the patriarch, was a Revolutionary War hero who'd made his fortune importing goods from Europe. And then there was the Silas Sedgwick House. The New Nineveh Historical Society called it "a Litchfield County architectural landmark," "a Colonial Revival gem." It had three stories, two rambling additions, and twenty-one rooms. Black-and-white photos on the society's Web site showed a spectacular mansion set behind towering trees with a formal garden. Peggy had hardly been able to believe her luck, even when she'd learned she'd be staying there with not just Luke, but his great-aunt, too—one big happy family.

"I know it sounds insane, Bex, but everything is falling into place." Peggy sat squeamishly on the coffee table, checking first to make sure it wasn't sticky. You never knew in Josh's apartment. "It'll be good for the store. It will be good for me and Brock. And it'll be good for you. I've been letting you take care of me for far too long. It's time I made a contribution. Besides, it's only until next September."

Bex had a fleck of tomato sauce on her cheek. "What if the old lady lives another twenty years? You'll never get to marry Brock. Not a huge tragedy in my opinion, but still, you're stuck in a sexless marriage to a random person you don't care about. Have you thought of that?"

"She can always back out, sweetie," Josh said. "The will just says if they're still married in twelve months, they'll get the house. There's nothing forcing them to stay together for life."

On Saturday, Peggy turned her rental car, a Pontiac this time, onto Church Street, toward the traffic light that swung on a cable over the center of town—the intersection of Church and Main. As she waited at the light, she leaned over the steering wheel to get a better look at New Nineveh. She couldn't get over how postcard pretty it was, with its picturesque churches and shops arranged around a central lawn. The single incongruity was a group of picketers on the grass. "Save Our Town!" their signs read. "Stop Destroying History!" It was surprising to find strife in this serene setting. She'd have to find out what they were protesting.

She peered up Main Street, trying to locate the Silas Sedgwick House, but the homes were set back behind yellow- and magenta-leafed trees. When the light changed, she turned left onto Main and counted houses in from the corner on the right: One. Two. And then, three.

Her arms broke out in goose bumps.

It was a breathtaking, magnificent white-clapboard structure. Two pairs of first- and second-story windows with black-painted shutters were set on either side of a grand front door flanked with four columns. Above the door, on the second story, a dramatic central window arched toward the third floor, where a smaller crescent window curved up toward a graceful, sloping roof. The roof was crowned with a flat widow's walk surrounded by an ornate balustrade.

Four sturdy chimneys rose, one from each corner. On the front of the house was a neat white plaque with black-painted lettering:

Silas Ebenezer Sedgwick
1796

The historical society photographs hadn't done it justice.

Awed, Peggy turned into the shallow semicircular gravel driveway between Main Street and the house so abruptly that the Pontiac's tires squealed. She stepped out of the car, locked the door, and stood in the fall air.

Balanced high on a ladder in the front yard, a frail figure was sawing branches from an oranging maple.

Peggy's breath caught in her chest. A low picket fence separated the front yard from the sidewalk, and she hurried through its gate and across the lawn, afraid of startling Miss Abigail off her unsteady perch. Why wasn't Luke pruning the trees? Really, why wasn't a gardener doing it? A house this size would have a gardener.

At the tree, bits of wood rained onto the lawn. Peggy stepped between fallen branches, dodging another that was plummeting to the ground. "Should you be up there? Isn't this considered strenuous—"

"Look out below!" Miss Abigail called. Another slender branch dropped near Peggy's feet. Miss Abigail regarded it with a cold eye and nodded. "That should do for today." She started down the ladder, disregarding the hand Peggy held out to her, passing Peggy the saw instead. "If Luke asks, our neighbor Mr. Fiorentino chopped off those branches, and I was not on that ladder."

For the first time since she'd called Luke two weeks and a day ago, Peggy felt an unwelcome pang of apprehension:

What have I gotten myself into? She made the decision to ignore it and carried the saw carefully as Miss Abigail hauled the severed branches to a small stand Peggy hadn't noticed at the edge of the front yard. A wooden box with the words *Honor System* on it sat on the counter next to half a dozen metal buckets. Miss Abigail panted a bit as she arranged the branches in the buckets, one eye on a woman who was coming up the sidewalk. "The Sedgwick maple is the oldest tree in town." She stopped as the woman arrived, then continued, "Silas had it planted when the house was built."

The woman, who was around seventy, wore impenetrable round sunglasses. " 'One dollar a branch,' " she read. "Hmm. Interesting. You've lowered your prices."

Miss Abigail smiled. "Mrs. Riga, may I present Mrs. Sedgwick."

Peggy didn't understand why Mrs. Riga was watching her expectantly. Then—oh, dear—was *she* supposed to be Mrs. Sedgwick? "Call me Peggy." She felt like a mouse under the woman's owlish stare.

"Call me Ernestine. My husband and I live back on Market Road, in what used to be the Sedgwick carriage house." The woman cocked her head to one side. "Let's see the ring."

Oh, dear. The ring. Still holding the saw, Peggy showed Ernestine Brock's promise ring uncomfortably. *I'm doing this for him,* she reminded herself.

"That from Star Jewelers, honey?" Ernestine listed to the left as her oversize designer handbag slid off her shoulder onto her arm. "Remember my grandma pin, Abigail—the one with all the children's birthstones? It took that place nearly a month to fix the clasp. A month! It's so New Nineveh. What else does that jeweler have to do?" She pushed the bag back up where it belonged. "Now, Peggy, I hear you're only here on weekends. Why?"

"Peggy has a little business in the city," Miss Abigail explained. "She sells mops and buckets."

"Well, *that'll* come in handy around the Sedgwick House." Ernestine sounded perhaps the tiniest bit contemptuous. It was hard to tell.

Peggy hesitated. She wanted to set the record straight but didn't want to be disrespectful to Miss Abigail. "It isn't mops and buckets, though," she said carefully. "It's called ACME Cleaning Supply, but we sell bath products, like soap."

"Well, it won't be forever, will it, dear? You'll be moving up to New Nineveh soon enough, I'm sure," Miss Abigail said. Peggy felt as if she were being interrogated.

It was Ernestine who ended the grilling. "I'm off. Peggy, you'll come over sometime for a look at my flower stand. See you at the party!"

Miss Abigail held on to her smile until Ernestine was well down the sidewalk. "I'll be introducing you at a small reception, dear, next Sunday afternoon. I presume your family is in New York? I'd like to invite them—your parents and brothers and sisters."

Peggy imagined the look on Miss Abigail's face when Max and Madeleine Adams parked their RV in Silas Ebenezer Sedgwick's driveway. "I'm an only child. We're from Northern California, but right now my parents are traveling. They'd love to be here otherwise."

It wasn't entirely false. Peggy's father had been a middle manager for a California department store chain and had moved from town to town, assignment to assignment, when the mood struck. Peggy had spent her last two years of high school, anyway, in Northern California. And her parents *were* traveling; a few years ago, Max had cashed in his retirement nest egg to finance his dream of crisscrossing the West in perpetuity in a recreational vehicle. Peggy suspected her parents' lifestyle choice would not sit well with Miss Abigail. It didn't sit well with Peggy, though the RV wasn't what bothered her—it was that their future was too precarious, too uncertain.

"Let's go inside." Miss Abigail started toward the house, her steps short and slow across the leaf-scattered lawn.

"Who'll watch the flower stand?" Peggy considered volunteering to stay outside. Her decision to remain married to Luke was seeming hasty and foolish. She doubted she could keep up the charade for an hour, let alone a year. "That box isn't locked. Anyone could walk off with your money."

"This isn't New York City, dear."

Up close, the Silas Sedgwick House front door was even more imposing than it was from the car—perhaps nine feet tall and broader than a regular door, with a weathered brass knocker set squarely in the center, a good foot above Miss Abigail's cotton candy head. But it also needed a paint job. Strips of black had peeled away, revealing bare wood underneath like the glimpse of shirt through the elbows of Luke's shabby sweater.

Miss Abigail threw her whole body against the door, and it creaked open. "Welcome," she said, ushering Peggy inside.

"Don't tell me you don't know what to say. You're a writer. Or so you claim." Nicki brandished her cell phone at Luke. "You know lots of words. How about these? 'Stop. Leave me alone, bitch. I'm backing out.' "

The couch opposite Nicki was littered with lacy pillows. Luke shoved them to one side and sat down. "I'm not backing out." This scheme with Peggy was repugnant and unseemly and went against every fiber of his being. It was also the best thing to happen to the family finances in half a century—and, to Luke himself, ever. He'd been shocked at first at Peggy's proposal and hung up summarily, but by morning he'd reversed his thinking and called her back. Hadn't he dreamed his entire life of living someplace where no one knew his business back for generations? Hadn't he longed to pursue his poetry, to break free of the Sedgwick name, to escape the ingrained notions of how to live, whom to be friends with, what to do? Now he could and, more crucially, ensure his great-aunt had the kind of medical care she deserved. "It's a winning situation for all of us," he told Nicki, sounding like one of the speakers at the Family Asset Management Conference.

Nicki waved the phone at him. "What's her number? I'll call her myself."

"Put that down," Luke said coolly. The third or fourth time he and Nicki had broken up, right here in her artist's loft in South Norwalk, with its bohemian view of the New Haven line train trestle, she'd thrown her coffee at him. It had hit the back wall and splattered to the floor, ruining the weaving project Nicki had been working on at the time, a shawl-like garment fashioned from what looked like pink barbed wire. Luke secretly believed he had saved the world from it.

Nicki shut the phone but didn't put it down. "What about me? I'm supposed to stay out of your life for a year?"

"Not if you don't want to."

"You mean if I want to sneak around, see you only during the week, and stay away from New Nineveh completely."

"You're at craft shows nearly every weekend anyway. And if you don't come to New Nineveh, you won't have to visit with my great-aunt."

Luke was worried about Abby. She'd returned from the hospital uncharacteristically docile, obediently following her doctor's orders to avoid taxing activities, like gardening, that she'd always enjoyed. She was more muddled, too; he'd tried to make her understand Peggy Adams was not related to the extinct Adams family of New Nineveh, which had once rivaled the Sedgwicks in importance, but she couldn't grasp it.

He frowned. "I'm afraid Abby might not be around very long."

"You'd better hope she isn't. It'll kill the old lady for sure when you dump that Vegas whore after a year."

"Don't call her that. It's unbecoming to you."

"Well, la-di-da."

"Anyway, we'll cross that bridge when we get there." Luke was thinking, suddenly, that he and Nicki should break up once and for all. Life would be considerably easier.

Then he thought, *Bridge*. The word brought to mind Peggy Adams. But why, he didn't know.

"What's she like?" Nicki asked. "The Vegas whor—"

"Her name is Peggy."

Nicki rolled her eyes. "What's she like?"

In a tray on the trunk Nicki used as a coffee table, scuffed nuggets of sea glass surrounded a dusty collection of candles. "I don't know. Nervous." Luke poked at the candles. "Why don't you ever light these things?"

"Is she pretty?"

He knew he should jump in with the objective truth, that given the choice between Peggy and a five-foot-ten-inch redheaded Amazon goddess, few men would notice Peggy was in the room. He had vaguely remembered Peggy as being vivacious and intelligent, but he'd seen none of that in Mayhew's office. Obviously his attraction had been to the situation. The liquor, a stranger in a strange city: The combination had proven a potent but all-too-fleeting aphrodisiac.

Aphrodisiac. The word had great rhythm—perfectly trochaic on its own, but ideal for iambic pentameter: *An all-too-fleeting aphrodisiac. An aphrodisiac that vanishes.*

"Don't think I don't notice you aren't answering my question. Which means you think she's pretty. You want to fuck her. Why else would you stay married to her?"

She was jealous. Nicole Pappas—jealous. Like a vulnerable child, she curled her legs underneath her. Her dark snake-eyes faded back to green.

"You have nothing to worry about." Luke, the product of a culture in which the unchecked display of feeling was proof of an insufficiently rigorous upbringing, was surprised by an overwhelming surge of sappy, sloppy affection for his girlfriend. Nicki was sexy, vulgar, and dangerous. She cared about him, in her own peculiar way. They understood each other. They had never promised each other more than they were able to give.

A pillow from the pile next to him tumbled into his lap. He flipped it onto the floor. "Come over here."

She stroked the arm of her chair. "*You* come over *here*."

Luke's nerves vibrated with the inevitability of what would happen next. He pointed down at the throw pillows scattered on the rug. "I'll meet you halfway. Right there."

"That's not halfway. *That's* halfway." She pointed to a spot on the floor a few inches closer to her side of the rug.

Luke's nerves began to vibrate a little less. Did everything have to be a dispute, every time?

Nicki continued pointing fixedly at her spot on the rug.

Luke glanced past her, at the rhinestone clock some artisan had given her in barter at a crafts show. He could stay and negotiate inches, or he could leave, drive the sixty miles back to New Nineveh, and get on with the charade.

"I'll see you next week," he told Nicki.

He left his girlfriend sulking in her chair and headed out to meet the wife he'd never wanted.

Peggy blinked. She and Miss Abigail were standing in a dim front hall. A simple iron lamp hung from a medallion in the center of the high ceiling; the weak flicker of its one working bulb did nothing to dispel the gloom. To the left and right, wide door frames led into twin front parlors. In front of them, a steep staircase made a right angle as it ascended to unseen floors above, while beyond it, on this level, a narrow corridor led farther into the house. Peggy's impression was that it was a beautiful entrance, if smaller than she'd expected for a house this grand. But as her eyes adjusted, she began to make out odd details: a brown water stain on the ceiling, a monstrous cobweb in the bend in the staircase. The house smelled of ten thousand spent fireplace fires, with notes of mildew. It occurred to her that she hadn't checked the date of the historical society photos. They could easily be fifty or sixty years old.

"Luke!" Miss Abigail called. "Do you have a valise?" she asked Peggy, rubbing her hands together as if summoning a genie. "I'll send Luke to fetch it. Luke!" The name bounced hollowly through the house.

Peggy prepared herself, but Luke didn't appear in a billow of magical vapor—or any other way.

"Never mind, dear. Would you care to freshen up after your journey?"

Peggy couldn't decide whether she was glad or offended at Luke's apparent absence. She settled on glad. "I'd like to see the house, please."

"Certainly, dear." Miss Abigail led Peggy to the doorway to the right. "We'll begin here, with the gentlemen's parlor, where Silas used to retire with his guests after dinner, and his wife, Dorothy, would go with the wives across the hall to the ladies' parlor." The rooms were shadowy, with drawn heavy curtains, but Miss Abigail spoke as if she had memorized the contents of each parlor along with the names of her ancestors. "The ladies' piano was a gift from Governor Wolcott in 1797. Silas's youngest daughter, poor Temperance, was reportedly quite gifted. Do you play?"

"Only 'Chopsticks.' " Peggy didn't want to ask what had become of poor Temperance.

"Lovely. We'll have music in the house again."

A floorboard creaked as Miss Abigail led Peggy out and down the corridor, deeper into the house. They emerged in a vast room, its size more dramatic because there was no one in it. There were two separate groupings of sofas and armchairs with tattered upholstery and sprung springs. On the outside wall of the room, a door, as massive and imposing as the one through which Peggy had entered the house, led to a side garden ragged with weeds.

"This is the grand parlor." Miss Abigail stopped in front of the cold fireplace. "The family has done some of its most important entertaining here. There's also an east parlor, but we don't use that part of the house anymore. It was built for members of the Sedgwick extended family, back when generations lived under the same roof. It's too big for just Luke and me and the cat."

"You have a cat?"

"Quibble," Miss Abigail said. "You'll likely never see him. He hides under my bed."

The Oriental rug on which Miss Abigail stood was worn down to its backing. Against the wall behind her, a dusty grandfather clock stood silently, its delicate black hands stalled at four twenty-three.

Peggy thought the room terribly lonely. "Why does the house have this other formal entrance?"

"That's not an entrance, dear." Abigail walked over to the

large side door and pressed her withered hands against it. "It's to take the coffins out."

Their tour continued into the dining room off the grand parlor and then to a library, where a man Miss Abigail identified as Silas Sedgwick glowered from an oil painting above yet another fireless fireplace. The house was damp and chilly, and Peggy would have liked a heavier sweater, but Miss Abigail, seemingly unaffected by the cold, led her down another hall and into a cluttered den populated with more painted portraits.

Everyone in these pictures is dead, Peggy thought. "I might go get my luggage now," she said.

"Suit yourself," said Miss Abigail.

Forcing herself to walk, not run, Peggy wound her way through the house and back out into the bright afternoon. *Get in that car,* a part of her whispered. In two hours she could be in the city, having dinner with Bex and Josh and laughing about her five minutes of impetuousness. She unlocked the Pontiac and slipped into the driver's seat, fumbling for the ignition.

"Going so soon?"

She jumped, a nascent scream dying in her throat. Luke Sedgwick had caught the edge of the car door in one hand. A battered Volvo sedan she assumed was his stood in the gravel driveway in front of her rental.

"I'm not going anywhere," Peggy lied. "I was about to pop the trunk." She reached down, intending to open the trunk dramatically as she said "pop," but she had to grope around. Her fingertips came into contact with a latch. She pulled up on it. The trunk stayed shut, but the car's hood rose.

Curved lines bracketed Luke's mouth, as if he were about to laugh at her.

"Could you close the hood?" Peggy would have liked to

tell him to wipe that smirk off his face, but the most important thing was for the two of them to get along. It would be a long year otherwise.

Luke let go of the car door and deftly shut the hood, and Peggy located the correct latch and disengaged the trunk. She had been prepared to carry her own luggage, but Luke lifted out her suitcase and set it at the top of the driveway. Peggy brought over two totes, a shopping bag, a gift basket for Miss Abigail of bath products from the store—tea rose, always a crowd-pleaser—and a pillow.

Luke looked at her strangely. "We have linens."

She decided not to try to explain her strange-bed phobia and followed him as he loped back toward the house with her suitcase.

At the front door, she paused. "Aren't you supposed to carry me over the threshold?" She laughed at her own joke, but Luke looked stricken, as if she'd just suggested they swing naked from the Sedgwick maple. She turned away so he wouldn't see her embarrassment, took a breath, and went in alone.

FIVE

Luke returned to his study, on edge. Yesterday had been a terrible day in the market. The Dow had fallen by five percent, which was bad enough, but he had managed to do even worse, losing seven percent from the already dismal Sedgwick family portfolio. At this rate, its most valuable asset would soon be the worthless few acres the family still owned out on the highway. In just the past two weeks, with his time and energy taken up by this marriage business, Luke had lost his focus completely. On top of it all, he had poetry running through his head. Phrases, lines, whole stanzas—as if a rusty tap had been reopened and water was flowing crazily every which way. All he wanted to do was sit quietly and write it all down.

"An aphrodisiac that vanishes," he whispered. "An aphrodisiac that fades away. An aphrodisiac that disappears."

Somebody coughed.

The sound startled him only slightly; in the back of his mind, he'd made note of footsteps clacking down the hall. He scrawled the aphrodisiac lines on the back of an envelope.

Peggy stood in the doorway. "I thought we should talk."

A talk already? Eight minutes into their marriage of convenience? "Have a seat." Luke sounded more genial than he felt.

"There's nowhere to sit."

She was right. The space was a cavernous rectangle—Luke

liked to annoy his great-aunt by threatening to convert it into a squash court—running the whole front length of the house, with a high, vaulted ceiling that followed the sloping roofline. It was empty except for his desk and chair and a massive old mirror leaning against a wall. He rose and offered his seat to her, but she declined. That meant he'd have to remain on his feet, because it would be impolite to sit back down. The two stood awkwardly next to the desk.

She looked around. "What is this room for, anyway?"

"It used to be the ballroom. That's the half-moon window you see from the street, over the big Palladian window on the second floor. I come here to work." He waited for Peggy to get the hint. Another line came to him: *Delusional, like permanence, or wealth.* And another: *A shimmering, as if love were a ghost.* He wrote both down.

"I want a room upgrade."

He put down his pen and laughed.

"Why is that funny?" She folded her arms across her chest.

He folded his arms over his chest, mimicking her stance. "I'm not running an inn."

"You gave me the worst room on the whole floor, with a twin bed and old seventies furniture. I counted three empty bedrooms on my way here. They all have queen-size beds and chandeliers and fireplaces."

"How do you know?"

"I opened the doors and looked."

He switched on his desk lamp. As a child, she would have been one of those thin-skinned, bookish girls who were almost too easy to tease, and certainly not the sturdy, suntanned field hockey player, of the sort he'd never been attracted to, with whom his parents and great-aunt had always expected he'd settle down nevertheless.

But Peggy's uneasy mix of shyness and aggression was interesting, in an anthropological sense. He studied her. "I know you're not an Adams, but you're not even a Yankee, are you?"

"Sure I am. I was born and raised in California."

He laughed again. "That doesn't count."

"If you're not from the South, aren't you a Yankee?"

"Only to people in the South," he said.

She looked out the crescent window at the waning afternoon. "Well, I'm a New Yorker now, and no self-respecting New Yorker would settle for that room." She faced him. "Like it or not, I'm not a guest. I'll be living here weekends until our year is up." By the terms of Miss Abigail's offer that would be next September, the day of their wedding anniversary. "And I'm your business partner with a legal interest in this house."

As if it had been waiting, the sheet of plaster that had been threatening for weeks to fall from the ceiling dropped resignedly into one corner.

"Um . . . ," Peggy faltered. "We also need to talk about your great-aunt's party next weekend—how we're going to behave as a, you know, couple." She was blushing again. "Like, what we'll do if people start tapping on their glasses. You know how people do that at wedding receptions? So the couple will"—she hesitated—"kiss?"

A reception. Just what he needed. Abigail hadn't mentioned a thing about it. Two hours of cocktails and small talk and pretending to be married. It would take a Shakespearean actor to pull it off, and Luke was no actor. He supposed Peggy was enjoying this, that she was yet another of those women, like Nicki, who thrived on drama. "There will be no glass tapping, I assure you. Lesson one about Yankees: We don't like public displays of affection."

"What a relief," Peggy said.

Luke thought of their wedding chapel photo, recalled suddenly the dress she'd worn—conservative in front, daringly low in the back. She'd knocked the breath out of him, he remembered now, this demure blonde with a smoldering sensuality lacking in any Yankee girl he'd ever met, but not overtly sexual, like Nicki. Sugar and spice. Naughty and nice. Intriguing. "Do you *want* people to tap their glasses?" He had to admit, the thought of kissing her wasn't at all offputting.

"No! Absolutely not!" She crossed her arms over her chest again and glared at him.

"All right, then." His unsavory thoughts vanished as quickly as they'd arrived. "Is there anything else?"

"I want a new room."

He was desperate to get back to his three lines of poetry. There were still a few minutes left to work on them before dinner. Abby liked to eat promptly at five-thirty, and he knew she was preparing something celebratory. He thought about explaining that he'd given Peggy the best room available, the one with the working heat and no evidence of mice. He'd spent the past three days cleaning it. He'd aired the mattress outside and rolled back the rug to mop underneath.

"Pick any room you like," he said.

Climbing the stairs that evening, Peggy couldn't decide whether she'd done well at dinner or not. Miss Abigail had been welcoming, regaling her with tales of the Sedgwick family history and of Luke's exploits as a teenager. But at one point, she'd set down her fork and beamed at Peggy. "I was fond of your grandmother Tippy, dear."

"Tippy?" Peggy had asked, swallowing, with relief, the last bite of a bland, leaden biscuit.

Luke said, "Tippy *Adams,* your grandmother."

Luckily, at least from a conversational perspective, Miss Abigail had just decided they needed more biscuits. When she'd left the room, Luke muttered, "Play along. She really believes you're a descendant of an old Connecticut family."

"But I'm not," Peggy protested. "My dad's family came over from Russia. They were named Adams at Ellis Island. I don't want to lie to her."

"What does it matter? It makes her happy. For all we know, there never was a Tippy Adams, and Abby's imagining the whole thing. Besides, we're already stretching the truth to the breaking point."

"Then I don't want to stretch it any more than we have to."

Miss Abigail returned with a refilled basket of biscuits. "Now, Peggy, tell me," she said. "How did you and my great-nephew meet?"

Peggy's mind went blank. In their negotiations over the past two weeks, Luke had provided her with the fictional outline of their phony romance, but just then, at the dinner table, she was unable to dredge up a single detail, except that she and Luke had supposedly dated for only a month before getting married. Peggy accepted another biscuit to buy time, and racked her brain for the gist of the story.

"Oh! Through our mutual friend, Thayer Whittaker!" she exclaimed at last, like a quiz show contestant. Luke looked up at the ceiling, as if praying for patience.

"Isn't that nice," Miss Abigail said, then wrinkled her forehead. "Remind me, please, dear. Who is Thayer Whittaker?"

Peggy was certain of this one. "He was a classmate of Luke's at Harvard."

"Yale," Luke said quietly. "She of course means Yale."

"I'm not sure I've met Thayer." Miss Abigail buttered a piece of biscuit. "Have I?"

"I don't think so," Peggy said. She knew for a fact that there was no such person.

The meal was a grayish roast with boiled potatoes and mushy green beans. Miss Abigail hadn't turned on the overhead light but had set a single candle on the long dining room table, and Peggy had used the near darkness to her advantage, shuttling the food back and forth across her plate instead of eating it. It had been too early for dinner anyway; she hadn't had much of an appetite. Now it was eight o'clock, and Peggy's stomach was growling. A small triumph—she had packed an energy bar in one of her tote bags.

She had chosen a new room a few doors up from her old one, with light blue floral wallpaper that, though peeling at the corners, was attractive and feminine. She ran her hand along the wall until she located the light switch, saw Luke had left linens on top of the bare bureau, and turned to the making of the bed. The mattress had no cover, and Peggy shuddered a little as she lifted it to tuck the sheet under a corner. When she dropped the mattress back down, it exhaled a cloud of dust.

She coughed and made the bed quickly, glad she'd thought to bring her own pillow. At last, she spread out the comforter. It was a hideous masculine plaid that didn't go with the room, but, Peggy thought, at least she'd busted out of her jail cell. Bex would be proud.

Something wasn't right.

Peggy awoke in pitch darkness, straining her ears for the noise. She heard nothing. She'd been dreaming. Sleep tugged at her, and she closed her eyes again.

There it was—a faint, sibilant whisper. A ghost, gossiping. A thing in her room.

She ought to flip on the light, to surprise it in its tracks, but doing so would mean getting up and putting her feet on the floor, where the Thing could grab her ankles and drag her under the bed. *Don't be an idiot. Get up and turn on the light.* She poked a foot out from under the covers.

Wait—was that it again?

Peggy jerked her foot back, her useless eyes stretched wide. It could be a burglar. Who knew if Luke bothered to lock the front door. On the way in with her luggage, when she'd relocked the car, he'd looked at her and said, just as his great-aunt had, "This isn't New York City."

The room was freezing. If the light were on, she'd probably be able to see her breath—quick, shallow gulps she was trying hard to silence. She strained to listen while noiselessly counting sixty one-one-thousands. She counted out another sixty seconds, and another. Surely, if the Thing was a burglar or murderer, he would have made himself known by now. *Count for five more minutes, and if nothing happens, it was your imagination. One, one thousand...two, one thousand...*

But the numbers tangled up in themselves, and she was back in Manhattan, in front of Brattie's Sports Pub on Amsterdam Avenue, which she'd been passing by on the rainy November afternoon she'd first met Brock. And then she was on their first date at Undine's, the warm, solid pressure of Brock's hand on her back as he escorted her to their table, making her forget how nervous she was. She thought about the wedding they'd have with the money she'd earn from sticking it out until next September twenty-sixth in this strange, cold house with a man she didn't know and didn't especially like. This was the deal she'd made. She pulled the ugly comforter up to her chin. *One weekend down,* she thought. *Only four dozen or so more to go.*

It wasn't a sound that woke Luke; it was the quality of the light. New Nineveh nights were black, especially when there was no moon, but tonight the darkness outside his window seemed illuminated artificially, as if a New York City streetlamp had sprung up among the trees that lined the sidewalk. He got up to look out the window. Below him, the side yard shone with bright streaks he knew were coming from the ladies' parlor windows. Odd, to be sure; he'd been the last to go to bed, and the house had been dark.

He tiptoed downstairs.

The entire first floor was lit up. Luke went to each deserted room, turning off the lights, knowing his great-aunt had turned them on for her own mysterious reasons. He called her name softly, searching for her, until at last he came to the library.

It had been ransacked. Objects from cabinet drawers were scattered in all directions. Shelves' worth of books had been flung onto chairs and carpets. In the middle of the chaos, Abigail drifted in bare feet and a flannel nightgown. "Gone!" she wailed. "Lost and gone!"

Luke shook the last cobweb out of his head. "It's two in the morning. It's freezing in here. Where are your robe and slippers?"

She looked at the floor, as if the robe and slippers had been there moments ago. "I've gone and lost it, Charles!"

Abigail had never before confused him with anyone else. "Let's rest awhile," Luke said, putting his arm around her shoulders.

She pushed it off, marched over, and took out a few more books.

"You shouldn't exert yourself like this. You heard what the doctor said." Luke swept aside a pile of detritus in a chair—the dial from an old telephone, a ball of rubber bands, a yellowed, half-finished needlepoint canvas tangled in thread. He would be up the rest of the night straightening the room. It would embarrass Abby to have Peggy see it like this. "Sit here and let me look."

Abigail was trembling, frustrated, and upset. This woman who'd never asked him to care for her, who'd never so much as spent a day in bed until her hospital stay last month, swayed on her feet and plucked at the sleeves of her nightgown. "But you can't help, Charles! You're gone, too!"

"Abby." Luke took a breath. "I'm Luke, your great-nephew. Trip's son, remember? Charles isn't here, but I am. Tell me what you're trying to find."

All at once, the frenzy left Abigail's movements. "Oh," she said in a small voice. "I've done it again, haven't I?"

A discarded book lay facedown on a side table—a faded copy of *The Story of Philosophy* by Will and Ariel Durant. Abigail picked it up and turned it around and around in her hands. Luke waited for her to tell him the story behind the book: which family member had acquired and owned it—perhaps his Socialist great-uncle William, of whom the family had been terribly ashamed; or Aunt Beebee, Luke's late father's late sister, who'd fancied herself an intellectual.

All Abigail did was set the book back down.

"What were you looking for?" Luke asked again softly.

"I don't know." Defeat etched his great-aunt's lined face. "I don't remember anymore."

SIX

Everyone at Brattie's Sports Pub called the bartender "the Commissioner," except for the regulars, who got to call him "the Commish." Peggy could never bring herself to use the abbreviated name. She was convinced the Commissioner hated her. It had started with an unfortunate incident early in her relationship with Brock in which, at the bar, she'd referred to the Los Angeles Dodgers and the Commissioner had pointed to the "B" on his stained baseball cap and avoided her eyes ever since. From then on, she'd let Brock go up and get the drinks.

But this Wednesday evening, Bex and Josh had joined her and Brock for a rare couples get-together, and Peggy intended to demonstrate what an insider she was at Brattie's, to impress her friends with her ease in this other world, Brock's world. Besides, Brock was at the foosball table. So here she was, waving her money, saying, "Excuse me," trying to get the Commissioner's attention. It was hopeless. Peggy smiled at her neighbor at the bar. "Could you please order me two soda waters?"

"If I could ask your opinion." The man held out his left wrist. "What do you think?"

"I think you're wearing two watches," Peggy said. One was all dials and gauges, like controls in an airplane cockpit. The other had a plain face with Roman numerals.

"Good eye. Which do you like better?"

Peggy pointed to the old-fashioned watch. It was not only simpler and more elegant, but it seemed familiar. She stared at it, trying to place where she'd seen it before.

The man laughed. "That's the one I'm getting rid of." He flagged down the Commissioner and ordered Peggy's waters.

Luke. That's what it was. Luke wore a watch like this. Peggy thought back to him on Saturday, in his enormous study, sleeves pushed up, the glint of red gold hair next to a leather watchband.

The man tapped the dials-and-gauges model. "I just bought this one. It's titanium, water-resistant to ten thousand feet, and look, it has an altimeter."

Peggy was chagrined to feel the blood rush to her cheeks—not from choosing the wrong watch, but from the memory of Luke. It wasn't as if he were attractive—all right, he was kind of nice-looking, but his personality was a disaster, and her weekend had hardly been a success. She'd slept far too late Sunday morning and had run to take a shower, only to discover that her bathroom had only a tub, had given herself a quick sponge bath when the tub appeared to be out of order, the water a feeble trickle from its lime-crusted faucet, and had rushed downstairs to cold white toast and stilted small talk. Luke had hardly glanced up from the business section of the *Hartford Courant*. She'd left for the city the moment she'd finished her lukewarm coffee, and he'd barely said good-bye. To think, starting this weekend, she'd be stuck with him Friday night and Saturday morning, too.

The Commissioner set two glasses in front of the watch man, who started to pay for them, but Peggy handed him her money and thanked him for his help.

"Thanks for *your* help..." The man waited for Peggy to introduce herself.

"I should get back to my friends," she said.

Bex was by herself at their table. "Look at my husband. Look at him." At the moment, Josh, still in shirt and tie from his day at Legal Aid, was doing a victory dance with a guy in a CBS Sports logo cap. "And to think I want to have that man's baby."

"He's just having fun." Peggy gave Bex one of the waters and took the other for herself.

Bex drank and made a face. "This isn't Perrier."

"We're in a sports bar."

"As I'm painfully aware. Hi, sweetie," Bex greeted Josh, who'd come to the table to stuff a chicken wing in his mouth. He belched loudly, laughed, kissed Bex's forehead, and returned to the foosball table.

Apprehension rose in Peggy's chest. In seven years she'd heard a thousand variations on Bex's theory that Brock brought out the worst in Josh. She didn't want to hear it tonight. "I bought a wedding ring for Connecticut," she said. "It doesn't feel right to wear Brock's ring there." She checked to make sure her boyfriend's attention was elsewhere and slipped a tiny velvet bag from her purse to show Bex what was inside: a glittering square stone framed in a marquee of tiny stones, with more dotting the slender band.

"Stunning," Bex said. "It's, like, five carats."

"It's fake." Peggy replaced the bag in her purse. "A simulated ring for a simulated marriage."

"Having fun, girls?" Brock appeared at the table, two other foosball players in tow, and put his big hand on Peggy's head and mussed her hair.

One of Brock's cohorts said to her, "Way to go. This is huge."

"Thanks, Sean!" Peggy was pleased. Brock must have told his friends of their pre-engagement.

"Huuuge." The other buddy socked Brock in the bicep.

"Peggy, if you start missing him too much, you can always come by my place."

"Or mine. Four months is a long time. A lady might get lonely." Sean squeezed Peggy's arm.

Brock laughed. "Cool it, guys, she doesn't know yet."

Confused, Peggy looked at Brock for a clue.

"Doesn't know what?" Bex asked.

"I'm not sure how to break this to you, friend."

Having lost his chips early, Hubbard, who was hosting Poker Night at his home in Westport, had appointed himself cocktail czar, pouring whiskey from an age-hazed crystal decanter into whatever odd glass he could find behind the bar. "Liddy got a card in the mail, a party invitation from your great-aunt. I'm afraid the dear girl has finally lost her mind. Not my wife, your great-aunt."

To Luke's relief, Abby had been her old self on Sunday morning, if still not able to remember what she'd been seeking so desperately the night before. She'd spent several hours in the library retidying Luke's work, rearranging the cabinet drawers with a methodology Luke had chosen not to question.

"Abby's fine," he told Hubbard.

Hubbard held a ceramic mug with a golf club manufacturer's logo. He refilled it and leaned against a wall. "She seems to think you've gotten married. To someone named Megan, Liddy said."

Despite his performance in Las Vegas, Luke wasn't much for liquor. On a normal poker night, he might have a single drink. *You're a disgrace to the tribe,* Hubbard would say, shaking his head. Tonight Luke needed to occupy his hands and fortify his resolve. He tipped back his glass, etched with the silhouette of a floating mallard. The Scotch tasted like turpentine. Perversely, this pleased Luke. "It's Peggy."

Hubbard raised an eyebrow a questioning millimeter.

At the table, Simmons, who had the dealer button, had paused, his hand angled toward Luke's empty chair. "You playing cards, Sedgwick, or working on getting laid over there?"

The other men in the room laughed, startling Toby, Hubbard's twelve-year-old golden retriever, who lifted his head, thumped his tail twice, moved to a spot closer to his master, and went back to sleep.

"You go ahead. I'll sit out this hand." Luke swirled the liquid in his glass, an amber lake rising to drown the etched duck. With their friends back to their hands, he muttered to Hubbard, "Her name is Peggy. Not Megan."

"Ha! You've gone and married a papist, no less. Isn't Peggy short for Margaret, or Mary Margaret, or Margareta Maria Madonna—"

"Get off it. She's not Catholic." *Or maybe she is*, Luke thought. "And what difference would it make if she were?"

Hubbard chortled, enjoying what he thought was Luke's joke.

"I'm serious."

Hubbard laughed for a moment longer, until it became clear humor wasn't what the situation called for. His mouth dropped open. "Christ." He topped off Luke's glass and led him to a pair of club chairs beneath a painting of one of Toby's dead relatives. "When? Why? Who the hell is she?"

Luke settled himself into a chair, downed his drink, and told the lie he'd rehearsed.

"She knocked up?" Hubbard asked when Luke was finished.

Luke stared down his friend over the rim of the empty mallard glass.

"Come on. A shotgun wedding to a girl nobody's heard of?"

There was a minor commotion from the table: Ver Planck was scraping a substantial pot to his chest. Distracted, Hubbard got up to pour himself another round, then brought the decanter to refill Luke's glass. He sat back down. "Is she us?"

The phrase was shorthand; no explanation was necessary. Hubbard meant, Did Peggy measure up to the coded list of criteria that determined whether a girlfriend or wife was "our kind"—a list compiled within, Luke imagined, five minutes of the Pilgrims stepping onto Plymouth Rock, dubbing themselves America's ruling class, and mixing themselves a congratulatory round of gin and tonics. It took into account family background, appearance, alma mater, occupation, hobbies, and behavior, plus scores of other, subtler cues someone not "us" would never think to look for—participation in the right childhood etiquette classes; a family beach key at Martha's Vineyard. To be "us" was to claim one's place in a club whose members were utterly convinced of their own moral and social superiority. A club that couldn't exist unless it excluded anyone whose background, religion, or genetic code didn't measure up.

Luke, as he always did, wondered why any of it mattered.

"Don't tell me she's a Tiffany," Hubbard continued, watching the poker table. It was a reference to Ver Planck's spouse, whom Hubbard secretly derided as a social climber.

An odd sensation prickled up the back of Luke's neck: *That's my wife you're talking about.* He looked at Hubbard, saying nothing.

"Damn, Sedgwick. Why? Why now, after all this time?"

The game was winding down; Ver Planck had most of Simmons's and Eaton's chips. Luke had been playing well before Hubbard had insisted on pouring him a drink. On a percentage basis, he'd made more this evening at cards than he'd made this week in the market, which for the past two days had fallen dizzyingly, risen again, and settled out at about where it had started. Luke was comfortable with his conservative portfolio, though he'd noted that a technology stock into which Ver Planck had bought heavily had doubled in value in forty-eight hours. Then again, it was easy to take Ver Planck–style risks, to make volatile investments, to marry a woman who wasn't "us," when you were Ver Planck and had more money than God.

Hubbard was still waiting for an answer.

"It just felt right," Luke said.

To his ears, the words sounded laughable, cheap, but Hubbard let it go. He leaned back in his chair. "Well, congratulations, old boy. I suppose Liddy will want to have her for tea or something." He rubbed the retriever's stomach with his foot. "Just one more question."

"What's that?"

"Does this mean Nicki's available?"

Brock didn't get it. He couldn't understand why she was upset. "It's not like I wasn't going to tell you," he kept repeating. He'd said it three times so far on their walk home from Brattie's.

Jog home was more like it. It wasn't easy to stay a few self-righteous steps ahead of a man whose legs were half again as long as yours. "When?" Peggy panted. "Packing to catch your flight to Sydney? 'By the way, I'm off to work on a surfing movie, see you in June'?"

"Come on." Brock had caught up and was at her side again. "You know I'm booked with football through the

Super Bowl. I'm not leaving for three months. I would of told you before then." Under the streetlights, Brock swung his camera-carrying arm, circling it first forward, then back, as he always did when he'd worked too many days in a row. "Anyway, it's Hawaii first, then Brazil, and then Australia."

"That's not the point." Peggy regarded him out of the corner of her eye. She wanted to poke him in the chin dimple, sock him in his Disney-prince jaw, tell him it was would *have*, not would of. "The point is we're a couple. Couples don't make big decisions without talking to each other first...."

Her indignation dissolved there, at the corner of Amsterdam and Sixty-eighth Street. Brock wasn't the deceitful one. He hadn't gone and accidentally gotten married. He wasn't conning an old lady. He wasn't carrying on a false relationship behind her back. Peggy was hardly in a position to claim the high ground.

She stopped walking, no longer angry. "Did you mean what you told me, that you're working to save money for our wedding?"

"Well," Brock said. "Yeah."

A block behind them, a trio of young women erupted in shrieks of laughter. They were falling all over one another, doubled up over some private joke. They were twenty-two or twenty-three, maybe. As she waited for Brock to elaborate, Peggy envied them. They had a few years left before it was time to agonize over where their lives were going.

"Brock." Peggy couldn't stand it. She couldn't wait any longer. She had to ask. "What if I paid for our wedding?" She had to know. "What if I could raise the money for the big wedding you say you want by, say, next fall?"

Brock swung his arm.

"Just theoretically. If the cost weren't a problem anymore, *then* could we get married?"

The three women broke out in fresh peals of laughter.

Brock turned to look at them.

Peggy wanted to scream, to run around him in mad circles.

He turned back to Peggy. She held her breath.

"I don't know," he said.

The trio walked around them on the sidewalk—split up and passed them on either side without looking at them, as if Peggy and Brock were no more than a physical obstacle in the landscape. A boulder. A sinkhole. A vortex that would devour them the way this relationship had devoured seven years of Peggy's life.

Seven years she wouldn't get back. And for what?

"I think I should move out," Peggy said.

Brock stopped rotating his camera shoulder. "Out of where?"

"Our apartment." Peggy couldn't believe she was saying it. "I can't do this, Brock. You and I want completely different things. I've been waiting and waiting, thinking you'd come around, that you'd come to want the life I want. But I don't think you will come around, and I'd be an idiot to wait any longer. You can keep the apartment. I'll move back in with Bex."

Brock scratched his head. "You want to take a break?"

"I think it's a break*up*." Peggy removed her pre-engagement ring and held it out to him, one part of her on the verge of tears, another amazed at how free she felt, a third aware that despite her resolve, Brock would try to talk her out of leaving.

She'd go to Bex's. The building was back in the direction she and Brock had just come. Peggy started walking. Brock would say something before she reached the end of the block. He would call after her, and she would explain, kind but resolute, that her decision was final.

But he didn't call, and she continued walking, until there

were so many blocks between them that she wouldn't have heard him if he had.

On Friday afternoon, after market close, Luke telephoned Nicki to set up a Monday-night date.

"Why can't I see you tonight?" Nicki countered. "There are all sorts of things I'd like to do to you..." She left the rest of the sentence to his imagination.

Luke was no longer listening. Out of nowhere, he'd remembered a line from his wedding vows in Las Vegas, something about committing himself constantly and faithfully.

"Come over tonight," Nicki repeated.

"I can't," he told her. Peggy was set to arrive in a few hours, and it would seem strange to Abigail if he wasn't home.

Yet Abby had long since retired to bed by the time Peggy showed up. Luke was immersed in paying bills when he heard a noise. He found her on the doorstep, pounding the massive knocker hard enough to wake the dead.

"I've been out here five minutes!" Her breath came out in angry white puffs. There were as yet unshed tears in her voice. "It's pitch dark! Anyone could have grabbed me and slit my throat!"

You had to pity her, so unnecessarily wound up. "Why didn't you let yourself in?"

He turned the knob to demonstrate that the door had been unlocked, but that didn't seem to appease her. He decided to let her pull herself together in peace and went out to her car to collect her suitcase, the same gigantic one from last week, except—he wouldn't have thought it possible—heavier. One thing she was right about: The light over the front door wasn't working. He'd have to check the wiring in the morning.

"You'll lock the house, right?" Peggy didn't sound any less upset when he returned.

"This is New Nineveh," he tried to reassure her.

By ten the next morning, Luke, Peggy, and his great-aunt were at what had once been the New Nineveh Grocery until it had been bought out and turned into a Stop & Shop, a change Abby had never acknowledged. Abigail waved the shopping list she'd painstakingly written in her spidery cursive and gave orders like a general.

"Luke, you get the crackers. Peggy, you get the spray cheddar, and a little Monterey Jack and some Brie, because it's a special occasion. And cream cheese, and celery..."

Peggy nodded. She had been uncharacteristically quiet since last night's harangue on the doorstep. Luke would have expected a few more complaints by now. He chuckled to himself. They'd surely come later.

"...bacon and two jars of mayonnaise and four cans of cream of mushroom soup," Abigail was saying. "Do we have toothpicks, Luke? I forgot to check."

"I'll pick up a box."

"I hate to waste the money." Abigail made a disapproving noise. She turned to Peggy. "Don't forget the celery, dear."

Caught trying to camouflage a yawn, Peggy dropped her hand to her side. Luke stared at it. She was wearing the most obnoxious, ostentatious diamond he'd ever seen. He wasn't one to pay attention to jewelry but couldn't imagine how he'd missed the ring before. Engaged to be engaged. That was the phrase Peggy had used when he'd called to tell her they were married. "I have a promise ring," she'd said. Well, it was one hell of a promise ring. The guy had to be from either Hollywood or the Mafia.

"I saw a cheese shop near Mr. Mayhew's office," Peggy was telling Abigail. "Should we get the cheese there?"

Here we go, Luke thought.

Abigail patted her pocketbook. "That store is for the weekend people, dear. The cheese here is much cheaper and just as good."

"It's a Yankee thing," Luke murmured to Peggy, who didn't answer.

Abigail didn't appear to have heard. "There's the Reverend Matthews. I'd like you to start coming with me to church tomorrow, Peggy. You too, Luke. You haven't been to a meeting since Easter." She started toward the condiments aisle, stopping to greet the pastor of the First Congregational Church of New Nineveh, who was loading his cart with bags of Snickers bars and a decorative spiderweb from the Halloween display.

"I should start on the crackers." Luke headed to the appropriate aisle.

Twenty minutes later, he and his great-aunt had reconvened in a checkout line, but Peggy was nowhere to be seen. Luke tracked her down in the pasta and rice section, gulping from a cup of store coffee. "I thought I'd make a dish or two for the party." She tossed a bag of beans into the cart.

"There's no need. Abigail has the food taken care of. There'll be the cheese and crackers, and she's making clam dip." He didn't have the heart to tell her that at WASP parties the food was little more than a decoration.

"I need garlic." She turned at the end of the aisle and was gone again.

Luke returned to his great-aunt in the checkout line. "Peggy would like to cook for the party. I believe she's worried we'll run out of hors d'oeuvres."

Abigail scrutinized him with her clever brown eyes. "She's a flighty one, isn't she?"

"A little." Luke focused on the magazines by the register, scanning the tabloid headlines. TROUBLE FOR THE ROYAL FAMILY, one proclaimed over a grainy photograph of a grimacing Prince William. Or was it Prince Harry?

"I know exactly why you married her."

Luke read more headlines. She couldn't possibly know. Could she? "And why is that?"

Abigail broke out in a raspy squawk of delighted laughter. "It's plain as day. You're exactly alike. In all my years I've never seen two people more suited for each other."

SEVEN

Peggy woke on Sunday, checked the time, and leaped out of bed. After returning from the market, she'd spent the rest of yesterday trying to rid the Silas Sedgwick House of two hundred years of dust. Afterward, she'd worked well past midnight making party appetizers in a kitchen utterly lacking in modern appliances. The whole house, in fact, was a graveyard of archaic tools. The vacuum cleaner had to be at least as old as she was. The sole television, in the den, actually had antennae; it got three snowy channels. There was a percolator instead of a coffeemaker. There was no dishwasher, an absence Peggy hadn't noticed until three o'clock this morning. Not for the first time since her breakup with Brock, she'd wondered as she cooked whether she should call off this deal with Luke, too. But that would be foolish. She might not have a wedding to pay for, but there was still the rent on the store to contend with.

She'd crawled into bed wearier than she thought she'd ever been but had slept fitfully. Her dreams had been full of Brock—of him standing under the streetlamp, watching her leave. She would wake periodically to the sound of the Thing in her room. *Why didn't he go after you?* Peggy imagined it was whispering. *Why didn't he put up a fight after seven years?*

And already, it was noon. It was clear by now the Sedgwicks were early risers, and bathing, putting on makeup, and drying her hair would delay her appearance in the kitchen by at least another forty minutes. Peggy decided to go down, apologize for sleeping late yet again, and then get cleaned up. But Miss Abigail wasn't at her spot on the rubbed-away patch of linoleum in front of the sink; and Luke wasn't rustling through the *Courant* or the *Litchfield County Times*. A slip of notepaper lay on the table, anchored with a porcelain sugar bowl matching the blue-and-white Sedgwick china:

Dear Peggy,

Luke is doing errands. I have gone to church.

Yours,
Abigail A. S. Sedgwick.

Peggy sighed. Of all the obligations to sleep through, church with her new great-aunt-in-law was probably not the one. She only hoped her party appetizers would make up for it and imagined the impressed look on Miss Abigail's face as she sampled Peggy's famous spicy Mediterranean artichoke squares, the old woman reassuring her that skipping church was understandable when one's cooking was this heavenly.

She meandered through vacant rooms toward a screen porch she'd discovered yesterday at the back of the house: a peaceful place in which to settle into a rocking chair and watch birds flittering in the garden on a summer morning. But the October cool crept through the lacy knit of Peggy's sweater, and a desolate feeling fell over her. She retreated back inside, retraced her steps through the kitchen, her bootsteps deafening in the grave-silent house, crossed the grand parlor she'd spent much of yesterday dusting and mopping, and started up the staircase—the third step from the bottom gave an unearthly creak—to the top floor.

Luke's ballroom-study, at the top of the stairs, was on the west, street-facing wall. Peggy had seen the other rooms on her side of the third floor but burned with curiosity over the hallway on the north side of the house. Luke's bedroom was there, and what else?

There was no reason she shouldn't find out. She clomped past the ballroom toward unexplored northern territory.

It was dim back here, and it took a while until the outlines of two closed doors revealed themselves. Peggy tried the first and saw the room had nothing in it but a few sagging cardboard boxes sealed with masking tape. She moved on to the next, reached out to open it, then hesitated. She knocked softly. This would be Luke's room. "Anyone home?"

The question ricocheted eerily off the far end of the corridor.

Peggy bolted, pounding back toward Luke's study. One of the double doors was slightly ajar, and she stopped, heart hammering, and tested the door with the tips of her fingers. It opened a few inches with an anemic *skreek*. Peggy whispered, "Are you in there?"

A soundless sliver of movement flashed behind her. *Luke!* Peggy whipped around, full of adrenaline, but there was no sign of him.

Once, at the store, a tourist whose first language hadn't been English had referred to goose bumps as "ghost skin." The phrase came back to Peggy as the flesh rose on her arms. If there were such a thing as ghosts, this house would have generations of them—malevolent spirits who would understand only that she was an outsider here, a Sedgwick impostor.

"This is absurd," she said, and because this time she was expecting the echo, it didn't frighten her. Not as much. She squeezed inside the ballroom. What did Luke do for a living, anyway? She'd not thought to ask. Despite herself, she wanted to know more about him. She had to have seen something in him that night in Las Vegas.

Luke's desk was covered with papers in messy piles. A pencil whose point looked to have been whittled, not sharpened, lay alongside a scattering of paper clips. Peggy picked up a scuffed glasses case, inspected it, and put it back down.

On the computer, a geometric screen saver morphed from cube to ball to helix and back again. Peggy tapped the keyboard; the screen brightened into a list of numbers and three-letter abbreviations—stock symbols. She lifted the corner of a sheet of paper lying facedown at the top of the biggest pile. "Connecticut Light and Power," it read; the electric bill. The bill underneath, "Naugatuck Fuel." But these had to be mistakes: The two bills totaled over two thousand dollars for September.

She scanned a smaller pile: opened envelopes, bits of wrinkled scratch paper, the corner of what looked like a photograph at the bottom. It was typical of a man. He'd have a lot more space if he'd throw away his trash instead of arranging it in piles. Why, for example, did he need the opened Connecticut Light and Power envelope? She started to set it aside, then saw penciled on it:

staid genes worked hot
from your electric charms

Peggy sat in Luke's desk chair and read the lines again and then again. Could Luke have written them?

It didn't seem possible, yet all of the bits of paper in this stack had things written on them: sometimes one line, sometimes several. On the back of a credit card receipt was a single word: "enchantment." The receipt, she saw, was from a restaurant in a place called South Norwalk. It was dated nine days earlier.

A hard knot formed in her chest. She slipped the receipt

back into its place, but as she did so, all of the papers moved an inch, revealing more of the photograph. Peggy slid it out.

The woman in the snapshot was leaning against the interior wall of what could have been a Manhattan loft—except it wasn't Manhattan; there were elevated train tracks behind it Peggy didn't recognize. The woman's lips were parted, and her face and upper chest were thick with freckles, like a Norman Rockwell character. But there was nothing cuddly about this woman, the feral waves of auburn hair, the cigarette dangling loosely from her long fingers. She was sexy. Treacherously sexy. The kind of woman you hoped never decided to go after your boyfriend.

Enchantment indeed.

Peggy thought of Brock, of the incident in Florida.

She glared at the woman. What was Luke doing with her? *Stay away from my husband,* she thought irrationally.

The anxiety expanded inside her chest, pressing on her lungs and gripping her windpipe. She studied the snapshot. Luke would study it, too, for inspiration, as he spun lines like—she shuffled through more scrap paper—"aching for your embrace; us turned to one..."

They had to be sleeping together. What man could see this woman and not want to—

She was being watched.

Peggy was sure of it. The house was observing her, reading her thoughts.

A low moan sounded from the far corner of the room.

Peggy turned toward the disturbance and gasped at another flash of motion. The moan was coming from behind the mirror resting on the floor. Miss Abigail's cat, or a poltergeist? Peggy didn't want to stay and find out. She caught sight, momentarily, of her fearful reflection before racing for her bedroom.

For heaven's sake, it was seven minutes to four; where was she? Punctuality was part of Luke's social code. It meant you cared enough about your fellow citizens to respect their time.

Abigail had been tsking and clucking, increasingly loudly, for twenty minutes. Now she came to Luke in the foyer. "Go upstairs and fetch her. They'll be here any minute."

There was no chance Luke was going to risk coming across Peggy in a state of undress. He took his great-aunt's elbow. "Let's get you a sherry."

Just then the staircase began to tremble, signaling the imminent arrival of someone descending it, and Peggy appeared. Her mouth drew into a shiny pink circle at the sight of Luke and Abigail waiting for her in the foyer. *Creak,* went the third step from the bottom as she placed one high-heeled shoe on it.

"You look festive, dear." Like any good Yankee hostess, Abigail revealed no trace of displeasure at her new great-niece-in-law's tardiness or choice of getup. Luke, who usually paid no more attention to fashion than he did to jewelry, was certain that Peggy's short skirt was wholly inappropriate for New Nineveh.

Though it looked pretty good.

"You're late. People will be here any minute."

"I thought the reception started at four." Peggy turned to Abigail, who was rearranging fall branches in a vase on the foyer table. "Won't everybody be fashionably late?"

Luke suppressed a smile. "There's no such thing as fashionably late in New Nineveh."

Peggy was uneasy. He could see that. It was intimidating enough for him, having to put on this act for people he at least knew accepted him. He couldn't imagine being in her shoes—he glanced at her feet, then jerked his head away. Those high heels were far too distracting.

"Well..." she hesitated. "I think the tub is broken. It took an hour to fill."

He decided some levity was in order. "You were lucky. It usually takes two hours."

Peggy didn't laugh. She probably guessed, correctly, that he was telling the truth.

"Your wife might care for a cup of punch. Why don't I get one for her." Abby hurried off.

"In any case," Peggy said with a sigh once they were alone, "perhaps I could shower in your bathroom from now on."

Luke laughed. "That *is* my bathroom."

"There's only one bathroom on the entire third floor?"

"There are only two in the house. Abigail's doesn't have a shower, either. But there isn't time for this." He checked his watch again. "We need to get our story absolutely straight. Now, a lot of the people coming today have known my family for generations. There's a group I went to prep school with—that's Phillips Academy Andover, but just call it Andover—and a few neighbors, and friends of Abby's and my late parents'. They'll all want to know about you. You moved around a lot as a child, didn't you?"

"Who told you that?"

He was perplexed. How *had* he known? "We must have talked about it..." *that night*. He hoped his discomfort wasn't as obvious as hers. "Did you live at any time in Palo Alto?"

"San Jose."

"I don't suppose you went to Stanford?"

"NYU."

"Art history?"

"English."

"Really?" It was the first thing aside from their shared

blunder in Las Vegas that he and Peggy had in common. Luke had majored in English and economics at Yale.

"Yes." Her words were clipped. "Really."

He wondered if he'd said something to insult her. "How did an English major end up selling soap?"

"I needed the money," she said.

He considered telling her he could relate, but time was wasting. "Just say you're from Palo Alto and have an art history degree from Stanford."

"What's wrong with San Jose and NYU?"

"I just already told a few people the first story." He had the distinct impression he was digging himself into a hole. "It's more, well, authentic."

"You mean your friends wouldn't live in San Jose or go to NYU."

"Luke, what was I supposed to be getting for you?" Abigail's question came from the dining room.

The distraction couldn't have come at a better time. "Punch, but we'll get our own, thank you." Luke lowered his voice. "All right, Peggy, quickly: After our private wedding in New York, we drove up to the Colonial Inn for the night, and—what?"

Peggy had raised her hand—a little facetiously, Luke thought. "When?"

"When what?"

"When was our wedding—the date? You remember, right? People will ask. And what is the Colonial Inn?"

"It's a bed-and-breakfast about ten miles from here." He shrugged. "People think it's romantic."

"Have you been there?"

"Sure." He'd taken Nicki to the Colonial's restaurant for dinner a couple of times.

Peggy was quiet for a few seconds. Then she repeated, "And when was our wedding?" She sounded offended. Luke couldn't imagine why. Before he could take a guess, she went on, "September twenty-sixth. I can't believe you, Luke."

"Of course." Luke couldn't imagine how he'd forgotten. "My mistake. September twenty-sixth. The day our year is over."

"I'm going to put the bruschetta in the oven." She started to leave, but Luke blocked her.

"This is important. Gossip gets around fast. If even one person suspects our marriage is anything but genuine, that it's a business arrangement, it'll get back to Abby, and she'll march straight back to Lowell and rip up the will so fast it'll make your head spin.... *What?*"

Peggy's forehead was furrowed, and an emotion he didn't understand radiated from her eyes, which were, he'd forgotten, the soft, complicated gray of a stormy autumn sky.

Eyes like skies that never cease to deepen—

The phrase came to him as if dictated.

Drown at twilight in them—drink their glow

"Do you remember anything at all about our"—she swallowed—"about that night?"

And then he did.

He hadn't noticed her, another face in the crowd, as he'd crossed the casino on the way to his room after the final seminar of the Family Asset Management Conference. He'd simply seen a figure crumple to the floor, and had rushed to help, and had found this unreal, ethereal creature. He could still picture the casino light gilding her forehead. She'd worn a wedding veil. A bride brought into being just for him.

"Rise, resty Muse," he'd quoted, taking her small, soft hand in his and helping her to her feet, breathing in, as he did so, the delicate scent of her skin, as if she were made of a thousand mysterious flowers and spices and fragrant fruits.

"Shakespeare." She'd smiled up at him and continued the line. "Rise, resty Muse, my love's sweet face survey..."

Immediately, viscerally, he had understood there was such a thing as love at first sight. Which had made his finding himself alone the next morning all the more bittersweet.

"Do *you* remember anything?" he asked, testing her.

"Just waking up and wanting to die." She was standing pigeon-toed in her high heels. "I obviously went temporarily insane that night. I'm sorry. About everything."

From the other side of the front door, the decisive clack of the knocker announced the party's first arrival.

"No need to apologize," Luke told Peggy, stung. "I don't recall a thing."

Nobody was eating the artichoke squares. They sat, cold and congealing, next to the untouched tuna-and-black-bean bruschetta. Earlier, Peggy had tried moving both dishes and the roasted vegetables from their second-tier spot against the back wall of the grand parlor. But they were faring no better here on the dining room table, next to Miss Abigail's peanut butter and bacon on Ritz crackers. Peggy felt somewhat vindicated that none of the food was getting much attention from the reception guests. Not so the booze. Not even in college had she known people who could put away liquor—and not even good liquor—this fast. The cheap Scotch and gin had been replenished a number of times; the crystal punch bowl, despite its oceanic proportions, had already needed to be refilled twice with Miss Abigail's whiskey-sour punch, by a uniformed, middle-aged maid named Erin whom Miss Abigail had insisted on hiring—with the money she must have saved buying grocery store cheese and no-name spirits.

A dainty, withered guest drained her cup in three gulps and held it out for more. Erin could barely ladle fast enough. After the woman shuffled back out into the grand parlor,

Peggy caught the maid's eye. "If you need a break, I'm happy to take over."

Erin stopped midladle and smoothed her uniform. "You enjoy the party, ma'am."

Peggy turned to see whom Erin was addressing. No one was there. She started to rearrange the artichoke squares one more time, caught Erin's disparaging look, and put down the silver serving tongs.

"That looks scrumptious!"

The speaker, a woman about Peggy's age whom Peggy remembered having been introduced to in the foyer, had the delicate handles of several empty punch cups hooked over her fingers.

"I can fix you a plate." Peggy reached for a deviled egg.

"Lord spare me the Yankee food. One of those." The woman nodded toward the artichoke squares. "It's okay. I can get it." She let Erin take the cups and, while the maid was refilling them, picked up a plate. "Look at that roasted vegetable salad. And bruschetta! Did you make all this?"

Peggy wanted to hug this person. She just wished she could remember her name. All the female guests at this party seemed to have the same first name that sounded like a last name, or a borderline-parody nickname like Topsy, and they looked alike, flat-chested and bony, with mousy hair and short-filed fingernails.

"Yes, I made it," Peggy said, "with help from Martha Stewart."

"It's delicious." The woman brushed a crumb from the neckline of her sweater. She was curvaceous and womanly, like a 1940s pinup girl, a healthy five or six dress sizes bigger than the other women and an exception to the mousy rule. Everything about her was gleaming and shiny and expensive-looking, from the prim angora crew neck she somehow made alluring, to the diamond-studded baby-shoe charm glittering around her neck, to the pearls that were larger and whiter than anyone else's. "Isn't Martha a doll? We lived near her in Westport when I was a kid, and once in a while she'd pop over with dahlias from her cutting garden. Did you grow up around here?"

"In San Jos—Palo Alto."

"Well, we're all thrilled Luke picked a nice girl to settle down with, finally. Why are you hiding? Come."

She set down her empty plate, thanked Erin, and gathered up three of the refilled cups by their spindly crystal handles. Peggy balanced the other three between her palms, her elbows pointing out like wings, and followed carefully, wondering what this woman had meant by "finally." They passed through the grand parlor, where Miss Abigail, in a long skirt and a high-necked blouse, was conversing with a hunched, elderly man in plaid slacks and a cashmere sweater in an eyeball-searing shade of ultraviolet. Lowell Mayhew stood nearby with his wife, whose name had also slipped Peggy's mind. Both smiled at Peggy, and she lifted her right elbow in greeting. A wave of punch broke onto her wrist, but she kept going, her eyes on her new friend's back. The woman's bouncy black hair curled at the ends like a model's in an old shampoo commercial.

"Peggy, over here!" a voice sang out.

A few steps away, under a pastoral painting with a gilt frame Peggy realized she'd neglected to dust, Ernestine Riga had spotted her. She'd been talking to a man and woman in their sixties who Peggy was pretty sure were the Sedgwicks' next-door neighbors, Annette and Angelo Fiorentino.

Ernestine caught Peggy by the sleeve with such enthusiasm, Peggy almost doused punch all over the Fiorentinos. "Emily Hinkley called—she's the president of the ladies' auxiliary," Ernestine informed Peggy and the bouncy-haired woman. "She wants our house to be part of the New Nineveh Home Tour! Emily says they're all impressed with our loving restoration of the former Sedgwick carriage house. We'll be the top-billed home. I hope we have time to spiff up the place—June isn't that far off!"

"What an honor!" Either Peggy's new friend didn't think, as Peggy did, that Ernestine Riga was a self-important show-off or she was too polite to reveal it. She held her punch cups steadily. "I've always fantasized about having my house chosen for a tour. Which reminds me, Peggy. I'll have to have you over for lunch soon."

Ernestine looked the woman up and down. "Aren't you married to that hedge fund mogul in Greenwich? That VanderSomething?"

"Tom Ver Planck. Yes, I am. I'm Tiffany. Please forgive me for not shaking your hand. Has the Sedgwick House been in a home tour, Peggy? I've always loved this place."

Peggy's elbows were aching from holding the punch cups, and her head was reeling from too many names, and she'd been distracted by a tear in the grimy wallpaper directly behind Ernestine's head. "Home tour?" she repeated stupidly. She wasn't sure what a home tour was, let alone if this house had been in one.

Annette Fiorentino's long gray braid thumped against her shoulder as she shook her head. "Oh, no. Abigail would hate all those tourists coming through. She doesn't like strangers in her home."

Angelo Fiorentino had a faint Boston accent. "I'm surprised she let *you* in, Peggy."

Peggy started to feel dizzy. But Angelo had been joking; Annette was laughing. "I know Miss Abigail is overjoyed that Luke found you," Annette said, serious again. "I don't think any of us expected him to marry."

"You plan to have kids?" Ernestine barked, but before Peggy could think of a polite way to suggest that Mrs. Riga mind her own business, Tiffany excused the two of them charmingly and gently led Peggy away.

"Thank you," Peggy said.

"Anytime. People can really be nosy, especially once you're married. They think you should start popping out the babies right away." Tiffany wove expertly past a table stacked with wedding presents. Peggy hadn't expected people to bring anything, and just looking at all the hopeful, pastel-wrapped boxes made her feel awful. Tiffany stopped and gave her a conspiratorial grin. "So. *Are* you two planning to have babies?"

Peggy felt her hands start to sweat. "No time soon."

"Smart thinking. You lovebirds need time to focus on each other. I don't think Tom and I have slept all night alone together since our son was born."

Peggy made a mental note not to repeat this story to Bex. "You have a son?"

"Milo." The woman's eyes softened. "He's two. You'll have to meet him."

Their path ended at the library, where a half dozen or so men and women huddled in a close circle, some standing, some leaning easily against the backs of armchairs. One man, whose wide, flat, boyish face was beginning to turn puffy with age and alcohol, held a bottle of Scotch in one hand while yanking a book from one of the floor-to-ceiling shelves with the other.

"What did I miss?" Peggy's ally passed out the punch. "I've completely forgotten whose cup was whose, but we're all friends, right? Hi, hon." She stood proprietarily close to another of the men, smacking a lipstick kiss on his shiny, tan cheek.

"I see, Sedgwick, that your bride has befriended our Tiffany." The puffy-faced guest looked at Luke, signaling something Peggy couldn't decode. He set down his bottle and introduced himself as Kyle Hubbard and the petite, thin-lipped woman next to him, who seemed vaguely affronted by Tiffany's abundant chest, as his wife.

Peggy remembered linking the short *i* in "skinny" with the woman's name. At last, she could greet a guest properly. "Lizzie, right?" With luck, she wouldn't have to reshake anyone's hand. Hers were tacky with sloshed punch.

"Liddy," Kyle's wife corrected, darting her gaze away from Tiffany. "Not to worry—you have a lot of names to memorize. That's Tom Ver Planck, Tiffany's husband. This is Topher and Carrie Eaton, and Bunny and Creighton Simmons." Her eyes crinkled as she tilted her head toward a preternaturally cute man and woman who looked like brother and sister. "Bunny and Creighton used to be our newlyweds, but you and Luke have dethroned them."

"I'm sure that's not true, Bunny," Peggy told the woman, whose headband and diminutive gold earrings framed round, stuffed-animal eyes in a face free of makeup.

"That's Creighton," Liddy corrected. "*He's* Bunny."

The circle erupted into laughter. Peggy searched for a sign of support from Luke, but he had missed the exchange completely. He and Tom Ver Planck had moved to a quieter corner and seemed deep in discussion. She clasped her punch hands across her elbows, then dropped them quickly. These people didn't need to know how uncomfortable she was.

"I had a hard time keeping them straight at first, too," Tiffany whispered sympathetically. "They do blend together."

The puffy one, Kyle Hubbard, cleared his throat. "But where were we? Ah, yes. Quit talking business, my brother, and recite us a little ditty."

Luke looked over and frowned.

"You leave me no choice." Kyle set down his drink and opened the book, flipping through the pages.

"You're holding it upside down," Topher pointed out, to more laughter.

Kyle flipped the book right-side up and began reading in a singsong voice:

When you are old and grey and full of sleep,
And nodding by the fire, take down this—

He paused. "Christ, this is dull."

"It's Yeats." Peggy didn't realize she'd spoken aloud until she saw Kyle look up at her. "It's one of the most romantic poems ever written." She didn't add, *And you're mangling it.*

"Then by all means, let's get your beloved to finish. Be a sport, Sedgwick," Kyle called loudly. "Your bride would like you to read this sonnet, or whatever it is."

"I don't, really," Peggy protested. *And it isn't a sonnet.*

"All right." Kyle sniffed and rubbed his pouchy eyes. "I'll do it. 'When you are moldy and grey, take down this book…' " Everybody but Tom, Tiffany, Luke, and Peggy laughed.

"Put that away, you philistine." Luke strode back to the circle.

Kyle held the book out of Luke's reach. "You read, or I will."

"Come on, Luke. Put him out of his misery," said Creighton.

Luke pressed his lips together, as if to keep from speaking impolitely, and took the book from Kyle's hand. He pushed his glasses back on his nose and straightened his rangy body and began:

When you are old and grey and full of sleep,
And nodding by the fire, take down this book,
And slowly read, and dream of the soft look
Your eyes had once, and of their shadows deep;

He didn't look happy, but he recited with a command of the poem that showed he was familiar with it. Peggy looked again and realized he wasn't reading at all but was reciting from memory, and she felt light-headed.

How many loved your moments of glad grace,
And loved your beauty with love false or true,
But one man loved the pilgrim soul in you,
And loved the sorrows of your changing face;

He was handsome. His quiet melancholy made Brock's broad-shouldered good looks seem cartoonish, inconsequential. He tipped his head forward in concentration, a lock of hair falling over one eye. He wore the same dark suit he'd had on when Peggy had woken up next to him in Vegas. It was hardly of the most up-to-date cut, but it was right on him.

This is my husband, Peggy thought. *He's my husband, and he's handsome, and he knows Yeats.* Her legs felt as if they might buckle under her.

And bending down beside the glowing bars,
Murmur, a little sadly, how Love fled
And paced upon the mountains overhead
And hid his face amid a crowd of stars.

He finished reciting, and the whole world faded away.

It could have been inadvertent. Or he could have intended to catch Peggy's eye. All Peggy knew was that he looked at her, and she looked at him, and all else receded—the party laughter and the tip of glasses, the rustle of fabrics—faded away, or never existed, and there were just the two of them, virtual strangers who had somehow become the only people in the world.

Once before, a man had looked at her this way. Once before, she'd gazed into a man's eyes and found in them this exquisite understanding: *We belong together.* But who had it been? She remembered the feeling, the moment, but, cruelly, not the man. *It was Brock. It has to have been Brock,* she told herself, knowing it hadn't been; that Brock Clovis had never seen her the way Luke Sedgwick was seeing her now.

Without thinking, Peggy extended her hand to brush back Luke's hair and might have done it had someone not reached out and caught her fingers.

"Look!" Tiffany cried, and the world came back into focus.

Peggy was weak with shame. Had she really been just about to touch Luke Sedgwick?

"It's exactly like mine!" Tiffany held out her hand, aligning it with Peggy's so their left ring fingers were parallel and Tiffany's flawless, starry-framed diamond aligned with Peggy's flawless, starry-framed cubic zirconia. Peggy stiffened, preparing for Tiffany to identify her and her ring as fakes, but Tiffany only giggled. "I take that back. It's exactly like mine, only bigger."

Everyone except Luke leaned in.

"So it is. I wouldn't have guessed you'd go flashy, Sedgwick," Kyle drawled.

Peggy stole a peek at Liddy and Creighton's wedding rings—plain bands as different from Tiffany's as the two women were from the glossy-mouthed, generously hipped Tiffany herself.

"That's the ring of a man who's deeply in love," Kyle continued. "Wouldn't you say, Ver Planck?"

It was becoming clear to Peggy that the more upset Luke was, the less he spoke.

"Actually, Hubbard, it's the ring of a man who is deeply in love and who's been far more successful as an investor than you have," Tiffany's husband returned. Liddy raised an unplucked eyebrow as Tom, Tiffany, Topher, and Carrie burst into fresh peals of laughter.

One thing was for sure. It was lucky Peggy didn't have an inkling of feeling for Luke, because if she had, she'd be insulted at his evident disgust over the suggestion they might be in love.

Kyle squeezed behind Peggy, caging her in a half hug around the shoulders. "You must be quite a girl, Mrs. Sedgwick, to have inspired this Ver Planck–like display of extravagance."

Peggy laughed politely and started to move away, but Kyle kept his arms locked firmly across her collarbone in an embrace less sexual than possessive. Surely this time Luke would step in, Peggy thought, but he simply shut the book—"That's enough of that"—and replaced it on the shelf. For the life of her, she couldn't tell if Luke meant he was through reading or that he'd had enough of his friend's behavior. Or was he saying he'd had enough of her? Was she embarrassing him by her mere presence among his friends? Was it clear to these people that she didn't belong?

"Do tell, Mrs. Sedgwick." Her captor's breath on the back of Peggy's neck bore the not entirely repugnant tang of whiskey and cigarettes. "How did you persuade our friend here to tie the knot?"

It seemed to overtake her, a desire to torture Luke a little. It was wrong, she knew, yet the urge reached out and wrapped its tentacles around her as if to strangle her. Or it could just be that Kyle had tightened his arms across her chest. Panic rose to take the place of the wicked feeling, but she laughed as if this sort of thing happened to her all the time. "Simple. I propositioned him. He couldn't say no. Could you, Luke?"

"I couldn't." Luke's easy tone seethed with warning. "You gave me no choice."

The men broke out in catcalls. Kyle squeezed Peggy harder. "Now recite one of your poems, Sedgwick."

"Oh, do! We've never heard a single one!" Liddy seemed undisturbed that her husband had Peggy in a choke hold. Was it, too, a "Yankee thing"—an arcane prep school hazing ritual? If so, there was no sense in struggling. She tried to relax in Kyle's clutches as the circle pressed Luke to recite.

"Peggy, you make him," Carrie Eaton called out.

In an instant, Peggy was in the crosshairs of eight expectant stares and a ninth, enigmatic one—Luke's. She was already sorry for teasing him and sure he would rather not be the center of attention, sure that these people hadn't seen his poetry because Luke hadn't wanted them to. Perhaps he thought his poems weren't good enough. She should be a good pretend wife and bolster his confidence, the way a real wife would. "Why not read the one about the sunveined southern winds? It's really nice—" She stopped herself, too late.

"You mean," Luke said, "the one on my desk, upstairs, in my study?"

Hubbard chose this moment to release Peggy, and she stumbled forward and felt one of her heels grind into Luke's foot.

Luke stepped back. "That poem isn't finished," he said.

Tiffany called, "Make one up!"

Peggy felt as if she'd just thrown Luke to the lions. These were Luke's friends, weren't they? Couldn't they see he was miserable? She wanted to tell them to stop it and leave him alone, that she'd made a terrible mistake, that she hadn't meant to go through his papers.

But Luke seemed to have recovered. "Good idea," he said. "I'll make one up. A poem for you, Peggy."

All had been forgiven, it seemed. Peggy thought, with a little thrill, that Luke might say something beautiful to her. After all, he had been there for the look they'd just exchanged.

Luke gazed off at a point in the distance, started to speak, then frowned, paused for a slug of his drink, and began again:

Single men, I have something to say
Don't you make my mistake, or you'll pay:
At the bar, stop and think,
Just say no to that drink
Lest you wake with a wife the next day.

He bowed, and the crowd applauded, the men slapping Luke on the back and the women crowding around him with cries of, "Bravo!" and, "How did you do that?" Peggy stood back, stunned.

When the ruckus died away, Luke spoke up. "You people didn't understand a single word I just said, did you?"

The crowd burst into laughter, and Peggy knew Luke was right: His limerick had gone over everyone's head but hers, as had been his intention. He knew Peggy understood: She was nothing but a drunken mistake, and any attraction between the two of them was a figment of Peggy's poor, foolish imagination.

EIGHT

November

Dr. Kaplan had pronounced it "a textbook stim." Bex's retrieval procedure had yielded eleven mature eggs, which had been whisked away to the lab overnight with what Josh was euphemistically calling his donation. This morning, the doctor had called to report that three eggs had fertilized. Assuming they stayed healthy, they would be ready to be placed in Bex's uterus in another three to five days. But standing in Josh's apartment, pointing at the sofa, Bex radiated joy, her olive skin glowing as if she were already pregnant.

"Start with that. Torch it, drive a stake through its heart, whatever you have to do." Behind Bex, the men-with-a-van Peggy had hired to bring over her things seemed puzzled. "I mean, get rid of it." Bex eyed Josh's coffee table. "You're next," she told it.

"But Josh won't have any living room furniture," Peggy pointed out as the two movers lifted Josh's frat-house couch, a herd of dust balls underneath flying to the four corners of the earth, and hefted it sideways out the door. Peggy could hear them stumping down all five flights of stairs.

"We'll buy a new one." Bex stared at the empty space where the couch had been. "I can still sense its evil spirit." She stood on one foot, resting the other on the doomed coffee table. "You know what we should sell at the store? Ritual products. Like candles that smudge away the demonic traces left behind by ugly furniture. One-Night-Stand-Erasing Linen Water. Bad-Neighbor-Begone Body Lotion with Garlic and Citronella."

Peggy laughed. "A home fragrance called Exorcism. Which I'd be the first to buy for the Sedgwick House."

"You don't *really* think it's haunted."

"Not literally."

Still, it had been two weekends since the wedding reception, two weekends of pervasive malaise in the house, four mornings in the kitchen drinking Miss Abigail's burned coffee while Luke hid behind the newspaper, hours of waiting in vain for him to apologize for treating her so shabbily at the party. The longer he'd kept silent, the more she'd begun to fume. She'd spent most of her time on the third floor, opening and cataloging an endless flow of wedding gifts, then carefully repacking each vase, candlestick, and teapot into its tissue-lined box, which she moved to the empty room next to Luke's. When the year and their marriage were over, she and Luke would have to return each gift to its giver. She wrote thank-you notes on stationery Luke's great-aunt unearthed for her in the house—the very same stationery, Miss Abigail said, that Luke's mother had used when she was a new bride. Peggy felt more a fraud with every word she put down on the cream-colored paper. "Dear Liddy, thank you for the lovely sterling cocktail shaker. Luke and I look forward to having you and Kyle over for drinks soon."

This past Sunday, just to get away from Luke and thank-you notes, she'd brought an alarm clock and woke in time to go to church with Miss Abigail—the meeting house, Luke's great-aunt called it—but it wasn't much of a respite. Peggy had worn a pious-seeming black dress but still had felt conspicuous as she followed Miss Abigail to the first-row

Sedgwick pew and when, at the beginning of the service, a worshipper Peggy didn't recognize stood up, said he had an announcement to make, and welcomed Mrs. Peggy Sedgwick to the congregation. At the coffee hour afterward, Peggy had smiled woodenly as cheery townsfolk shook her hand, congratulated her, and then looked around for Luke.

"You know my great-nephew. Not one for church. But"—Miss Abigail would lean in toward Peggy and the stranger, as if conspiring—"I'm counting on his wife to talk sense into him." And the anxiety would rub itself, catlike, against the inside of Peggy's lungs. Even if Luke had cared to address her in anything besides monosyllables, she was the last person to get him back to the First Congregational Church of New Nineveh. Beyond a few weddings and funerals, Peggy had no experience with organized religion. Her father, an athiest, raised Jewish, hadn't set foot in a temple since his thirteenth birthday; her mother was vaguely Christian. Peggy had a passing familiarity with Abraham and Isaac and Jonah and the whale but had felt like an impostor stumbling her way through the hymns, reciting from her program what everybody else knew by heart: "Give us this day our daily bread, and forgive us our debts, as we forgive our debtors." After she'd drunk the communion grape juice (not the wine she'd expected), she'd accidentally dropped her thimble-size glass. It hadn't broken, but it had bounced on the meeting house's wooden floor with a sharp *clackety-clack*. At least she hadn't had to sip from a shared cup. She rubbed her nose, which tickled at the thought of catching a stranger's cold.

"Tell me about it. The man hasn't dusted in years." Bex walked to her husband's window, which faced the building across the street. "And you wonder why I don't let him move in."

Josh's phone rang, and Bex skipped over to it. "Hi, Mom!

Can you believe it? I'm trying not to get excited, but I'm excited!"

"I'll go get us lunch." Peggy walked two doors down to 5J, Bex's apartment, the one Peggy had once shared and would officially begin sharing again today, after having slept here for the past three weeks on nights Brock wasn't traveling.

Nicki took a drag on what had to be the day's twentieth cigarette and blew smoke sideways out the cracked-open car window. She tapped a column of ash into Luke's empty travel mug, which she held steady between her thighs. With her left hand, she caressed the gearshift.

"I drink out of that cup." Luke punched the radio buttons from a Crazy Carl Kirkendall carpet commercial to a staticky country song to WNPR National Public Radio. He glanced at the sun-cracked dashboard, noting that the Volvo, twenty-five years old and inherited from his father, had long passed two hundred thousand miles. It also had less than a quarter tank of gas.

Nicki let the smoke curl provocatively from her nostrils. She looked exactly as she had the first time he'd met her—the hair, the lips, the suggestive fingertips. When she spoke, her words trailed the smoke out into the curiously warm afternoon. "Are you staying over?"

A mint-condition Big Healey convertible roared past in the left lane. As the car flashed by, Luke caught a glimpse of the driver: silver-haired, arm draped across the back of an empty passenger seat. A man enjoying his freedom; a man who, unlike Luke, hadn't spent half the day driving his girlfriend to a particular yarn store in Great Barrington, Massachusetts, to pick up a certain type of special yarn that looked like any other yarn, nothing worth crossing the state line for.

Nicki was still teasing the gearshift, stroking her index finger lightly up, over the top, and down again. It was doing nothing for him. But then, none of Nicki's old tricks was working these days. "I can't stay over," he told her. They were on the interstate, ten miles from Nicki's place in South Norwalk. It would take him an hour to get back home, and he had a volatile market to contend with, storm windows to put up, half a dozen unfinished poems languishing on his desk, and the inexorable sense of time passing—not just the afternoon, but the earth itself cooling at the core while the surface melted; the universe stretching to its limits and preparing to fold back in on itself. He thought of the look he'd exchanged with Peggy at his great-aunt's party, how time had come to a standstill, until he'd let his temper get the better of him in such uncharacteristic and unseemly fashion.

"I'm out of Merits." Nicki stubbed out her cigarette and dropped it in his cup.

Luke wondered how he'd tolerated her smoking habit for so many years. He took the next off-ramp, drove into a Hess station, and got out to pump the gas. He knew full well Nicki assumed he'd go inside for her, but he played oblivious until she gave up hope and climbed out.

He probably wouldn't have called Peggy, but the sign at the pump forbidding the use of cell phones seemed, contrarily, like an invitation. Luke took his from his pocket and dialed Peggy at the shop. After four rings, a woman he recognized only as the wrong one answered. Nicki came back outside, taking a cigarette from the new pack. Luke hastily pressed the "End" button.

"Who are you calling?"

Damn. "Abby." He didn't know why he'd wanted to speak to Peggy, only that suddenly she had seemed a soothing antidote to Nicki's hard, glittering toughness. He shouldn't have attacked Peggy like that at the reception. Nicki would have given Luke the finger, told him to fuck off, but Peggy was sensitive. He opened the passenger door, holding his palm above Nicki's fiery head in case she got too close to the door frame. He climbed in and shut his own door. The Volvo smelled of gasoline.

Luke eased the car back onto the highway and drove for several miles without saying anything, listening to a current-affairs show out of Hartford, smoke swirling around his head. He passed the bloody carcass of a deer, twisted and broken at the edge of the road.

Luke turned off the radio. "This isn't working."

Nicki coughed. "What's not working?"

"We. Us. This." He didn't want to look at her. If the Medusa head weren't already there, it would be after he said his piece. "You've meant a lot to me, and we've had our good times, but—"

She laughed. "We just got back together." She flicked more ash. "We have a good two months till our next falling-out."

"No." As if in punctuation, something—a pebble, probably—struck the front windshield with a small, sharp crack.

"I give you three weeks before you come knocking on my door," Nicki said.

The pebble had left a pock in the windshield just big enough to make the glass vulnerable to cracking in the coming winter cold. Yet another thing to fix. "Not this time, Nicki."

There it was—the Medusa face. Luke stopped being preoccupied with the windshield ding long enough to see the amusement drain from Nicki's eyes and fury flush her cheeks. He hadn't planned to have this talk right this minute, here in the car, but it might well be the ideal location: private, contained, and completely within his control. Just in case she got the urge to throw it, though, he casually took the travel cup and slid it underneath his seat.

"It's her," Nicki hissed. "You're—what? In love? All torn up inside about cheating on your wife? Starting to take this marriage a little too seriously?"

He had been about to say his decision had nothing to do with Peggy; that the simple fact was, he and Nicki were incompatible everywhere but in bed, had been incompatible almost from the day they'd met; that they had stayed together far too long, and both of them knew it. But he wondered if there might be a grain of truth in what she was saying.

Before he could form his thoughts into a coherent sentence, he heard a small sniffle, and when he saw tears in Nicki's eyes, he was stunned. Nicki didn't cry. Not when they'd broken up in the past. Not during her sister Heather's breast cancer scare. Not at *Field of Dreams* on cable.

"You never asked *me* to marry you," she said in a pathetic, watery whimper that made it clear he was a monster.

"But you knew the rules!" He made a conscious effort to dial back the defensiveness in his voice. "You knew I didn't want to get married," he began again. "Not to anyone. I was honest from the start. And you didn't want to get married, either. You've insisted ever since our first date." He was doubting himself, second-guessing what he had or hadn't said; whether in five years he'd unintentionally led Nicki to believe he'd felt anything he didn't. Gentlemanly behavior was as much encoded in his DNA as were the Sedgwick nose and the Sedgwick propensity toward heart afflictions, and it upset Luke to think he might have made a misstep along the line.

Nicki had turned toward the window, her shoulders shaking. He stopped in front of her building and cut the ignition.

"Marry me," he said.

She stiffened, still facing the window.

"I can get an annulment in ninety days." He felt as if he were choking, as if Nicki's yarn were unspooling in the backseat and twining around his throat. "We'll elope and move to New York or Paris, in time, and I'll write poetry and you can work on your art."

She turned back around, tears suspended on her face, tiny pale crescents underneath her flared nostrils, her eyebrows furrowed in...Luke couldn't tell. Not grief. Definitely not happiness.

He had no desire to marry Nicole Pappas. *But if she says yes, I'll do it. I'll do it because it's the right thing to do.*

Nicki opened her mouth, shut it, and blinked away her tears. Luke realized what she looked like—as if she'd been caught in a lie. The same look he would have had on his face when he was sixteen and his great-aunt had nailed him to the wall on the flower boxes. Then a greater truth dawned. *She doesn't want to marry me. I've put her on the spot.*

Nicki worked a cigarette out from her pack.

"Don't light that in my car," he said.

The spell was broken.

Nicki gathered her special yarn from the backseat. "So long, Luke. It's been fun." She swung her long legs onto the pavement. "Have a nice life." She stepped out onto the sidewalk, not bothering to close the car door behind her.

Luke watched her strut away, her body to lust after, her auburn hair dazzling in the sun. He reached down under his seat for the ash-filled travel mug. He leaned across to shut the door and turned the car back toward New Nineveh.

Peggy walked to West Seventy-ninth and Amsterdam and bought avocado-and-cheese sandwiches for herself and Bex at their favorite organic lunch place. Here in New York, the change in seasons was just beginning, and there were still days—today was one—where it was warm enough to sit outside without a coat. Suddenly too hungry to wait, Peggy decided to eat her lunch in the little park behind the Museum of Natural History. She made herself comfortable on an empty bench and unwrapped her sandwich, swinging her feet. On summer weekends, this place was full of museum-goers, but on a weekday afternoon in fall, things were quiet. A nanny and two children walked by. A homeless woman slept on another bench; her dog, curled on top of a pile of rags and trinkets, raised its head as a man in an untucked shirt and jeans went past, chattering animatedly to an invisible companion. Peggy observed this man with mild interest until it became clear he was talking not to himself, but into an electronic device hooked, cyborglike, over his ear.

The cyborg stopped in front of her bench. "Well, look who's here!"

Midbite, Peggy looked him over. It appeared he was trying to communicate with her face-to-face.

"The watch, remember?" He held out his wrist, and Peggy recognized him as the man she'd met three weeks ago at Brattie's. He had a beard—not a beard, exactly, more a precision-trimmed dark stubble. On his belt, a blue electronic light blinked from inside a leather case. He said, "I'm Jeremy."

Peggy swallowed and introduced herself, shielding her mouth with her hand in case she had alfalfa sprouts in her teeth. She made room for him on the bench. He seemed to be expecting her to.

He sat next to her. Even outdoors, she recognized his aftershave, a blend of key lime and cedar she was sure was from Gaia Apothecary. He said, "Twice in forever I'm north of Fourteenth Street and I see you both times. That's worth dinner, don't you think?"

Nobody had asked her out in seven years. She was saved from having to say no by an insistent cell phone. She waited for Jeremy to slip on his earpiece again and answer, but he pointed toward her purse: It was her phone, not his.

It was probably Bex, wondering what had happened to her. "I should answer that." Peggy caught the phone on the second to last note of its generic, musical ring.

"Have you seen *Field of Dreams*?" Luke asked on the phone.

Jeremy removed his gadget from its clip on his belt and consulted it. Peggy slipped off the bench and stepped a few yards down the path. "Pardon me?"

"Have you ever seen *Field of Dreams*?" Luke repeated.

Was he calling to apologize, at last? If so, this was a strange way of doing it. "I'm not sure what you mean," she said.

"*Field of Dreams*. A guy builds a baseball diamond in a cornfield—"

"I've seen *Field of Dreams*." Thanks to Brock, Peggy was reluctantly familiar with every sports movie ever made—*Rocky*, *Raging Bull*, *North Dallas Forty*. It might well be his only lasting legacy. She was pretty sure she was getting over Brock. It made her question why she'd stayed with him so long in the first place. The first two weeks had been rough, but this week she'd had the urge to cry only once. Her tears had been cursory, lasting less than a minute.

"Did you cry?" Luke asked in her ear.

She was baffled; it was as if Luke were reading her thoughts. On the bench where she'd left him, Jeremy was chattering away again into his reattached earpiece. "Did I cry about what? Why are you calling?"

"Did you cry at *Field of Dreams*?"

"Everybody cries at that movie." She was losing patience.

What did this have to do with his behavior at their wedding reception? "Of course I cried."

"I thought as much. Good." He hung up without saying good-bye.

By seven, Peggy had her new-old room in reasonable order, and she and Bex sat in the living room, toasting to roommates and fertility and success at the store. "And to your new single life. And the death of Josh's couch." Bex clicked her sparkling cider against Peggy's champagne. "Can you believe it's gone from the sidewalk already? Who would take that hideous thing?"

"Careful. I'm grieving. And Peggy isn't exactly single." Josh, just home from the office, set down his briefcase on one of Peggy's packing boxes. He kissed Bex and pecked Peggy on the cheek, then rummaged through a drawer in the kitchen. "So I thought of names for the baby." He emerged with a fistful of takeout menus and plopped down next to Bex. "I'm thinking Shlomo if it's a boy, Tzeitel if it's a girl." He squeezed Bex so hard, Peggy could have sworn Bex's eyes bulged out.

"Oh, nice. " Bex smiled at him. "What if we have two boys?"

"Shlomo and Yehuda."

Bex laughed. "Or two girls? Or triplets?"

"I haven't gotten that far."

Bex ruffled his hair.

They had the exact relationship Peggy had always wished for. As she had so many times in the past, she forced herself not to be jealous. "Were you two always this cutesy-poo?"

"Always were, always will be, and now that you're living

with us, you're going to be subject to shows of cuteness that will amaze and astound you." Josh gave his wife a second, flamboyant kiss on the lips, then leafed through the menus. "Who's hungry for Szechuan Palace?"

"I have a date," Peggy blurted.

The two stared at her. "When?" Josh asked, at the same time Bex was asking:

"With whom?"

"Next week." Peggy shuffled menus aimlessly while she recapped her afternoon. She left out Luke's phone call and didn't mention the only reason she'd agreed to go out with Jeremy was that when he'd again asked her to dinner, an image of Luke sharing a glass of wine with the redheaded woman in the photograph had flashed into her mind.

When she was finished, Bex proposed a toast: "To new beginnings."

"New beginnings." Peggy inclined her glass in Bex's direction. What did Luke matter, anyway?

"But you're married," Josh said.

Bex sighed. "I believe Peggy knows that, sweetie."

NINE

The apple harvest had ended last week, yet, with classic city-folk enthusiasm—born of the distinctly urban assumption that one's every whim could be satisfied, no matter the time of day or the season, at some nearby shop or club or restaurant—Peggy and Tiffany Ver Planck had insisted on going apple picking anyway. Luke waited as the two tried to persuade the proprietor of Bethlehem Farms, who was selling cider and doughnuts behind the counter at his farm market, to give them a basket and picking pole. The old-timer had already warned there wouldn't be any fruit left, at least none worth eating. But he gave them what they'd asked for, and Peggy and Tiffany hauled themselves up into Ver Planck's gargantuan black Escalade, on either side of the Ver Plancks' sleeping toddler, with Luke in the front seat and Ver Planck driving the two hundred feet to the apple orchard. The two women disappeared over a ridge into the misty Saturday afternoon.

Luke and Ver Planck walked the circumference of the orchard parking area, a dirt lot rutted with tire prints, one car door open in case Milo woke up. "Pick your own apples—it's genius," Ver Planck said. "Plant trees, and people pay for the privilege of playing migrant farmworker. Low overhead, low labor costs."

Luke squelched through a muddy patch. "Low profit margin."

"True." Ver Planck stopped to survey the haze-shrouded farm, rows of fruit trees undulating with the curves of the hills; sun yellow scarecrow globes painted with menacing eyes keeping guard from wires strung over the spent cornfields. He framed his fingers into a rectangle and looked through them as if through a viewfinder. "Better to raze and subdivide."

Luke detected no irony in his friend's comment. He walked ahead to the top of the ridge. Below him in the orchard, the doll-size figures of Tiffany and Peggy flitted from tree to tree like butterflies. Far beyond them, to the north and east, were Hartford and Providence and Plymouth Rock and Provincetown, and the Atlantic Ocean and ultimately England, where the bones of Silas Sedgwick's fathers slept.

Ver Planck caught up. "You own the land, don't you, next to that Pilgrim Plaza on Route 202? It's part of the holdings you manage, right? You can do with it as you wish?"

Luke nodded. The land to which Ver Planck referred was the last piece of Sedgwick property the family still possessed—twenty acres of fallow pasture bordered by a crumbling stone wall. A vocal group of preservationists, organized by Annette and Angelo Fiorentino, had picketed there during the construction of Pilgrim Plaza on the adjacent woods that had, until half a century ago, also belonged to the Sedgwicks.

"Ever thought of developing it?" Ver Planck asked. "I played Sebonack last month with Grant Atherton. You know him."

"The name sounds familiar." A crow landed a couple of feet from Luke and hopped a few steps on the deserted field. *The only moving thing / Was the eye of the blackbird,* Luke thought: Wallace Stevens.

"Atherton was a few years behind you at Andover. He's head of new-store development at Budget Club. I told him he ought to talk to you. They're looking to put a store in this area."

"You think there should be a discount superstore on my family's land?"

"Why not? The property's just sitting there, going to waste. You give Budget Club a ninety-nine-year lease, and you can still call the land yours. That strip mall next door is already pulling in customers, there's a new traffic light—just the infrastructure a retailer like Budget Club is looking for." He clapped Luke on the shoulder. "Think about it."

Luke thought about it. For half a second. "No thanks," he said. The crow cawed as if laughing at them both.

The farmer hadn't lied: There was nothing left on the trees. Peggy wound through the orchard, eyeing the crooked, barren branches. There had to be one good apple left. She wanted only one.

She'd been delighted that morning when the Sedgwicks' telephone had rung and Miss Abigail had come to get her in the dining room, where she'd been writing a thank-you to a Mrs. Digby Twombly for a set of seasonally themed tea towels. "Tom Ver Planck's wife, for you, dear," Miss Abigail had announced. It was Peggy's first call at the house. She'd followed Miss Abigail to the den, where the phone, black with a rotary dial and a bell, squatted on a cluttered end table, its heavy receiver balanced on a stack of yellowing telephone books.

"Tom wants to visit with Luke, and Milo is obsessed with going to a farm," Tiffany said. "Why don't we make an afternoon of it?"

Now Peggy appraised the orchard systematically. "Maybe we should go farther down the hill. There might be a tree no one else noticed."

Tiffany took the picking pole, a strange tool that resembled a broom handle with a small net attached to a metal ring at the top. They walked together, the flat tracks of Tiffany's pink rubber Wellingtons next to the deep holes left by Peggy's impractical boot heels, until Tiffany stopped. "Do you hear crying?"

Peggy listened. "I think it's a crow cawing."

"Oh." Tiffany exhaled. "You're right." They started walking again through the damp air. "Poor little Milo. He was the one who wanted to come to a farm, and now he's going to nap through the whole thing."

Peggy was quiet, thinking of Bex. This morning she'd had the transfer procedure. All three embryos were now inside her. It would take about a week before Bex would know if any were growing, and the news could easily be bad—the embryos had failed to divide; Bex wasn't pregnant; all the money and time and hope had been for nothing, and she and Josh would have to start the process all over again. How many tries could their emotions and bank account take?

"There's one!" Tiffany pointed up into a tree. "Wait, it's all pecked at."

Peggy drew her leather jacket tighter around her and looked back up toward the ridge. On top, she could make out Luke and Tom, pacing back and forth. It was the most animated she'd seen Luke all day. He'd returned to his tight-lipped self, without so much as a mention of his phone call last week. On the ride over to the farm to meet the Ver Plancks, he'd spoken twice: to ask if she had closed the car door all the way, and to offer an insightful remark about the weather. Now there he was, waving his hands, pontificating.

"What do you suppose they're talking about?" Peggy wondered aloud.

Tiffany's laugh had a tiny, adorable snort at the end. "Business. Always. I always say, unless my husband is asleep, he's putting together a deal, and if he could figure out how, he'd make deals in his sleep, too. Last night he dreamed he bought the Brooklyn Bridge."

"What does he do, exactly?"

"He manages the family investments, just like Luke."

"Like Luke?" As soon as she asked, Peggy wanted to kick herself—if she were really Luke's wife, wouldn't she know this already?

But Tiffany just regarded her with a quizzical expression. "Well, you know, they all call it something different. Tom has his hedge fund, and Luke has his investment portfolio, Kyle has the Hubbard Family Foundation, but really each of them is just playing around with the inheritance."

Tiffany couldn't be right, not about Luke. People with inheritances to play around with didn't live in mansions that were falling to pieces. Peggy wished she could ask Tiffany all sorts of questions about Luke, about how he'd come to be living with his ninety-one-year-old great-aunt, about his poetry, about the sexy redhead in the photograph on his desk who was so obviously the subject of his poems. "Why is everyone so surprised Luke got married?" she blurted. "All people keep saying is, 'I can't believe he settled down!' "

Tiffany was gazing up through the mist into a tree. "I've known Luke ten years, and he never talks about it, but my sense always was he had no interest in carrying on the Sedgwick name, or living in the Sedgwick House, or anything else associated with people like him."

"You mean, like you—and me," Peggy corrected herself quickly. She too was supposed to belong to this group.

"Oh, yes, 'people like us.' " Tiffany laughed. "I'm not

'people like us'; I'm from Queens. Anyway, I always told Luke as soon as he met the woman of his dreams, he'd marry her in thirty seconds. And, voilà, I was right!"

More right than you know. It had taken a little longer than thirty seconds for Peggy and Luke to get married, but Tiffany wasn't far off, even if, really, what had done it for Luke wasn't meeting his ideal woman, but being rip-roaring drunk. But wait a minute. "I thought you grew up in Westport."

"I did. From age two to age eight, until my dad ran out on my mom and me, and poof—we were back in Flushing, living with my nana."

Peggy smiled. It was a good joke.

"I'm not kidding. Does this help? 'My muthah bought me a sweatah,' " Tiffany said in a nasal accent, giggled, and went to search more trees.

Peggy laughed, still not sure she believed Tiffany, and mechanically scanned the next apple tree in the row. Its bowed branches arched darkly against the sky and brought to mind a familiar shape she couldn't quite put her finger on, the Gothic windows of a cathedral in Italy, or the base of the Eiffel Tower, or...

"Last night he dreamed he bought the Brooklyn Bridge," Tiffany had said.

The Brooklyn Bridge.

Peggy was walking across it, an otherworldly midnight stroll, the air balmy on her skin, the bridge's double arches framing cables strung with white bulbs, like Christmas lights. And—she closed her eyes and concentrated—she was hand in hand with somebody very special, asking him a question. And the first real details of her night in Las Vegas surfaced like a long forgotten dream.

She and Luke had run out of cash, left the roulette table at New York New York, and ridden the hotel's roller coaster outside, across the desert sky. They'd wandered onto the Brooklyn Bridge—not the true bridge, a scaled-down reproduction leading nowhere, a platform running along Las Vegas Boulevard.

"I don't like bridges," Peggy had admitted, and Luke had asked her why. She'd looked out across the traffic-snarled Strip, where engines idled to the tuneless bass throbbing of car stereos. And she'd told Luke about the time she'd walked across the real Brooklyn Bridge; and about how, when she'd reached dead center, at what had felt like a mile above the East River, it had struck her that there was nothing underneath her but air. She didn't tell Luke she'd been with Brock at the time.

Luke had taken her hand. "And yet you're not afraid of a roller coaster."

"My mind is a roller coaster," she'd said—melodramatic but true. Precarious pitches and unexpected curves felt ordinary to her.

"You don't have to be afraid on this bridge." Luke had put his hand on her waist. The night had been warm, windy, lush with possibility. "I'm going to give it to you as a gift. You'll own it, and then you won't be scared of it."

"That's so generous." Peggy had thought this the most romantic, the most madly improbable moment of her life. "But why?"

"For knowing Shakespeare. For blowing all my money on roulette. For making me ride the roller coaster."

"You could have done that without me."

"No," Luke had said. "I couldn't have."

And then, because there couldn't be another scene as romantic as this, there was no other appropriate step but to ask the question every hopeful romantic longed one day to ask. And who could resist saying yes on this stage set, in this unreal, idealized place where the Brooklyn Bridge was only a few feet off the ground and strung with Christmas lights; where it, and love, and marriage, were better and cleaner and simpler than the real thing?

Even if it was the woman asking the question?

Peggy couldn't breathe. Seriously—there was no air coming into her lungs. Her throat was closing, and her hands felt disconnected from her body. She was going to suffocate here in this spent orchard, and Tiffany, who was deep into another row of trees, wouldn't return until it was too late. She attempted a small, shallow breath and then a larger, deeper one.

She had proposed to Luke on the fake bridge. She'd held both his hands and looked up into his eyes, her face a moving image reflected in his glasses. "Will you marry me?" It had slipped from her mouth, but once the question was out, she knew she'd meant it. And when he had answered instantly, she'd known he'd meant it, too. For one instant of absolute clarity, they'd seen the future in each other's eyes.

Peggy braced one hand against the cool, rough bark of the apple tree and smiled in spite of herself. No chain of events could be less suited to people like her and Luke.

Damn. Those had been strong martinis.

She was about to call to Tiffany, suggesting they give up, when she looked into the tree one last time. There it was. She circled the tree; the apple was perfect from every angle.

"I found one!" Peggy shouted, abandoning her thoughts of Luke. Tiffany came running with the pole and demonstrated how to position it under the apple and squeeze the handle so the metal rim closed around the fruit and captured it in the net.

Luke watched them come marching up over the ridge, the upright pole between them, a small object swinging at the top.

For a good ten minutes, Ver Planck had been following Milo as the child zigzagged back and forth across the parking area. Ver Planck's eyes lit up with relief. "Look who's back, sport."

"Hi, peanut!" Tiffany waved.

"Mummy!" The child took off at a stiff-legged run, stepped into a tire rut, and fell, sprawled on his stomach, a few yards from Luke. Luke stood still. He looked back at Ver Planck and then at Milo getting himself to his feet and staring wonderingly at the mud on his pudgy, starfish hands.

"Baby!" Tiffany shrieked. She let go of the pole, dashed up the last few feet of the ridge, and swooped Milo into her arms, his muddy front pressed against her jacket.

Milo began to wail. Tiffany looked at her husband—accusingly, Luke thought.

Luke rushed to Ver Planck's defense. "Milo's fine," he told Tiffany, trying to reassure her. Out of the corner of his eye, he saw Peggy scramble to the top of the ridge.

"Why didn't one of you pick him up?" Tiffany was wild-eyed as Milo continued to scream.

Peggy was out of breath. "What's happened?"

"It's nothing." Luke could see how quickly Peggy's concern would turn to panic if someone didn't show some common sense. "Milo fell a little. He's okay."

The Ver Plancks were both hovering now, Tiffany clutching their howling child to her chest while Tom shepherded them both toward the car.

Peggy reached up to get the apple from its net. She started toward the Ver Plancks, leaving Luke to hold the picking pole. He watched her approach the trio cautiously and hold up the apple to Milo as one might offer food to a shy animal.

To Luke's amazement, Milo stopped in the middle of a shriek. He extended a muddy hand. Tiffany took the opportunity to swipe it clean with a disposable cloth from a plastic container.

"Isn't it pretty? Your mommy and I picked it for you," Peggy crooned, as if calming a screaming child were the most natural thing in the world to her.

"Hold it." Milo spread his fingers wide. Tiffany wiped his tear-streaked face.

"Would you like to hold the pretty apple?" Peggy passed the fruit to the boy, and Luke saw Tiffany mouth the words *Thank you.*

At the farm market, Peggy waited by the cars with Tiffany while Luke and Tom took a now placid Milo to look at the cows. Peggy was in no hurry for their return. She dreaded the empty afternoon awaiting her at the Sedgwick House nearly as much as she did the silent drive back with Luke.

"Are you really from Queens?" she asked Tiffany. "Or were you joking back there?"

"Oh, it's no joke," Tiffany said. "Nobody jokes about being from Queens."

Peggy took a breath, screwed up her courage. "Can you keep a secret?"

Tiffany was leaning against her mountain-size vehicle. Her quilted, corduroy-collared jacket was caked with mud. "Absolutely."

"I'm not 'people like us,' either."

"I know," Tiffany said.

"You do?" Peggy's heart beat faster; she hadn't expected this. A gust of wind picked up, and she shivered; her own jacket was simply no match for the foggy dampness. "How?"

Tiffany came closer, catching Peggy's jacket hem between a thumb and forefinger. "There are clues. Your clothes, for example. Don't get me wrong; they're gorgeous. But look at Liddy and Carrie and Creighton. It's wool, not leather; navy, not black; flats, not heels; loose, not tight; ChapStick, not lipstick—"

"You wear lipstick."

Tiffany giggle-snorted again. "I get my hair colored, too—very *not* 'people like us.' You can take the girl out of Flushing, but you can't take Flushing out of the girl." She smiled. "Where are you really from?"

"Nowhere. Everywhere. It's a long story. Luke knows, but do you think Liddy and the others can tell I'm not one of them?"

Tiffany shook her head. "I don't think so. But if Luke doesn't care, does it matter? Tom loves that I'm from Queens."

Peggy wished she could tell Tiffany the truth about her marriage. "It matters," she said softly. "I can't tell you why, but it does."

Luke was quiet on the drive back to New Nineveh. Peggy watched the houses go by. With the trees half-bare, the hidden homes emerged, unmasked: beautiful old clapboard Colonials with leftover Halloween pumpkins grinning on the porches and fall wreaths on the doors.

"Why are all the houses white with black shutters?" The volume of her own voice startled her. She'd not meant to speak aloud, to get between Luke and the silence that fell over him whenever they were alone.

But—"Didn't you know? It's the newest color combination," Luke replied right away, pleasantly, as if all this time he'd been waiting for her to start talking first.

"It's new? Really?"

"As of about 1880. In Connecticut that's new." His eyes

tilted up at the corners in what might be a smile—as rare and unexpected as the last apple in an orchard. "In case you hadn't noticed, we're not so good with change."

"So hating change is a Yankee thing."

"Exactly."

"Then I must have a little Yankee blood. I hate change more than anything."

"Really?" Luke looked at her. "One wouldn't know it by your actions. Would you consider painting a house beige?"

"Beige?"

"To a Yankee, a beige house is flamboyant."

"Then how do you Yankees give directions to your houses?" Peggy parried back, enjoying the camaraderie. "Do you say, 'Turn right at the white house with black shutters, pass the white house with black shutters, and then make a sharp left at the white house with black shutters?' "

Luke smiled—definite, genuine. " 'Once you pass the white house with black shutters, you can't miss our house. It's the white one with the black shutters.' " His front teeth overlapped slightly. The flaw suited him. He had the appealing, unfussy confidence of a man who knew who he was and had nothing to prove.

"Wait!" Peggy returned to the view outside the car. "There's a white house with dark green shutters."

Luke slowed to a stop and leaned over a steel travel mug wedged next to the gearshift to look out her window. He said, his voice hushed, as if murmuring across a pillow in the dark, "Their neighbors must whisper about them."

He was so close. She could have touched his sleeve or laid her hand on his leg.

"What would they whisper?" Peggy almost whispered this herself.

"The neighbors? Oh, that those people are bohemians.

Troublemaking nonconformists. Or, worse, Democrats." He looked over the tops of his glasses at her, as if they were real friends sharing an inside joke. She could imagine the softness of his threadbare khaki pants under her fingers. He smelled of shampoo and clean laundry and wool. A real man's scent—not bottled.

She had to stop. *I am not attracted to Luke Sedgwick.* This was simply a reaction to weeks of celibacy. Luke had been the man of her alcohol-addled dreams for a few hours of one night. What had he done since then to deserve any admiration on her part?

Luke accelerated past the green-shuttered house, left arm on the car windowsill, right hand loosely, lazily, on the steering wheel.

I am not attracted to Luke Sedgwick, Peggy repeated to herself.

It wasn't working. She evidently had a thing for emotionally unavailable men. That would explain why she'd fallen for Brock and why she'd taken it upon herself to pop the question to Luke outside a casino after too many martinis. Tee many martoonies, as she and Bex used to say in college.

Well, no more. The next man she had a relationship with—Jeremy, maybe, or one she hadn't yet met—would be friendly and personable not just when the whim struck. The next man she got involved with would care about her. And besides, Luke was taken.

The NEW NINEVEH, POP. 3,200 sign flew by on the left, and Luke turned onto Church Street. They stopped at the traffic light. On the green, picketers marched with their signs. Annette Fiorentino was among them. Peggy waved and started to ask Luke about the demonstrations.

But Luke was pointing at a spot past the group. "I grew up in that white house with black shutters."

Peggy followed the line with her eyes. "Which?"

"The smallish one with the potted mums on the steps."

"I thought you grew up in the Sedgwick House."

"No, just in its shadow." The light turned green, and Luke turned left on Main Street, past two white houses with black shutters. Peggy craned her neck to take in Luke's childhood home: solid, handsome, traditional. Like Luke, she realized.

I do not have a crush on my husband.

She bit the inside of her cheek and remembered Luke standing by nonchalantly while Milo flailed in the mud. She saw him in the library, reciting his petty limerick. *Don't you make my mistake, or you'll pay.*

"I don't understand why you didn't help Milo," she said. When he didn't answer, she repeated herself, louder.

After the third time, Luke said, "He wasn't hurt. He didn't need help." He pulled into the driveway of the Sedgwick House, white with black shutters, and cut the engine.

"He was crying!"

"Only after Tiffany fussed over him." He got out and walked around to open Peggy's door.

"She was not fussing! She was helping Milo up, the way I'm sure your mother picked you up when you fell down." She checked herself. Good—her brief moment of attraction was gone.

At the front door, Luke stood back so she could enter first, but once inside, Peggy felt lost. She wasn't ready to face the disrepair, the drafty parlors, her lonely room. The time stretched out endlessly until tomorrow afternoon, when she could return to the city.

She'd go for a walk in town. She'd been meaning to see what was down there anyway and to find out what Annette and the others were protesting, and there was a good hour left until dark. She'd just go up to her room to get a warmer sweater and check in with Bex.

"It went perfectly. I feel fine. I'm in bed, and, look, here's my husband, bringing me cookies and milk on a tray. Thanks, Josh, sweetie," Bex said.

More relaxed already, Peggy changed sweaters, put her jacket back on, and hurried back downstairs, nearly bumping into two figures in the dusky entryway.

"I have it!" Miss Abigail was saying to Luke. She was holding out her right hand, which was clenched, as if she held something.

Luke reached out to take whatever it was.

Miss Abigail pulled in her fist. "Follow me. You, too, Peggy." Without waiting for an answer, she disappeared into the house.

Luke hesitated, then followed.

Peggy groaned to herself. She was vaguely curious about what Miss Abigail was holding, but once she let the house swallow her up, she'd never make it back out for the afternoon. On the other hand, it would be rude not to follow, and Miss Abigail was intimidating, even though Peggy could probably bench-press her. At least she could have at one time, when she was in better shape. *I have got to start going to the gym,* she thought.

The den, when they arrived, was in a greater state of disarray than normal. The portraits on the walls hung at odd angles. The fireplace mantel and the tables had been cleared, and the floor was littered with tarnished silver candlesticks, a ceramic ashtray with a picture of a ship on it, a scattering of pennies, dozens of faded copies of *Life* magazine, and a needlepoint pillow that read: "Use it up / Wear it out / Make do / Do without." Luke gaped. Peggy confirmed her own suspicion that she, too, had her mouth open and closed it.

Miss Abigail seemed oblivious to the mess. Luke caught his great-aunt's elbow before she could step squarely on top of the May 1981 *Life,* featuring Ronald Reagan in a cowboy hat, and tried to guide her to a chair. As usual, she didn't sit. Instead, she picked her way with surprising steadiness to a tilted painting of a young woman whose oval face was framed with wings of dark hair.

"This is Elizabeth Coe Sedgwick, the wife of Silas's favorite son, Josiah. Elizabeth bore Josiah five children, four of whom, tragically, died. Elizabeth herself passed away giving birth to the fifth."

"How awful." Peggy tiptoed up to the painting and leveled it. Of all the portraits in all the museums she'd visited in her life, it had not sunk in before that the people in them had once been real, flesh-and-blood human beings with lives and loves and losses. She searched Elizabeth's gently curved lips and placid eyes for a clue that this woman understood her fate and was at peace with it. Luke, meanwhile, was stooped over, restacking the magazines mechanically, as if he'd sat through Miss Abigail's story a thousand times.

"That fifth child was Luke Silas Sedgwick. Our Luke, as you're aware, is Luke Silas Sedgwick the Fourth."

Peggy hadn't been aware. She glanced at Luke, who was returning the magazines to their place on a low shelf.

"That makes Elizabeth your husband's great-great-grandmother. This portrait was painted the year she was married. The brooch she's wearing was a wedding present from Josiah. Now it's my wedding present to you."

Miss Abigail opened her hand. On her palm gleamed a small, dome-shaped gold flower, with a single perfect pearl at the center. It was indeed the same pin fastening the delicate lace cape that lay across Elizabeth Coe Sedgwick's ivory shoulders.

Luke was paying attention now. His freckled, ruddy face was pale. "Abby, where in the world did you get that?"

With tears in her throat, Peggy touched the brooch longingly. What stories might it tell of the parties it had attended, the women whose dresses it had adorned, all long departed through the coffin door. "It's lovely," she said, "but I can't accept it."

Miss Abigail pressed the brooch into Peggy's hand. "Nonsense. You're a Sedgwick. That's the end of the discussion."

"Thank you. It means a great deal to me," Peggy said sincerely.

"Then for goodness' sake, young lady, put it on. Luke, help your wife."

"I can do it myself." The idea of forcing Luke to pin this precious family heirloom on her was more than Peggy could bear. She caught his eye and held the gaze for a long beat, desperate to make him understand, to signal that she would return the brooch to him and in no way felt it was rightfully hers.

But Miss Abigail was also staring at Luke in that intense way she had, leaving Luke no choice but to do her bidding. Peggy slowly took off her jacket, and Luke leaned in, the back of his hand grazing her cheek. At his touch, Peggy felt her breath catch. Luke fastened the brooch to her sweater. Could he hear her clamoring heartbeat? Could he see into her thoughts, know she'd been reliving their moment on the make-believe Brooklyn Bridge? She stepped back hastily.

Miss Abigail regarded Peggy with suspiciously bright eyes. "It looks well on you, dear."

She was a remarkable woman. Peggy couldn't imagine how, at ninety-one, Miss Abigail could keep straight all those names and dates and events. How sad must she be to watch the family die off, to be at the end of a breed of fragile dinosaurs?

On impulse, Peggy darted forward and wrapped her arms around Miss Abigail's rigid body. *I'm sorry I won't be giving you an heir,* she wanted to say. *I'm sorry we're deceiving you. You have to believe it's in everyone's best interest. I want you to be safe as much as Luke does.*

Miss Abigail patted Peggy's back awkwardly and retreated to a safe distance. "I'll take my sherry now," she announced, and left to fix herself her nightly glass.

Peggy picked up a candlestick and replaced it on the mantel, then knelt and gathered up a fistful of pennies. "Where should I put these?"

Luke laughed humorlessly. "In a sack. Then take the sack down to Seymour's Hardware and tell them the Sedgwicks finally have enough to get their roof replaced." He turned back to the bookshelves. Peggy searched for a suitable coin container and settled for the empty copper firewood caddy on the cold hearth. The pennies clanged to the bottom.

She brushed off her hands and got to her feet. "You can have the brooch back. As soon as our deal is up, I'll return it, I promise. I know it isn't mine."

Above her, dead Sedgwicks peered out from their frames. Peggy watched Luke return a silver cigar box to its place next to the magazines. If only she knew what he was thinking.

"We should probably talk about the house," she said, "and how we should go about selling it." She lowered her voice so the portraits of Luke's ancestors wouldn't overhear. "And what needs fixing before we do."

"That's easy, everything," Luke began as Miss Abigail returned with her drink.

"What's that, young man?"

"Never mind," he said.

Miss Abigail sipped from her diminutive sherry glass.

"That brooch looks lovely," she said to Peggy. "Almost as if it were made for you."

"I have work to do." Luke excused himself and left, his footsteps disappearing down the hall.

He didn't appear the rest of the evening. At six, Peggy and Miss Abigail ate frozen beef potpies and peas together in the kitchen, on the blue-and-white china, and Miss Abigail shared more tales of the Sedgwick ancestors—about two of her own older brothers, Henry and George, who'd succumbed to influenza in 1918, the year she was born; and her oldest brother, Luke Silas Sedgwick the Second, who was Luke's grandfather. And about Luke's father, the Third, known as Trip, who in midlife had married Nan Woodruff, from an old Maine clan. The Sedgwick family had assumed the couple would have no children, until to everybody's surprise, including Trip and Nan's, Nan had given birth to Luke at the shocking age of forty-seven.

"They're both gone now." Miss Abigail dabbed at her lips with a dinner napkin showing evidence of multiple mendings. "It's a pity. They would have been pleased Luke found you."

Peggy wasn't so sure. She speared a cube of beef with her fork. "Have you . . . Why did you not . . . ?" *Get married,* was the ending of the question. She caught the look on Miss Abigail's face and wished she hadn't begun.

Miss Abigail's eyes were blank. Her lower lip trembled. She held a forkful of peas halfway to her mouth. "Who are you?" A few peas tumbled off her fork, bounced off her chipped plate, and rolled underneath the table. "What are you doing in my house?"

Peggy had just bitten into a piece of crust. It was dry and salty, and she had to force herself to chew and swallow, willing the food not to get stuck in her suddenly unyielding throat. "I'm Peggy. Luke's . . . wife."

She flinched as Miss Abigail's fork fell to the table with a nerve-shattering clatter.

"He's dead!" Half howl and half shout, the cry filled the kitchen. Miss Abigail tried to lift herself out of her chair. Peggy wasn't sure whether to restrain her or help her up. She felt sure asking whom Miss Abigail was referring to—Silas Sedgwick? Luke's father?—was the wrong thing to do.

"Charles is dead!" Miss Abigail shrieked. "Gone!"

What had Peggy said? The anxiety dug its bony fingers into Peggy's lungs, wringing them, twisting them, making each gulp of air an exercise in mind over matter. *Breathe, Peggy. Breathe.* "I'm going to get Luke. Please, just stay in your chair. Okay?"

Miss Abigail gazed ahead vacantly, but at least she didn't move.

"Don't leave. I promise to be right back." Peggy walked calmly from the kitchen, breaking into a run the second she was out of Miss Abigail's view. She tore down the hall toward the front staircase and had just about made it into the front entryway when she slipped on a bare spot of wood, lost her footing, and fell with a crash. Pain shot through her right leg, but she ignored it, picked herself up, and sprinted up the stairs.

The tea had served its intended purpose. After finishing it, Abby had agreed to change into her nightclothes, ordering Luke out of her room. He took the cup and saucer downstairs to the kitchen, which was otherwise spotless; Peggy must have done the dishes and cleaned up Abby's mess. By the time he'd gotten to his great-aunt's side, Abigail had managed to spill most of her food and knock over her drinking glass, and water had been cascading off the edge of the table onto the floor below.

When he returned to Abby's room, she was in bed, snoring gently under a blue-striped Hudson's Bay blanket Luke remembered from his childhood as the roof to many a rainy summer Saturday fort. He tucked the blanket around Abby's shoulders as Quibble jumped onto the bed and prowled it silently, a black shadow with a tail arched into a question mark.

Luke lined up Abby's slippers at the end of her bed, where she would find them in the morning, and crept out of the room, leaving the door open a crack and turning on the hall light. He climbed the back stairs to the third floor, hoping to catch Peggy in her room, but the door was closed. After he knocked and she didn't answer, he opened the door cautiously. All he found inside was the barest whisper of her flower-and-fruit fragrance. He stood still, trying to capture the scent in his nostrils, to take apart its components and decipher its mysteries, then shut the door with a soft click and went downstairs.

Peggy was in the den, her back toward the door, her face inches from the portrait of Elizabeth Coe Sedgwick as if she were memorizing every paint crackle. Luke coughed, and she spun around, her left hand flying to the brooch on her sweater as if to check that it was still there. The diamond sparkled on her fourth finger. It was almost too much to bear, the sight of another man's engaged-to-be-engaged ring covering the wedding present Abigail had given Peggy in good faith. "You're a Sedgwick," his great-aunt had declared, and he'd had to turn away; Peggy might not be a real Sedgwick, but just then, wearing that brooch, she'd looked like a Sedgwick, and the image had been a shock. It made no sense to him that he could simultaneously rail against his heritage and be so taken by the way this woman seemed, through no conscious effort of her own, to embody it.

Peggy moved back from the portrait. “Is Miss Abigail all right?”

“She’s fine. I made her chamomile tea.” He didn’t add that he had fortified it with a healthy shot of sherry. “She can get like that when she’s overtired or overexcited. It upsets her when it happens. She thinks it’s undignified.”

“But she can’t help it,” Peggy said. “She’s ninety-one. No one expects her to keep up appearances every minute of the day.”

She expects it of herself,” Luke told her. “Keeping up appearances is what Sedgwicks do.”

Peggy dropped into a chair now free of the items Abby had spread throughout the room. Luke realized Peggy must have cleared those, too, and put back the remaining books and trinkets. For the first time, he was thankful to have someone else helping him look after his great-aunt, even if Peggy was here only because she knew eventually she’d be compensated for it. She must be as desperate for money as he was.

Who was she? Luke wondered. He imagined Peggy had enjoyed a childhood full of ordinary pleasures, of brothers and sisters and neighborhood friends riding their bicycles on an unremarkable suburban cul-de-sac, their futures wide open, their choice of college and job and mate entirely within their own control.

She got up again to straighten a portrait of a young girl in a party dress.

“That’s Abigail,” Luke said, and Peggy smiled. The child version of his great-aunt had short, dark hair and a playful look in her brown eyes that suddenly reminded him of somebody; he couldn’t remember who. “I suppose you would like to know who Charles is,” he said.

She nodded.

“Charles Finnegan lived two houses north of here. He

was the son of the housekeeper at Number Five Main Street. When Abigail was a schoolgirl, she and Charles were the closest of friends. My great-grandparents didn't like their only daughter fraternizing with a servant's boy, but the friendship only strengthened, and when she turned sixteen and he was eighteen, they secretly got engaged."

Luke hadn't planned to air his family's laundry, but if Peggy was to be witness to Abby's outbursts, it was best she understood them. He continued, "Soon afterward, her brother, my grandfather Luke the Second, discovered their plan to elope and ratted out Abigail to my great-grandfather, who secretly arranged a job for Charles. He used his connections to get Charles work building the Bourne Bridge in Massachusetts. This was during the Great Depression, and good jobs were hard to come by. Charles would have needed to save money for his marriage—a marriage that wouldn't include a dowry—and my family knew he couldn't and wouldn't say no. Charles promised Abigail he'd return to her once the project was completed, but the family was counting on Abby coming to her senses before he got back.

"But things turned out better than my great-grandfather had hoped. Charles had been working only a few months when he fell off the bridge into the Cape Cod Canal."

Peggy gasped.

"Abigail wasn't the same. No matter how many suitors her parents brought home, she swore she wouldn't marry, and she didn't."

"That's the saddest story I've ever heard."

"I don't know. To me, it's all very Miss Havisham."

"How remarkably unsympathetic," Peggy said.

Luke straightened in his chair. "I guess I don't understand how one could be so dependent on another person that to lose him or her could ruin one's life."

"You've never...?" Peggy looked into the empty fireplace. "You've never been...?"

"Consumed? Obsessed? No." He found he was again eyeing her ring. He supposed she was consumed with love, or whatever she thought passed for love, for the cretin who'd given it to her.

"You wanted to talk about the house. What is it you want to know?" He took off his sweater and tied it around his shoulders. "I suppose you'd like a sense of how much it's worth—"

"Three million, according to the tax assessment."

So she'd done her research. He had a brief flash of admiration for her business instinct that was quickly eclipsed by a fierce Yankee disapproval of which he hadn't known he was capable: This outsider was digging into his family's private affairs, placing a dollar value on something to which she had no true right. He reminded himself that he didn't want the Sedgwick House and sat back down. "If we could sell it for that much, it wouldn't be without a lot of work, which we need to start doing. We can't afford a new roof and a paint job, but I thought I'd draw up a list of chores we can tackle. It'll take months to get this place into selling shape, and it won't be any fun. No offense meant, but you don't strike me as the kind of woman who..."

"Who what? Who enjoys being insulted in bad rhymed verse at her own wedding reception?"

Where the hell had that come from? Despite his reluctance to bring it up, Luke had expected to have this discussion sooner or later, given the way Peggy had avoided him and acted sulky the two weekends before this. But not out of nowhere, during a discussion about unrelated matters, when just this afternoon she'd given the impression that she wasn't mad at him anymore. He considered his response, not knowing what she expected him to say, not wanting to get it wrong and start a whole lot of unnecessary unpleasantness.

But Peggy was already bombarding him with a barrage of, "Don't you have any feelings?" and, "Where were your manners?" and, "You had no right."

"I apologize. It won't happen again." It was a frank sentiment. She didn't seem appeased, so he groped reluctantly. "As you already know, I guess, I write a little poetry now and then. But it's nothing like... what you heard. That was a spur-of-the-moment poem. It was... I don't know..." *For chrissakes, Luke, find an adjective.*

She got up. "It was bad. 'Say, pay, day.' You could at least have used 'dismay' or 'betray' or 'radioactive decay.' "

"Thank you for your valuable poetic suggestions. It was a limerick. I'd had a few drinks. Ever done anything you regretted when *you* were drunk? Say, married someone wholly inappropriate?" He was annoyed at himself for letting his annoyance show.

She got up, as if to go upstairs, walked to the doorway, and turned back around. "You know," she said, "my relatives came here the same way yours did—on a ship. Just because it wasn't the *Mayflower* doesn't make you better than me. Now, if you'll excuse me, I'm going upstairs to plot more ways to wreck your life."

Before he knew he'd made the choice to go after her, he was on his feet, following her to the front staircase, knowing she was aware of him a few feet behind—as usual, the house kept no secrets; his footsteps were thunderous—and was refusing to acknowledge him. Just as she started up the staircase, he stepped onto the landing and reached out to grasp the hem of her sweater.

"It was the second *Mayflower*," he said.

She stood, balanced on the very edge of the squeaky third step, the extra inches putting her face above his eye level.

"The original *Mayflower* landed in 1621. Another ship, also called the *Mayflower*, arrived here eight years later. My relatives were on that ship."

He'd always thought of her as delicate, in need of protection—yet at this height, she seemed neither.

"So you see, as far as the original Pilgrims are concerned, the Sedgwick family is sloppy seconds. And, so you're clear on this, I don't think I'm better than anybody." He waited for her to storm up the stairs.

Instead, she offered him the smallest smile. "You must need this money pretty badly," she said.

"I do," he admitted. "My great-aunt needs to go into a nursing home. You saw her tonight. She's only going to get worse. Unless we sell the house, there's no way I can afford it."

"Then it would be nice," she said, "if until this is over, we could try and get along. We don't have to be best buddies, but it would be good, at least, to have a united front."

"By which you mean . . . ?"

"That you don't embarrass me in front of your friends. And you stop making me feel unwelcome. And talk to me once in a while. I'm sorry I snooped in your office. But I only did it because I don't know a thing about you."

"I talk to you."

"You do not."

"I'm talking to you now."

She raised her eyebrows at him. "Luke, I'm not stupid. It's clear you don't want me here. I don't blame you. But you agreed to this marriage, and you're going to get what you want in the end, and it would be nice if you could try to tolerate me for the next year."

"Eleven months. We've done a month already. I only have to tolerate you for eleven more."

"Actually, it's ten months. And nineteen days."

"But who's counting?"

She looked different when she laughed. The shadows, the scrunched-up forehead, vanished, leaving a lively, intelligent face with a big smile and those warm gray eyes—eyes, he realized with a shock, that held the same playful expression as the little-girl Abby's. Here was the woman Luke had met in Las Vegas. That he liked seeing her again was more than he cared to admit to himself.

TEN

Peggy felt as if she'd made a diplomatic breakthrough. Something had changed today. Between Luke's unexpected friendliness in the car, their cooperative effort to help Miss Abigail, and their exchange just now on the staircase, she thought she could look forward to a little less chilliness from her temporary husband. Tomorrow, if her courage held, she might see if he had any memory of their walk across the bridge.

She shivered. Speaking of chilly, her room seemed much cooler than the rest of the drafty house. Didn't an unexplained pocket of cold mean a ghost was present? Peggy could practically hear Elizabeth Coe Sedgwick moaning, "Give me back my brooch . . . I want my broooooooch. . . ."

"You don't scare me." Peggy unpinned the brooch and put it safely in her nightstand drawer. She resolved to order long underwear and was getting into her pajamas when it occurred to her a ghost might be watching her undress.

She buttoned her top hurriedly and distracted herself with a chorus of "Ninety-nine Bottles of Beer on the Wall" on her way to the bathroom. "Take one down, pass it around . . . ," she sang, lining up her cleansers and moisturizers—this for her cheeks, that for under her eyes—on the edge of the rust-stained sink and then clipping her hair off her face. "Ninety-eight bottles of beer on the wall." The water was freezing, but by now she knew to brush her teeth in the time it took to warm up. She squeezed organic toothpaste onto her imported Italian toothbrush with the ergonomic handle and brushed, humming through the foam, and then sang between splashes of water as she washed her face, and sang some more while she moisturized, and sang as she raced down the hall to the relatively ghost-free shelter of her ugly plaid comforter.

In the morning, Luke was at the kitchen table, as always, buried in his newspaper, as always.

"Good morning!" It was a lot of cheer to muster before ten a.m., but she was determined to start off her new phase with Luke on the right foot.

"Mmm." Luke didn't stop reading.

"Have you seen Miss Abigail? Is she better?"

"Mmm-hmm."

"Thank goodness." The news made Peggy enormously happy. She guessed she'd grown fonder than expected of Luke's great-aunt. She poured herself a cup of bad coffee, threw away Miss Abigail's used teabag from last night, and sat at the table across from Luke. She had prepared herself. It was time to bring up the marriage proposal. "I'm glad we cleared the air last night. Aren't you?"

Luke continued reading.

Peggy toyed with the salt and pepper shakers. Mr. Pepper and Mrs. Salt, her mother called them. They were married, and when you passed one, you were supposed to pass the other as well, so the two wouldn't be separated. "Building bridges. That's what some people call it." She emphasized "bridges."

Luke's newspaper rattled as he turned a page.

"You know what Tiffany said yesterday? She said Tom dreamed he bought the Brooklyn Bridge. Isn't that funny?

The Brooklyn Bridge, like, 'And if you believe *that,* I'll sell you the Brooklyn Bridge.' "

"Mmm-hmm."

Peggy's enthusiasm ebbed. There wasn't a trace of recognition in Luke's response. There wasn't a trace of yesterday's openness. As if their breakthrough hadn't happened. She asked, "Is anything wrong?"

"No," Luke said from behind the newspaper.

"You're acting quiet."

"I *am* quiet." A pause. "And I'm not a morning person."

"Me neither. I guess you've figured that out." A squeaky, skittish giggle escaped before Peggy could stop it. It was awkward, this one-sided dialogue. *Help me out, Luke,* she thought. *Give me something to work with.*

Miss Abigail bustled in, wearing her going-out clothes and her coat.

"Good morning!" Peggy sang out for the second time in three minutes. "Are you feeling all right?"

The old woman stared at the counter. "Young man, where did you put my teabag?"

"That was me," Peggy said. "I threw it out."

"But it was still good for two or three more cups." Miss Abigail looked certifiably puzzled, then brightened up. "It's nearly time for meeting, dear; you'd best be getting your coat."

During church, Peggy sat quietly next to Miss Abigail and tried to pay attention to the service, but her mind wandered to Tiffany enumerating the ways Peggy stood out from the Connecticut crowd. In their pearls and low-heeled pumps, the women in these pews, no matter their age, seemed to have stepped out of another time. The fashionable crowd in New York would consider them laughably conservative—dowdy, even—but Peggy thought they looked exactly right in the clean, plain meeting house. And Tiffany had been correct about this, too: No one else here was in black. Peggy might as well have been out all night clubbing and worn the same outfit to church.

The Yankees, their heads bowed in unison, began to recite the Lord's Prayer. What would these people think if they knew Peggy was just going through the motions? She said her own silent prayer instead. *Please put an end to war. Please make all the sick people better. Please stop global warming. Please give Bex a baby.* It seemed too much to ask for, even from God.

Luke was waiting at the curb to drive them home when Peggy and Miss Abigail emerged into the sunshine, but Peggy told him she'd walk. She'd finally explore downtown New Nineveh, eat lunch with Miss Abigail at the house, and go back to New York early to see Bex. She'd had good luck with the Sedgwicks this weekend and didn't want to push it.

"Downtown" was far too ambitious a description of New Nineveh's handful of storefronts and churches. They were arranged in a ring around a central green—an oval of lawn studded with autumn-hued trees, an aged iron cannon, several war memorials, and some benches on which Peggy had so far seen not a soul sitting. A flag fluttered red, white, and blue on its pole; a shaggy pine tree pointed like an arrow toward the sky. On this crisp morning the area was deserted, except for people going home from church: the white wood Congregational building she'd just left, the red-roofed Victorian Methodist church on the south side of the green, the neo-Gothic stone Episcopal church to the east. People chatted on the leaf-covered granite sidewalks and returned to their cars. Walking the green, Peggy understood why no one had lingered. The town was pretty; it would have been a perfect setting for a boutique like Peggy's. But there was little to do here. Three-quarters of the buildings were either real estate offices or posh antiques dealers—not places that invited casual browsing. The few other stores weren't the sort that brought in droves: Seymour's Hardware, the Cheese Shoppe, a small Italian restaurant called Luigi's, and the Toggery, where two WASP mannequins posed with his and hers camel-hair coats draped across their shoulders. Establishments were shuttered, too—an old coffee shop, a dentist's office, and a store whose faded gold window-lettering proclaimed: "Star Jewelers, Since 1909." Taped directly above was a sign: "Come see us at our new location in Pilgrim Plaza!"

Despite finding long johns at the Toggery, Peggy returned to the Sedgwick House discouraged by the state of the town.

Annette Fiorentino was in her front yard next door, raking leaves. She greeted Peggy. "What do you do all week? Ernestine says you work in the city."

"I own a little bath products shop," Peggy answered. "Why are you picketing?"

"You own a little shop!" Annette wore a Baja pullover—a hooded Mexican jacket. Peggy hadn't seen one since she was eleven and had lived for eight months near the beach in Ventura. The non-Yankee garment made her like Annette that much more. "I'd love to recruit you for our protests," the neighbor continued. "We picket on Saturdays when the weather is good, more often when there's a specific threat."

"Threat to what?"

"To our town. To its rural character, its history. To the health of our small local businesses—I'm sure you can relate." Annette scraped a few leaves off the tines of her rake. "We started picketing when the zoning commission approved Pilgrim Plaza out on Route 202. We want to remind people that once you pave a place over, once you bring in the Starbucks and the Gap and the McDonald's, you can't go back. Please, join us. So far our group is mostly weekend people from New York and people like Angelo and me who moved to New Nineveh from other places. Getting a local on board would be a big coup."

Peggy would have loved to help Annette. "Miss Abigail would have a fit," she told the neighbor sadly, and returned to the Sedgwick House.

She changed into jeans, tidied her room, set her purse and tote bag at the top of the stairs, and knocked on the ballroom door. As she'd expected, Luke was at his desk, his head bowed over his work. Probably writing poems to that redhead. For someone who claimed never to have been consumed by love, Luke wrote some convincing verse. *Maybe he's just in lust with her, not in love,* Peggy told herself, but felt no better.

"I thought I'd fix Miss Abigail lunch," she said.

"She's taking a nap," Luke answered.

"In that case, I'm heading back to the city."

Luke lifted his head. "Why?"

"I feel like I'm"—she didn't know how to explain it—"in your way."

"You're not."

He took off his glasses and rubbed the lenses on his shirt. Without them, his eyes had a directness that reminded Peggy of Silas Sedgwick's commanding gaze in the library portrait. Even more than the people in church, there was something not of this time about Luke. It was hardly a stretch to imagine him in a high-collared eighteenth-century jacket and ruffled dress shirt, exuding that same "my name is my destiny" confidence, presiding over generations of descendants as yet unborn. Except that Luke, Tiffany had said, was unhappy in the world his family had created and which Miss Abigail guarded so ferociously.

"You asked why I didn't help Milo yesterday." Luke replaced his glasses, and the effect was gone. "This is why. When I was ten, my mother got a second-degree burn on her thumb. We were at a clambake. She rinsed it with seawater, wrapped a towel around it, and that was that. My father was an attackman on his lacrosse team at Yale. One time he got hit on the head so hard that he passed out on the field and then came to, brushed himself off, and scored the winning goal on a behind-the-back shot. There are two guiding Sedgwick family principles. Number one..." He counted them on his fingers. " 'If it's easy, you're doing it wrong.' Number two, 'Pain builds character.' So my parents didn't swoop in if I stepped in a mud puddle."

Peggy felt sorry for him. "That's sad. And strange."

"It's the way I was raised." He spun the chair so he was facing her, not the desk. "Also, I don't talk for the sake of talking. You need to know this if we're going to get along. If I'm quiet, it means I have nothing to say. I'll discuss financial concerns affecting you, but personal issues are off the table. This has nothing to do with you. It's simply who I am."

"I understand."

But she didn't. Brock had been easy. When he was happy, he was happy, and when he wasn't, she'd cook dinner and hand him a beer and he'd be happy again. She'd never had to decipher the moods of her parents, who broadcast, to the point of exhaustion, each thought, feeling, and, in her mother's case, worry the moment it came up. Nothing in her experience had prepared Peggy for friendship with a person so reserved.

She dropped off her rental car and arrived at the apartment to find Bex in pajamas in front of the microwave. "What are you doing out of bed?" Peggy looked around. "Where's Josh?"

Bex stretched. "Out with his brother. I gave him a reprieve. Meanwhile I'm so tired of resting I want to run up and down the stairs about a thousand times. How was your weekend?" She kept her eye on the cup of instant cocoa revolving inside the microwave.

Peggy hit the "pause" button. "Don't drink that. It's all chemicals. I'll make you real hot chocolate. Keep resting." She placed her hands firmly on Bex's shoulders and steered her protesting friend back to bed. She fluffed up Bex's pillows, smoothed the sheets, and stood back so Bex could get in.

"You're becoming me, all bossy and full of yourself," grumbled Bex.

"I take that as a compliment." Peggy tucked her in and returned to the kitchen to search the cabinets for cocoa and sugar and cinnamon. Ten minutes later, she was back in Bex's room with a steaming mug.

Bex sipped appreciatively. "You're right. This is so much better. Now, how was your weekend?"

Peggy sat on the edge of the bed. "Luke and I are friends. That's what we're saying, anyway."

"I don't get it. What were you before?"

"I'm not sure. Hostile business associates, I guess." Peggy pointed at the mug, and Bex passed it over. The hot chocolate tasted heavenly, like comfort. She passed it back to Bex. "What do you think Luke saw in me in Las Vegas?"

"He's your husband. Why don't you ask him?"

"Right. He'd never say. He never says anything, really."

"What do you expect, sweets? He's a WASP. Withholding, unemotional, wears tweedy jackets, drinks too many gin and tonics. That's it!" Bex pushed away from her pillow, nearly spilling her cocoa. "Opposites attract. You're everything he isn't! That's what he sees in you."

"I don't think so." Luke could be warm and funny when he wanted to be. And he had emotions—he wrote poetry. *But not to me,* Peggy reminded herself. Anyway, what was the point of dwelling on what she and Luke had or hadn't seen in each other? This wasn't a relationship; it was a financial agreement. *I will not develop a crush on Luke Sedgwick.* "I'm surprised at you, using stereotypes," she told Bex.

"All stereotypes have a basis in reality."

"So you're Jewish. I guess that makes you . . . what?"

"Oy." Bex laughed. "Cheap, loud, and demanding. So when can I see this schmancy house of yours?"

"You don't want to, trust me. It's a wreck."

"Then would you at least get me a cookie?"

This time Peggy rolled her eyes, but she returned to the kitchen just as her phone began playing its music in her purse. She answered and was greeted with an earsplitting din punctuated by air-horn blasts and an announcer over a loudspeaker.

"Hey. I'm in Philly," her caller shouted.

"Brock?"

"Big Eagles-Redskins game tonight. We've got about twenty minutes to kickoff and the crowd is going nuts. Must be a full moon."

"Brock," Peggy shouted back, "what are you doing?"

"How about dinner next week?"

"We're broken up," she bellowed, perhaps louder than necessary, just as Josh came in, taking earphones from his ears.

"Hi!" Josh hugged her. "Missed you this weekend."

"Who's that?" A beep from Peggy's call waiting drowned out Brock's question. It was typical: Either nobody paid her the slightest notice or the entire world needed her at the same time.

Josh winked at her and went to check on Bex, faraway

music still spilling out of his dangling earphones. The call waiting beeped again.

"I just heard a guy say he missed you," Brock persisted. "Are you with some other guy?"

"Yes." Peggy's heart beat faster at the half-truth. "It's over between us, Brock." She switched to the other call, ending her conversation and any remnant of her former relationship with the press of one small but decisive button.

The waiting caller was, unmistakably, Miss Abigail.

"Dear? I'd like your parents' address in California." She would be in the den, standing, not sitting, somehow able to hold that two-pound phone receiver to her ear. "I'd like to ask them to Thanksgiving dinner. It's time we met."

Peggy tried to shift mental gears. At least she could hear what Miss Abigail was saying. The Sedgwicks' old phone got crystal-clear reception. "That's kind of you, Miss Abigail, but my parents can't come for Thanksgiving."

Thanksgiving. Peggy had not considered what she'd do on holidays. For the past seven years, while Brock worked at some football game or another, she'd had dinner with Bex and Josh at Bex's parents' apartment. Peggy roasted the turkey; Bex's dad, Allen, baked mincemeat pie; her curly-haired whirlwind of a mom, Sue, zipped around trying to locate the gravy boat; her sister, Rachel, who was a vegan, picked at the meal and sulked. For Christmas, Peggy generally traveled alone to Texas or Arizona, wherever her parents had parked their RV. More often than not, Brock worked on that holiday, too, and on New Year's Day. She spent New Year's Eve with Bex and Josh, or alone, with a good book.

"We'll have them for Christmas instead," Miss Abigail declared. "They'll spend the week with us. Their address, please?"

Peggy thought fast and gave Miss Abigail her parents' last

permanent address, the house they had sold years ago. She hoped Luke's great-aunt wouldn't notice the location wasn't Palo Alto but San Jose, and that the post office wouldn't send the letter back. Peggy would forge a note back from her mother, sending regrets, and bring it to New Nineveh, claiming Madeleine had accidentally mailed it to her instead of the Sedgwick House. It wasn't the most elegant solution, but it would have to do.

Optimism wasn't a state of mind in which Luke often found himself. He wasn't altogether comfortable with the sensation, though it was interesting, almost enjoyable. He wondered at its source but came up with no answer.

An hour or two after Peggy had left Sunday afternoon, Luke had heard coughing and come upon Abby in the shut-down east addition, trying to drag the dust covers off the furniture. "It's gone! Lost and gone!" was his great-aunt's familiar, distressed refrain, but then she'd dropped the search, seeming, blessedly, to forget about it, and had been in a cheerful mood since. Luke was still trying to decide exactly when and how to tell her he and Peggy planned to start fixing up the house without tipping her off that they were already set on selling it. But if her mood held, it might help soften the blow.

He slept better. He made a couple of daring trades. He wrote two poems with images of bright skies and birds on the wing—poems so sunny, he couldn't believe they'd come from him. They weren't any good, but he'd finished them. It was a boon he wasn't questioning.

He went from room to room in the Sedgwick House with a legal pad and a gimlet eye, cataloging everything that needed to be fixed or attended to, beginning with the ruffled fungus fanning from the corners of the basement and finishing with the splintery balustrade around the widow's walk on the roof of the main house. He stayed on the roof awhile, looking out over the garden and then across to the Rigas' place on Market Road. For much of his life he'd come up here simply for the fun of it, not to check for leaks or to clear birds' nests from the chimneys. At eight, he'd liked to stand alone, high above it all, Zeus on Mount Olympus with an armful of lightning bolts. He'd spent his eleventh summer at the balustrade, throwing water balloons at passing cars. The summer he was sixteen, he'd lost his virginity up here to a tape of "Margaritaville" with Ann Marie Scoggs, a girl from Torrington High School, she of the tenth-grade cynicism and clove cigarettes. Not surprisingly, his parents and great-aunt hadn't approved of her, and she couldn't comprehend them. In August, just before he'd returned to Andover, Ann Marie had told him, "Your conservative shit bums me out, and Jimmy Buffett sucks," and broken up with him. It had taken him half the year to get over her, but now he looked back on the experience with fondness. If this roof could talk.

Back on the first floor, he came across Abby in the ladies' parlor, having a discussion with her cat. "Nonsense." She held out a hand so a purring Quibble could rub it with his whiskery cheeks. "I'll find that nest egg and then the only way they'll be able to take me out of here is through the coffin door—" She stopped talking as Luke came in.

"Find what?" he asked.

Abby petted the cat carefully.

Luke crouched down next to her. "Is it possible you've hidden more jewelry around the house?"

Quibble twitched the tip of his tail and darted from the room.

Abby chuckled. "All that jewelry was sold long ago. It's just Elizabeth's brooch left, and..."

"And what?" Luke mentally spun through all the jewelry he remembered. There couldn't be anything of value left. Could there?

"There's a box," Abigail went on. "With a star. From Charles."

It all made sense. This was what Abigail had been so keen to find lately. This was why she'd been tearing the house apart, for an obscure gift from her lover Luke had never before heard about. More likely, he suspected, it was Abby's dementia talking, and there was no box.

But this was a fortunate break for him. "I'll tell you what." The mystery was solved, and he could use it to his advantage: a harmless white lie to appease his great-aunt. "Peggy and I will find the box for you. On the weekends we'll look for it, one room at a time. We'll do a little tidying and patching up as we go, too."

Abigail's gaze gave way to her piercing look. "You're a credit to the family, Luke."

Luke felt like anything but. He thanked her anyway.

Peggy couldn't have imagined she'd see the day when Brooklyn would become a destination for people who lived in Manhattan. But when the taxi dropped her off for her date with Jeremy at the corner of Bedford Avenue and North Sixth Street, under an orange flag that spelled "twig" in lowercase fuchsia letters, Peggy realized her simple black dress was as wrong here as it had been in New Nineveh, if for entirely different reasons. Williamsburg was teeming with thrift store girls in brocade coats and lace-up boots and scruffy boys with artfully disarranged Guatemalan knit hats. Peggy decided she hated trying to keep up with trends. She probably always had.

She hung back on the sidewalk outside the restaurant, took

out her vial of emergency Ativan, shook a tiny white house-shaped pill into her cold palm, and swallowed it without water.

Jeremy was waiting at the bar, absorbed with his electronic gadget. Next to him a group was singing "For She's a Jolly Good Fellow" to a tattooed woman in a "You Say Dyke Like It's a Bad Thing" T-shirt.

"I hope you weren't waiting long," Peggy apologized to her date. She could only imagine how Luke—Luke again; why did she insist on thinking about him?—would react to her being six minutes late, stranding him next to a raucous hipster birthday party.

"Not a problem." Jeremy rose and kissed Peggy European style on each cheek. "We're here now," he told the hostess, who tossed her blond, waist-length dreadlocks and walked them to their table. Peggy clandestinely wiped her cheeks with the backs of her hands. She supposed this was one good thing about being a repressed Yankee: Luke wouldn't subject anyone to an overly familiar Euro-kiss.

With a jolt, she realized he must have kissed her. She tried to recall how his lips had felt on hers. Was he a good kisser? Did the Yankee restraint hide a passionate heart? The partial poem on his desk had made it seem that way. *Staid genes worked hot from your electric charms*. He might be with his girlfriend right now. She pushed the unwelcome thought from her mind as Jeremy pulled out her chair.

It was Luke's turn to host poker night. At seven o'clock on Wednesday, half an hour before the rest of the players arrived, he ushered Ver Planck into the gentlemen's parlor. Ver Planck produced two comically oversize cigars. He clipped off the end of the first one with a gold Dunhill cutter and offered it to Luke. "Montecristo A. Best smoke money can buy."

"What's the occasion?" Luke accepted the cigar.

"No occasion. Just a taste of what you could enjoy if you'd reconsider this Budget Club idea."

Luke took a puff. "You talk like there's something in it for you."

"Only the glory of your success," Ver Planck said. "You could stand to be more aggressive with your assets, Sedgwick, and this is perfect for you. You'd just be leasing the land, not selling it."

"Maybe so." Unlike with the Sedgwick House, there was nothing saying he couldn't lease the Sedgwick land. "But Abigail would still have my head."

The air in the room was blue by the time Kyle Hubbard, Topher Eaton, and Bunny Simmons arrived. Hubbard breathed in deeply, exhaled with a theatrical "Aaaaaaaah," and tossed his coat across the back of the couch. "Miss the wife during the work week, Sedgwick?" Hubbard laughed. "You've got the right idea, friend, with this weekend-only deal. A man would kill for that kind of setup. Too bad it can't last. She's planning to move up here, yes?"

"Eventually."

Luke was a burgeoning expert at lies and dodges. Yesterday, Ernestine Riga had asked him when he and Peggy were going to have children, and he'd deftly changed the subject to the New Nineveh Home Tour. Ernestine had forgotten her question entirely and launched into an exhaustive account of the repairs and upgrades she and her husband were doing to prepare the former Sedgwick carriage house for its social debut. What a paradox, Luke had thought: The better-preserved Sedgwick house was the one that no longer belonged to the Sedgwicks.

"Enjoy your freedom while you can," Hubbard said. "Speaking of Peggy, Liddy and I want you two to come to the Game with us. We'll tailgate, the whole thing. Topher and Carrie are coming, too."

"Oh, I don't know," Luke said.

"Loosen up, Sedgwick. Besides, we all want to get to know the little lady." Hubbard headed toward the Scotch and called across the room, "I trust you brought Cubans for the whole class, Planky?"

The specials at twig were written in chalk on a monstrous blackboard on the back wall. Jeremy had to turn in his chair to read it, and while he did so, Peggy scrutinized the back of his neck. How quickly her dating days were coming back to her, when she and Bex had used the neck-nails-shoes system to rate men. Jeremy had earned a point for his nails already: They were neither bitten nor dirty nor manicured. His shoes were marginal: They weren't run down at the heels, but they were motorcycle boots—pretentious, Peggy thought, unless you were actually riding a motorcycle. Half a point. That left his neck: Was it properly groomed or slovenly and unshaven? She leaned over the table to get a look.

Jeremy turned back around. "The ostrich carpaccio looks good." Peggy jumped back, toppling the table votive with her sleeve. The candle singed the tablecloth before Jeremy smothered it with his salad plate and grinned. "No girl has burned down a restaurant to get out of dinner with me before." He flipped over his digital gadget, glanced at it, and flipped it back facedown.

Peggy subtracted one point for the gadget, two for living in a neighborhood too trendy for its own good, and another for the ostrich carpaccio, which sounded just plain nasty, but she gave him two for self-deprecating humor and decided she'd been on first dates far worse than this. She and Jeremy had an uncanny number of things in common. He was an entrepreneur as well, with his own business setting up computer networks for small companies. He had moved to New York the year after she had. When she asked where he'd grown up, he said, "Sunnyvale, California. It's near—"

"San Jose." Maybe it was the pill she'd taken, but she could feel herself unwinding, her edges blending into the scene around her. "I lived there a couple of years."

They learned they'd graduated from rival high schools, that Peggy had taken ballet lessons half a mile from Jeremy's house. "Do your parents still live there?" she asked once the six-foot-tall, shaved-bald waitress had set down their appetizers.

"They liquidated everything and moved to Costa Rica." Jeremy grimaced. "I know what you're thinking. Normal people wouldn't do anything that nuts."

"My parents' retirement nest egg is an RV with a bumper sticker that says, 'Driver Carries No Cash—He's Married!' " Peggy took a bite of her salad. It was a shame she'd ordered so timidly. After weeks of high WASP cuisine, she should be up for something adventurous. "I think they should have gone with the one that said, 'Driver Carries No Cash—He Blew It All on This RV!' "

"I swear, we're the same person." Jeremy tucked into his carpaccio. At least he wasn't eating a frozen potpie and canned peas. Peggy decided to reinstate his food points.

When dinner was over, Jeremy walked her to the corner and told her he'd like to see her again. He moved in closer. She stayed still, trying to decide whether to lean forward an inch so he'd kiss her or back an inch so he'd shake her hand.

A car roared past on the street behind her. She could hear

snippets of conversation on the sidewalk: a woman summarizing a column in the day's *Times,* two teenagers giddily debating whether to go to this party or that movie.

She leaned forward.

It was a fine kiss. Decent softness with respectable pressure—enough to show he was interested, but not intrusive. It was good to be kissed after so long, and her body began to respond even if her heart remained stubbornly detached, her arms wrapping around his neck—shaven, it turned out.

When the kiss had run its course, Jeremy asked, "What are you doing this weekend?"

She felt dazed. Why wasn't she melting with desire?

"My friend's band is playing Saturday. Want to go?"

"Okay," she heard herself agree, then remembered. She couldn't go anywhere this weekend, next weekend, or any weekend for another ten months and—fourteen now—days. "I forgot. I can't. I'm—" She bit off the rest of the sentence. How could she explain?

"How about..." He removed the gadget from his belt, touched the screen, and studied it. "Next Tuesday?"

"Okay." Was it okay? She guessed so. She and Jeremy had so much in common. She hailed a taxi and let Jeremy kiss her on the cheek before she stepped alone into the car and felt her edges merge into the cracked vinyl seat.

ELEVEN

Bex felt funny.

"Funny how?" Peggy asked.

"Different. I can't explain. It might mean...you know." Even over her cell phone, with its usual bad New Nineveh connection made more crackly today by a November wind howling outside, Peggy could hear the emotion trembling in her friend's voice.

She slipped her old, holey NYU sweatshirt over her head. "That you're...?" She didn't want to say it, either. She didn't want to jinx it.

There was a knock on Peggy's door. "Ready?"

"In a minute." Peggy pulled the sweatshirt the rest of the way on. "That was Luke," she told Bex.

"Where are you crazy kids going?"

"To clean fungus in the basement. It's a nonstop party around here." Peggy paused. "You'll keep me posted, right?"

"You'd better believe it," Bex said.

Peggy had only a passing familiarity with the basement. She'd taken a peek at it during the exploratory phase of her first weekends at the house. But it was even darker and spookier than the rest of the place, and as a rule, Peggy considered a basement to be like a spleen: You knew it was in there, you knew it served an important function, but you had no desire to see it. "In California, they don't have basements," she told Luke. In one rubber-gloved hand she carried a plastic bucket that had long ago held five gallons of interior house paint. With the other, she clutched the rickety banister and followed Luke down a cramped, plunging pine staircase on which she could imagine breaking her neck. "They build houses on concrete slabs, right on top of the dirt."

"No basements?" Luke, who carried a broom, a shovel, and a flashlight, reached up over his head to pull a lightbulb chain Peggy hadn't known was there. "Then where do Californians store their radon gas and toxic mold?"

They went deeper into the basement, past the finished section with painted walls and a cracked cement floor. Here, the walls were stone and draped with spiderwebs, and the floor was packed dirt, and the damp, stale odor she'd smelled faintly in the house enveloped her. She covered her mouth and nose with her hand. "Maybe we should save this for another day. We could get a couple of those surgical masks." *Better yet, gas masks.*

The basement ceiling was the underside of the floor above: broad boards supported by rough beams. It was low, and Luke walked a little hunched over. "Relax." He skirted a lumpy shape Peggy identified as a hideous, harvest gold upholstered side chair of the same era as the furniture in the upstairs bedroom Luke had led her to on her first day. Behind it was a dingy antechamber filled with what appeared to be row upon row of folding chairs. "It's not toxic mold. It's just basement smell. I've been in and out of here all my life, and I'm fine." He led her past a pile of stacked wood Peggy assumed was for the no-longer-used fireplaces.

"What are we doing back here? I thought we were starting in the laundry room," she said.

Luke was standing next to the strangest door Peggy had ever seen. It was made from vertical boards of unfinished wood, with hammered, triangle-ended black metal hinges extending across horizontally to hold the wood together at the top and bottom. It was like the door of a medieval castle. Luke reached up for another invisible chain above his head, but no light came on. "Guess the bulb's burned out." He flipped on the flashlight.

She set down her bucket. "What's this, the Silas Sedgwick memorial dungeon?"

Luke held the light under his chin, casting his face in ghoulish shadow. "You guessed it. We throw all the Sedgwick wives in here once we're through with them."

"That's not funny!"

"Peggy, you could really learn to be less nervous."

"I'm not nervous. That just wasn't funny."

Luke grinned. "Well, this isn't a dungeon; it's the wine cellar. I need to go in for a minute. Want to come?"

Peggy most definitely did not. The only thing she wanted to do less was wait out here alone in the dark. "Sure."

He disengaged the black metal latch and waved one hand in an "after you" gesture. Inside, he turned on another overhead lightbulb.

Peggy had expected a dusty trove of bottles, but the room was empty, with its gray black stone walls and rows of vacant wine cubbies. She went to inspect a decaying, iron-banded oak barrel at the far end of the room. "Where did all the wine go?"

"I'm pretty sure into my dear uncle Bink's liver, may he rest in peace." Luke had to duck to keep his head from hitting the ceiling. "But come over here." He knelt in front of one wall and removed a stone, revealing a small, irregular opening. Inside was a black bottle encrusted with grime.

"It's 1934 vintage port. The last of the Sedgwick supply. Somewhere along the line, one of my relatives stashed a bottle in this hiding place. I like to think Abby did it to keep it away from Bink. I wouldn't put it past her. In any case, Hubbard, Eaton, and I stumbled across it one summer when we were kids. I've been saving it ever since."

"Saving it for what?"

"The right time." He reached out and grasped the bottle in his long fingers. There was a scrape of glass against granite as he slowly took it from its place in the wall. "Would you hold this, horizontally, please? Careful, the cork is shot."

Peggy cradled the filthy bottle against her sweatshirt, glad she had thought to wear her rubber gloves but not as disgusted as she might have been. This port had been in this house through World War II, the Kennedy assassination, the moon walk, the Gulf War, the collapse of the World Trade Center, the election of Barack Obama. And Luke had chosen to share it with her. She watched him, still kneeling in front of the empty space in the wall. Could it be he cared about her more than he was letting on? And why was the possibility so tantalizing? His gesture seemed packed with meaning, despite his having said nothing.

Still, he sure was acting peculiarly. He reached into the alcove as if feeling around inside it.

"What are you looking for?" She hoped she didn't sound overeager.

He got to his feet without replying. "Thanks. I can take that now." He retrieved the bottle and slid it back into place. He replaced the rock in the wall and wiped his hands on his knees. "You ready to tackle some fungus?"

It seemed that special moment wouldn't be with her after all.

The fungus in question was growing up and out from the laundry room baseboards in undulating waves like the ruffles on an old-fashioned petticoat. Luke explained its presence meant there was water seeping in from outside.

"Euw." Peggy couldn't look at it. Her skin was crawling.

"Do you want the shovel or the broom?"

They spent the next hour attacking the fungus, Peggy knocking it off with the broom, Luke picking it up with the shovel and depositing it into the paint bucket. When they were done in the laundry room, they moved through the rest of the basement. After a while, because she couldn't stand not sharing the news with somebody, Peggy asked, "Did you meet my friend Bex in the casino? You know...that night?" She shut her eyes and whacked away at a particularly large fungus formation. When she looked again, she saw with a shudder that the fungus had flown four feet in every direction.

"I'm not sure." Luke scraped the shovel along the floor. "I vaguely remember a woman with curly black hair trying to get you to go upstairs."

"That was Bex." Peggy followed Luke as he moved the bucket a few steps down. "She's my best friend, and she might be pregnant. She and her husband have been trying for so long, and..." Peggy blushed. Luke didn't want to know the intimate details of Bex's life. Or hers, for that matter. Personal issues were off the table. "Well, anyway, we're hoping she is," she finished self-consciously, and turned back to her chore.

"Then I hope so, too," Luke said.

Surprised, Peggy shut her eyes again and swatted another patch of fungus with her broom.

When they'd filled the bucket to overflowing, and Peggy feared the fungus's mushroomy odor had settled permanently onto her skin, Luke took the bucket and they climbed out of the basement, blinking, across the windy back garden.

He set down the bucket near the far edge of the lawn,

which was bordered with trees. Freshly raked leaves were piled at intervals, the wind lifting some and blowing them away; Luke must have gathered them up during the week. It had become clear to Peggy ages ago that the gardener she'd assumed took care of the grounds was as much a fantasy as the ghost that whispered and rustled in her bedroom at night. In fact, she was pretty sure the ghost would appear long before a gardener did.

"We can dump it here." Luke made no move to pick up the bucket. Peggy couldn't tell if he was waiting for her to do the honors. The fungus was heaped so high, one good gust would easily spray it across the yard or onto Peggy. She didn't want to touch the bucket. She wanted to go inside and boil herself.

Luke squinted at her.

"Is something wrong?" she asked.

"You have a big glob of fungus on your face."

"Where?" Peggy swiped frantically at her cheeks with her forearms. Nothing fell away. She swiped again, hopping up and down, desperate to get it off.

Luke picked up the bucket. A few repulsive gray brown chunks of fungus tumbled onto the lawn at her feet. She shrieked and was sprinting to safety a few steps away when a thought occurred to her and she turned back around. Luke stood, a smile playing at the corners of his mouth.

"There's no fungus on my face, is there."

He exploded into laughter.

Infuriated, embarrassed, she turned again, intending to storm up to the house. But a leaf pile caught her eye and she ran toward it instead, catching up an armful and dumping it on his head. "Ha!" she yelled with victorious glee, and darted to one side as he heaved his own hastily scooped armful. It missed her entirely, the leaves dancing and swirling in the damp wind, which was delicious with smoke from the Fiorentinos' chimney. She grabbed up two more handfuls of leaves and lunged, smashing them against the front of Luke's sweater with a satisfying crunch. She whooped again, leapt out of the way, and sprinted for the house.

He caught up with her at the kitchen door. He was grinning, crinkles at the corners of his eyes, red patches on his cheeks. "Impressive," he panted.

She laughed, also panting. "You have leaves all over you."

He brushed off the front of his sweater, his sleeves, his sides. "Any more?"

"Here." Feeling daring, she took a bit of leaf from his hair and held it out to him. He carefully accepted the tiny piece in his fingers, held it out, and let the wind carry it away.

She was breathless for reasons that had nothing to do with her sprint across the back garden.

"So I take it your friend Bex knows the truth about us—about this," Luke said after a time.

"She and her husband, Josh," Peggy told him. "And Padma, our salesgirl at the shop. But they're all sworn to secrecy."

"That's it? No one else knows?" Luke was watching her closely. "You said you were engaged to be engaged. Surely you told your boyfriend."

Peggy blushed. "Don't worry about him." She was about to explain to Luke that she and Brock weren't together anymore, but Luke wasn't interested in her personal life, and she decided she wasn't interested in rehashing it anyway.

Luke was silent.

"Have *you* told anyone?" she asked, the wind whipping a strand of hair into her mouth.

"Just a friend."

"Who?" Peggy couldn't imagine. "I thought I met all your friends at the party."

"She wasn't at the party," Luke said as a sprinkling of raindrops fell across the porch.

It was turning into quite a storm. The rain had started in earnest after Abigail and Peggy had retired to their rooms for the night and Luke had gone up to his study to crunch numbers. Now it was well into the night—early morning, actually—and the wind was hammering cold rain against his bedroom window and lashing the branches of the maple trees, which by dawn likely would be bare. He lay awake in the dark, his mind full of thoughts like ricocheting tennis balls.

"Did you find it?" Abigail had asked over dinner. Luke had been about to help himself to seconds of Abby's signature casserole, a childhood favorite, the one made with chicken, celery, mayonnaise, and cheese and topped with crumbled potato chips.

Peggy had looked up with interest.

"No," Luke had answered, distracted. Peggy had cleaned up after their day in the basement and wore a soft pink sweater pinned with the Sedgwick brooch; she looked uncannily at home at the Sedgwick dining table. Still, he'd changed the subject to the water problem in the basement. Peggy might pass for a Sedgwick, but she wasn't one and didn't need to know about Abigail's box with the star. That counted as personal business. He'd had a flash of inspiration that Abby might have hidden her "nest egg" in the same secret spot as the last of the family port, but it was possible, he realized, that Peggy had thought he was getting out the bottle to share it with her. He would have to phrase things more carefully in the future so she wouldn't think he was attracted to her. That wouldn't do at all.

But spending the day with Peggy hadn't been bad. She'd been a sport about the fungus and had taken him by surprise with the leaf attack.

Another tennis ball sailed over the net: water in the basement. Luke couldn't begin to guess how much that would cost to fix. He would probably have to leave the task to the house's new owner. He mentally knocked twenty thousand dollars off the asking price.

Still, the sale of the property, if added to his meager investment portfolio, would go a long way toward allowing him a new life, modest but unfettered at long last from his family name and New Nineveh. He would never leave while Abigail was still alive, but eventually...He envisioned his possible future home. A Hemingway cottage in the Florida Keys, a cabin in the Rockies, a sailboat to dock in any port that appealed to him. He'd do his investing during the day and write poetry at night. Nothing to fix, no obligations, nothing to do but figure out who he was.

But just as he mentally ran to return that imaginary lob, a real and particularly strong gust of wind rattled his bedroom window. He cursed himself for not having brought the rain bucket to the mudroom. Distracted by the leaf fight, he'd forgotten it down on the lawn. He'd had a little fun and now would pay for it. He turned over in his bed with a groan. The bedsprings creaked sharply. His predecessors would sneer at him, wallowing in self-pity over having to venture outside for a bucket and going on about finding himself. *You are Luke Silas Sedgwick the Fourth. There is nothing else to know,* Silas Ebenezer Sedgwick scolded in Luke's imagination. *Cease this self-indulgent melancholy. And get that rain bucket at once. I fear for your character.*

The fantasy tennis balls fell to the clay and stayed there. Action was the best antidote to worry, and there was an immediate problem to deal with: the infamous three-floor Silas Sedgwick House leak.

Luke got out of bed in the dark, put on a sweater over his T-shirt and pajama pants, and jammed his feet into his slippers. He padded past his study and then past Peggy's closed door to the linen closet near the bathroom, where he got the third-floor bucket, set it in the spot where the rain had already soaked through, and descended the new staircase to the second-floor closet where he kept the second-floor bucket, placed it in its spot under the water dripping from the third floor, and went down the final flight to the first floor. It was black as a tomb down here, but he knew the house's every twist and turn. It wasn't until the dining room that he turned on a light, startling Quibble, who fled—perhaps toward the mudroom, where Abby kept his food dish. Outside, the wind howled and rain pummeled the house. He strained his ears, and there it was: the *tap, tap, tap* of rainwater in the front entry. He stood, indecisive. He really should retrieve the bucket.

No. He'd take a chance, just this once.

The punch bowl was in the buffet cabinet, filled with folded table linens that Luke stacked neatly on the dining table. He carried the bowl into the foyer and set it on the floor under the hanging lamp. At once the timbre of the drip changed, from *tap, tap, tap* to *tink, tink, tink* as it cascaded off the lamp into crystal instead of onto wood.

Satisfied, Luke climbed the front stairs, avoiding the creaky step. On the top floor he hesitated, and instead of turning toward his own room, he tiptoed up to Peggy's door. He moved closer and pressed his ear to it, straining to hear... he wasn't sure what. Perhaps a sign that he wasn't the only one swatting at mental tennis balls at two in the morning. But the *tink, tink, tink* of captured rainwater echoed below, and the storm howled above, and Luke's shame eclipsed his curiosity, and he retreated to his vacant bed.

The paperweight was the only misstep, and who would notice it? A palm-size dome of glass with the three-dimensional pattern Peggy remembered was called *millefiori*, it wasn't the first, second, or tenth object any other Sunday afternoon lunch guest at the Ver Planck family compound would see—not when there were so many other breathtaking things to look at. Such as the sculpture in the corner: a ten-foot heap of tangled, rusted wire out of which reached a single pink-resin arm; or the rug fashioned from loops of wool the diameter of rope; or the art on the soaring walls. From her spot on a geometric red sofa, Tiffany pointed. "That one with the giant blue splotch drives my nana up a tree. She says she could do it herself blindfolded." She laughed her infectious snorting laugh. Through the wall of glass behind her, a sinuous steel sculpture took the place of honor in a goldening meadow of tall grass that had surely been landscaped to look unlandscaped.

But Peggy kept returning to the paperweight on the coffee table, and at last Tiffany picked it up and passed it to her. "My mom gave it to me for my sixteenth birthday. Chachi—that's our decorator—he hates it. Tom made him let me keep it, but when Chachi comes in here he always goes"—she sang—" 'One of these things is not like the others...one of these things doesn't belong...' Remember, from *Sesame Street*?"

Peggy thought Chachi would sing the same thing if he saw Peggy herself, small and incongruous in her own chair, a gray upholstered spiral whose twin she was certain she'd once seen at the Museum of Modern Art. She clutched the paperweight. It was solid, feminine, comforting.

"I'm so happy you could come," Tiffany said. "I'm sure you don't like to be apart from Luke. You're separated so much as it is." She stopped and drew together her eyebrows in concern. "Are you cold? I could turn up the heat."

Peggy shook her head. It was overwhelming—the lunch prepared by an invisible chef and served by a housekeeper; this airplane hangar of a house, with its pitched angles and lofty ceilings. Peggy's parents could park their RV in Tiffany's living room. Peggy suspected she'd uttered no more than a dozen sentences since she'd driven this week's rented car up the sweeping driveway and spotted Tiffany waiting for her at the front door, bouncy haired and smiling in pressed jeans and cheetah-spotted needlepoint slippers.

"Peggy, please." Tiffany glanced at the wireless baby monitor next to her on the sofa cushion. "I know this place is a little much. It has this effect on people; they kind of clam up and stare. But we have exactly forty minutes left until Milo wakes up from his nap, and then it's all over. Didn't you have questions? Please, ask!"

"I don't know where to start," Peggy began. "I don't know about anything Yankees are supposed to know about. I don't even understand the difference between Yankees, preppies, and WASPs. I haven't a clue about prep school or sailing or polo. I'm not descended from Pilgrims, and my family doesn't live like..." she waved her hand around the room.

"This," Tiffany finished the sentence. "Okay, I'll tell you a secret. Liddy, Kyle, Topher—they don't live like this, either. When they come here, they're appalled. They think it's all very showy and tacky and new money, just like me."

Peggy was shocked. "They say that?"

The housekeeper glided in with a tray of gemlike cookies and two glasses garnished with twists of orange peel.

"Ooh, yummy! Thanks, Clea. Try the water, Peggy. It's infused with citrus and ginger." Tiffany took a drink as Clea glided back out. "Anyway, no, they don't say that. They're too well-bred to talk trash. But they all think I'm a social climber. It doesn't help that the first time they met me, I was slinging burgers at J. G. Melon."

Peggy knew the restaurant. It was on the Upper East Side. "You were a waitress?"

Tiffany touched her nose, the Charades gesture that meant Peggy had made the correct guess. "They used to meet up there after work on Thursday nights, back when everyone was young and single and living in Manhattan. Well, everyone but Luke—he'd gotten a place in Hartford. Funny..." a faraway look came into her eyes. "You'd think Luke would have left Connecticut the second he had the chance." She reached for another cookie. "Anyhow, I thought Tom was so hot that one night I made the hostess seat them all in my section. To them, I'm sure, I'm the gold digger who stole their friend. Which, for the record, I'm not. A gold digger, I mean."

"How do you know they think that?"

"I grew up among the Yankees, remember? I understand their ways. Tom says Liddy and Kyle and the others are boring and insular and doubts he'd be friends with them anymore if they hadn't all grown up together. Except for Luke, who doesn't seem to buy the old-money-versus-new-money, us-versus-them garbage, either." She took a miniature meringue from the cookie assortment. "The funniest part is, Luke and Tom have the bluest blood of the bunch."

Peggy selected a diamond-shaped shortbread. "They all seem pretty blue-blooded to me."

"But they're not. Not by their own standards. Topher

Eaton might wear Nantucket Reds and mix a mean Bloody Mary, but his mother is Argentinian, which hardly makes him a WASP. And Bunny Simmons's parents belong to the Maidstone Club, but—ever heard of Crazy Carl Kirkendall?"

"Connecticut's Carpet King?"

"Creighton's dad. Talk about an outsider. People say he had to agree to resurface the school tennis courts before Choate would let her in." Tiffany slipped a lacy wafer off the cookie tray. "Kyle Hubbard is a swamp Yankee, two generations removed."

Peggy took another cookie as well; she couldn't help it. "Swamp Yankee?"

"A Connecticut redneck. I'm not saying these things to be mean. Lord knows I have no pedigree. My mom was a stewardess before she met my dad, and now she's office manager for an orthodontist. My dad was—probably still is, wherever he is—a swimming pool contractor. But Tom is from this ancient Dutch family that settled in New York when it was still New Amsterdam. He thinks it's hilarious when those people make their cracks about how our car is too flashy or our house is too modern or our son's name is too trendy, or that Tom is far too interested in making a buck than befits a gentleman."

Peggy shifted in her chair. "I would hate it if people criticized me like that."

"Trust me. Tom doesn't care. Neither do I. Neither does Luke, probably because he has the best credentials of all. He's an authentic white Anglo-Saxon Protestant, and he went to an approved prep school, and he can trace his roots all the way to the Pilgrims, which means he's hit the trifecta: He's a WASP and a preppy and a Yankee. They don't make 'em like Luke anymore."

"But I don't care about any of those things," Peggy said.

"Aha!" Tiffany planted her slippered feet back on the floor. "That's exactly why he's so wild about you!"

Peggy, who had just popped a sixth—or was it seventh?—cookie into her mouth, inhaled a little too sharply and got a crumb in her throat, leading to an eye-watering, face-reddening coughing fit that went on for far too many mortifying minutes. Tiffany pounded her on the back, exhorted her to raise her arms over her head, assured her she wasn't choking, because if she were, she wouldn't be able to cough, and finally, when the fit began to wind down, instructed her to drink some water.

"Whew!" Tiffany exclaimed after it was all over. "Was it something I said?"

Peggy laughed feebly.

"Here's the thing, Peggy. Liddy and the others, they already assume you're one of them. Unless they sense you're trying too hard, they probably won't figure you out. And if they do, so what?"

Outside, the golden grass waved silkily. The baby monitor was still silent. If there was a time for Peggy to tell Tiffany the whole story behind her marriage, this would be it. It would be a tremendous relief to have a friend to confide in.

"What's bugging you?" Tiffany asked.

Peggy thought, with a stab of conscience, of Bex. Hadn't her best friend been remarkably supportive? Hadn't she listened with interest to Peggy's tales of the Sedgwicks and their idiosyncrasies, and of the Sedgwick House with its creaks and moans and things that went bump in the night? Last night had been particularly creepy, with the storm outside and ghostly footsteps up and down the stairs. She'd even felt something outside her door—*felt* it: a silent presence waiting for her. Bex was the only person who wouldn't laugh when she related the story this evening.

Yet Bex was in New York, and possibly pregnant. Tiffany was closer to the situation, intimately familiar with the cast of characters.

"I don't know"—Peggy spoke haltingly—"that our marriage, mine and Luke's, will last very long."

Tiffany's eyes lost their glow.

It was the first time Peggy had seen her new friend unhappy, and she lamented having begun this confession that would now need to be spun out and explained. Too late, Peggy realized that admitting she'd wed Luke for financial gain probably wouldn't endear her to a woman who'd spent her adult life trying to prove she hadn't done that very thing.

Peggy picked up the millefiori paperweight. "We got married quickly, and we're from such different backgrounds and—"

She wasn't at the party, Peggy remembered. Luke had dropped that "she" so casually yesterday. Who else could "she" be but the redhead?

"—and I think he's seeing another woman," Peggy said. Hearing the words aloud made her ill. She hadn't realized how deeply the idea bothered her.

Tiffany laughed—a magnificent, snorting giggle. "Peggy Sedgwick, welcome to WASPville. We all think the same thing about our husbands, I guarantee you—me, Liddy, Creighton, Carrie Eaton, all of us. Want my advice?" She leaned forward. "Be really good in bed. No whips or leather, mind you—this, as you know, is preppy sex we're talking about, very white bread with mayonnaise—but my theory is, if Tom's happy and satisfied, he won't *want* to go anywhere else. Are you with me?"

"Mummy!" Milo's distant cry sounded on the baby monitor. "Mummy!"

Tiffany pressed a button on the monitor and spoke into it

soothingly. "I'm coming, baby. Be right there." She got to her feet and looked at Peggy. "I hope this helped a little."

"It's good to have someone to talk to," Peggy assured her. "Thank you."

Tiffany brushed her hair back from her shoulders and picked up the baby monitor, cradling it as if it were her child. "I'm sure your marriage will be fine, Peggy. I really am. Just remember, people can pretend to be lots of things. But the way Luke looked at you at your wedding reception—after he read the Yeats poem? I've never seen him look at a woman that way. That's why they call it true love, Peggy. There's not a man in the world who can fake that."

TWELVE

For the next week, Peggy had all the work she could handle at the store. December was approaching, their best sales month of the year, and she spent hours receiving new inventory and restocking shelves in preparation for the holiday rush. But even as she tried to keep her mind on her tasks, she'd catch herself ruminating on what Tiffany had said: "I've never seen him look at a woman that way." Each time Peggy replayed those words, the same electric current thrilled through her. It was a sensation both enthralling and repellent, and she reached for it again and again, the way, as a child, she would press her tongue against a loose tooth. Then she'd remind herself that Tiffany, perceptive as she seemed, knew nothing of Peggy and Luke's business deal, and a soft, smothering gloom would blanket her.

Worse, she couldn't understand why she cared whether Luke had a girlfriend or not. *I must be lonelier than I thought,* Peggy told herself.

It was good, then, that she had Jeremy.

On Thursday afternoon, a flicker outside the shop door caught Peggy's eye, and a deliveryman came in, dwarfed by a floral arrangement wrapped in layers of tissue and protective plastic, a small white envelope stapled to the front. Peggy saw autumn leaves peeking over the top of the tissue paper, and the current electrified her spine again.

She acted blasé until the man had gone, then she ripped the

card from the bouquet and prepared herself: Luke couldn't, wouldn't have sent it. The flowers would be from Jeremy; she'd seen him yesterday as well as the day before. She sighed and peeled open the Lilliputian envelope.

On the front of the card was printed, "Thinking of you." On the back, in unfamiliar handwriting Peggy assumed was the florist's:

Missing you,
Brock

So the flowers weren't from Jeremy after all. Peggy should have been upset that Brock kept trying to contact her. At the very least, she should have been troubled by the redundancy of "thinking of you" and "missing you." Strangely, she was touched—even relieved. It made sense now why she'd been so blue. She must have subconsciously remembered November was the month she and Brock had met. Today could even be the day....

A glance at the calendar confirmed it. It was November 19, the eight-year anniversary of her first date with Brock.

Without thinking, she dug out her phone.

"You got the flowers?" From the clanking and grunting behind him, Peggy guessed Brock was at the gym. "Are they nice?"

Peggy had forgotten to look. She hastily tore the plastic and tissue from the arrangement. There were roses in peach and russet, accented with the autumn leaves and clusters of deep red berries. "They're perfect," she said. Brock's flowers always were. "I guess you know what day it is."

"Couldn't forget. Remember we went to Brattie's after dinner?"

"That was fun." Peggy softened at the memory. She had

enjoyed that night, slumming at the sports pub in her going-out clothes, listening to stadium rock anthems on the jukebox, and drinking beer. All night, guys had come up to Brock to ask, And who's this lovely lady? "Meet the girl I'm going to marry," Brock had told one of his cameraman pals, and Peggy had gone home with that phrase and the tune of "Who Let the Dogs Out?" playing on an endless loop in her brain.

The shop door opened and shut, opened and shut, opened and shut, as three people came in one after another. Peggy smiled and nodded at the third, a regular who came in almost weekly for a particular type of mint pedicure scrub; Peggy and Bex had speculated that this woman must have the softest feet in New York.

"How about dinner sometime?" Brock asked.

"I don't think so," Peggy said, with genuine sadness, as the store phone began to ring.

"Peggy received a telephone call," Abigail told Luke when he came downstairs for lunch on Thursday.

"Why would people be calling her here?" It was rare enough that Luke got a phone call at the house.

"Why wouldn't they? She is your wife, after all." Abby had a peculiar expression playing around her eyes—not quite the Look, but close. It occurred to Luke that she might be aware of more than she let on. "The message is by the telephone," she said.

The caller had been Liddy Hubbard, asking whether Peggy and Luke planned to tailgate with them and the Eatons at the Game. The regrets would have to come from Peggy. Fielding social invitations also was part of what wives, at least Yankee wives, did.

He dialed Peggy at the store.

"Do you have a minute?" He slouched into his favorite shabby chair near the phone, the one directly across from the portrait of Elizabeth Coe Sedgwick in the flower brooch Peggy now wore on her sweaters at dinner, where its luster in the candlelight rivaled Peggy's luminous skin....

"A minute." Her voice wasn't unfriendly, but she sounded busy. He told her about Liddy's invitation.

"The Harvard-Yale game? When?"

"Yale-Harvard," he corrected; an automatic response. "This Saturday." The game was always the weekend before Thanksgiving.

"And a tailgate party? Did she say if we're supposed to bring anything?"

Her reaction exasperated him. The last thing he wanted to do was spend a Saturday afternoon listening to Hubbard, who'd also gone to Yale, and Eaton, who'd gone to Harvard, relive their glory days and argue, with increasingly liquored fervor, over whose alma mater was superior. "Do you even care about football?" he asked Peggy.

Luke heard the click of a door closing, and the background noise grew muffled, as if Peggy had stepped into a small, private room. "I haven't been to a tailgate party," she said. "It's always sounded like so much fun."

"It isn't." From the facing wall, the painted eyes of Elizabeth Coe Sedgwick bored into him.

Peggy said, "You and I should get out more."

"Why?" He pictured her saying the same thing during the week to her boyfriend.

"Also, I'd like to invite a few people over for Thanksgiving. Maybe the Fiorentinos. They seem nice."

He stared right back at the portrait, defiant. "I'd rather keep it the three of us."

"Why? So we can sit shivering in the dark, eating that chicken-and-potato-chip stuff?"

"We have turkey. But what's wrong with Chik-N-Chip Casserole?"

Peggy made an odd noise, a sort of laugh crossed with a sneeze.

"I just don't want a big fuss," Luke said. "The more we socialize with people, the more chance we'll make a mistake and be found out."

"Fine." Peggy sneezed—a definite sneeze this time. "No guests for Thanksgiving. But we're going to that tailgate party."

Shaking her head and sneezing for at least the twentieth time, Peggy stepped back out into the store, glad to escape the cloying algebra of fragrances in the supply closet: lemon plus patchouli to the power of bergamot times beach grass plus vanilla plus tangerine plus green tea divided by gardenia squared. She replaced the phone in its cradle by the register.

"Where'd you get the flowers?" Bex, who'd come in just before Peggy had taken the phone into the closet, was standing near the front window, pretending to be a customer, picking up items and examining them. Her theory was that shoppers were lemmings; they were more likely to come in when other shoppers were already inside.

"Some sales rep." Peggy wanted to tell Bex about her recent contact with Brock, her sense that he might be trying to win her back. She wasn't sure how to start. Bex was so pleased about their breakup.

"Lucky us," Bex said. "Who was that on the phone?"

"Luke. Mister Uncongeniality. Thank heaven we aren't

a genuine couple. If it weren't for me making him go out, I don't think he'd leave his study."

"Men." Bex sighed. "It's like, as soon as a man meets a woman, she becomes his only friend. We're all that's saving them from being lone wolves."

"Brock wasn't a lone wolf." Maybe now was the time to broach the topic. "He always had lots of friends."

Bex didn't take the bait. "By the way..." She gestured at the now empty store across the street where Black and White Books had once been. A FOR LEASE sign had been posted on the window. "I called about the rent on that place."

"How much?" Peggy allowed herself to hope.

"Let's just say we don't have a prayer in the world of affording it. Our rent increase is a bargain by comparison. You don't plan to back out of this deal with Luke, do you?"

"Not a chance." Luke might be a lone wolf with a thing for red foxes, but Peggy could put up with him for half of three million dollars.

"You're a lifesaver." Bex stood contemplating the inside of their own window. "So what should we do for the holiday decorations this year?"

"Holiday" reminded Peggy that she still owed her great-aunt-in-law a forged note from her mother, declining the invitation to the Sedgwick House for Christmas. It was amazing how much paperwork was involved in being married.

Then she had another idea. "What are you and Josh doing on Christmas Eve?"

"You mean after we close up shop? Ordering Chinese and going to a movie. Just like we always do. Why?"

"How would you like to spend it with the WASPs?"

THIRTEEN

She would never get this right. Peggy sank down, turtlelike, into her scarf and tried to hold her coffee cup steady with wind-chapped hands retracted into the sleeves of her coat. She was shivering uncontrollably in a grassy parking lot outside the Yale Bowl, with two hours to go before game time, surrounded by Ivy Leaguers who didn't seem to notice it was thirty-three degrees out here—one of New Haven's coldest game days on record, according to the radio on the way up. Luke, Topher, and Kyle stood in a loose circle, Topher and Kyle swapping jokes. Luke wordlessly observed them.

"How many Elis does it take to change a lightbulb?" Topher, in a dark red Harvard baseball cap, was asking. "The entire student body. One to change the lightbulb and everyone else to tell him he did it just as well as a Harvard student."

A few feet down, next to a car to which had been affixed a sun-faded Yale 1962 flag, a fur-coated crowd Peggy's parents' age was gathered around a table with a silver candelabra and steaming silver chafing dishes, singing what sounded like "Boola! Boola!" over and over again. There were so many of them, they effectively drowned out the din from the student-tailgate field across the street, where a visiting New Haven radio station was blasting hip-hop and intoxicated students danced in Yale sweatshirts and down vests, oblivious to the cold.

"How many Cantabs does it take to change a lightbulb? Just one—to hold the bulb while the rest of the world revolves around him." Kyle wore yellow corduroy pants and a black bowler hat to which he'd affixed one of the "Proud Yalie" stickers passed out by the alumni association. He sauntered over to Peggy, sucked on his cigarette, and exhaled smoke in the direction of her coffee cup. "Let's put a little brandy in that."

Peggy sniffled. The weather was making her nose run. "It's ten in the morning."

"Exactly. You're hours behind."

At the Hubbards' Land Rover, Liddy was setting up a folding table she'd taken from the trunk. At a second folding table, Carrie Eaton and her second grader, Paige, arranged stalks of celery in a cup next to a spare jug of Bloody Mary mix. Peggy asked, as she had three times already, whether she could do anything to help, but Liddy waved her off. Peggy was heartened slightly to see that the tin of shortbread she'd brought was open and sitting nearby. So she'd gotten that right.

The group of older alumni sang, "They will holler boola boo!"

"Did you two go to Yale—and Harvard?" Peggy added quickly, in Carrie's direction.

"Babson for me." Liddy extracted from the car a stack of blue plastic Solo cups nearly as tall as she was and set it on the table. "Carrie went to Lake Forest."

"Oh!" Peggy said brightly. She hadn't heard of either school.

"I have a way you can help, Peggy." Carrie gave a piece of celery to Paige, who stuck it into the hole left by her missing front tooth and ran off between the parked cars to terrorize the Hubbards' four- and six-year-old boys. Barclay and Bradley, Peggy remembered: blond and blonder. "Liddy and I are co-chairing next year's Daughters of New England Night of Hope," Carrie said.

"It benefits the Families Can Foundation." Liddy brought a pan of seven-layer dip to the table.

"We thought you might enjoy chairing the goody bag committee," Carrie continued. "It's a wonderful way to meet people."

"And a chance to help those less fortunate." Liddy sank a chip into the dip and nibbled it daintily. "You could really shine with the goody bags."

"Last year, the goodies were chintzy," Carrie said. "Should we put out the chili, Liddy?"

Peggy gazed with longing toward the covered barbecue grill a family was lighting three cars away. She wanted to crawl inside. She wanted Liddy and Carrie to turn their backs so she could steal a napkin to wipe her nose. She hoped she was conveying neither of these desires. The last corner of her brain not yet frostbitten was already assembling goody bags filled with products from the shop. "I'm f-f-flattered," she eked out through chattering teeth.

"We'll sponsor you for Daughters. We know you'll fit right in." It was Carrie's turn to pick up the conversational relay. "All of our friends participate on one committee or another. Creighton Simmons is always in charge of the table centerpieces. They were gorgeous last year, weren't they, Liddy?"

"Creighton does have a flair for choosing flowers," Liddy concurred. Peggy wondered if the two women secretly felt superior whenever they heard a Crazy Carl Kirkendall commercial.

Lemon would be a nice, crowd-pleasing fragrance for the goody bags. Everyone loved lemon. Peggy could almost hear the oohing and aahing. "What d-does T-Tiffany d-do?"

Liddy pried the lid off a container of baby carrots. "Tiffany isn't in Daughters of New England."

Peggy's stomach sank.

"She and Tom come to Night of Hope, though," Carrie said. "They buy a table every year. It's next October, by the way. May we count you in?"

"I'm sorry." Peggy was. Sorry and glad at the same time. "I'll be gone by then."

Paige and the boys ran past, shrieking.

"Where will you be?" Liddy asked.

The football sliced across the sky, soared over the tidy rows of SUVs and station wagons, an off-course pigskin missile bound for the head of some unsuspecting reveler—in this case, Hubbard. Luke reached up to pluck the football out of the air and looked around for its owner, who turned out to be a kid in his mid-twenties, obviously a recent graduate.

"Sorry, man." The kid stood poised, impatient, wanting the ball back.

Luke threw it and sought out Peggy, who was hunkered inside her coat, her cheeks and nose pink from the cold, and had missed the scene entirely.

Her entire appearance had changed. He'd hardly noticed over the past several weeks that the heels and tight jeans had gradually fallen by the wayside until she'd come down this morning in chinos, driving moccasins, and a barn coat, outpreppying his preppiest friends.

"Where'd you get the clothes?" he'd asked. She'd even gotten the broken-in part right; though he assumed everything she wore was new, it looked as if she'd owned it all for years. He'd been stunned at the transformation, impressed at her chameleonic powers.

She'd widened her eyes at his question. "Is something wrong?"

He'd considered telling her he liked the way she'd always stood out from the crowd, that the conservative outfit didn't suit her because now, except for the flashy diamond ring he wished she would leave back in New York, she looked exactly like everybody else.

"Not at all," he'd said at last.

Luke left Hubbard and Eaton and walked over to Peggy. As he got closer, he could see her agitation. She looked cornered, shriveling under the scrutiny of the other wives. He didn't care for Liddy and Carrie. They brought to mind pterodactyls, with their predatory eyes and sailing-and-skiing-weathered skin.

"Where will you be?" Liddy was cross-examining Peggy. "Luke, where will your wife be that she can't help the Daughters of New England at our Night of Hope?"

"It's n-next October." Peggy's words came out in white clouds.

Luke understood at once.

He laughed and put his arm around Peggy's shoulders. "You two wouldn't rob us of our honeymoon, would you?" He clutched Peggy tighter. She was shivering. "We were married so quickly, we didn't go on a romantic getaway, so we're taking it for our anniversary instead. Aren't we, Peggy?"

Peggy looked up at him. She sniffled.

Liddy and Carrie were exclaiming, "How sweet!" and, "Where are you going?"

"Hawaii," Peggy chattered.

"Bermuda," Luke corrected. Peggy might look like a WASP, but Hawaii was no WASP vacation spot. For good measure—and to shock Carrie and Liddy with a public display of affection—Luke brushed his lips against Peggy's cold, fragrant hair. He pocketed a leather-covered flask somebody had set out on the tailgate. "Come, darling. Let's go for a walk." His arm still around Peggy's shoulders, he seized her back from the jaws of the pterodactyls.

The top of her head was burning. The spot where Luke had touched her—had it been a kiss? did that count as a kiss?—still radiated a small, insistent pulse that warmed her nearly as much as his arm around her shoulders and the gulp of brandy he'd insisted she swallow. It took resolve not to succumb to the sheltering curve of his arm, not to lean her body into his. If she did, she suspected he would move away, and she didn't want him to. It wasn't just because she was feeling warmer than she had since climbing from the Hubbards' car into the frigid New Haven morning.

They slipped out through a space in the chain-link fence separating the alumni tailgate area from the road and walked on the shoulder for a few yards, scuffing through heaps of yellow and orange leaves.

"Want to see the real Yale?" Luke shouted as they crossed the road to the student area. The noise was deafening. The students were glassy-eyed, flushed, staggering across acres of trampled grass littered with squashed cups and foam plates and lined with U-Haul vans Peggy guessed they'd rented just for tailgating. The girls had painted blue Y's on their cheeks, and the boys wore "Fuck Harvard" baseball hats. An ambulance, lights flashing, whooped behind Peggy and Luke as it entered the student lot. The reek of stale beer rose from the ground.

"Did you do this sort of thing when you were here?" Peggy asked.

"Never."

"Were you in one of those secret Yale societies, like Skull and Bones? I've always wondered what the members do."

"They get together on Thursday and Sunday nights and tell their life stories."

"That's it?"

"More or less."

"So you were in one?"

"No. I lack the preppy social gene." He took his arm from around her shoulders.

She almost grabbed it and put it back, but instead she accepted another belt of brandy from the flask; the weather was starting to overtake the warm spot on her head.

He took off his coat. "Put this on."

"You don't need to do that," she tried to protest, but he settled the coat around her.

It was a barn coat like the one she'd had sent over from the Toggery, but his was flannel lined and heavy and already held his heat. He uncoiled her scarf and rewound it so it covered her ears, and he crossed the ends in front of her throat and buttoned up the coat. "Hardly fashionable, but it'll help."

"But what about you?" It was the first chatter-free sentence she'd uttered for forty-five minutes, and she was torn between gratitude and concern. Surely Luke wouldn't be able to walk around out here without his coat.

He shrugged in his ragg wool sweater. "WASPs withstand cold. It's what we do. We call it having thick blood."

"And here I thought it was blue blood."

His laugh warmed her more than the coat.

She floated through the rest of the day, fortified at lunch time by Liddy's chili (spicy hot, no; temperature hot, yes) and a few more swigs from Luke's flask. At game time, she sat in the wooden bleachers of the Yale Bowl, a blanket across her knees, with Luke on her right, hoping he'd take her hand, although he didn't.

In the fourth quarter, with Yale ahead by fifteen points, Kyle leaned forward drunkenly and called down the row to Topher, who was sitting on Peggy's left, "Somebody'ssss buying me a Porterhouse!" He added to no one in particular, "When we win, Crimson over there is taking ussss to dinner."

Carrie was sitting on her husband's other side, with Paige. "You didn't make another bet, did you, Toph?"

Topher hiccuped. "There's still time."

From his side of their row, Kyle drank from his smuggled-in flask and guffawed.

Peggy leaned forward and called to Kyle, "Topher's right. In '68, Harvard got two touchdowns and a two-point conversion in the last forty seconds. Anything can happen." She reached out to return Topher's high five.

Luke looked astonished.

"I'd worry if I were you, SSSedgwick." It was remarkable Kyle hadn't passed out. His face was florid, his words slurred. "Seemss your wife is consorting with the enemy."

Peggy drew the blanket tighter around her knees. "My point was, it ain't over till it's over." A Harvard player fumbled, then recovered, the ball. The Harvard side of the bowl roared. Barclay and Bradley, too, squealed with excitement until Liddy shushed them, saying, "Wrong team, boys."

Kyle raised his flask. "A toast. To life."

"You're the only one with a drink, Hubbard," Topher said.

Kyle ignored him. "To life. Y'never know where iss gonna take you."

"That's bull." Luke spoke up. "There are no surprises."

"Notsso," Kyle slurred. "Didjou know lassyear you'd be married?"

"He's got a point." Topher raised an imaginary glass. "Anything can happen."

"I'll drink to that." Kyle took a swig.

"You'll drink to anything," Luke retorted, but Peggy saw he was smiling.

She couldn't get to sleep.

It might have been the alcohol. Peggy hadn't felt drunk, but she'd lost count of how much brandy she'd had over the course of the day, and she supposed it could be affecting her sleep. Or the cold could be the problem; it had settled back into her bones as soon as she and Luke had returned to the Sedgwick House. It might be that her room felt haunted again, full of the whispery noises that quieted if she consciously listened for them. Or was it she who was haunted? She couldn't get Luke out of her mind—the embrace of his coat around her shoulders, the way he'd looked almost proud when he'd asked her, on the way out of the Yale Bowl, how she knew so much about football.

"I dated a sports fanatic—a long time ago." She still couldn't decide why she'd added the qualifier, except she'd thought she'd seen Luke frown. It was that disapproval that had her tossing and turning. Was it possible Tiffany had been right after all? Luke couldn't really have feelings for her, could he?

A noise, a soft *cheep*, came out of the darkness. Peggy stopped breathing and listened. The room was silent once again.

He couldn't. It wouldn't make any sense if he did. He'd not ever showed a shred of romantic interest in her. He could have held her hand today during the football game if he'd wanted to. None of the others would have thought anything of it.

Cheep, came the sound again, and Peggy realized what it was: her cell phone, telling her she had unopened voice mail. For once glad for, rather than annoyed by, a communiqué from the outside world, she reached out for the nightstand. Soon a dispassionate electronic voice was informing her she had four new messages.

The first was from her mother, more tense than usual. "Peggy, call us." The second was from her mother. "Peggy, call your dad and me." The third was from her mother. "Patricia Ann Adams, why in the world don't you answer your phone? Call us right now." The final one was from Bex. "Peggy, will you please call your mother? She's been leaving messages at the store all day."

Airless lungs contracting, a litany of potential Adams family disasters whirling across her imagination, Peggy punched in her parents' number.

Her mother didn't bother with hello.

"*When were you planning to tell us?*" The yell was earsplitting. Peggy suspected Miss Abigail could hear it on the second floor. She dove underneath the ugly plaid comforter. The phone's illuminated screen flickered like a fire in a primitive cave.

"Tell you what? Mom, what's the matter?"

"What's the matter? It seems you've gotten married. At least, so says a person named Abigail Sedgwick in a letter inviting your father and me to Christmas in Connecticut. My only child gets married and doesn't invite us to the wedding? What about Brock? Who is this Sedgwick woman? Are you in trouble, Peggy? Have you joined a cult? Do you need us to deprogram you?"

"You got the letter?" It was as if Peggy's brain were on a ten-second delay.

"The post office forwards our mail. We're in an RV park, Peggy, not on Mars."

It took Peggy nearly an hour to recount to her mother, and then her father, the now familiar, fictional tale of her and Luke's whirlwind courtship and marriage; to explain that she and Brock had broken up.

"We can't understand why you didn't tell us about this." It was her father's turn on the line. "Unless you're ashamed of us."

Peggy could hear her mother in the background: "It's typical Peggy, Max—not thinking of anyone but herself."

"She was always ashamed of us," her father said. Peggy could tell he had his hand over the phone mouthpiece, but she could hear every word. "That's why she hasn't let us meet her husband."

I'll be getting a massage this week, Peggy thought. Her neck ached from hunching over in the blanket cave. She stuck her head out for air and lay on her back, eyes wide in the darkness. She repeated, "I'm sorry," and, "I didn't mean to hurt you," and, "Of course I love you," until they were meaningless lines. "You'll meet him sometime." It was a last-ditch effort to appease them. "I promise."

"Oh, we'll meet him." Her mother had retaken control of the phone. "Over Christmas, when we come to Connecticut."

Luke turned onto his side in his bed, uncomfortable, and folded one leg up and out from underneath the covers. The room, though cold, was stuffy, as if the air had been sucked out of it. The bright light of a half-moon shone through his window. He was restless. He couldn't remember the last time in his adult life he'd been without a woman this long. This, he knew, was why he'd not been able before to break away from Nicki. It had been easier to put up with her moods, her shallowness, her cigarettes, than to do without the pleasures of silky skin and pillowy lips and soft hair. For the first time since their breakup, he wondered what Nicki was doing. Was she, too, lying awake? He could call her. It was after one in the morning, but she was a night owl.

His phone was in the pocket of his pants, which were draped across the chair next to his bed. He dialed and listened, his breath quickening. Nicki's line rang once, then twice, then three times with no answer. He hung up and slipped out of bed. Nicki wasn't the one he wanted to speak with anyway.

That he'd known the door would be shut didn't quell his disappointment when he found it so. He couldn't imagine what he'd expected on this, his second middle-of-the-night foray to Peggy's bedroom. Did he think the door would be ajar? That Peggy would be beckoning in a diaphanous nightgown? Still, he lingered in the hallway, not ready to admit defeat, telling himself if he stood here long enough, she might sense that he was missing her after their day together, hoping to talk to her, and come out. Quibble, on his way down the hall from somewhere, mewed softly and brushed up against Luke's leg in the dark, but by the time Luke reached down to pet him, the cat was gone. Luke was just about to return to bed when he detected Peggy's muffled voice from behind her closed door.

She was awake! He leaned closer, as he had during his last late-night wandering. This time there was no muffling rain, and he could distinctly make out a one-sided conversation. Most of the words were unintelligible, but he heard her say, "...love you..."

She had to be talking to *him*.

Discouragement pressed upon Luke's shoulders. He didn't like the idea of Peggy with another man and a life outside of New Nineveh. Strangely, he had started to think of her as belonging to him—his to share the burden of caring for Abby, to work with in easy silence. He'd been flattered the previous weekend in the basement, when Peggy had confided in him about her friend Bex's possible pregnancy. As they continued their chore, Peggy had added that Bex was her business partner and that her husband lived down the hall.

"Sounds like the perfect marriage," he'd said. "All that time alone."

She'd knocked off a particularly stubborn piece of fungus with her broom. "What's so great about being alone all the time?"

He hadn't known the answer. He was thinking were he ever to settle down for real, after his and Peggy's annulment, he'd like it to be with someone like Peggy. Someone who was a friend first.

From down the hall, his phone rang. Nicki. She must have seen his missed call and was returning it. He stood, torn, straining to catch more of what Peggy was saying. His phone rang again. Perhaps all of this was a sign that he was, as Nicki had said, taking his marriage more seriously than he needed to. Peggy wasn't his. She was someone else's. Why should Luke have to forsake all others? Why should he cut Nicki out of his life altogether because of some misplaced sense of husbandly loyalty?

By the time he'd made it back to his room, the ringing had stopped. He debated with himself, climbed back into bed, and dialed.

"Where are you?" Nicki was using the husky, come-hither voice that always made him want to come hither.

"In bed." He ignored the "this is wrong" ache in the pit of his stomach. "Where are *you*?"

"In bed."

The sex had been matchless with Nicki. There was no doubt about it. His ex had eroticism to spare, and she was fearless.

"In bed, naked," she continued.

He could practically feel her breath, close in his ear. It would be so easy to ask her to go on.

"Should I go on?" she asked.

Yes, he thought. *No.*

He couldn't believe it. He didn't want her to. He wanted to hang up and pretend the phone call had never happened. What a pussy.

"I knew you'd call, Luke." The barely discernible flick of a cigarette lighter igniting. A pause; an inhale. "It's almost three weeks on the dot." An exhale. "Told you so."

"Nicki, when I called a minute ago—it was a mistake. I hit the wrong button. I apologize for disturbing you." He prepared himself for a barrage, but Nicki, displaying a degree of self-discipline she'd never managed while they were together, hung up without a word.

FOURTEEN

Peggy no longer minded Luke's silence at the breakfast table—she'd grown almost comfortable with it—so when he spoke to her Sunday, it caught her unawares. She stuttered a greeting and reached up to comb her bangs with her fingers.

"I trust you slept well." He let his newspaper flutter to the table, stifling a yawn as he did so.

"I did, thank you." She hadn't, but this time instead of listening for ominous noises, she'd agonized over the prospect of her parents' visit. It wasn't only that she couldn't imagine the Adamses mixing with the Sedgwicks. It was that this was all turning out to be infinitely complicated. When it came time for Peggy and Luke to go their separate ways, it would be difficult enough telling Miss Abigail. Now she'd also have to break the news to her own family. It seemed marriage, even a marriage of convenience, was not to be entered into lightly.

"Well, I didn't." Luke picked up his cup and stared into it, as if hoping more coffee would appear. "It wasn't very restful around here last night. There was a lot of talking, coming from your side of the house."

Peggy felt her face redden. She hadn't known Luke could pick up on a phone conversation all the way in his room. Worse, if he'd overheard hers, he must know her parents had found out about him—that now there were two more people she and Luke would have to lie to.

"I feel terrible, really. I've tried to keep this relationship a secret—" She broke off, self-conscious at using "relationship" to describe their arrangement. Luke would think she liked him. She glanced toward the doorway, hoping for the fortuitous appearance of Miss Abigail, telling her it was time to leave for church. "I mean, I've tried to keep this life in New Nineveh separate from my, well, real life. I was hoping the two worlds wouldn't collide." She sighed. "So what should we do with my parents at Christmas?"

"Your parents?" Luke's face changed from tired and grumpy to bewildered.

"Right," she said. "When they come to visit."

Luke stared at her. "Your parents are visiting? Here?"

"Yes, Luke. Here." She couldn't understand his confusion. Hadn't he just said he'd overheard her on the phone? "Your great-aunt told my parents we got married. Naturally, they want to meet you. So how do you want to handle their visit?"

Luke's face was white. "I shouldn't have agreed to this. It's beyond dishonest. It's morally wrong." He stood up and started out of the room, but Peggy caught him by the sleeve, hurt at the way he unfailingly made her feel like the corrupt one, like the interloper. Here she'd thought they were getting to be friends, and he still assumed the worst of her.

From afar, she could hear measured footsteps: Miss Abigail was approaching at last.

"Do you think"—Peggy kept her voice low—"that I like this loving couple act any more than you do? Do you think I enjoy duping your great-aunt, and your friends, and my parents? Do you think I don't wish every day this were over?"

"Good morning, Abby," Luke said.

Peggy let go of his sleeve. Miss Abigail stood in her shabby cloth coat that couldn't possibly keep her warm enough, if it was as cold today as it had been yesterday. The old woman glanced from Peggy to Luke and back again. "Good morning," Peggy said, frozen in Miss Abigail's searching eyes.

"It's time for church, Peggy," Miss Abigail said at last. "I trust you both slept well?"

Later that afternoon, Peggy bundled up against the weather as well as her wardrobe would allow and was outside loading her bags into the car, shivering, when Luke came around from the back garden. He carried a cache of reflective stakes over his shoulder, like arrows; Peggy knew the stakes were to mark off the edges of the driveway to help guide the snowplow once winter finally arrived. He handed her half of the bundle, saying, "We should have done this weeks ago when the ground was still soft—it's probably near frozen already, after yesterday."

Peggy sighed to herself and spent the next half hour helping Luke plant the stakes. When they were through, instead of thanking her, he said, "Let's go to the roof. There's a leak I've been meaning to investigate."

"I can't. I have to get back to the city."

"I see." He was not happy. She could tell. He put his hands in his pockets. Across Main Street, a green Volkswagen Beetle slowed as it passed by, as if it could sense an interesting skirmish developing on the Sedgwick House lawn.

"What's the matter with you?" Peggy couldn't understand it. They'd gotten along so beautifully yesterday. What had changed? He'd seemed so annoyed that she'd been on the phone last night. So she'd ruined his beauty sleep. Why couldn't he let it go?

"Nothing's the matter," Luke said.

The green car made a U-turn at the traffic light and started slowly up their side of Main Street. "Good, then." Peggy walked toward her own car. "I'll see you late Wednesday night. I'll come up for Thanksgiving, but I have to go back to the city right after dinner." She was about to explain that she couldn't abandon Bex at the shop on the day after Thanksgiving—"Black Friday" in the retail world, the busiest shopping day of the year—when she saw Luke was no longer listening. The Volkswagen had turned into the Sedgwick House driveway.

Peggy watched it, too. Were Luke and Miss Abigail expecting a visitor?

But the driver didn't get out of the car. She leaned out her window, a woman with long red hair and a smoking cigarette. Peggy knew in a flash who this was.

"Hello there." The redhead disregarded Peggy entirely, turning her face to Luke. "I hope you got to sleep last night." She flashed Luke a seductive smile, pulled her head back into the car, and drove away.

Heading back to the city, Peggy clutched the steering wheel and punched the accelerator aggressively, but nothing could get the sight of that woman out of her mind. It was one thing for Luke to have a girlfriend, another thing entirely to rub said girlfriend in Peggy's face. It was humiliating. It didn't matter that the marriage wasn't real; she'd still ended up with a husband who was cheating on her. *Welcome to WASPville.*

"Thoroughly uncalled for," Bex agreed when Peggy got home. "At least *you* keep your extracurricular affairs to yourself."

Peggy was not consoled. How liberating it would be to call off this deal with Luke, to tell her parents the invitation to Christmas had been a big mistake, to no longer have to care whether Luke was seeing that floozy or not.

"How were things at the store?" Peggy asked, perusing her closet. She was due to meet Jeremy in an hour.

"Not good. We had maybe three people all afternoon. I sent Padma home early."

So much for calling off her fake marriage. "People are probably just staying home because it's cold," Peggy said, heavy-hearted.

"I have two other pieces of news. Ready? Guess what competing chain store is moving in across the street? Bath."

Bath was the bath-and-body chain based in Ohio. Peggy felt as if she'd been hit with a two-by-four.

"They might as well name it Put ACME Out of Business," Bex continued.

"Bloodbath," Peggy suggested, and laughed, though it wasn't funny. She couldn't imagine what the second piece of news was. How much worse could it get? "What was the other thing?" she asked.

Bex's smile lit up her whole face.

"I'm pregnant," she said.

"You smell delicious." Jeremy's breathed words were steamy in her ear. "What are you wearing?"

"Nothing." Peggy fumbled with her key and unlocked the apartment building door, and the two stumbled, attached at the lips, into the building's day-bright hallway with its institutional white walls and pitched staircase. "I mean"—she felt the need to clarify—"I don't wear perfume. Obviously I'm not wearing nothing, as in no clothes." *Peggy, shut up.* "What did you think of the movie?"

"It was okay." Jeremy kissed the side of her neck.

She made a split-second decision. "Would you like to come up?"

"God, yes," he said, and she led him up the stairs, hoping she didn't have panty lines, that her skirt didn't make her appear too broad in back, that he wouldn't be turned off by the view. *He'd* better not be ambivalent about what was about to happen, even if she was. No—she wasn't ambivalent. Not since her twenties, before she'd met Brock, had she gone so long without sex. She felt as if she were about to lose her virginity for a second time. It would be good for her. She could move on from Brock and get over what seemed to be a growing obsession with Luke. And Jeremy was a nice person. And they had so much in common.

They were both out of breath when they reached the fifth floor. Peggy applauded herself for making a rational choice in love for the first time in her life and opened the door.

"How'd it go?" Josh called, his eyes on the television screen.

"Come watch with us," Bex added. "It's *The Philadelphia Story*. You've seen it, right? Katharine Hepburn has to choose between three men..." She turned around. "Oh! Hi!" She elbowed Josh, who finally took his eyes from the movie. The two got to their feet and shook Jeremy's hand. Peggy felt as if she'd been ambushed by her parents.

She led Jeremy back out into the corridor.

"They're never awake this late. They don't even sleep here, usually." Peggy felt sheepish. "But Bex got good news today and—"

The blinking gadget on Jeremy's belt emitted a piercing beep. Peggy held her breath, sensing an uncontrollable fit of church giggles coming on.

"I have an idea." Jeremy absently checked the gadget. "If we're going to do this, let's do it right. Let's go away for a weekend. This coming Saturday."

"But this weekend is Thanksgiving," Peggy said, and cleared her throat to cover up the last vestige of giggle.

Jeremy touched her arm. "Then the weekend after. I read about this great country inn, totally hidden away. Let's go there."

It was the holy grail of dating: a man who wanted to whisk

her off on a romantic rendezvous. In all her years with Brock, his schedule had allowed them perhaps two weekends away together. And this would be a weekend off from Luke.

"It's a date." She smiled at Jeremy. And kept on smiling, out of real pleasure or of habit she wasn't sure, as he kissed her good night and left in a cloud of his cedar-lime aftershave.

Monday at the store brought browsers but few buyers and a new batch of flowers from Brock—a raft of speckled orchids that left Peggy depressed. On the card he'd invited her to dinner the Saturday after Thanksgiving weekend. She was glad to get Brock's voice mail when she called and left a terse message that she couldn't see him the Saturday after next because she'd be out of town. Peggy wished already she hadn't agreed to the weekend away. Her heart wasn't in it, and now, alone at the shop, she understood why. Each time she thought about it, she pictured not Jeremy but Luke—Luke sharing a romantic dinner, kissing her in front of a roaring fire, leading her to bed, and undressing her slowly, sensually, as if unwrapping a gift...

"I assume you'll take this back."

Peggy hadn't heard the customer enter. The woman was perhaps a decade older than Peggy, carrying a handbag with a yapping dog inside. She held out a half-used bar of blue soap in a hand Peggy couldn't help but notice lacked a wedding ring.

"It was bright cobalt when it was bigger. As you can see, it's faded to azure, and it clashes with my powder room. I had a dinner party last night and was humiliated to notice, minutes before my guests arrived, that my soap was off."

Peggy refunded the woman's money grimly. *This is me in ten years,* she thought. *Single, with a purse-dog and a soap obsession.* It occurred to her that after ten years, she might be tired of peddling bath-and-body products to uppity New Yorkers.

She had to stop this mooning over Luke, too. From now on she'd be polite to him, nothing more.

She decided she'd better give Jeremy a chance.

His desk had gotten out of hand. It was overrun with paper, weeks' worth of orphan lines of poetry. On Wednesday, Luke rummaged through opened envelopes, bill stubs, Seymour's Hardware receipts, torn bits of yellow legal paper. His eyes lit on the flyer he'd politely accepted at some point from one of the picketers on the town green—was this it?—and flipped it over to read:

The soggiest grand smear of autumn leaves,
rain-polished, dank, wind-streaked across my path,
can brighten in an instant. I believe
in fortune changing too, the fates' pure wrath
gone soft without warning. Success at last!

Irritation with himself burned like bile in his throat. The repetitiousness of "rain-polished" followed by "dank" perturbed him; the end of line five, which he'd liked at first, was hackneyed—a corny greeting card sentiment written two weeks ago in a fit of foolish optimism. He slipped the flyer, poem-side down, into his wastebasket and kept searching his desk, stumbling onto a photo Nicki had given him back in the spring, taken in her loft. They'd argued that day; Luke couldn't recall why. He studied Nicki's sexy, strong-featured face, testing himself, and found no attraction to it. He put the photo into a drawer and continued his excavation until he uncovered the shard he was searching for:

An aphrodisiac will disappear,
delusional, like permanence or wealth
a shimmering, as if love were a ghost

As he'd hoped, it had held up well. He added a fourth line:

and yet my passion for you seethes and sears

And reread the words until they blurred together. He'd written the first three lines the day Peggy had arrived at the house. Her appearance in his life had coincided with the most productive writing bout he'd had in years. It figured. Maybe she was his muse, and here she was telling another man "I love you" on the telephone in the middle of the night.

Luke wondered if he was writing this poem for Peggy.

For the rest of the afternoon, he walked up and down the ballroom, unable to concentrate. He was glad for his poker game that night; by the time he arrived home to find Peggy's rental car in the driveway, he knew she had long since gone to sleep.

He stayed upstairs as long as he could on Thanksgiving morning and came down to find Peggy and his great-aunt in the midst of dinner preparations.

"Would you like anything in the stuffing other than celery?" Peggy, in one of Abby's old aprons, dumped a bag of stuffing mix into a bowl. "I like to put water chestnuts and mandarin oranges in it. It's really good."

Abby, looking only as nonplussed as propriety would allow, slid an intact cylinder of canned cranberry sauce into a crystal dish. "Celery will do, dear. We've always made it that way."

He kept catching himself watching Peggy—in the kitchen, as she sprinkled French fried onions onto the green bean casserole; over dinner, where she spoke little and ate less; as the three of them washed dishes together afterward and Abby chattered about how pleased she was Peggy's parents were coming for Christmas. Luke had assumed there would be an opportunity to take Peggy aside and tell her he was sorry for the way he'd behaved on Sunday. But she wouldn't meet his gaze. And if she had, and if he had been able to confess he'd been jealous, plain and simple—then what? She was with another man who was clearly not going away.

Peggy left for the city as soon as the kitchen was clean and Abby had gone to bed, and returned again two days later, late Saturday night. Luke was up in the study listening for her car in the gravel driveway; when she drove up, his heart seemed to catch, then resume beating at double speed. He rushed downstairs to meet her.

She was hauling her bag out of the car.

"Let me help you," he said.

"I've got it. Thanks. You can go back inside."

"It's dark. I'll walk you to the door."

"No need. This is New Nineveh, remember?"

He accompanied her in silence back to the house.

On Sunday, it was as if she were going out of her way to stay busy and keep Abby close at hand. When it was time for her to leave again Sunday evening, he followed her to the front door, helpless, as she carried her own suitcase. He stepped aside to let her out and said to her back, "I'll see you next weekend."

She stopped and turned around. "Actually, I thought I'd skip next weekend."

"What do you mean, skip it?"

"I thought we could use some time apart. If that's all right with you."

Luke could see her mind was made up already, that whether he approved the decision or not was immaterial. So he assured her, WASPily, that he couldn't agree with her more and ushered her out the imposing front door into the frosty, star-spangled darkness.

FIFTEEN

December

It had all gone remarkably smoothly, Peggy thought the following Friday night, when she'd normally be driving to New Nineveh—from telling Luke she wouldn't be coming up, to securing Padma to work extra hours so Bex wouldn't be stuck there if she started not to feel well, to successfully booking an eleventh-hour leg-waxing appointment. A different, sunnier person, a Bex or a Tiffany, would take all this as a sign her weekend with Jeremy would be lovely. But Peggy could see only portentous omens. She was stumped over what to wear to bed (silk nightgown, too sexy; cotton pajamas, too not-sexy). Now that it seemed she would be disrobing in front of a new man, she seemed to have gained five pounds. And Luke had been entirely too quick to agree to a weekend apart. Why did *he* need a weekend apart? She couldn't bear the answer—to spend it with that detestable redheaded hussy.

On Saturday morning, an hour before Jeremy was due to pick her up, she returned from a desperate, last-minute trip to the gym to find Bex on the couch, grim-faced, the telephone clutched to her ear, while Josh lingered nearby. "Uh-huh, but it doesn't feel normal. I can't get out of bed," Bex was saying.

"She's talking to her OB. She slept sixteen hours last night," Josh whispered. "Says she's never been this tired in her life."

Peggy's heart *whooshed* into her shoes.

Bex hung up. "She says I'm probably working too hard and should go ahead and sleep as much as I need. No, Peggy, do not cancel your weekend. And Josh, don't start telling her she shouldn't go because she's married."

"But I *am* married." Peggy's legs were already aching from her spin on the elliptical trainer. What had she expected after not exercising in aeons—that she'd sail through her workout like a marathon runner?

"Get out of here," Bex ordered. "Have fun. I'm going back to bed."

At twenty minutes to pickup time, with wet hair and a half-packed suitcase, Peggy answered her cell phone. It was Brock, performing a desperate monologue: "I have to see you. I can't stop thinking about you!"

Bad omen number two. Peggy pleaded a bad connection, turned off her cell, and left a note for Josh and Bex that she'd call with the number of the inn. She used Bex's phone to call Padma and told her the same thing, leaving her strict instructions not to bother Bex with any minor problems.

"Okay, have a blast," Padma said. "Where are you staying, anyway?"

"I don't know. He wanted it to be a surprise."

"Oooh. He must really like you."

Jeremy showed up fifteen minutes late, apologetic, wearing his cyborg earpiece, saying he'd tried her cell but hadn't gotten an answer. They brought Peggy's suitcase down to the street. There was an orange parking ticket on the windshield of Jeremy's double-parked rented car. *Bad omen number three.*

Jeremy stuffed the ticket into the glove compartment and started the car—outfitted, Peggy noticed, with every electronic accessory yet invented. She looked out the window as

Jeremy obeyed the generic female voice of the global positioning system and maneuvered onto the Henry Hudson Parkway, the same road Peggy took out of town on Friday nights, although he didn't turn off onto the Cross Bronx Expressway as she did. After two months of driving to New Nineveh, Peggy was again used to being behind the wheel, but she was glad to relax in the passenger's seat, to enjoy the view of the Hudson River.

She addressed Jeremy's profile. "Where is this mysterious place you're taking me?"

Jeremy slowed to pay the toll on the Henry Hudson Bridge. "The Colonial Inn, about two hours north." He fiddled with the satellite radio. "It was written up in *New York* as best weekend spot. Heard of it?"

Oddly enough, Peggy had, but she couldn't remember how. She turned her phone back on long enough to leave Bex and Padma the inn's toll-free number, then turned it off again and continued to admire the scenery—people had already begun to decorate their homes for the holidays—as Jeremy sped through the northern suburbs of New York City. She listened to him describe his Thanksgiving and thought about how perfectly nice he was, exactly the kind of man she'd told herself she wanted, and he was interested in her—though she did wish he would take that cyborg thing off his ear.

They were an hour into the trip when Peggy spotted a green highway sign with a familiar state outline.

"Connecticut?" she wheezed through constricting lungs. She hadn't known you could get there this way.

"Merge...onto...Interstate...Eighty...Four...East," the cool, modulated GPS voice instructed.

Jeremy's tone was light. "You have a problem with Connecticut?"

She laughed. "Not at all." *Fiddle-dee-dee. It's just that my husband lives here.*

Jeremy took his right hand off the wheel and laid it on Peggy's left knee.

Peggy felt it there, heavy, and told herself not to be silly; Connecticut was a big state. But half an hour later, when the GPS lady exhorted them to "exit...onto...Route Two... Zero...Two," the alarm bell rang in her head. "We aren't going to Litchfield County, are we?"

Jeremy exited onto Route 202. "You have a problem with Litchfield County?" He was taking all of this as banter. She started to tell him she was serious, but she couldn't. Anxiety had paralyzed her vocal cords, and she had no credible reason for needing to go back home to New York this instant. Besides, Jeremy was still talking: "...have lunch in the inn restaurant after we check in. Or we could go for a drive. There are a lot of really pretty towns up here: Litchfield and Norfolk and New Nineveh."

"I'm not feeling very well." It was nothing if not accurate.

"Really?" Jeremy looked at her. "When we get to the inn, you can relax, get a massage at the spa."

"Turn...right...on...Roxbury...Road," the GPS lady cooed. Peggy felt like slapping her.

And then she remembered: the Colonial Inn.

She and Luke had supposedly stayed there on their wedding night.

Connecticut probably had hundreds of romantic inns. Thousands, scattered over the countryside between the picturesque farms and the antiques stores. The entire state was a weekend getaway paradise. America's Founding Fathers had probably set it up that way when choosing it as one of the original thirteen colonies: *Two hundred years hence, these vistas shall be a tonic for stressed-out New Yorkers.* And in this state bursting with bucolic quaintness and charming country retreats, Jeremy had chosen the Colonial?

"You . . . have . . . reached . . . your . . . destination," the GPS lady announced.

Jeremy drove up to the rambling wood-shingled inn, with its twin gambrel roofs and evergreen-swagged porch. As they crossed the lobby, festive with white poinsettias and a floor-to-ceiling Christmas tree that filled the room with the aroma of fresh pine, and Jeremy went to check in, Peggy found she was feeling better. She could handle this. She would handle this. What was her alternative—to crumble? Moreover, the inn was a beautiful old place—lovingly restored, exquisitely appointed, all that the Sedgwick House ought to be. No wonder Luke had chosen it for their fictional—

Ernestine Riga was walking across the lobby. She stopped, spotted Peggy, and stared.

Peggy darted around the corner into a wood-paneled library nook. Maybe Ernestine hadn't actually seen her. Maybe she'd been looking at someone else. No such luck: Ernestine, in a pastel tracksuit, appeared around the corner. "Why, Peggy, what brings you here? Are you and Luke having lunch?"

Peggy's heart pounded wildly. Jeremy was going to appear any minute, and the jig would be up. She couldn't let that happen, not this far into it. "He's parking the car." Peggy was starting to perspire. Was Ernestine here for lunch, too?

"Isn't that romantic." Ernestine gave her a syrupy smile. "My daughter-in-law gave me a gift certificate for a massage. Matter of fact, I'm due at the spa this minute. Toodles!" She patted Peggy on the arm and hustled out of the library nook, the legs of her nylon pants scritching together loudly. Peggy was beyond grateful for this stroke of good fortune.

Jeremy rounded the corner, his cyborg ear still attached.

"We're all checked in. Want to take a quick look around the place? We could walk through what's left of the garden." He handed Peggy a brochure.

"Let's go upstairs," she said.

Peggy drew the hood of her coat lower over her forehead. In a first, she'd come properly prepared for cold country weather, and she needn't have. The day had turned summery warm; the other hotel guests strolling the grounds wore shirts and light sweaters. The zero-degree attire was for disguise only, in case Ernestine was still around. The alternative was being upstairs with Jeremy in a room dominated by a canopied, down-quilted bed so seductive that she couldn't look at it. She'd be expected to make use of that bed in a few hours and wasn't ready. As Jeremy had settled in, she'd decided to go for a walk to clear her head, promising to be back in half an hour. "No problem," he'd replied, and plugged in his computer.

The brochure had shown the garden maze in its summer glory, a circular layout of immaculately sculpted boxwoods and groomed gravel paths. But most of the surrounding plants had gone dormant for winter, and the hedges were bleak and tatty. Safely outside, Peggy took her phone from her pocket and dialed the Sedgwick House. The sound of Luke's voice, when he answered, was like deliverance.

"How are you?" she asked. *Do you miss me, even a little?*

"The flashing around the northwest chimney is shot," he said. "It all needs to be ripped out, and the mortar, too."

"Maybe we can do that next weekend." Peggy didn't have the slightest idea what flashing was.

He laughed curtly. "It's a job for a professional."

She waited, but he didn't elaborate. Above her, migrating geese crossed the sky in a moving V.

"If anyone asks," Peggy said finally, "you and I had lunch today at the Colonial Inn."

"Who's going to ask that?"

"Someone might."

"Where are you?"

"Just please don't forget."

She hung up and took a few steps into the maze, contemplating whether Luke had ever been here with that redhead, made love to her upstairs in one of those giant beds. Behind Peggy's dark glasses, tears sprang to her eyes. She brushed them away, angry at herself. She had to stop thinking of Luke as anything but a husband in name only. He wasn't hers. His heart belonged to another. When their year was up, she'd never see him again.

She walked deeper into the maze, trying to summon every piece of advice she'd ever gotten. Would Jonah, her acupuncturist, diagnose her as afraid of moving ahead with her life? Would Orsolya, her Hungarian facialist, call this thoroughly unrequited fixation on Luke more proof that Peggy only fell for the wrong men? Or was Peggy just creating fantasies in her head to keep from dealing with this more pressing concern: that Jeremy wasn't right for her?

Because he wasn't. Jeremy was likable, treated her well, wanted to be with her—and she wasn't attracted to him in the slightest. She looked around for a bench, desperate to rest her workout-weary legs. The realization felt unbearable. If she couldn't muster up any enthusiasm for this man, who was everything she'd thought she wanted, there was no man on earth for her at all. She'd be alone for eternity, while everyone else around her—Bex and Josh, her friends from college, Tiffany and Tom, Liddy and Kyle, Luke and the redhead—every last human being but her paired off. Even Miss Abigail, tragic as her story was, had had a taste of true love. Peggy had no one, not even a memory.

With nobody around to see, she took off her sunglasses and buried her face in her hands as tears spilled over her cheeks.

"Peggy!"

The sound of her own name grew closer and louder, an intrusion into the peace of the inn gardens, accompanied by the rhythmic crunch of running footsteps over the gravel paths. She was just able to dry her eyes before Jeremy burst through an opening in the hedges. She didn't want him to see her crying.

It wasn't Jeremy.

"Peggy!" Her pursuer was rasping, breathless. "I need to talk to you!"

SIXTEEN

The sight of Brock Clovis at the Colonial Inn in Litchfield County, Connecticut, was so exotic that for several seconds Peggy just took it in. Yes, it was Brock all right, his face shiny with exertion, a massive bouquet of roses in his equally massive hand.

"I've been looking all over for you. I called the store, and they said you were staying at this place, so I drove up and..." He leaned forward at the waist, trying to get his breath back. How strange that a person who appeared as fit as Brock did could be winded from running around a garden maze. Peggy opened her mouth, ready to suggest he spend more gym time on cardio and less on weights.

Brock was now breathing more normally. "I want to set some stuff straight."

"Why aren't you working?" It hadn't yet occurred to Peggy to wonder why he was here, just how.

"I took a day off. I didn't appreciate you enough when I had you, and now I realize—big mistake. You're a sweet girl, Pegs. There aren't a lot of girls as sweet as you. I shouldn't've messed with what we had."

"Thanks. That's nice." What if Ernestine Riga was watching and recognized her parka? What if Jeremy happened to look out the window of their room and saw her here? Jeremy might not be Mr. Right, but she dreaded hurting his feelings any more than necessary.

"I brought you a present."

Peggy's eyes went straight to the roses Brock was holding. The words tumbled from her mouth. "I don't want to be mean, and it was nice of you to drive all this way and go to this kind of trouble to apologize, but I'm not here alone, and so you can see why it would be impolite of me to show up back in my room with flowers—"

Brock wasn't listening.

What he was doing was producing a box—a small blue box—and getting down on one knee in the gravel, surprisingly graceful for such a big man, like a circus elephant she'd once seen as a child balancing delicately on one massive, columnar foot.

As if in a dream, she took the box and, with fingers suddenly twice their normal thickness, tugged at the ribbon—back on Fifth Avenue, she imagined, a mischievous salesgirl was laughing at how tightly she'd tied this bow—and removed a smaller inner box just like the one that had held her promise ring. "He couldn't give you the real deal?" Bex had asked when Peggy had come into the shop wearing it.

This wasn't a pre-engagement ring. This wasn't a fake wedding ring. This was, in fact, the real deal.

Brock struggled to his feet, less nimble than he'd been while sinking to his knees, to help Peggy shove the ring over her unaccountably swollen knuckle. He took her hand in his and held it out as if displaying it to her.

"What do you think, Pegs?"

Luke didn't hang up when Peggy did. He held the dead receiver in his hand absently, mulling over their brief exchange, attempting in vain to decipher why Peggy had brought up the Colonial Inn, until the phone made its insistent, earsplitting off-the-hook signal. He replaced the receiver and went out to Charity's Porch. Through the screen, he watched Abigail walking in the back garden and tried to picture what Peggy was doing in New York this weekend and whether she was doing it with her pre-fiancé, and the solution to his problems materialized with such immediacy, Luke couldn't believe he hadn't thought of it before. Peggy wasn't taken, not really. She wasn't engaged. She was merely engaged to be engaged. *Which means she's fair game,* he thought. *There's no reason I can't pursue her myself.*

And there wasn't. There was no reason at all. He resolved to put some effort into making Peggy Sedgwick his own. She was his wife, after all.

The roses lay abandoned in the gravel. Peggy was sure they had no fragrance but pitied them all the same. She steered her mind back to the matter at hand. She again had the sensation of watching herself: Peggy Adams mulling over a marriage proposal. Only—*was* this a proposal? Had Brock asked her to marry him?

Footsteps crunched from a few feet away, and Jeremy appeared through the hedges—half man, half cyborg. "Peggy, are you in here—" He stopped short.

Brock was still holding her hand. She pried his fingers off hers.

"Who the hell is this?" Jeremy put his hand on his waist-tethered gadget. He looked for all the world about to unsheathe it for a digital duel.

"This is, uh, my ex-boyfriend, Brock. Brock, this is…" Peggy didn't know how to introduce Jeremy. Or why she felt compelled to introduce these two at all.

Brock nodded wordlessly at Jeremy and said to Peggy, "So how about we go for it? Let's get married, Pegs."

"But I just made dinner reservations," Jeremy said.

Brock looked apologetic. "Oh, man. Sorry."

Here was Peggy's choice made flesh: dating men like Jeremy, telling her life story over and over, breaking up or being broken up with, or marriage. An eternal, fruitless quest for an as-yet-unmet Mr. Perfect…or the opportunity to stop searching. At no moment had her life been as black and white. Brock or nobody? Quit looking or keep trying?

But what about Luke?

She was an idiot for thinking it. Hadn't she just realized Luke wasn't a choice? And what did he have to do with anything? Whatever she felt for him wasn't real. People didn't form relationships with men they met during drunken blackouts. Here was Brock, whom she'd loved for seven years, who had clearly changed, whom she would surely grow to love again, who was asking her to be his forever.

Forever.

She was ready for forever.

"What do you say, Pegs?" Brock's question floated through the air.

She'd imagined this moment differently. She would be wearing a dress, not a down parka. She wouldn't have brought a date along. She wouldn't be petrified of being caught by Ernestine Riga. She wondered, amazed, why she wasn't crying. She'd always assumed she would cry.

"Okay," she said. "Let's go for it."

After reimbursing Jeremy for his expenses, Brock wanted to stay at the inn, but Peggy was intent upon getting home. She barely remembered the drive back, what she and Brock had talked about, whether they'd talked much at all. Her dazed mind raced through a long list of quandaries: How profusely apologetic she should be with Jeremy. Whether he'd prefer the apology to be in person, over the phone, by e-mail, or via text message. How to break the news to Bex. How to tell Luke about Brock; *whether* to tell Luke about Brock. How to tell Brock about Luke. And the wedding date, which Brock was already pressing her to set.

"End of January." He maneuvered the car in front of her building, munching on the remains of an extra-large order of fries from a drive-through just across the New York State line. "After playoffs, before the Super Bowl."

Already, the logistical problems were piling up. "As in eight weeks from now?"

"Yeah, why not? If we wait past that, we're getting into February and I'll be leaving to do the surf documentary, and then by the time I'm back it's summer and baseball season, and then it's August and football, and by the time that's over we're talking January a year from now. Who needs an engagement that long?" He offered her some fry crumbs.

Peggy shook her head. Who needed a long engagement? She did, to be sure her other marriage was annulled first. This was the ideal time to tell Brock about Luke. But that would spoil the moment, wouldn't it? "Let's not set a date just yet—mmmmf," she answered as he kissed her, familiar and salty, until a taxi behind them honked its horn and Peggy moved away.

He reeled her back. "Go pack a suitcase and come stay at our place."

"I'd better take a rain check." She gave him a quick hug. "I should tell Bex the news first."

But not tonight. In the stairwell, she slipped Brock's diamond ring into her handbag. In the span of a couple of months, she'd gone from a woman without a ring to a woman with one ring too many.

SEVENTEEN

The Holidays

Peggy had changed. She wasn't being sullen or hostile, just distant. Luke found it maddening. How could he win her over when she wouldn't speak two sentences to him? He tried inquiring about her health, her work. "Fine, thank you," she'd answer, no matter the question. He'd been able to pull out of her that Bex was indeed going to have a baby. He'd asked Peggy to pass along his congratulations. "Okay, yes, sure," she'd replied distractedly.

He began to test her, asking her opinion just to take the opposing view. When Abigail inquired which vegetable they would prefer with dinner, Luke would wait until Peggy said peas, and then he would say carrots, but she wouldn't argue. One Saturday afternoon, passing the picketers on the way back from a trip to Seymour's, he asked which side she was on.

"Theirs. I think development is ruining the character of the town."

"If you lived here and had to drive forty-five minutes to the beauty parlor, you might think differently." It was juvenile, he knew.

She only laughed. "*Salon,* Luke."

He suggested every long, involved chore he could think of. They recaulked the bathtubs, spread a blue tarp over the leaky roof and around the northwest chimney; there was no money to have the roof properly repaired. They spent hours shuffling across the floor of each of the house's twenty-one rooms, listening for squeaks, hunching over to nail down the loose boards. The work was repetitious and dull; talking would have passed the time. Still, Peggy barely spoke. Her mind, he could see, was elsewhere.

Nicki called every so often, a cell phone siren trying to lure him back onto the rocks. If he answered his phone at all, he kept the talk light. More often, he ignored it. Late one weeknight, lonely, he drove halfway to Nicki's place in South Norwalk, turned around, and came home. She wasn't the one he wanted.

New Nineveh prepared for Christmas. Colored lights appeared on the pine tree on the green, the volunteer fire department trimmed its station with a wreath, and the brokers at the real estate offices set dishes of red and green Hershey's kisses on their desks. But this year, most of the local shoppers had flocked to Pilgrim Plaza, and the town center was sad and deserted. The only steady sign of life came from the small huddle of Saturday picketers who marched across the still snowless green.

But when Peggy returned on the weekends, which were filled with more social invitations than he'd ever received without her—and left him little time alone with her—Luke's dolor deepened. Whether they were drinking hot chocolate at Liddy Hubbard's Christmas cookie party or passing under the mistletoe—mistletoe! there to torment him!—on the way into the Rigas' holiday open house, Luke scowled at Peggy's ring. His plan to court her was getting nowhere.

On the morning before Christmas Eve, Luke was untangling the cords of Miss Abigail's decorative electric candles, setting one onto the sill of each window as he had every December 23 as far back as he could remember, when an oversize pickup truck towing an outsize trailer pulled up in front of the house as if sidling up to a dock. A man and woman climbed out and walked toward the front gate. From his window in the gentlemen's parlor, Luke could make out their astonishment as they gazed at the house's facade. He continued working—it was not unusual to have tourists stop to ogle the house—but in another few moments the door knocker sounded, and he reluctantly went to answer it.

"Is this the Silas Sedgwick House?" The woman had faded blond hair pulled back from a worry-lined forehead.

Luke said it was, patiently pointing out the plaque.

"Wow." The woman's eyes were wide. "Really, wow."

Luke waited for more questions and hoped the two wouldn't ask to come inside for a tour. It was remarkable how many did.

The husband was balding and bearded, with a souvenir New Mexico sweatshirt and a pair of shorts. It was a mystery to Luke why tourists wore shorts in the winter. Perhaps handling that big pickup was more strenuous than it appeared. "If this is the Sedgwick House, then you must be Luke," the man said, and before Luke could answer, he was caught in a bear hug; and the wife, too, was exclaiming how thrilled they were to meet him, and it dawned on him who these people were.

"We know we're a day early." The man answered Luke's next question before he could think it. "We made great time through Maryland and Delaware, and we were going to stop there awhile, but then we decided, why wait? Why not drive straight through to Connecticut?"

"Absolutely." Luke took the first opportunity he could to retreat to a safer distance. Yankees did not hug and kiss total strangers, even their new in-laws. *Holy hell,* he thought, *I have in-laws.*

"Who's at the door?" Abigail called.

"If you're not ready for us, we can camp out in the rig." The woman took her eyes off the house for a moment to flutter a nervous hand toward the trailer.

"We wouldn't think of it. I'll get a room ready for you on the second floor. Come in, Mrs. Adams, Mr. Adams."

"Please." Peggy's father rested his hands comfortably on his round, solid belly. "Call us Mom and Dad."

"But that can't be," Peggy said into the phone. She was at the shop and made an effort not to shout. "They're not supposed to get there until tomorrow!"

"Then right now, two strangers who arrived towing something called a Kustom Koach are drinking eggnog with my great-aunt in the library."

"What do I do?" Peggy pressed her back against the storage closet door. On the other side, the store buzzed with activity and Bing Crosby carols; there was a line at the register, and Padma was frantically wrapping gifts. "I can't leave the store. It's crunch time and Bex is at the doctor."

"Don't worry. I can handle your parents. You come up tomorrow night, as planned."

"That's very sweet, Luke. You can't handle them. My mom will worry about everything, and my dad will wander around the house in cutoffs."

"He already is. Cutoffs and bedroom slippers. And he gave Abby a big kiss on the lips." Luke had to admire Peggy's father. Unlike his daughter, he didn't seem the slightest bit self-conscious.

Peggy groaned. "They won't be able to get over the house, and how big it is. Then Miss Abigail will start asking about their connection to the New Nineveh Adamses, and they won't have the faintest idea what she's talking about, and our story will be blown to bits."

"I'll handle it."

Peggy opened the supply closet and peeked out. She had little choice but to trust Luke to take care of things. "Okay, honey. Thanks."

"Honey?"

"I meant okay, thanks." She hung up and emerged red-faced from the closet. *Honey.* She'd gotten mixed up and thought she was talking to Brock. Juggling two relationships was not proving easy. Once she'd nearly called Brock "Luke," and last Friday night she'd walked halfway to the car rental place before realizing she had slipped on not her phony wedding ring from Luke, but the real engagement ring from Brock, which she kept stashed in her jewelry box alongside the Connecticut decoy. She'd had to go back and switch them. Making matters much worse, she hadn't found a way to tell Bex and Josh about her betrothal. She wore Brock's ring only on their dates one or two nights a week—evenings Peggy let Bex assume she was having dinner with Jeremy.

Peggy would have insisted, had anyone asked, that she was keeping her engagement secret for her friend's sake, that Bex was in no state to handle the shock. Bex was constantly nauseated—a good sign, Bex said; it meant her hormone levels were good and strong. "I might be carrying more than one," Bex had confided the night before. "You should come with us to the six-week ultrasound and see... oops... wait... hold on..." She clapped her hand over her mouth and rushed from the room.

But it wasn't Bex's delicate condition that was keeping Peggy from sharing her own good news. She just wasn't ready to hear her friend's well-argued reasons why Peggy was making the biggest mistake of her life. *Which I'm not,* Peggy told herself, taking Padma's place at the register. Brock had been nothing but accommodating. Over sushi the night after the proposal, he'd suggested she move back into their apartment, and Peggy had put him off.

"I've been thinking we shouldn't sleep together until we're married," she had interrupted before he could finish. She had already decided not to tell Brock about Luke. What was the point? Brock would be hurt and wouldn't—couldn't—understand, and since he was gone weekends anyway, and working as usual over Christmas, he didn't need to know. But Peggy couldn't be sleeping with one man while she was married to another. She had to have some integrity.

Brock had been speechless through a mouthful of hamachi-maki.

"It will seem more special that way," she'd continued.

"Then can we at least get married in January? You never did give me an answer."

Anxiety squeezed her temples. "I promise, we'll set a date soon."

But "soon" still hadn't arrived, and Peggy's troubles weighed on her as Christmas grew closer. In just twenty-four hours, she and Luke would have to act out their charade at Christmas Eve dinner. She didn't know how much longer she could keep it up before it all folded under her like a Sedgwick House of cards.

Again, Luke was struck by how exponentially big his life had become in such a small amount of time.

Last year, still living in his apartment in Hartford, he'd barely noticed the holidays. He'd spent Christmas Eve with Nicki at her place and driven to New Nineveh Christmas Day for a quiet dinner with Abby. Now here he was in the Sedgwick dining room with a tableful of people he'd only just met. To his right, Madeleine—he couldn't bring himself to call her "Mom"—was describing life on the road to Peggy's friend Josh, while Bex poked cheerfully at the takeout Indian dinner Peggy had brought from the city and chatted with Peggy's dad. The only two who didn't seem to be enjoying themselves were Abigail, who was fanning herself and taking liberal gulps of water between polite tastes of lamb curry, and Peggy, seated across from him with a pained expression as her father rose from the table, his dinner napkin slipping to the floor from the lap of his denim shorts.

Max tapped his lowball with his butter knife. Luke noted with amusement that Peggy's father, who'd arrived asking for a wine spritzer, had adapted quickly to Abigail's limited choice of Yankee beverages: tonic water, Harvey's Bristol Cream, gin, and Scotch. He'd stopped seeming cowed by the house. It was as if he'd been in this world all his life. *Next thing you know,* Luke thought, *he'll be collecting duck decoys and playing bridge.*

"A toast to Peggy and Luke," Max announced, "and the merging of the great Sedgwick and Adams names...."

Peggy glanced at Luke. He shook his head as imperceptibly as he could and still get the visual message across: *Don't worry.* Peggy's concerns that her parents would ruin their story had, so far, been unfounded. Since the Adamses' arrival, Luke had managed to steer the discourse elsewhere whenever it began to turn—usually through Abby's prompting—to matters of heritage. Just this afternoon, when Abby had suggested driving past the former Adams mansion on Church Street and then visiting the Adams family plot at New Nineveh Cemetery, Luke had jumped in asking for a tour of the Fifth Wheel—RV slang, he'd learned, for a towed trailer—and Max had proudly obliged, showing off its compact kitchen, living area, and full-size bed. Luke had been intrigued. Maybe this was what he would do when he was rid of the Sedgwick House—take to the open road.

When they'd emerged, Ernestine Riga had been passing on the sidewalk. "How was your lunch?" she'd asked Luke.

"Lunch?" he'd repeated.

"At the Colonial Inn. Peggy didn't tell you I saw her there?"

He'd kept his cool. "Lunch was great, thanks." He'd introduced Ernestine to Max and Madeleine, and Ernestine had eyed them with inordinate interest until he was able to herd them safely back into the house, swallowing his jealousy and shock. So Peggy had wanted a weekend off to spend it with another man at *their* theoretical honeymoon spot. It had taken every shred of his self-control to push the thought from his mind. He did so again now.

Max had finished with his toast. "Mazel tov!" He polished off his Scotch.

Abby craned her neck toward Luke. "What did he say?"

Peggy coughed forcefully. Her mother jumped up from her chair and ran around to thump on her shoulder blades. "Are you choking? Are you all right?"

"Fine!" Peggy gasped, and Luke could tell she hadn't been choking at all—just trying to distract all assembled from the fact that her father had said "mazel tov."

Max raised his glass again. "Whoops, I forgot. May they be fruitful and multiply!"

"Hear, hear!" Madeleine sat back down at her place.

"And soon!" Abby added. Everyone looked at Bex and Josh as if waiting for them to agree.

"Oh!" Bex said hurriedly. "Hear, hear."

"And what about you two? You've been married how many years?" Max asked Josh.

"Please pass the naan," Peggy said.

Madeleine passed her the dish. "Really, Peggy, you're not getting any younger. If you two start trying now, it could be a year or more before anything happens. Before getting pregnant with you, I had a terrible miscarriage—"

"Mom, I know!" Peggy barked, and glanced quickly at Bex, who seemed to be keeping her condition secret.

"Want some curry, honey?" Max offered a forkful off his plate to Bex, who turned green and ran out of the room.

Everyone stared at her empty chair.

"She's fine," Josh assured them. "It's nothing."

Max put the forkful of curry into his mouth. "You'll have to move to New Nineveh full-time first, Peggy," he continued. "It's hard to make babies when you're a hundred miles apart!"

"Please pass the samosas," Peggy said loudly.

"When *are* you moving up here, dear?" Miss Abigail was more energized than Luke had seen her all day. And no wonder: The Adamses were posing the tough questions Abby couldn't ask on her own. "The town is starting to talk. The Reverend Matthews asked for you at church on Sunday."

"Church?" Max Adams repeated.

"And in the Grocery," Abigail went on, "Emily Hinkley wanted to know why she doesn't see you around town more often."

"Peggy, Luke, listen to Abigail." Madeleine Adams contributed her two cents as Bex came back in and took her seat. "It's not healthy for a couple to live apart. Is it, Bex?"

Peggy put her head in her hands. Luke, remembering that Josh and Bex maintained separate apartments, longed to laugh but refrained.

Madeleine didn't wait for Bex's response. "The closer together you live, the better. Look at your father and me. We're practically living on top of each other and our love life has never been more satisfying!"

Don't think about it.

Peggy was having an impossible time following her own advice. No matter how hard she tried, she lay in bed, unable to erase the evening from her mind. Could it have gone any worse? Okay, it could have gone worse. Her father could have worn white shorts, for example, a no-no after Labor Day. Her mother could have insisted on recounting each harrowing detail of the miscarriage story, reducing Bex to tears. Miss Abigail could have choked on her aloo gobi. Everyone at the table could have uncovered her and Luke's lie—

There was the ghost again. The Thing. She could hear it rustling.

Don't think about it.

It could be worse. She could have twenty more months of this to endure, instead of just nine. Yet how much lower could she sink than she had tonight, lying so outrageously to her parents? When Bex and Josh had left for the city, whispering to Peggy how amazing the house was, and Peggy had announced she was going to bed, Luke had said, "Think I'll turn in, too," and they'd made a big show of going upstairs together just like a real married couple, only to separate on the third-floor landing. Peggy had opened her bedroom door to discover that all her belongings had vanished. She'd padded indignantly to Luke's study, where he'd explained that he had hidden her things so it wouldn't appear as if they were sleeping in separate bedrooms. "In case your parents decide to go exploring on our floor," he'd said. And Peggy had thought, *This is what it's come to.* The Christmas she'd never had but had always dreamed of, a holiday with family and friends all gathered around a table, and it was nothing but an illusion.

Rustle, rustle, whisper. The ghost noises erupted full force.

Peggy tried to calm herself. It could be worse. So the Thing was more active than usual. If it had wanted to make contact with her, wouldn't it have done so by now?

An unearthly yowl erupted from the blackness. And then—*thud!* The Thing landed on her feet.

Peggy screamed. She leaped off her bed and flung herself in the direction of the door. When she made contact with the doorknob, she threw open the door and shrieked again. It filled the house, rolled down the dark, empty third-floor hallway, frightening her more, until suddenly she was almost at Luke's door and lights were blazing and Luke was running toward her.

"Ghost!" She could barely get the word out. "Ghost!"

Peggy's mother appeared at the top of the shuddering back stairs. "What is it? Peggy, are you all right? Did you say ghost?"

Through her panic, Peggy realized with dismay that her own hysteria-tinged voice sounded nearly identical to her mother's. And that her father, right behind her mother, was wearing an undershirt and boxer shorts. What was wrong with her parents? Why couldn't they be dignified?

The staircase rattled again, and Miss Abigail came into view. "What on earth is going on?"

"You aren't supposed to be climbing stairs!" Luke scolded.

Peggy told her, "There's a Thing in my room!"

"*Our* room," Luke said warningly.

Peggy held her breath. Had anyone noticed?

It appeared they hadn't. "Is this house haunted?" Madeleine was demanding.

Miss Abigail blinked. "Of course it's haunted."

"Everyone calm down," said Luke, who, like his great-aunt, Peggy noted, was appropriately attired in a robe. "Peggy, what thing?" But as Luke was asking, the Thing itself streaked past them and down the stairs into the chasm of the house below. A cat. A cat with a small, furry object in its mouth.

Peggy screamed again.

"Get hold of yourself, dear," Abby said. "It's only Quibble, with a mouse."

Peggy shuddered at the thought of the limp, gray thing in Quibble's mouth. There were mice in her room? Mice—their revolting pink feet scrabbling across her pillow, their disgusting tails...

Two patches of black appeared before Peggy's eyes. They doubled, then redoubled, until her field of vision was riddled with blackness. She rubbed her eyes, swayed a little on her feet...heard her mother, from far away, suck in her breath...

Luke grabbed her shoulders. She rested her head against his chest. *Nice.* She closed her eyes. *Strong. Safe.*

"What's the matter, Peggy? Talk to me!" Her mother rushed over, but Luke held on to her.

"She needs to lie down."

Luke was right. She needed to lie down. She forced her eyelids apart, stood up straight, and shuffled back in the direction she'd come, toward her room.

"This way." Luke put his hands on her waist and turned her to face his room.

"Yes. Right." She wasn't as faint, but she was all too aware of Luke's touch.

"Why don't you go back to bed," Luke told her parents and his great-aunt: a command, not a request. "I'll take care of her from here."

And with her parents and Miss Abigail watching, Peggy allowed Luke to steer her into his bedroom. He closed the door behind them and patted the foot of his rumpled bed. "Rest here a bit. Get your bearings back. You'll be all right."

She did, jarred by the sight of her belongings, the candle she'd brought from the shop, her snapshots of Bex and Josh, in Luke's otherwise unadorned chamber. He must have caught her looking, because he shrugged. "I know. It's like a hotel in here."

"Why don't you have any mementos or photos?" *Like that one I saw of your girlfriend in your study.*

"I don't plan to stay here long." He touched her forehead. "You looked about to pass out back there."

She moved away from his touch. She was a taken woman. "I'm fine."

"Spoken like a Sedgwick." He opened the door an inch and peeked out. "Coast is clear if you want to go back to your room now. Don't worry. You scared a couple of lives out of the cat. I doubt he'll be back in there for a while."

Peggy stood up slowly and left, closing Luke's door behind her. She was halfway down the hall when she hesitated, turned back toward Luke's room, turned back again toward her room, and then made a decision and knocked softly on Luke's door.

It opened instantaneously, as if he'd been waiting for her.

"I can't sleep in my room."

"Why not?"

"I, uh..." He was gorgeous. Really. Tall and lean and gorgeous. How had she been able to resist him all this time? "Uh..."

He had his glasses in one hand and was polishing them idly on his pajama top. He raised an eyebrow.

"Mice in there," she finished inarticulately.

"I'd say it's safe to assume, at least for tonight, that your room is mouse-free."

Few men could pull off plaid flannel pajamas. Luke Sedgwick not only could, he was positively sexy in them, with his sleep-tossed hair, squinting at her knowingly without the glasses, as if he could see straight into her soul…and it hit her.

She was wearing thermal underwear.

And nothing but. Long johns and a matching top printed with a ditsy floral pattern and cut close to the body—for warmth without bulk, according to the aged Toggery saleswoman. They clung to every curve, bump, and bulge, leaving nothing to the imagination.

Luke slipped his glasses back on.

Peggy dove into his bed, yanking the covers up to her neck.

"Make yourself comfortable," he said.

"This isn't what it looks like."

"What *does* it look like?"

"Like I just jumped into your bed. Which is not what I did. Well, it's what I did, but not for the reasons you might think." *Peggy, please, shut up.* She began again. "I'm not properly dressed. If you wouldn't mind loaning me your robe, I'll be on my way. Just don't look."

"I pretty much saw. In the hall. My eyes aren't *that* bad."

Don't think about it. "A robe, please."

His robe was camel colored, like the coats in the window of the Toggery. He held it out to her and averted his eyes, and she slithered out of his bed and into the garment, which enveloped her in Luke's clean, manly smell.

She was as light-headed as she had been in the hallway, only this time it had nothing to do with panic or anxiety and everything to do with this feeling of being in Luke's bedroom, in his bathrobe. She cinched the belt tightly around her waist. "I'll return it tomorrow morning." She started again for the door.

"Wait." He removed a wrapped present from the closet. "It's past midnight. Christmas Day. You can open it."

Peggy was touched and ashamed. She'd blown most of her

holiday budget on an overpriced rolling suitcase for Brock, leaving little left over. She'd found items from the shop for her parents and the Ver Plancks. But she'd hesitated over Luke—what did one give a husband of convenience? In the end, she'd bought a joint gift for him and Miss Abigail. Now she wished she'd tried harder.

"All I got you was a cookie basket," she admitted.

"That's fine." Luke sat on the bed. "Go ahead, open it. It won't bite you."

She sat, too, and tore away the wrapping paper to reveal a book: *William Butler Yeats: Early Poems*, its cover faded, its pages yellowed, a leather bookmark marking the poem "When You Are Old."

"It's the book I read from at the party," Luke said. "I thought you should have it. To make up for my behavior the rest of that evening. It belonged to my aunt Beatrice. We called her Beebee."

Peggy turned the book over in her hands. "But this should stay in your family."

"Well, you're in the family."

"Only for now. I can give it back to you, along with the brooch, when I—" The word caught in her throat. "When I leave."

"It's all right," he said. "You can keep the book."

It was the best present anyone had ever given her. Peggy knew this without hesitation. She didn't know how to thank him. She saw he was searching her face, his hazel eyes deep and serious behind his glasses. In the house's stillness, she imagined she could hear his heart beating in time with hers. *If he were my husband for real,* she thought, *this would be when I would throw my arms around him.*

She looked away. "I can't believe I was scared of a cat. I

almost forgot he existed. How can a person not see a cat for three whole months?"

Luke's laugh was hoarse, almost nervous. "He pretty much keeps to himself."

"Like you," Peggy said quietly. "Alone in your study so much of the time. My being here must be hard on you. I'm so sorry."

"I'm not in there to hide, Peggy." The lamp lit the edges of his hair into a halo around his face. *I should get out of here,* she thought. "I write poetry. Or I try to. And I'm responsible for what's left of the family money—for making more of it—a talent it seems I don't possess. I'm in there trading and dealing, trying to stop this house from falling down and to keep Abigail and me fed and clothed. And I'm failing miserably at both—poetry and Family Asset Management. I don't know why I'm telling you this. You can't do anything about it."

"Sometimes just talking about it can make you feel better."

"Not in my world," he said.

He rose from the bed. She was disappointed until she realized it was only to take a sweater from his bureau. She was surprised when he began to talk again. "It's cold in this house," he said, pulling the sweater over his pajamas. "If I kept it any warmer, the bill would be four or five thousand dollars a month. There are property taxes I can barely keep up with and maintenance costs I clearly can't keep up with, and all these obligations fall on me. I was born into them, and from the moment I was aware of my family name, I knew, like it or not, I would inherit them. When I really wanted to be like . . . you."

"Me? Why?"

"You're free. You can live wherever you want and work at whatever you want. You haven't had several generations of your family telling you from birth, 'You will choose a career in finance, and you will live in the Sedgwick House,' and this is the college you'll attend, and these will be your hobbies and here's whom you'll be friends with. You're not tied down to a family home—hell, your parents don't even have a home." He sighed. "Abigail would call what I'm doing complaining. We Sedgwicks don't complain."

"Well, it is complaining. If you're so worried about money, why don't you get a job?"

"I had a job. I was an economist at Hartford Mutual. I left to care for Abigail and this house. Even if I'd stayed, I didn't make nearly enough to keep this place running."

Peggy tried to imagine Luke playing office politics, going on team-building retreats, golfing with his superiors on weekends. She couldn't picture it, any more than she could picture herself in that kind of environment. Still, she couldn't fathom why he would want to trade lives with her. "We all have obligations, Luke. All right, I got to choose mine, but they're still obligations. In a few months, the rent on our store will double, which we're pretty sure will put us out of business, unless the competitor moving in across the street ruins us first. And when I was growing up, we moved seven times. The minute I got used to a new school, my dad would decide he was bored and we'd be off to a new town. I think you're the luckiest person in the world to live in a place where everyone has known you from before you were born, where your presence actually matters. Okay, end of tirade." She took a breath. Luke was staring at her. She buried her face in her hands.

With exquisite tenderness, Luke peeled her hands from her face and tilted up her chin with the tip of a finger.

Before she could waver, before she could say a word, before she could clarify what was happening, he moved closer—the bedsprings creaking absurdly—cupped her face in his hands, and touched his lips to hers.

They were soft. Impossibly soft and warm, and it was the softest and warmest of kisses, the sexiest, most romantic kiss ever, the tip of Luke's tongue tracing her lips, his hands playing across the small of her back, his longing hidden behind a restraint Peggy knew would soon dissolve—evolve—into devouring hunger. Peggy and Luke were there within moments, falling onto the bed, he loosening the sash of her robe and slipping his hands beneath her long underwear to brush against her skin, she with her arms tight around him, drawing him closer... until the phony diamond on her prop wedding ring snagged in his sweater.

It took all her willpower to disentangle herself and move away from the kiss.

"What is it?" He was breathless.

She didn't want to say it. More than anything she wished not to have to, or that, at the very least, she could have kissed Luke Sedgwick for a few more minutes until reality intruded and ruined everything.

EIGHTEEN

She might as well have sucker-punched him.

Luke scrambled up from the bed to a less vulnerable position, glad the conservative cut of his pajama bottoms allowed him to preserve his dignity. God bless Brooks Brothers. "You're engaged?" He was like Milo, teetering on the edge of a tantrum. "You told me you were engaged to be engaged, and now—"

Peggy appeared to flinch. "When did I tell you that?"

"In September. The first time we spoke on the phone." He pointed at her hand, at the hated gaudy diamond. "I take it you're now calling that an engagement ring, not a promise ring?"

The flash of Peggy's eyes was reminiscent of Nicki when she was angry. "This isn't an engagement ring. It's supposed to be my wedding ring. Mine, from you."

Luke was stunned. He gathered himself, surveyed his room, bare except for Peggy's knicknacks. "You don't know me at all," he said, more for his own sake than hers, then asked wearily, in his normal voice, "Who is he?"

"His name is Brock." Peggy was looking at the floor. "He's a sports cameraman."

"Ah," Luke said. "The football fan."

Her palpable misery gave him no satisfaction. The lips he'd savored moments before were trembling, the bright heat in her cheeks might have been the flush of passion, not shame.

He yearned to take her in his arms and peel off her long underwear—how had he never considered how erotic long underwear could be?—and make love to her until she forgot there was any other man in the universe.

She adjusted her—his—robe where the lapels had fallen open in the front. "It wasn't sudden." She sounded far steadier than she looked. "We've been together for years."

"If he loves you so much, why did it take him this long to propose?"

Peggy's shoulders dropped, her face fell, and she wrapped her arms around herself in the self-protective way he recognized. Some writer he was. He couldn't imagine being able to articulate how sorry he was, how to say he was angry not at her, but at himself for letting her get away; but before he could try, she began to uncrumple before his eyes, raising her head and unfolding her arms. "I broke it off with him in October, right after my first weekend here. But you didn't do the same thing with your girlfriend, did you? You think it's perfectly fine to keep seeing her. That redhead."

He was surprised. "Nicki?"

She flinched again. "If nothing else, don't you think your great-aunt might hear gossip around town?"

He should set the record straight—explain he'd ended his relationship with Nicki soon after the wedding reception, that since then he, unlike Peggy, had honored their wedding vows. "What about you? I suppose you were with the sports fan at the Colonial Inn the weekend you decided you and I needed some time apart." The jealousy he'd forced down erupted in him again. "Whose brilliant notion was it to go there, so all of Litchfield County could see you? Why not just pitch a tent with him on Ernestine Riga's lawn?"

"Great idea. Then that Nicki person could have driven by in her little green car and waved." She rewrapped her arms around herself. "Just tell me. You *have* been seeing her, haven't you?"

"Fine. Yes." Luke was tired of arguing. He was just plain tired. In an hour or so, it would be light outside. "Are we done here?"

"We're done." She crossed to his door for the second time in the past hour. The poetry book he'd given her lay forlornly on his bed. "We may be stuck with each other until September, but as far as I'm concerned, this friendship—whatever you call it—" Peggy glanced back at the book one last time. "It's over."

The morning of New Year's Eve, after half a dozen wordy parting speeches, much sloppy bear hugging and cheek kissing, and twenty minutes devoted to backing the Fifth Wheel painstakingly out of the narrow service driveway along the north side of the Sedgwick House, Peggy's parents drove off, back out west, into the warm weather. Luke was sorry to see them go. Peggy had returned to New York on Christmas afternoon, and without the distraction of Max and Madeleine there was nothing to do but think, only one thing to think about, and he didn't want to think about it. The house seemed more forlorn than ever. He spent the morning buying and selling stock and came downstairs to pick at the last of the overcooked Christmas leftovers. When he stepped on the squeaky third step in the front staircase, it seemed to whimper.

Luke was despondently jotting poetry in the margin of one of Abigail's grocery lists when his great-aunt came into the kitchen to fix herself a cup of tea. She scorned his offer of help and shuffled to the sink to fill the old kettle and set it on the stove. There was the *tick-tick-tick* of the old gas burner struggling to ignite, and then a ring of blue flame leapt up to meet the kettle.

"Quiet in here," Abby commented.

"Very." Luke put down his pen. He'd been thinking of a walk in the woods he'd taken with Abby one New Year's Eve afternoon when he was a boy. On that afternoon, the sun had already begun to set behind an ancient tree whose snow-dusted branches bowed, veil-like, toward the forest floor. The Widow in the Woods, Abby had called the old oak, and pointed out the carcass of a second oak nearby: Only the trunk remained, destroyed by lightning years earlier.

"Mr. and Mrs. Adams certainly are exuberant." Abby took her soggy, used teabag from its stained saucer on the counter and set it in her cup. Then she turned on Luke with the Look.

Luke decided to ignore it. "Would you care for a gingerbread man? There are a couple left in Peggy's cookie basket—" He stopped. His heart was heavy at the thought of the widowed tree, and of Peggy, and Abigail was not about to stop looking at him. "All right. What is it?"

"What's wrong with your marriage?"

The directness of her question threw him—he wondered whether a bit of Max and Madeleine's freewheeling, get-it-all-out-in-the-open style had rubbed off on her. He wouldn't mind so much if it had, although perhaps not regarding this particular subject. His brief kiss with Peggy had stirred something in him; he had, for a gossamer instant, finally known what real love was, why people chose to marry and pledge forever to each other. He recognized the desire to prolong that forever with children who carried forward one's name, and with it the promise of eternity.

And then the moment had ended, and he understood that with Peggy there would be no forever.

Abigail was observing him; he could tell. He spun lines in his imagination, stalling for time: *Her light-struck mate turned to moss. Her bolt-cracked mate transformed to moss.* The widow tree would be gone now, he thought, bulldozed for the Pilgrim Plaza parking lot.

"I asked a question, young man."

"I don't know what you mean." He didn't, truly. There was so much wrong with his marriage. It could be anything.

"Why did she leave on Christmas? Why didn't she stay the week?"

"People who own stores can't up and leave work for a week." Especially the week after Christmas, when stores were filled with shoppers spending their gift money and buying themselves everything they hadn't gotten for the holidays. Peggy had explained this to Luke when he'd asked the question himself.

"They do in New Nineveh." Abby's face had that set, stubborn look.

"New Nineveh isn't New York."

His great-aunt clucked her tongue. "And why is Peggy still living in New York? She shows no interest in moving in with us permanently. Meanwhile Ernestine spotted that Pappas girl driving past the house last month. This is no way to conduct a marriage." She stopped for a breath of air. "Neither do I believe Peggy's parents are of the New Nineveh Adamses."

Luke knew he was squirming under her unflinching certitude.

"I've been thinking"—he slipped the shopping list with his poetry into his pocket—"that we—Peggy and I—might be better off ending things."

"Ending your marriage?" Abby rubbed her ears, as if she'd heard wrong.

"We're nothing alike."

The old woman *tsk*ed.

"It's true. We shouldn't have married in the first place, and we shouldn't have stayed married. We rushed into it without considering whether we were good for each other." Each word was a blow to Luke's already battered heart. But admitting the truth to Abigail was, in its own way, cathartic. "I know you care for her, and I know you want me to settle down, but..." That was as far as he could go. He could hardly explain he couldn't stay married to Peggy because she was engaged to another man.

The teakettle whispered breathily.

"Do you care for her?"

The kettle's whisper climbed a few decibels.

"Yes," Luke replied after a moment. "But it's not that easy."

"If it's easy, you're doing it wrong."

The kettle had worked up its full head of steam. "I'd like you to consider changing your will again," Luke continued more loudly. "Now that you're more comfortable with the idea of selling the house, we could still sell it—"

Abigail took the kettle off the burner.

"—without Peggy!" Luke shouted into the now quiet kitchen. He stopped, gestured at the stove, and continued in his regular voice, "The burner." It was still on.

Abby poured boiling water into her cup and poured the rest, hissing, down the drain. "My will stands." She set the empty kettle in the sink basin. "You and Peggy are to remain married for a year."

"The burner, Abby." Luke pointed.

"Otherwise there's no selling the house." She sat at the table across from him. Behind her, the burner continued to blaze, a perfect crown of fire.

"Abigail, the stove!" Luke shoved his chair back and, with

hands he hadn't realized were clenched into fists, twisted the burner knob to "Off." "You can't just forget the stove is on! Do you want to burn the house down?"

"It was a mistake." His great-aunt stirred her tea. "You were here to take care of it. Now, you do understand me about the will?"

"You can't make that kind of mistake!" It was unfair to shout at her, but he was weary of pretending everything was fine. Everything was not fine. Everything was an abject disaster. "We have no insurance, Abby. I had to let the policy lapse. If this house burns, you'll have nowhere to live and, more to the point, nothing to live on! Do *you* understand?"

"We have my box with the star. We can live on that."

"There is no box." He looked her straight in the eye. "I've been searching for weeks. I've found nothing. If Charles did give you a gift, and I'm not saying he didn't, it can't possibly have any value. I'm sorry, Abby." He was simply unable to fly off the handle. To remain even-tempered was too deeply ingrained in him.

Abigail simply sipped her tea. "A box with a star," she repeated, and for the second time Luke wondered if some of his great-aunt's dementia was an act. If she wanted a way to distract him from his talk of divorce and selling the house, she couldn't have chosen anything more effective. He dropped the subject.

Brock was a born host. He strode across his father and stepmother's New Jersey living room, utterly at ease, stopping every few steps to shake a hand, clasp a shoulder, or freshen a drink. He was brilliant at it. So different from—

No way. Peggy would not waste her New Year's Eve thinking about Luke.

"Refill. Who all needs a refill? Bex? Josh?" Brock had a big voice Peggy could imagine bouncing off the room's vaulted two-story ceiling during more intimate gatherings. He held a champagne bottle and tilted it toward Bex.

Bex put her hand over her plastic champagne coupe, which Peggy knew held sparkling water, and declined without explanation. Bex still hadn't gone public with her pregnancy and wouldn't until the first trimester was over. It was one of many secrets Peggy felt terrible about keeping from Brock, especially since she'd already confided in Luke. *Dammit, Peggy. Stop thinking about him. Him and Nicki.* She wished she didn't know that woman's name.

"Josh, then. Here you go, big guy." Brock paused as Josh polished off the last of his champagne, then he refilled Josh's glass to the brim. "Glad you both made the trip out here. We should move to Jersey, Pegs. Look at how much space this house has. And our kids will need a yard to play in."

Peggy couldn't argue with the space, but the house was horrible, with its hollow decorative columns and wood laminate floors and gas-burning fireplace, all brand-new and synthetic. It, and the other identical houses in its development, seemed to have sprung up fully formed, like shiny plastic pieces in a Monopoly set. But the place was in excellent repair; she'd give it that. Luke would kill for the ceiling, a pristine expanse of white plaster free of stains and bulges. Sealed, watertight perfection. She blinked back the floating circles the sunken lights had left in front of her eyes. "We'll see," she said. She had no intention of living in a house like this.

Brock was already moving toward the next group of guests. Most were people Peggy didn't know: friends and business associates of the Clovises. She spotted Brock's brother, Brent, a shorter, blond version of Brock who'd be best man—the only other member of the wedding party besides Bex. A few of Brock's former football teammates from high school were swapping stories with Brock's father, Ron, while the friends' wives stood separately, eating shrimp from an icy heap of seafood on the dining table. Peggy realized this was the difference between WASP parties and everybody else's parties: Here, people ate the food.

She scanned the room some more. There were no cameraman buddies; except for Brock, they were all over the country, setting up for tomorrow morning's bowl games.

"See how he's changed? He turned down work on New Year's just to be with me," Peggy pointed out to Bex and Josh, as if the two had been criticizing Brock—when neither had made a single disparaging comment since Peggy had finally told them of her engagement. They'd been supportive and complimentary and all the things Peggy had hoped they'd be.

"I noticed." Bex settled into a bony reproduction armchair, not even taking the opportunity to comment that earlier, Brock's stepmother, Sharon, had pretentiously described it as "Louis Quatorze."

"Me too." Josh took another gulp of champagne.

It was bizarre.

"I'll be right back." Peggy dodged through the crowd toward Ron and Sharon's media room, where guests' mink coats lay in perfumed strata along the backs of the couches and chairs and rhinestone handbags littered the seats. Peggy found her own plain bag and stood, her phone to her ear. On the wall-mounted flat-screen television, people cavorted live in Times Square, the sound on mute.

"Happy almost New Year," she greeted Luke when he answered.

"The same to you." His matching polite, distant formality bothered her, which was stupid. It wasn't as if she'd called to whisper sweet nothings in his ear.

"Where are you?"

"You called the house," he said. "You didn't think I'd be out in a cardboard hat, singing 'Auld Lang Syne'?"

"I guess not." She laughed, feeling foolish. "How's your great-aunt?"

"She went to bed hours ago."

And where's the redheaded strumpet? Peggy thought. She took an anxious breath and let herself be mesmerized by the televised revelry. She and Bex and Jen and Andrea and a few other college friends had actually gone to Times Square the first New Year's Eve after Peggy had moved to Manhattan. It had been tightly packed with people, and every so often, just for fun, Peggy had lifted both feet off the ground and let the crowd carry her along.

"Is there anything you wanted to say?" Luke asked.

"Yes. I think we should call it off early. Our, uh, arrangement." She couldn't bring herself to say "marriage." "I can't keep hiding this from my fiancé—"

"What about the money?"

The complete absence of hurt in Luke's voice left Peggy more confused than she had been before she'd picked up her phone; she'd thought the conversation would ease her mind. "I don't care about the money." She pictured Luke in the chair he liked in the den, the one by the telephone table. "I'll find some other way to save the shop. This isn't worth it."

"You're right. I'll find some other way to take care of Abigail. We can tell her as soon as Mayhew draws up the papers."

"Great." Her throat ached. "I have to go."

Back at the party, the football wives were still attacking Mount Seafood and Brock was still chatting it up with his friends, though Josh had joined them.

Bex, in her chair, looked up as Peggy approached her. "What's wrong? You look upset."

"Not at all. I'm happy." Or would be, once the numbness

wore off. And once she had broken the news to Bex. "Luke and I are calling it off early. I hope you can understand, Bex. I just can't pretend to be his wife anymore. Not now that I'm engaged. Luke will have his lawyer draw up the papers right away, and we'll break the news to his great-aunt together." Miss Abigail. What would become of her? Peggy refused to acknowledge the growing choking sensation in her throat. Miss Abigail wasn't her responsibility. She was Luke's relative, Luke's concern.

On the opposite side of the room, one of Brock's friends was reenacting a dramatic football pass. "He goes long... long... and..."

Peggy turned away from the distraction. "The money will be a problem, I know. But we'll figure it out, Bex. There has to be another way to keep the store. We did pretty well this holiday." They had; sales had been up over last year, according to Peggy's accounting. "Maybe we can do a little advertising. And look for a new space. On a side street, where the rent is lower. I can't be married to Luke and engaged to Brock. It's just wrong. I hope you understand."

"Five minutes to midnight!" a guest yelled.

"I understand." Bex rested her hands in her lap.

"You're not upset?"

"Why would I be upset? You've got to do what's right for you." Bex smiled, a little wistfully, perhaps. "It's too bad, though. If I were you, it would kill me to lose that house."

"I would have lost it anyway," Peggy reminded her.

"And here's the other future Mrs. Clovis!" Brock's bronzed, blonded, surgically enhanced stepmother swept up and clutched Peggy's upper arm enthusiastically. "I'm so excited! You have to set the date, Peggy. Don't keep us in suspense!"

"Four minutes!" came the call.

The room felt packed to the walls, the guests tipsy enough that each seemed to occupy twice as much space as before.

Peggy squeezed between the flailing arms and swaying bodies and touched Brock on the shoulder. His friends hooted and catcalled as she led him toward the glassed-in patio Sharon called the lanai.

They were alone.

"I'm ready to set a date. Is there a day you can take off in June, when you're back from your documentary?" By then, her annulment would be final. Her sadness at the thought of Luke got lost in the bursts of laughter and premature honking of party noisemakers coming from the party room. "What do you think?"

"Ten! Nine!" the guests shouted. "Eight . . . !"

"Let's go for it." Brock grabbed her and squashed her to his machine-toned pectorals, his movie-star lips locking on hers as the party guests on the other side of the glass embraced each other. The New Year had begun.

NINETEEN

Midwinter, January

A few days after New Year's, Luke met with Lowell Mayhew, who warned that once Abigail understood he and Peggy were dissolving their marriage, she would reinstate her previous will. Luke again asked who the beneficiary would be, as he had almost four months ago, but Mayhew still wouldn't tell him.

"Do you think we could talk Abby into letting me sell the house without Peggy?"

Luke read the answer to his question in Mayhew's downcast eyes. "I wish you'd reconsider," the lawyer said. "I wasn't keen on this arrangement in the beginning, but Peggy is a lovely girl, and you seem fond of her. Surely you can tolerate each other until September. Why break up now with so much at stake?"

"It was her idea," Luke said mopily.

He thought long and hard and went to play tennis at Ver Planck's club. "I'm ready to talk to Grant Atherton," Luke said with no preamble as they strolled onto the indoor court.

Ver Planck didn't ask what had changed Luke's mind, as Luke had known he wouldn't. He took the lid off a can of tennis balls, which emitted a vacuum-sealed *whoosh.* "I'll set you two up with a meeting."

Luke had half hoped Ver Planck would tell him it was too late, that Atherton had found another plot of land. He imagined what his great-aunt would say about their farmland being turned into a parking lot and a Budget Club. But there was no use fretting about it. He needed the money. The land was part of the family portfolio and Luke's to do with as he wished. The house was not his to sell. A quick windfall from Budget Club would go a long way toward solving his financial problems. He could get the roof fixed before it fell in on their heads and hire an attendant for Abigail, a nurse to help him care for her.

The annulment papers named Luke Silas Sedgwick IV as the plaintiff and Patricia Adams Sedgwick as the defendant. Luke brought them home from Mayhew's office in a legal-size folder and left them on Peggy's bed for her to sign. In the ballroom, he stared alternately at the computer screen saver and out the window. He longed for snow, to lose himself in the physicality of shoveling the driveway. But there had been none so far this winter; the landscape was brown and dead. He got up from the computer and went downstairs.

His great-aunt was in the mudroom, picking up rain boots and snow boots one at a time and holding them upside down. She didn't turn around, and he watched her work awhile, then asked, "Any luck?"

She picked up a garden clog and shook it.

Luke removed the umbrellas from their tarnished brass stand. A spider scuttled out; otherwise the canister was empty. He searched the pockets of the ancient coats and slickers hanging along the wall and found a Swiss Army knife he thought he'd lost ages ago, but no box with a star on it. "Do you really think you hid it out here?"

"No," Abby admitted. "I still think it's in the library." They went inside.

He started at the top of the room, rolling the library ladder and taking several books at a time from the uppermost shelves and shining a flashlight behind him. His great-aunt did the same on the bottom shelves, and for a while they worked together companionably.

"My hands ache," she complained after about forty minutes, and put down the books she was holding. "I guess I'm getting old."

Luke hid his concern. It was the first time he could remember his great-aunt admitting to pain. For the rest of the afternoon, he searched the library—deciding, after a time, that he might as well dust the books while he was at it—and spent the whole of the next day, too, working mindlessly, removing, looking behind, dusting, and reshelving. By midday Thursday, he had dusted the entire roomful of books and had found nothing hidden behind them but more dust. He moved on to the closed-off and long neglected east addition, vacuuming and polishing. He searched every nook and cranny, under every cushion, in every drawer. At last, empty-handed, dirt caked, and aching, he climbed the stairs to the third-floor bathroom. When he emerged from the blackened bathwater, it no longer mattered to him whether Abigail's treasure existed or not. She believed it did, and he would keep looking for it. It was the only wish of hers he still held the power to grant.

The computer screen flickered in the dark room. Peggy watched intently, trying not to blink. Was this normal—a shifting, grainy pattern; snow against blackness?

"I'm not seeing anything," Josh said beside her, but just then a denser pool of darkness appeared.

"That's your uterus." Bex's obstetrician waved her free hand in front of the circular void on the ultrasound screen. "And . . . wait . . ."

From her position on the table, a pink medical drape covering her from the waist down, Bex craned her neck. Josh reached for his wife's foot and squeezed it.

"There's Embryo A!" The doctor waved her hand again. "And...good...we have a heartbeat...nice and strong. See that flicker, Josh?"

"Maybe," said Josh.

"I do! Nice and strong!" Bex repeated.

Peggy could make out a blurry, lambent mass, nothing more, but she was happy to take the doctor's word for it.

"Wait..." The doctor's face turned serious, and Peggy's chest ached as she braced for bad news.

"Here's Embryo B. It looks like you're having twins!"

On the subway home, Peggy and Josh sat on either side of Bex. No one spoke for many stops; Peggy guessed her friends were in shock. It was one thing to consider the possibility of more than one baby. It was another to prepare for the reality.

The train came into Columbus Circle, and passengers crowded on. A woman and a boy squeezed onto the bench next to Peggy. The boy leaned his head against his mother's shoulder. "Mommy. Mommy. Do you know who the goddess of home and family is?" His smile was a mismatch of adult and baby teeth. "Hestia."

His mother snuggled him closer. "Is she mortal or immortal?"

"We need to buy an apartment." Josh spoke up first. "We can't raise twins living down the hall from each other. We have to work as a team twenty-four hours a day, seven days a week, and neither of our places is big enough for four...." He stopped talking; Bex was crying. "Come on, Bexie, it won't be that bad. I promise to be neater and—"

"Can you name the names of all nine Muses?" the boy asked his mother.

"Can you?" she returned.

"No, but I know what they do, at least most of them. There's one of music, and one of drama, and there's one of history. They're the goddesses of hobbies."

Peggy patted Bex's hand. "You'll be able to afford it. There has to be one apartment in New York under a bazillion dollars." If she'd been able to stick it out with Luke, she realized, she could have lent Bex and Josh a down payment.

"Except for history. History isn't exactly a hobby," the boy continued.

"That's not it…" Bex produced a ragged tissue from her coat pocket. "Poor little Embryo C! What happened to little Yehuda?"

A lump rose in Peggy's throat. "You can't think that way. You have two babies! It's a miracle!"

"I know!" Bex sobbed, and then laughed, and Peggy and Josh laughed, too, wiping their faces and clearing their throats, and then the train was at their stop, Seventy-ninth Street.

"You should hold the handrail," Josh told his wife as they walked toward the subway station steps. "You're carrying precious cargo."

"I'm not ninety years old, sweetie." Bex took the handrail, but it was too late for Peggy; her friend's response had reminded her of Miss Abigail, and the thought of Miss Abigail had led her to Luke, and the thought of Luke was making her want to cry some more, a luxury she would not allow herself, because the idea of wanting to cry over a human being as unimportant to her as Luke Sedgwick was driving her mad. Especially when she loved Brock.

At her appointment with Jon-Keith the next day, she studied herself in the salon mirror as the colorist picked at her eternally lifeless hair.

"We need to get you on a schedule right away," he pronounced. "You'll want your last set of highlights no more than two days before the wedding, so there are absolutely no roots. Do you know what happens if you have even an eighth of an inch of roots? Your part shows up in all your photographs as a black line down the center of your head. It's a nightmare. Are you doing color photos or black and white? It's worse with black and white."

"I don't know."

Jon-Keith looked at her in disbelief. "Okay, anyway, what I do with my brides is count back from the final appointment and book all your previous appointments at six-week intervals. When's the wedding date?"

"I'm not sure." Peggy scrutinized her forehead. Maybe it was time to get those wrinkles fixed. Brides weren't supposed to have worry lines. "We only just decided on June."

Jon-Keith narrowed one eye, which made him appear more piratelike than usual. "You have *got* to choose a date. Already, the good venues are probably booked up. Do you know how long it takes to get a dress made? Months. You should have chosen your gown, like, yesterday, and you can't do that until you decide where you're having the wedding, because the setting dictates the tone of the whole day, and Lord help you if you end up at a beach ceremony in a black-tie dress. You're getting *me* all stressed out, and I'm not the bride!" He slid a piece of aluminum foil under a few strands of hair and painted on the highlights with a brush. Peggy felt like a turkey being basted.

The next day after work, Peggy stopped at a newsstand to pick up all the bridal magazines she could find, came home, and settled herself at the coffee table. "What do you think of this dress?" She tore out a page and held it up.

Bex was on the couch, engrossed in *What to Expect When*

You're Expecting. "It says here I should eat six hundred extra calories a day, three hundred per baby. I eat six hundred extra calories a day just at breakfast!"

"Oh, no!" Peggy let her magazine page slip to the floor. "In June, you'll be a month away from your due date!"

"Actually I may be giving birth. The doctor revised my date; she says most multiples are born early."

Peggy felt the familiar anxious tingle in her lungs. How could she marry without Bex? "We could push the wedding back." She felt better just saying it aloud. In the excitement of New Year's Eve, she'd forgotten another detail: how to explain to her parents that in a matter of a few months she not only would no longer be Mrs. Sedgwick, she would become Mrs. Clovis. How her parents would react was the big question. They'd always liked Brock but seemed to have grown attached to Luke and Miss Abigail over their Christmas visit. And they'd be stunned at the quick annulment.

"We could have the wedding in the fall instead," she suggested to Bex.

"During football season? That'll never work."

The perfect model-bride on the magazine nearest Peggy beamed up as if to ask, *What's wrong with you?* Peggy flipped over the magazine. "We could wait until next January, then."

Bex turned pages in her book. "Don't be silly. Get married in June. You've been waiting your whole life for this wedding. Why put it off?"

As the news of Peggy's engagement spread, there were excited calls and frenzied e-mails from the Las Vegas bachelorettes. Andrea, now married, chirped, "It was the guy in the casino, wasn't it? You told Brock and worked him into a jealous frenzy, didn't you? Nice job!"

Brock, out of town covering football playoffs, called

constantly from the road. “Hey, Pegs,” he’d say. “Whatcha up to?”

“I’m at the store,” she’d tell him. *Just like I was two hours ago.*

They settled on a date—the first Saturday in June. For a few hours, Peggy was glad to have at least made one decision. Then came a new flurry of calls from Sharon Clovis, who peppered her with questions about menus and guest lists. By Friday afternoon, Peggy had switched off her phone and had stopped dreading her trip to New Nineveh. Signing annulment papers and crushing Miss Abigail with news of her impending split from Luke seemed preferable to another moment of wedding talk.

But when she drove up, the Sedgwick House was empty.

“Luke? Miss Abigail?” Peggy stood in the frigid foyer, her call reverberating back at her. Why hadn’t they left the light on? Where would they be at ten o’clock at night? Luke wasn’t in his study, and Miss Abigail’s bedroom door was wide open—only she wasn’t in it, or in the kitchen, or in the library—

She was standing next to the black phone in the den when its bell broke the silence. Too worried to be startled, she grabbed it up before the first ring had finished.

“You’re there.” It was Luke. “We’re at the hospital.”

It was like a recurring bad dream in which she kept returning to Torrington General, hoping Miss Abigail would be all right. The emergency room waiting area was exactly as it had been last time—the same sea-foam green walls, a similar cast of unhappy patients and their companions, the same dog-eared issues of *AARP* and *Field & Stream*. A nurse motioned Peggy past the triage area toward a drawn curtain. Behind it,

Miss Abigail was in bed, asleep, a bloodied dressing on her forehead and a cast on one arm.

"You should have heard her when they went to stitch her up." Luke looked drained. "'No lidocaine,' she said. The doctors took it as a sign of dementia, but I told them, no, that's just my great-aunt."

They'd been cleaning out Miss Abigail's bedroom, Luke explained, searching for something, and she'd tripped or lost her balance. She had a fractured wrist and a gash from scraping her forehead against a drawer pull on her dresser. She didn't seem to have a concussion, but the doctors were keeping her again for observation. "The concern is that she may have had another one of those practice strokes."

Peggy patted Miss Abigail's good arm and smoothed her hair. *She doesn't belong in here. She should be home, in her own bed.* For the first time in months, she understood that this indomitable, seemingly indestructible old woman couldn't have more than a few years left. Soon Luke really would be the only living Sedgwick.

Luke motioned Peggy away from his sleeping great-aunt. "I'd like you to do me a favor," he whispered. "I wouldn't ask if it weren't for..." He nodded toward the bed to finish the sentence.

Peggy was shocked at how weary he appeared. She longed to take his hand, to let him rest his head on her shoulder. "Whatever you need."

"I don't think Abigail can handle the idea of an early annulment."

Peggy's mood soared. It was exactly what she had been thinking. How could they break up now, with Miss Abigail in this weakened state?

She'd postpone the wedding. Brock would be upset, but she'd think up a reasonable excuse. It was her duty. She'd stay married to Luke until September, fulfill the promise she'd made, do the right thing by Miss Abigail. By then, too, she'd be more used to the idea of marrying Brock. She'd be excited about her dress and her wedding and the napkin colors and all the things brides were supposed to be excited about. She would be ready.

"That would be fine," she told Luke. "We'll stick to the original plan. September isn't that far off anyway. I'll wait and get married after that." If Brock couldn't spare a weekend, they'd go to City Hall on a weekday, between his assignments.

Luke didn't seem appeased; his eyes held a sadness Peggy couldn't remember having seen before.

What was wrong with her? She had that "I have a crush on Luke Sedgwick" sensation again. She racked her brain for an unflattering memory of him but could remember nothing—nothing but Christmas Eve in his bedroom, his hands under her laughable thermal top, his lips on her throat. For the first time, she let herself not force the thought to one side—to imagine what Luke Sedgwick might be like in bed. "White bread with mayonnaise," Tiffany had once said. Peggy didn't doubt her friend's authority on the subject of preppy sex, but she had to think, from the way Luke's kiss had left her aching for more, that making love with him would be anything but bland.

"P-pardon?" She snapped back to reality. Luke had just spoken, and Miss Abigail was not two feet away in a hospital bed with a cast on her wrist and stitches in her forehead. How could Peggy think about sex at a time like this?

"You won't have to wait for September," Luke repeated. "I wasn't suggesting we put off the annulment."

"You weren't?" She avoided his eyes, glancing down at her hands, at the phony Connecticut wedding ring she'd once thought so spectacular. It wasn't right. Luke wouldn't have given her a ring like this. It was too big, too shiny, too—just *too*. Too everything.

"You're getting married, aren't you?" He sounded impatient, almost harsh. "You'll sign the papers this weekend and Mayhew will file them next week, as we discussed. I wasn't suggesting we postpone *getting* the annulment—" He left off; Miss Abigail was muttering something in her sleep. When she seemed to settle, he finished in a ragged whisper, "Only that we put off telling her about it."

A nurse came in. "Why don't you two go home and get some rest? She's stable. We'll call you if there's any change overnight."

There were only a handful of cars left in the parking lot. Luke walked Peggy to this week's rental, and Peggy searched for the key in her purse before finding it in her coat pocket. Her face was stiff in the frozen air. "So what you're saying is, we fake being happily married for ninety more days until the annulment goes through, and *then* hit your great-aunt with the bad news? Why do you assume in three months she'll be in better shape to handle it?"

"Do you have a better suggestion?"

She lifted her arms and dropped them against her sides.

"I didn't think so." He drove out of the lot behind her, his car's headlights on her back like accusing eyes all the way to New Nineveh.

After a sleepless night, Luke returned with Peggy to the hospital Saturday and found Abigail in a regular room, awake and insisting on a second helping of creamed chipped beef. Luke assured the nurse that Abigail's appreciation of the hospital food was also not a sign of dementia. He saw Peggy had her hand pressed over her mouth as if trying to suppress laughter and surmised she was thinking Abby's own cooking wasn't far off from hospital food. He couldn't disagree.

There was good news from Abby's doctors: Their tests showed no sign of another ministroke, and they concluded her fall had been a simple accident. "Go home, Miss Sedgwick," one said. "You'll probably outlive all of us."

Luke settled his great-aunt into her bed, surrounded with propped-up pillows, and Peggy brought up a tray with tea and crackers, and together they kept her company into the early evening as she reminisced about her privileged childhood, about the summer lawn parties and winter sleigh rides and games of hide-and-seek with the staff's children.

"The Sedgwicks had it better than most," she said just before she fell asleep. "But I learned the value of a penny saved. A few pennies over time can add up, you two. Don't forget that."

Peggy retired wordlessly to her own bedroom not long afterward, and soon Luke could hear the muffled sound of a one-sided telephone conversation. He shut himself into the ballroom, in the pool of light cast by his desk lamp, going over his budget until the numbers became meaningless. Then he turned from his computer and began to write.

Widow in the Woods

A hundred years or more, she's bent her crown
in storm, in sun, in moonsplashed midnight breeze,
surviving all the random vagaries
of this harsh world. A dense-twigged veil drifts down
from crown along her trunk—mourning slow wood
that rustles, tattered, in a hint of wind
this January dusk, cloudy, purpling
the ground with sudden shadows.

How she broods—
you speculate—on dark surprise and loss,
alone these many years, despondent, bent,
her bolt-cracked mate transformed to splinters, moss.
Though not alone, you feel the sadness of
a twilight breeze. There's never enough love;
the widow nods to you. Her branches moan.

The sky had grown lighter by the time he'd finished Sunday morning.

He should have been exhausted, but he was more energized than he had been since—really, since Christmas Eve. He read the finished sonnet twice, three times, four times. For once, he didn't want to change a word or consign it to the garbage.

Avoiding Peggy's room, he took the back staircase to the second floor to peek at Abigail, snoring steadily under her Hudson's Bay blanket with Quibble curled at her feet, then continued to the kitchen. He rested at the chilly table, his head in his hands.

"What are you doing?"

Luke blinked. Peggy was in the kitchen doorway. Wintry sunlight dappled the sweater and skirt she often wore to church.

"Your great-aunt would like tea and a poached egg on toast. If I didn't know better, I'd say she's enjoying being waited on." Peggy took a pot from the rack. "I wish I knew why it's called a poached egg, as if it had been stolen."

Luke wished he knew how Peggy could be so chipper at five in the morning. He wished he knew how Peggy could be *awake* at five in the morning. Or how the sun could be full in the sky when ten seconds ago it hadn't yet risen. "What time is it?" His throat was dry and creaky.

"Nine-thirty." She took from the bread box a loaf of

Pepperidge Farm Original White, the same bread Abigail had been eating for Luke's entire life. "What happened to you? Did you sleep here all night?"

"I wasn't asleep." But he must have been. And now Peggy had caught him.

Peggy put two slices of bread in the toaster. "I thought I'd go to church alone, if you don't mind bringing your great-aunt her breakfast. And I signed the annulment papers. They're on my dresser. For heaven's sake, please tell Lowell to make sure Geri doesn't see them."

"Thank you." Luke knew Peggy wouldn't suspect how painful the words were to say. He was trained to keep his emotions in.

TWENTY

At the end of January, Bath opened across the street. "I bet that store doesn't last three months," Bex scoffed. "They can't be that smart if they couldn't open in time for the holidays."

"I think I'll write them a note to welcome them to the neighborhood." Peggy brushed a fine layer of grit from a piece of the store stationery they kept near the cash register.

"But they're the competition!"

"We should still be polite," Peggy insisted. But her confidence waned when she went to deliver the note and introduce herself, and the store manager, rail thin and imperious, neither opened it nor offered her own name. A few days later, Peggy spotted an ACME Cleaning Supply regular, the mint foot-scrub woman, leaving Bath with a shopping bag in each hand. Already, Bex and Peggy were noticing a downturn in business.

They reminded each other that it was always slow in the dead of winter; shoppers didn't venture outside when it was cold, and it had been particularly frigid for the past couple of weeks, with temperatures in the twenties. As the month came to a close, Peggy envied Tiffany, who had migrated to Palm Beach shortly after Christmas. Even Brock was in Florida, setting up for the Super Bowl.

Florida. Peggy tried not to dwell on it too much.

"Do you think if a man cheats once, he'll be a cheater for life?" Peggy asked at her next massage appointment. As always, she was glad to be facing down, speaking toward the floor through the doughnut-shaped face rest.

"I had a boyfriend once who was a yoga instructor. I'm pretty sure he slept with every one of his students." Marlene pressed her fingers into Peggy's spine. "The man could not keep his prana in his pants. Is Brock cheating again?"

"Not at all. I was asking theoretically—ouch!"

"Sorry, Peggy. You've got that same knot in your shoulder you had two years ago."

It occurred to Peggy that instead of trying to massage away what was bothering her, she could face what was bothering her. On the bus home, she called Brock. There was nothing to arouse her suspicions. The hollow sound of the stadium was behind him: the noise and exclamations of cameramen and sound technicians setting up their equipment. Nothing to worry about. He was at work, where he'd said he would be. "Just called to say hello," she told him. A few days later, he left for Hawaii to work on the surf documentary. He'd travel to Brazil after that, and then Australia, and be away until shortly before their wedding.

And so it would go in their marriage. She'd be without Brock for days, weeks, possibly months at a time. Even if Brock weren't unfaithful, could she tolerate the loneliness? Was her mother right about husbands and wives needing to be physically together to stay together?

Maybe other couples did, Peggy concluded, but she was used to Brock's lifestyle.

She continued to spend her weekends in New Nineveh, keeping Miss Abigail, still bandaged and in a cast but long past convalescing in bed, entertained and out of trouble. Luke rarely came out of his study, except for meals, and Peggy was glad. The less she saw of him, the clearer it was that marrying Brock was the right decision.

Still, she couldn't get past her guilt over Miss Abigail.

"Luke will need you here every day once I'm gone," Luke's great-aunt announced one Saturday afternoon as she oversaw Peggy in the kitchen.

Peggy shook paprika into the casserole she was preparing, an old Sedgwick recipe. "You're not going anywhere."

"That boy wouldn't eat if he didn't have someone to make him supper. Now mix in the celery and two tablespoons of onion flakes, and then you'll put it in the casserole dish and top it with the bread crumbs."

Peggy knew better than to ask if Miss Abigail had considered using fresh onion instead of dried; she got the onion flakes from the spice cabinet. It was true: Miss Abigail took care of Luke as much as he took care of Miss Abigail. His great-aunt gave Luke direction and purpose and kept him in touch with his family history—a history Luke might claim to disdain, but which defined his every action. Luke's ancestors had surely displayed the same reserve, the same truculence and seeming inapproachability. You could see it in the portrait of Silas Sedgwick in the library. But the Sedgwick genes carried equal parts kindness, humor, and respect. Peggy measured and stirred her casserole, a little envious that Luke's whole life was here for him, while her own was fragmented, left behind in a succession of California tract homes.

"Luke says you aren't good for each other," Miss Abigail said.

Luke had been discussing her with his great-aunt? Peggy occupied herself spreading an even layer of bread crumbs over the casserole. Disturbed, a tiny bit flattered—she couldn't decide which she should feel. She settled on disgruntled. What did Luke mean, they weren't good for each other? She'd been a perfect wife.

Miss Abigail took a sherry glass from a cupboard. "I don't abide by all the modern foolishness about husbands and wives having to be friends. And Luke can be hard to like, with his brooding and moping. Nevertheless, what matters is, he cares for you."

"I don't think so." Peggy couldn't believe she was having this discussion.

"Hogwash, young lady. Put the casserole in the oven, please, and pour me a sherry."

Luke made an informal deal with Grant Atherton over hamburgers at the Nutmeg Coffee Shop, which had been a downtown fixture for over half a century. The business had recently relocated to Pilgrim Plaza, to a brand-new building done up to look like a fifties diner, with diamond-patterned chrome walls and red vinyl booths. Luke missed the original, shabby Nutmeg on the town green. It had been a genuine fifties diner.

For the formal deal, Luke put on his dark suit and parked the Volvo in the garage under one of the many glassy, mid-height office boxes that gave downtown Stamford, Connecticut, its ambitious bluster, as if it knew it couldn't compete with New York but was damn well going to give it the old college try. Atherton's office, on the ninth floor of the corporate headquarters of Budget Club International, looked out over a visual riot of shopping malls and I-95 and the railroad tracks and the wind-whipped, whitecapped Long Island Sound. Luke signed a contract, returned to New Nineveh, went up to his study, and stayed there for most of the next three days.

Each year at this time, Luke was reminded how quickly a New England winter could reduce his world, as freezing temperatures and layers of snow and ice confined him, and everyone, to their homes. This year, even without the snow, Luke's life seemed smaller than ever before. His great-aunt, his investments, his writing—there was nothing else. Except for the Fiorentinos, who stopped in two or three times a week to visit Abigail, he saw no one. Poker night had been temporarily suspended as its members left for ski vacations and winter homes. In years past Luke hadn't cared, but this year he thought it might have been good for him to leave the house once in a while.

He supposed he'd learned this from Peggy.

Peggy's appearance on weekends might have lifted his spirits, but he couldn't enjoy her company. Avoiding her was difficult—the freezing cold meant she, too, stayed at home, leaving only to accompany his great-aunt to the Stop & Shop or to church. "You don't need to take us places anymore," she told him. "I can drive Miss Abigail myself."

On a Friday in mid-February, he stepped out for a rare excursion to the post office. To his astonishment, the cold had disappeared. It was unseasonably, unreasonably warm. On the town green, the picketers were back, protesting in shirt-sleeves. A few birds chirped, as if it were spring. When Luke stepped up to the post office counter—refusing to capitulate to the dishonest weather, steadfastly wrapped in hat, gloves, and scarf—Jeff, the postmaster, crowed, "Nice day, huh?"

Sure—for May, Luke wanted to say.

"And I'm sure that'll all blow over soon." Jeff pointed in the direction of the green.

Luke nodded, not knowing what the postmaster was referring to.

"How's Peggy?" Jeff set Luke's roll of stamps on the counter. "I see her in church but not during the week. You keep her locked up in the house?" He chuckled, a big, hearty rumble that shook his burly chest. "Great girl, Peggy. But you knew that."

"I did. Do," Luke corrected himself.

Back on the green, he stood in the sun, sweating in his February clothing, idly watching the demonstrators. Norma Garrison and her husband, Mike, had moved to New Nineveh from New York after the terrorist attacks, seeking a safer life. They held "Protect Our Town" signs. The woman in the black cowboy boots was a writer, originally from Los Angeles, Luke thought. She held up a copy of the *Litchfield County Times*. And the owner of the Cheese Shoppe had an octagonal-shaped sign. When she marched back around so that the sign faced Luke, he almost exclaimed out loud. There, in five-inch-high white letters on a red background, was "STOP the Sedgwicks."

At home, Abigail was having tea with Annette Fiorentino. "...hasn't snowed all winter, and now this, and I don't like it one bit," his great-aunt was saying. "It's unnatural."

"I agree. How some people still doubt global warming is beyond me." Annette looked up. "Luke, what's the matter?"

Moments later, Luke and Annette were on Charity's Porch.

"I had no idea they were out there." Annette put her hands in the pockets of her faded jeans. "I guess they got excited, what with the warm day today and the article in the paper."

A spider was spinning its web in the corner of the screened-in porch. It was a futile exercise; the spider would die out here when the cold returned. "What article?"

"You didn't see the *County Times*?"

Luke hadn't. He rushed into the kitchen. The local weekly, which always arrived on Friday, lay unopened on the drainboard, with his own name looking up at him: SEDGWICK LEASES LAND TO BUDGET CLUB.

Luke had spent his whole life listening to his family tell him the only three times it was accceptable to have one's name in print were at birth, at marriage, and at death. He picked up the paper and read standing up:

> NEW NINEVEH—Four decades ago, plagued with financial woes and facing bankruptcy, William Elias "Bink" Sedgwick sold off all but 20 acres of his venerable family's real estate holdings, a stretch of farmland a mile west of the town green. Now, pending almost certain approval by the Planning and Zoning Commission, the remaining Sedgwick acreage will become home to a new superstore. Luke Silas Sedgwick IV has agreed to lease the land for 99 years to Budget Club, International...

If all the flues hadn't been sealed, Luke would have started a fire with this article, to ensure neither Peggy nor, worse, Abigail happened upon it. He made do with tearing the entire front page into confetti-size bits. He asked Annette, "Has Abby seen this? Does she know I've made this deal?"

"You haven't told her?"

"Did you say anything?" Luke persisted, and when it became clear Annette hadn't, he let himself relax slightly. "You have to stop the picketers," he told her.

"I'll go down there right away. How long do you need to break the news to your great-aunt? I'm sure they'll stop for a week or two."

"A week or two? I need you not to picket at all! You know me, Annette. Those people know me. I'm not some evil force out to destroy New Nineveh."

Annette touched his shoulder. "But that's what most of us think will happen if you put a Budget Club on your land."

"Luke? Annette?" It was Abby, wondering where they were.

Luke threw the torn newspaper into the garbage. "So you're going to keep picketing?"

"I'm sorry, Luke. I can't censor them. Please understand it's nothing personal. I hope we can still be good neighbors."

Luke nodded. In a small town like this, there was no sense in starting a feud.

"Oh, it's just..." Sharon Clovis leaned against a column for support and groped for the word.

"Spectacular." The saleswoman patted Sharon on the arm. "Now, don't cry. Watch the mascara."

Sharon blinked and smoothed her gold-buttoned knit jacket. Peggy was fascinated. She'd not realized how skinny Brock's stepmother's neck was. Sharon had the skinniest neck she had ever seen.

Peggy stood at the three-way mirror, unsure of what to do with her hands. Clasping them together, prayerlike, seemed wrong, as did crossing them over her chest. They dangled at her sides as if unconnected to the rest of her. Outside the reflected floor-to-ceiling windows, multitudes of New Yorkers shoved past one another in their rush to enjoy the nineteen-degrees-warmer-than-average Friday afternoon. Peggy seemed to be the only person in the world unsettled by the temperature.

The saleswoman joined Peggy on her gray-carpeted pedestal. "The fabric is exquisite. Eighteen yards of silk peau de soie, imported from France, not China, and light as a feather." She lifted Peggy's train and gave it an expert snap. It billowed up and settled back to earth. "And it's versatile. You could do cathedral wedding, garden wedding, downtown wedding, princess wedding."

In the mirror, Peggy watched the saleswoman and Sharon share a proprietary smile in triplicate and tried not to think about how hungry she was. Across the hushed room, another, younger bride preened in a beaded gown with a plunging neckline that ruled out any option besides strip club wedding. Peggy's dress was nice enough, she supposed, not too ornate, and she was weary of bridal boutiques. And time was ticking. As it was, she'd have to pay a rush fee to have the dress ready for June. She tugged the bodice farther up onto her chest and pressed her arms against her sides to keep it from slipping.

The saleswoman produced a silver clamp and used it to section off a few inches of fabric at the middle of Peggy's back. The bodice stretched taut across Peggy's chest. "There," she said. "How does that feel?"

Peggy wanted to ask if it was normal to feel nothing.

On the telephone a few hours after his talk with Annette Fiorentino, Luke received assurance from Wesley Buckle, the town's zoning commissioner, that ground breaking for the new store could begin after mud season, which was usually around April or May but this year seemed likely to happen early, Luke thought. He'd noticed that a number of trees had started to bud, and crocuses had pushed up through the soil. It was as if nature was fast-forwarding through winter.

Luke deposited his first check from Budget Club. The fact that the deal would go a long way toward shoring up the Sedgwick coffers failed to cheer him. He was only grateful the picketers had gone home. He could only hope that Angelo and Annette would talk sense into the demonstrators. With luck, Abby wouldn't find out there had been a group of people on the town green with "STOP the Sedgwicks" placards and he could break the news to her when the time was right.

His hope was short-lived. When he returned home from the bank, Ernestine Riga was speaking gravely to Abigail in the ladies' parlor. When he stopped in to greet the neighbor, he saw Abigail held a copy of the *County Times* with the article he'd destroyed; Ernestine must have brought it over. Abby was smiling, but her eyes were terrible. They said, *We'll discuss this in private, young man.*

Luke should have known better than to think Abby wouldn't find out on her own. The only surprise was that it had taken a few hours, not a few minutes.

On Saturday in New Nineveh, Peggy took Miss Abigail on their weekly grocery outing. Cal Seymour Jr., the third-generation owner of Seymour's, was leaving the Stop & Shop as the two came in. He looked right past Peggy as they passed. In the soup aisle, Peggy greeted a woman she recognized from church, who uttered a brief hello and excused herself. But at checkout, the cashier seemed thrilled to see her. "Don't worry, Mrs. Sedgwick. Lots of us who grew up here think it's time this town finally moved into the twenty-first century."

"What's going on?" Peggy asked Miss Abigail in the parking lot.

"You mean Luke didn't tell you, dear?"

When she got home, Peggy took the stairs two at a time, burst into the ballroom, and yelled, "What do you think you're doing?"

Luke looked nothing short of cornered.

"The green is already a ghost town, thanks to Pilgrim Plaza. And if that Budget Club goes in, it'll be the end of everything. Why shop at the Toggery when you can get cheap polo shirts at Budget Club? Why go to Luigi's when you can bring home frozen Budget Club pizza? Can't you understand? It's going on all across America, Luke—these big retailers marching into towns and cities and destroying them."

Luke had on a yellow oxford shirt. It was the first time in months she'd seen him without a sweater. With the freakish temperature, there was no need. "There's such a thing as progress," he said. He pushed up his sleeves as if he were too hot.

"It's not progress, it's greed. It's you trying to make a buck at the expense of an entire town. And it's exactly what's happening to my shop!" She caught a glimpse of herself in the mirror against the wall, surprised at how furious she looked. "Don't you care at all who you are and where you come from? Don't you realize there are almost no places like this left in America—places not overrun with chain stores? Don't you realize how lucky you are to live here?"

He looked unwell. His skin was dry, and there were hollows under his eyes, as if he'd been staying up all hours in front of his computer, not getting enough to eat, losing contact with the outside world. She was furious at herself for caring.

"The deal is done," he said. "Ground breaking begins in late spring. Or sooner."

"Do Annette and Angelo know this?"

"People were picketing yesterday afternoon. Annette got them to stop, but soon they'll be back out in full force. You should be prepared. They carry 'STOP the Sedgwicks' signs."

He seemed to be waiting for her to react, but she had nothing left to offer.

"I'm doing what's best for my family," he said eventually.

"Then I'm glad I won't be part of your family much longer."

She ran back down the stairs, the creaky third step screeching as she landed in the foyer. She left through the front door, running through the front gate and down the granite sidewalk to the Fiorentinos' black-shuttered white house next door, hammering their door with both fists until it swung open with Annette Fiorentino on the other side, her braid askew, her compassionate blue eyes scrunched with worry.

"I'm ready to join you," Peggy said, panting. "I'm ready to join the demonstration. Just tell me when you need me and I'll be there."

TWENTY-ONE

False Spring

Winter never returned. After a while, even those who'd been fretting about it soon gave in to unabashed pleasure at having dodged two more months of cold weather. In New York City, the daffodils bloomed in February instead of March, the tulips bloomed in March instead of April, and the city dwellers cheerfully put their snow boots and parkas in storage and brought out the spring coats and shoes that didn't usually emerge until after Easter. Peggy felt like the morose guest at a party.

"I feel like a traitor for saying this, but right now I don't mind." Bex stuffed her down coat into a bag for the dry cleaners. "I can't button this around me anymore, and I didn't want to have to buy a whole new one. Not that I need a coat anyway. Your father has the right idea, Peggy. I'm so hot I'd wear shorts if I didn't think people would faint from horror at my elephant ankles."

Bex had passed the first trimester, and the twins by all benchmarks were developing normally. At fourteen weeks, brimming with joy, Bex was announcing her pregnancy to customers, to the UPS guy, to anyone who would listen. She was already in maternity clothes, two or three sizes bigger than other women at her stage of pregnancy—publicly, definitively, proudly fertile. But she tired easily, and as she and

Peggy traipsed from empty retail space to empty retail space, trying to find a new home for their shop before the lease ran out, she had to rest every few minutes.

"I don't know why I'm dragging you all around," Peggy said, sighing, as they rejected yet another hole-in-the-wall with outrageous rent. "There isn't a single place on the Upper West Side we can afford, and it's all my fault." She couldn't help feeling she had killed their business by backing out of her deal with Luke. The ACME Cleaning Supply lease was set to expire the last day of May, and Peggy and Bex had yet to renew it. Without that Sedgwick House money, and with the competition from Bath, it was impossible to justify staying where they were, paying twice as much for the same space.

"It's not your fault. This city is too expensive. We working people can't afford it." Bex reached both hands behind her lower back to give herself a massage. "It's too bad you're not around weekends to go apartment shopping with Josh and me. Talk about depressing."

Bex was mistaken. Depressing was trying to explain to a ninety-one-year-old Yankee why you'd decided to demonstrate against her family on the town green. Peggy tried again and again to plead her position to Miss Abigail: "I mean no disrespect to you or Luke. But I know you can't approve of what Luke is doing with that land."

"I'd like my sherry now," was all the old woman would say.

Peggy spent four Saturdays marching, shouting slogans, and chanting until her voice gave out. She got stares—and a scowl or two—from plenty of passersby; the Realtors, especially, seemed to shoot daggers at the picketers marching past their offices. But just as many other people waved or nodded their approval. Debby Doff, owner of the Cheese Shoppe, brought the group samples—dabs of Brie on French bread or local cheddar with sliced apples—and Luigi, from Luigi's, gave out cans of soda. The shop owners understood, Peggy knew, that their livelihoods depended on keeping downtown vibrant.

But it wasn't easy for Peggy. In church, she could feel rows of eyes on her as she took her seat. She could imagine what people were thinking—that Peggy and Luke Sedgwick had turned against each other. Miss Abigail didn't seem aware of the whispers. Peggy began to think there might be a small silver lining in this apparently worsening dementia—if it prevented the old woman from being hurt. But then, Miss Abigail could be just being her usual, stiff-upper-lipped self.

"You have to tell her about the annulment," Peggy told Luke during one of their rare exchanges; she'd nearly bumped into him on the way back from brushing her teeth before bedtime. She was fully clothed, thank goodness. She'd learned her lesson after getting caught in her long johns.

Luke promised he would say something soon, but Peggy knew he was as reluctant to upset his great-aunt as she was. She let it go, hoping an opportune moment for the conversation would materialize. They had barely a month left until their annulment hearing, until this entire foolish endeavor would be behind her. She tried not to think of Miss Abigail, growing older, her health eventually fading, with only Luke to look after her; of what would become of the Sedgwick House; of Luke, free to be with whatever woman he chose.

On the last Saturday in March, Peggy was out picketing in the still too warm weather when a female voice spoke her name. She turned to see Liddy Hubbard, holding a leash to which was attached a graying golden retriever.

"Well, hi!" Peggy exclaimed, confused over why Liddy would drive an hour from Westport to New Nineveh to walk her dog. Just then, Peggy spotted Carrie and Creighton behind Liddy—nor did either one of them live anywhere near New Nineveh. For a moment she thought, *They've come to demonstrate.*

"Peggy, what are you doing?" There wasn't a trace of compassion in Liddy's thin, humorless mouth.

"Picketing, I guess," Peggy said stupidly. She waggled her "Save Our Town" sign. "See, we're protesting against the commercial interests who want to destroy New Nineveh's character to further their financial—"

Liddy narrowed her eyes. "We know what you're *doing.* What we don't understand is *why.*"

"People are talking." Carrie grimaced as a sudden cold gust ruffled her hair. "You're calling too much attention to yourself. Connecticut isn't a big state. Word gets around."

"Foolish names and foolish faces often appear in public places," Liddy interjected. "As my grandmother used to say."

"Exactly." Creighton, who had been patting the dog, stood back up and readjusted her headband—kelly green today, to match her grosgrain belt. "You're embarrassing your husband."

The snake of anxiety that had been slithering into Peggy's windpipe vanished—replaced by indignation. She set down her sign and led the trio away from the knot of demonstrators, toward the marble obelisk commemorating the New Nineveh soldiers lost in the Civil War. Peggy knew from Miss Abigail that the memorial included the names of three Sedgwicks.

She wished she had a coat. The temperature seemed to have dropped ten degrees in as many minutes.

"This isn't the sixties." Liddy buttoned up her jacket. "The hippie era ended for a reason, you know."

"It was tacky," Carrie said. "The polyester and the facial hair."

That was the problem with people who had everything, Peggy thought. They'd never had to fight for anything.

"I have a right to free speech," she insisted. "It's what this country was founded on. I'm not embarrassing Luke—not trying to, anyway. I just disagree with what he's doing."

"Listen." Liddy put her leash-free arm around Peggy's shoulders. "This isn't the sort of thing we would normally discuss, but, well, if you and Luke are having problems..."

Peggy was paralyzed with anger.

Liddy continued, "You know, Peggy, no marriage is perfect. I'll admit, Kyle and I have our differences now and then. But we don't parade those differences all over town."

Of course you don't, Peggy thought. *Not when you could have a couple of drinks and ignore it.* She wanted to defend herself, but what could she say, really? Besides, there seemed to be agitation among the demonstrators, who'd all set aside their signs and were huddled in a discussion. Peggy stopped listening to the preppy trio and tuned back in to her own group in time to hear Annette say, "That's it for today, folks. See you all tomorrow, weather permitting," and to discover that, at long last, snowflakes were falling.

"Luke!" Abigail shouted from downstairs. "Luke!"

Luke looked up from the poem in front of him. There was an almost agreeable sameness to Abby calling for him this way. He put down his pencil. A new piece of plaster dangled from the ceiling. For once, the house's decrepitude didn't bother him. It was almost endearing the way that piece of ceiling clung there tenaciously, defying gravity and time.

"Luke!" Abigail shouted as the staircase rattled.

Luke ran to the landing in time to see his great-aunt appear.

"What are you doing? You shouldn't be climbing—" He stopped himself.

Abigail's wrinkled cheeks were flushed with excitement. A mischievous sparkle lit her faded eyes.

"Winter is back," she said.

Peggy saw the two of them in Luke's study before they saw her. She started to ask how Miss Abigail had gotten up the stairs but forgot the question as she watched them confer together at the computer.

"You see, that's the storm coming in." Luke, in the straight-backed chair Peggy remembered from his bedroom, pointed to the display.

"What's this?" Miss Abigail was in Luke's desk chair, her tiny body craned toward the screen.

"If I click on it, it shows the snowfall over the next few hours. See? By three it will be steady, and by five it will be heavy. You can get all that on the Internet."

Miss Abigail snorted. "Or you could just look out the fool window."

Peggy laughed, and the two raised their heads, noticing her. "That was funny," she said, giggling. "Good one, Miss Abigail."

"Humor was not my intention, young lady." But instead of the glared rebuke Peggy had expected, a smile spread across Miss Abigail's face. "It's wonderful to be in the ballroom again. Mother and Daddy had such parties here. The chandeliers sparkled, and the musicians would play, and it was a fairyland." Miss Abigail hummed a tuneless melody.

"It's nice to see you in such a good mood." Peggy, too, could feel happiness stealing over her. As long as she was in this house, she was safe—from the prying comments of Liddy, Carrie, and Creighton; from the controversy over Luke's land; from the fact that the business she'd poured her life into was withering away. No wonder Miss Abigail loved the house so much. And, Peggy supposed, she could understand, too, why Luke might yearn to leave behind this cocoon of comfort to stretch his wings. Didn't everyone struggle between the desire for the familiar and the equal desire to break free? *Try to think what it is you're really anxious about,* Birch had said in that long-ago meditation class. Was it just that Peggy still hadn't found the right balance? Was this why she'd always been so eager to get married, as if marriage were the sole promise of safety in a cold, stormy world?

Miss Abigail was struggling to get out of her chair. Luke, still demonstrating the Internet's many weather-measuring capabilities, wasn't paying attention. "May I help?" Peggy asked, knowing what the answer would be: *Nonsense.*

"Yes, thank you." Miss Abigail fluttered her tiny hand onto Peggy's arm, and Peggy supported her as she rose slowly from Luke's desk chair. It was the first time the Yankee woman had ever needed her, and Peggy was glad to be able to help at long last. "It's time to start dinner," Miss Abigail continued. "Peggy, would you take me down the stairs?"

Their voices and footsteps faded, and then all was quiet. Quieter than quiet, hushed by the snow now falling in goose-feather flakes. His great-aunt was right, of course. Who needed a computer when one could simply look outside? Luke stood near the half-moon window, winter cold stealing in through the panes despite his best efforts to seal it out. The false spring was over. One needed to look no further than the New England sky, pregnant with snow.

It was time to get ready.

"What's Luke doing?" Peggy asked. For the past fifteen minutes he'd been passing by the kitchen, descending into the basement and emerging again with tarnished brass lanterns, plastic jugs of kerosene, and old shoeboxes with the stubs of candles. "He's acting like the world is about to end."

"There's a nor'easter blowing in." Miss Abigail surveyed the back garden out the kitchen window. Nearby, Quibble wove his black body around and between the table legs.

Something wasn't right. Nothing about this day felt normal, not the unexpected change of weather, not Luke's manic energy, not Miss Abigail's unusually good mood, not Quibble rubbing against Peggy's calves agitatedly, as if there were nothing the least bit odd about his being out and about at this time of day. Peggy opened the fridge. It was virtually empty. In all her focus on the demonstrations, she'd forgotten about her weekly trip to the market with Miss Abigail. There was a carton of eggs and, in the crisper, what looked like a bag of celery.

A clatter sounded in the basement, as if Luke had dropped something. The cat jumped two vertical feet in the air and streaked out of the room.

"Damn!" Luke cursed from down the stairs.

"Do you suppose he's all right?" Peggy started to get up, thinking she should offer him some assistance, but Miss Abigail touched her elbow.

"Let him be. He needs the distraction."

Distraction from what? Peggy didn't ask. She knew what Miss Abigail meant.

"This hullabaloo on the green is bothering him, dear. The Sedgwicks don't enjoy attention. It isn't in our nature."

"I have a right to free speech," Peggy responded, for the second time that day. "Forgive me, Miss Abigail, but this is what your own ancestors died for in the Revolutionary War—so future generations could speak their minds freely, even when it was difficult and painful. This is no easier for me than it is for you, or Luke. But I can't sit by while Luke ruins New Nineveh in the name of progress. This place is too special for me not to at least try and—"

Luke was passing through the hallway again.

"—change Luke's mind," Peggy finished when his footsteps were far enough down the hall. Self-conscious, she opened the refrigerator again. "How about scrambled eggs?"

Miss Abigail turned from the window. "You're a real Sedgwick, Peggy."

Peggy set the eggs on the counter.

"Our family's women have a long history of speaking their minds and standing up for what they believed in. Had Charles not passed away, I would have married him even if it meant losing my inheritance. Sedgwick women aided slaves on the Underground Railroad and marched at Seneca for the right to vote. Elizabeth Coe Sedgwick, whose brooch I gave you, was a vocal abolitionist. It nearly killed Josiah at first, but he came around." Miss Abigail grinned. "If you ask me, Sedgwick men have always been attracted to uppity women. Clearly my nephew is no exception."

Was Miss Abigail having one of her episodes? Peggy wasn't sure—and was blushing so badly, she wanted to hide in the refrigerator. She tugged at the celery in the vegetable drawer, but it was wedged in tightly, and she gave up. Even Miss Abigail couldn't want celery in her scrambled eggs.

Luke clomped into the kitchen, a dusting of snow in his hair. "The lamps are filled, the flashlights have fresh batteries, the shovels are in the mudroom, and the cars are in the garage. Anything I've forgotten, Abby?"

"Well," Miss Abigail said, "you never told me Peggy wasn't a Yankee."

Luke and Peggy stared at each other. It was the first time he could remember meeting her gaze in weeks. She was so pretty, he thought, before a less affectionate conclusion intruded. *You told her?* he mouthed. Peggy widened her eyes and mouthed back, *No.*

Luke couldn't imagine what to do. All he knew was Abby was wearing her "don't take me for a delusional old lady" look.

"Aren't you two going to explain what's going on?" Despite her stern words, Abby's tone was mild, almost amused.

This was the perfect time to tell her. Not just that Peggy wasn't a New Nineveh Adams, but about the annulment. About all of it—their accidental marriage in Las Vegas, their ridiculous plan to finance her long-term care by selling the house.

"Abby..." Luke looked at Peggy long and hard, willing her to understand. "Peggy and I have a number of things to discuss with you. Things about our marriage—the circumstances behind it, and decisions we've made about it." He glanced at Peggy for confirmation.

In the window behind her, snow pelted the ground. Peggy would be lucky to get home tomorrow, Luke thought; if the nor'easter kept up at this pace—the news was predicting a blizzard—it could take the snowplow crews all day to clear the roads.

Finally, Peggy nodded. "Maybe we should move to the den. It's more comfortable there."

Luke couldn't believe his luck. "Great idea, Peggy. How about it, Abby?"

His great-aunt peered into him. Not *at* him; it was as if she could see through his skin into his muscles, bones, bloodstream, into the DNA at the center of each cell.

"On second thought," she said, "I don't need to know right this minute."

"It would be best if you did," Luke pressed.

"He's right." Peggy put her hand on Abby's arm. "It's time."

"Nonsense," Abby declared. "It's time for dinner."

The meal was festive. Peggy made eggs, and Luke fixed Abigail her sherry, and Abby set out the family china, and the three ate as darkness descended on the garden outside, and the wind moaned, and snow collected in U-shaped drifts against the steamy windowpanes.

Peggy's skin gleamed golden in the overhead light. "Isn't it late in the season for a freak snowstorm?"

"It's not unheard of, dear. One year it snowed on Memorial Day weekend. Nineteen seventy-seven. Remember, Luke?" Abigail chuckled. "You and the Hubbard boy went sledding on your mother's silver tea tray."

Luke laughed aloud at the forgotten memory. The confession he'd so urgently wanted to make to his great-aunt half an hour earlier no longer seemed necessary. Why spoil the moment? He and Peggy still had time until the annulment was final. They had two more weeks....

Only two more weeks.

He pushed away his plate. Peggy was laughing, too, as Abby embellished the sledding story. This time next year, Peggy would be married to someone else, with an entirely new life, while he, Luke, remained in the life he had, except without Peggy.

Without the woman he loved.

Because, heaven help him, he loved her.

I love her, he repeated to himself with wonderment as the kitchen light blinked off and then on again like a heart fluttering to life, so quickly that he was sure he was the only one who'd noticed it had blinked at all. *I love her long underwear. I love that she found the only damn apple left in that orchard. I love that she's afraid of the basement but pretends not to be. I love that she has the guts to picket against me and that all the people in town like her better than they like me—*

The house went dark.

"Oh!" Peggy exclaimed.

"It'll come back on in a minute." Abby sounded unconcerned, but she and Luke both knew if the storm had already knocked out the power lines, there was little that could be done about it until at least tomorrow morning. "Meantime, Luke will light us a fire," she said.

Luke goggled at his great-aunt in the dark. "Abby, the flues have been shut for years."

"Then open one. Peggy is cold. She's been cold since the first day she came here. How about the library? I've always been partial to a fire in the library."

Luke got up and groped along the drainboard until his hand connected with the flashlight he'd left there. He flicked it on and set it in the center of the table, where it threw off an embracing circle of yellow light.

"It's all right, Miss Abigail," Peggy said. "I'm not cold anymore. I think my blood has gotten thicker."

"Nonsense. Luke, fetch the firewood. While you're at it, bring up that port you've been hiding. I don't know what you've been saving it for."

"You weren't the one who hid the port?" Luke was surprised. "Then how do you know about it?"

Abby tilted her head to scrutinize him. It must have been

an optical illusion, a trick of the flashlight, that made her appear no older than she did in her portrait in the den. "I know everything that goes on in this house," she said.

Twenty minutes later, a fire was crackling in the library. Luke heated the family port tongs and used them to cleanly break off the neck of the bottle underneath the cork. He decanted the port into a crystal vessel, the dusky scent of vanished time coiling up from the amber liquid. "We should drink it right away," he announced to no one in particular; Abby and Peggy seemed lost in their separate thoughts.

From her chair, his great-aunt gazed through the flickering shadows at the mantel portrait of Silas Ebenezer Sedgwick. "I believe I'll go upstairs," she said dreamily. "It's been a long day, and I'm tired."

Peggy stood with her back to the fire. "But what about the port?"

"I've never cared for port, dear."

Luke moved forward, but Abigail held out a hand to keep him at his distance and stood on her own. She nodded at him, and he gave her the flashlight, knowing better than to try to escort her to her room. Luke's heart swelled with admiration for his great-aunt—her resilience, her strength. *She's the last of her kind,* he thought.

Peggy, too, looked as if she would like to reach out to Abby, to touch her arm or pat her hunched shoulder, but she held back, Luke suspected, out of respect for Abby's reserve and simply said, "See you in the morning, Miss Abigail."

Abigail paused, as if to speak. Then she turned and made her way down the corridor, her fading footsteps punctuated by a faint protest from the squeaky step as she climbed the front staircase to her bedroom, before the darkness swallowed up the sound.

"Did something seem not right to you?" Peggy asked once she was sure Miss Abigail was far enough away.

Luke blinked as if waking from a dream—as if, Peggy thought, he'd been mesmerized by the flames. "What do you mean, not right?"

"I mean... It's not important." She'd been about to say everything about this day had been surreal, as if she, too, had seen the day's events from inside a dream instead of experiencing them as they'd unfolded, were unfolding, right now. In a giddy, irrational flash, it occurred to her that all of this might be a dream; and if she concentrated hard enough, she would wake up with Bex in their Las Vegas hotel room and return to New York City to apologize to Brock for giving him that stupid marriage ultimatum, and life would be just as it was before she'd gotten herself into this mess... and yet, she was aware it wasn't a dream, and furthermore, she didn't want it to have been.

Luke poured port into two cut-crystal glasses and reached one out to her. When she took it, their fingers brushed, and she drew back in surprise. Had he meant to touch her? She stole a peek at him, but his face was inscrutable in the half-light of the fire. Outside were darkness and the unseen storm.

"We should toast." Luke's voice was quietly gruff. "It doesn't seem right to drink this without ceremony."

She held the gleaming glass, hesitating. "I feel bad that you opened it. This is hardly the perfect time."

"Maybe Abby's right, and it's as good a time as any." Luke brought his glass to his nose and inhaled.

Peggy did the same, but the port's caramel aroma gave up no secrets. She said, "We really should prepare ourselves. It's been waiting so long. It could be terrible."

"It could." Luke raised his glass and tipped it toward her, as in a toast. "Or it could be every bit as good as we've imagined."

He touched his glass to hers, and she let herself fall into the complex depths of his eyes and understood he was no longer talking about the port.

She looked away, her heart racing, her airways narrowing with a feeling that wasn't anxiety, and sipped. And swallowed. And, when she was sure her face wouldn't betray her emotions, looked up. "Mmm."

Luke was taking his second sip of port. He held it in his mouth, then swallowed. "Hmm."

She drank again, the thick, flat liquid coating her throat. "Mmm-hmm."

"What do you think?" He was surveying her intently, as if all things hinged on her opinion of the Sedgwick port.

She smiled at him in a way that hopefully gave the impression of sincerity, took another sip, and swallowed it. "It's..." She was at a loss for words. "I—" She coughed. "I like it."

"Really?" He smiled back at her, a dazzling, lopsided, endearing smile that rendered her barely able to remember her own name. "Because I say it's swill."

She burst out laughing. She set the Sedgwick crystal onto a side table and draped herself against a bookshelf, giggling helplessly. Luke, too, began to laugh, with a depth and commitment she'd not heard in all their months together, and the more he laughed, the harder she laughed, until the two of them were clutching their sides and gulping for air as the fire popped and crackled and cast shadows across the portrait of Silas Ebenezer Sedgwick so that the great patriarch himself seemed to muster a smile at the scene below; to observe with lenient eyes as the family's last hope pulled his wife of convenience into a kiss from which Silas, had he been able, would have averted his eyes. But Peggy wasn't thinking about Silas Ebenezer Sedgwick. She wasn't thinking of picketers, or soulless superstores, or disapproving preppy wives; of ACME Cleaning Supply and its precarious grip on profitability; of lease negotiations or wedding dresses—or, least of all, of her fiancé. She surrendered to Luke's embrace, to his soft (so impossibly soft) lips, to the sweet roughness of his hands unbuttoning first his own Toggery corduroys and then hers and pulling her down with him onto the shopworn rug in front of the fireplace, as she tried with trembling hands to take off his sweater, and the frayed oxford shirt underneath, and the faded polo underneath that, until she looked up in frustration.

"How many layers do you have *on*?"

"It's a Yankee thing," he whispered, and kissed her again, hugging her to him and wrapping his long legs around her as they proved to each other, at long last, that something longed for and anticipated could indeed be better than either could have expected.

TWENTY-TWO

Of all the beds in the world, none could be as sublime as this. The sheets were silky, the pillows soft, the covers cozy and protective. Peggy stretched luxuriously, turned from her left side to her right, and, when she felt ready, opened her eyes.

Watery gray light trickled in through the snow-plastered windowpanes as snow continued to fall, tranquilly now. The world was otherwise still. Peggy recalled the line from Robert Frost: "The sweep / Of easy wind and downy flake."

Asleep next to her, Luke looked as he had the first morning she'd seen him: His chest—bare this time—rose and fell with his breathing, his lips were parted slightly, his reddish lashes fluttered as his eyes moved beneath his closed lids. It was all so familiar, she thought, curling her body into Luke's. This scene, and the fit of this man's body against hers, both now and last night. She shivered involuntarily, remembering their lovemaking, and then the full impact of what she had done hit her.

She'd slept with Luke.

She'd betrayed Brock and hadn't thought of him once as she'd done so.

And—her fingertips went cold, her lungs threatened to collapse—she had officially put her annulment in jeopardy. She and Luke had consummated their marriage, and there was nothing to keep Luke from telling that to the judge, if he wanted to cause trouble for her. She imagined having to call off her wedding to Brock, cancel her wedding dress order, unbook the church. If she was lucky, Brock might agree to reschedule the wedding for next year or the year after, once Peggy had gotten a full divorce—she could still file for divorce, couldn't she, even if the annulment could no longer be granted? But she couldn't imagine Brock forgiving her once he learned what a conniving liar she was, not just a woman who'd had an affair, but one who'd had an affair with a man to whom she'd secretly been married for months.

Peggy slipped out of Luke's bed, dressed quickly in last night's clothes, and tiptoed to her own room, hoping Luke wouldn't wake before she was able to get to her car and drive away. Safely in her own room, she called Bex.

"You did?" Bex started to laugh. "Really? Padma," she called, "you owe me twenty bucks!"

"Peggy slept with Luke?" Peggy heard Padma shout. "Woo-hoo!"

Peggy was horrified. "Bex, are you at the store?"

"Where else would I be at noon on a Sunday?" Bex answered. "Not that it matters. Thanks to the snow there's no one on the street. I was just about to send Padma home."

It was noon? Good grief, Peggy thought, she and Luke had made Miss Abigail miss church. Mortified at the thought of Miss Abigail sitting alone in the kitchen, no doubt aware of exactly what had happened last night, Peggy told Bex she'd see her at the apartment later.

"You'd better look outside."

Peggy drew aside one of her room's lace curtains.

The world had turned black and white overnight. Snow lay in thick white stripes on the bare black branches of the Sedgwick maple, which stood out, eerily beautiful, against the white gray sky. Main Street was entombed in snow; the black-shuttered white houses along it were heaped with snow; the Sedgwick front yard had disappeared. Peggy couldn't see the garage on Luke's side of the house, but she knew that the driveway leading to it would be buried as well.

"Looks like I have some shoveling to do," she told Bex, and hung up. There would be no way to get her car otherwise; no way to get home. She tiptoed down the front staircase, carefully avoiding the squeaky step, thinking she and Luke really ought to fix it, wondering why they hadn't thought to do so on any of the weekends they'd spent nailing down every other loose board in the house.

Well, the stair would have to be Luke's to fix now. She would not be coming back to New Nineveh until the court hearing in April. She couldn't face him any more than she could face the thought of what she'd done. She would tell Miss Abigail about the annulment today, whether Luke wished her to or not.

Miss Abigail wasn't in the kitchen. She wasn't in the ladies' parlor, still waiting, two hours past meeting time, in her Sunday clothing with her hands folded. She wasn't in the den or the library—Peggy could barely look into that room, at the decanter and glasses that still held the undrinkable port, without going weak at the memory of last night. She carried the glasses and decanter into the kitchen and set them on the drainboard. It was odd—there was no used teabag, no cup in its usual spot. The kitchen was undisturbed, as if Miss Abigail hadn't eaten at all today. Where could she have gone without breakfast or lunch?

What if she'd gotten it into her head to shovel the driveway?

"Miss Abigail!" Peggy dashed back down the stairs and into the mudroom, where shovels stood at the ready. Had the old woman taken one and gone out into the cold? Peggy yanked at the mudroom door, which opened toward her with a slide of snow onto the slate floor. "Miss Abigail?" she yelled into the monochrome garden, but nobody had come this way; the snow was untainted by footprints. Peggy ran to the front of the house and opened the main door. There were no footprints here, either. Calmer, she climbed the stairs to the second floor. Miss Abigail would be in her bedroom. Why hadn't she thought of that in the first place?

She knocked on Miss Abigail's door. "It's me. Are you in there?"

No one answered. She knocked and called again and then opened the door a crack. And there was Miss Abigail lying in bed, facing her, an amused smile on her lips as if she were about to share her deepest secret.

"There you are!" Peggy smiled back at her, still breathing heavily from running through the house, still too glad to have found Miss Abigail to think it strange that she was in bed this late. Peggy flipped the switch near the door—the room was dark—but the ceiling light didn't come on. "I'm sorry we didn't make it to church. But I'm not sure there's a meeting today, anyway. The power is still out, and have you looked outside? We're completely snowed in! Is that why you decided to stay in bed? I bet this is the first time in your life you've slept past noon."

Miss Abigail continued to smile.

"By the way, the port? You didn't miss anything. I'm sorry to say, not everything improves with age. It's a shame, but it was fun trying it." Was that why Miss Abigail was smiling? Had she suspected as much all along?

There was no answer. It was as if the old woman were in a trance.

"Are you all right?" Apprehensive, Peggy tiptoed up to the bed. "Can I get you anything? Are you not well today?"

He should have known. Luke sighed and rolled over. It was the second time in his life he had awoken full of peace and anticipation, thinking Peggy was next to him, only to discover she had gone. He had hoped to put his arms around her, to make love to her again. He wanted to tell her they belonged together. He wanted, using any and all measures necessary, including pleading or asserting his husbandly prerogative, to persuade her to call off the annulment. *We haven't been married very long*, he would tell her, an appeal to her common sense. *Let's give it more time*. He'd wanted to do and say all of these things before the day and its responsibilities intruded, before the magic of their night together had faded away. But, he reassured himself, dressing quickly in last night's wood-smoky clothing, it wasn't too late. Surely he could still take Peggy aside this morning and say his piece.

"Luke!"

His name rocketed toward him.

"Luke!"

His hopes soared again. Peggy was calling for him. It wasn't too late.

And then he realized she wasn't calling, she was shrieking.

He knew his great-aunt was gone before he touched her still, bloodless cheek. He didn't know what to do next. Dully, he dialed the Fiorentinos, and within minutes, Annette and Angelo had waded through what had to be waist-deep drifts in their front yard and were in Abby's bedroom, snow still caked on their jeans. Angelo helped Luke cover Abby with a clean white sheet, and then went out to shovel the Sedgwick House front path, while Annette spoke in low tones on Luke's cell and Peggy wept quietly in the corner. Luke was desperate to catch her eye, to calm her with strength he knew it was his duty to show, but she wouldn't look at him. Luke knew she was avoiding him on purpose.

And he was ashamed for thinking about last night while Abigail Agatha Sarah Sedgwick lay dead.

For Peggy, the afternoon passed slowly, excruciatingly, in hushed words and cups of undrunk stovetop coffee and untouched sandwiches from Annette, who'd traversed the snowy garden, back and forth, bringing provisions and supplies. As dusk fell, Peggy was sitting alone in the ladies' parlor, crying over the tea rose bath products she'd brought Miss Abigail, which she'd found unopened in Miss Abigail's bathroom, when Annette came and put an arm around her shoulders.

"Listen," she said, and Peggy tuned in to the thunderous scraping she'd barely registered coming from a distance outside. "The snowplows are nearing Main Street. It should be clear within the hour."

Soon, Peggy knew, people would come and take Miss Abigail away.

She called Brock. She longed for the familiar sound of his voice. She caught up with him in a hotel in Victoria, Australia. Peggy wondered momentarily if he was surrounded by blondes in bikinis, then concluded she had too much else to contend with to worry about it. "I miss you," she said. "I really wish you were here right now."

"Me too, Pegs." Brock said his good-byes; he was due downstairs for breakfast. Peggy next dialed Bex, who offered sympathy and counseled Peggy to stay and comfort Luke as long as he needed her to.

"Trust me. He doesn't need comforting. The man is made of stone."

"Stay anyway. You don't want to come back here and face the reality of our failing business."

Peggy hadn't thought she could feel worse. "It's that bad?"

"I finished the bookkeeping, which was easy because we had no customers today. We've officially had the most dismal first quarter ever."

Peggy returned downstairs. Ernestine and Stuart Riga, the Fiorentinos, and Lowell Mayhew were all in the grand parlor in their snow boots, speaking to Luke in hushed tones. In typical New Nineveh fashion, the news had traveled quickly. The visitors would have had to hike through the snow to get here.

A solemn Mayhew took her aside. "I'm sorry for your loss. She was a remarkable lady, and I know you made her happy."

Peggy started to cry again.

Mayhew fumbled in his pocket. "You just take your time, and when you're ready, you and Luke should bring in the will, and we'll all go over it together. There's no rush." He produced a handkerchief and held it out to Peggy.

She twisted it in her hands, wanting to wipe her face but not knowing what she would do with the hanky once she had. "I have no right to this house. We never even told her about the annulment. If we had, she would have gone back to her old will. I was going to break the news to her this morning, but—" She cut herself off with a sob.

"The agreement was you were to remain married for a year or until Miss Abigail's demise. Legally you've met those conditions. You may inherit her estate as outlined in the will." Mayhew chuckled sadly. "Provided you can find it."

Had Peggy been coherent, had she cared about anything beyond wanting Miss Abigail back, she might have asked the lawyer what he meant. As it was, two uniformed men had just arrived with a gurney, and she followed Luke to the foyer to escort them to Miss Abigail's room. But the men said it was fine; there was no need to go upstairs again, they would find their own way.

Peggy couldn't help judging Luke's demeanor. He was relaxed, serene, impassive—just as he'd been that first day in Lowell Mayhew's office. Just as he'd sounded over the phone New Year's Eve, when he'd effortlessly agreed to separate, as if their marriage, friendship—however one might describe it—had been meaningless. And now Miss Abigail was gone, and even that didn't seem to matter.

"Don't you care?" Peggy hissed to Luke as the men navigated the gurney around the bend in the staircase. "Don't you see what we've done? In one night, we ruined everything."

"She didn't die because we slept together, Peggy," Luke said with uncharacteristic directness. He didn't make his hands into fists and put them in his pockets. He didn't slide his glasses onto his forehead and rub his eyes, didn't exhibit any of the telltale behaviors Peggy now understood signaled his discomfort. As far as she could tell, he felt nothing about anything. Bex was right. Repressed, withholding, unemotional—*emotionless*—the stereotype fit Luke.

"You are the coldest human being I've ever met in my life." She stalked back to the grand parlor with Luke behind her, grief rolling over her in terrible, relentless waves, along with the knowledge that her life in New Nineveh had at last come to an end. She would likely never see these people again. Cowardly as she knew it was, she couldn't face saying goodbye to them. Explaining what had become of her would have to be Luke's problem, too.

After a time, the two men in uniform came down the new staircase. Miss Sedgwick had died peacefully of natural causes in her sleep, they assured Luke. They walked the gurney toward the front foyer and had nearly lifted it across the threshold when Peggy remembered something.

"Stop," she said. "This isn't right."

She led the men back to the door in the grand parlor, the coffin door. She opened it. More snow tumbled in; the drift was chest-deep. "We'll have to shovel it out," she told them.

"No, Peggy," Luke said. "That will take too long."

"So be it." Peggy was determined. "Miss Abigail was a Sedgwick. And this is the only way a Sedgwick leaves this house."

TWENTY-THREE

Mud Season

Late March snow, no matter how ferocious its arrival, tended to depart quickly, and the vast drifts that had paralyzed the town dwindled rapidly into dense, icy islands on lawns and roadsides. Even before the roads and sidewalks were clear, the condolence calls began, and Luke went through the motions as every person he had ever met came through the house with casseroles and sympathy until he had lost his appetite for both. He waited for an uninterrupted moment with Peggy, a chance to tell her all the things he'd wanted to for so long, but the morning after the funeral, he awoke to discover she had left for good, her room bare except for Elizabeth Coe Sedgwick's brooch and a brief note on the dresser: "I'll see you at the hearing." He left messages on her cell phone, asking her to please call him, but she didn't.

They met at the courthouse two weeks later, on what turned out to be the first day of a week of torrential April rain that would hammer away the last of the ice heaps and leave all of New England knee-deep in mud. It was in this downpour that Luke said good-bye to Peggy for what he knew would be the last time, after they had both perjured themselves and testified that they had not consummated the marriage, and the judge pronounced the annulment final: The marriage no longer existed, had never existed, at least in the eyes of the state.

Afterward, Luke walked Peggy to her car, rain dripping from his hair, his fingers wrapped around Elizabeth's brooch, which he had put in his pocket. "Mayhew and I are going to his office to discuss the will. You should come."

Peggy looked across the green to Mayhew's office and, as he'd expected, shook her head.

"We need to get a plan together, too, to sell the house," he persisted. "It would be good to get it on the market soon, so the summer people can see it."

"Whatever you think is best," Peggy said, her voice flat.

Luke was glad he'd brought the brooch. He took it from his pocket and held it out to Peggy, hoping she would take it and that when she did, she would let her hand linger in his.

She didn't move.

"Abby would want you to keep it."

"It belongs to the family. I'm not family anymore." Black rivulets of eye makeup flowed down Peggy's cheeks—rain, Luke knew, not tears. Peggy had not cried since the day they'd discovered Abby—not at the funeral; not afterward, when Abby's casket was lowered into the Sedgwick plot at New Nineveh Cemetery; not during the condolence calls, where she never let on she was anything but Luke Sedgwick's steadfast, capable wife. After nearly seven months as a Sedgwick, Peggy Adams, overemotional New Yorker, had turned into the consummate WASP.

It was a shame.

The rain fell. Peggy gave Luke a long look, and he knew the time to tell her all he'd left unspoken had passed. "At least take the brooch."

"I can't."

She got into the car. Luke remained on the sidewalk in the rain, watching her go, hoping she might look back, knowing she wouldn't.

It was fitting that her last visit to New Nineveh would be on a day as dreary and stormy as the day of her first visit. Peggy turned the windshield wipers to top speed and tried to brush away the rainwater that had collected in the driver's seat as she'd gotten inside her final rented-car-of-the-week. At the stoplight, she looked up Main Street one last time. Soon some new family, no doubt wealthy New Yorkers longing to play country-house on the weekend, would buy the Sedgwick House and fill it with televisions and blaring music. They would outfit the kitchen with status appliances and granite countertops, and install showers in the bathrooms and hire an exterminator to kill the mice, and stop off at Budget Club on the way back to the city Sunday evenings to buy bulk laundry detergent and flats of diet soda. Luke would move who knew where, free of the Sedgwick burdens. Would he someday regret giving up the house? Peggy peeked into the rearview mirror. He was still in front of the courthouse, a lone figure in the rain, newly unburdened, soon to be independently wealthy again. Peggy guessed there was no regret. She only hoped he'd find a good home for Miss Abigail's cat.

Mayhew emerged from the courthouse as Luke lost sight of Peggy's car. "You ready?" Luke asked, eager to stop dwelling and put his mind to something practical.

"If you're up to it."

Luke nodded his assent, and the two sloshed across the green to Mayhew's office, where Geri greeted Luke and asked for Peggy. "Where has she been? I haven't seen her since the funeral, poor dear."

Luke walked around behind the desk and took both of

Geri's freckled hands in his. He had to start somewhere, he supposed. "Peggy and I have split up. She's gone for good. I wish it weren't the case, but it is."

He watched Geri's eyes well up.

Stay strong. You're a Sedgwick, Luke instructed himself. He had let down not just himself, but the entire community. The news about Peggy and him would be around town by the end of the day.

Mayhew cleared his throat and patted his secretary on the shoulder. "Luke, let's go into my office. I presume you brought it?" He waited, as if expecting Luke to produce something from inside his slicker.

"Brought what?" All Luke had was Elizabeth's brooch.

"The will," Mayhew clarified.

"But you have one on file. Don't you?"

Luke sat at the kitchen table, his head throbbing, his stomach growling. It was three o'clock in the morning and there was nowhere else to look. After five sixteen-hour days of turning over every last metaphoric stone in this house, pulling out every drawer, turning back every rug, peering under every cushion and between every mattress, there was nothing left to do but concede defeat. The only copy of Abby's new will, which his great-aunt had apparently insisted on taking home with her for safekeeping against Mayhew's counsel, had vanished into thin air. And without it, without this updated version that gave Luke and Peggy co-ownership of the Sedgwick House, Luke knew, the previous version would prevail. The version Mayhew had tried to warn him about months ago at Seymour's. The version leaving the house and everything in it, all of Abigail Agatha Sarah Sedgwick's earthly possessions, to a single beneficiary who, at the moment, was padding silently across the drainboard.

"I salute you, friend," Luke said to Quibble. "It's all yours."

Quibble's yellow eyes glowed in the reflected light. He leapt to the floor and darted from the room.

It was all unfolding as it should. Luke didn't want to live in this house, had never wanted to, and now wouldn't be able to. Abby's will had seen to that: It called for Mayhew to hire a caretaker, using funds from the Sedgwick Family Trust—someone to come in every day, feed Quibble, and see to it the house wasn't overtaken with cobwebs and dust. Abby hadn't forgotten Luke, though. "To my devoted nephew, Luke Silas Sedgwick IV, I bequeath my box with the star, so he may be free to pursue his poetry and live where he wishes," she had written in the will. Luke had been moved by the gesture. The box didn't exist, but she had recognized his desires and had done her best to grant them.

His stomach growled again. When was the last time he'd eaten? Luke opened the refrigerator, but he had long since gone through the casseroles, and the shelves were bare: a bachelor's fridge. He remembered having seen celery in the vegetable crisper; it might still be good.

The drawer was stuck, as if somebody had tried to cram it with too much food. Luke tugged and tugged at the bag of celery. It took some doing, but he managed to get the bag out—if only because the celery had rotted. So much for that. He threw the celery in the garbage and went back to close the drawer, but there was something else inside, a brown paper bag.

Luke opened the bag and took out a small jewelry box.

It was old, made of black leather dry and cracked with age.

"Star Jewelers" was stamped on the lid in gold letters.

Luke wouldn't allow himself to hope. He spoke aloud into the kitchen. "The box." It had to be. A small box with "star" on top. Almost exactly as Abby had described.

He opened the lid a crack, and something gleamed. He lifted it all the way and beheld what was inside.

It was a platinum engagement ring with a tiny, delicate sapphire set off by two diamond chips. Charles's gift, Luke knew, to Abby. Elegant and simple, just as she would have wanted. Charles would have had to save for it for years.

And, though Luke was hardly a jewelry expert, worth two or three thousand dollars at most.

The inheritance.

His inheritance.

"On the bright side, you said you were sick of soap." Bex placed a "50% Off" placard next to their soap pyramid and returned to the chair in which she now spent most of her workday, resting her hands on her belly. At twenty-one weeks, the twins were kicking constantly. Bex said it was like hosting soccer practice in her uterus.

Now she held a bar of wasabi-ginger soap and waved it at Peggy. "You'll never have to smell me again," she made it say in a squeaky voice.

Peggy didn't laugh, but she knew they were making the correct choice—the only choice—by closing the store. There was no money left, no way to save it, no new location they could afford. And they'd had a good run. So many small shops didn't last more than a few months, let alone a decade.

She hadn't believed Luke at first when he'd called with the news about Miss Abigail's lost will. She'd thought it was a ghoulish Yankee practical joke. When she finally understood he was being serious, she'd had to repeat the information over and over. "You're saying Lowell didn't have a copy? Don't all lawyers keep copies of important papers?"

"Not if their clients tell them not to. She always insisted on keeping her own records, Mayhew said. There's not a shred of Sedgwick paperwork anywhere, he told me. I suppose she was worried about the family's privacy," Luke had explained tonelessly.

"And she left everything to Quibble? Can't you contest it?"

"I could. And I'd probably win. But I don't want to. If you do, I can't stop you."

She had declined without a second thought. She might not get her million dollars, but she'd be able to sleep at night.

"How are things?" Luke had asked.

She wanted to tell him it felt strange to spend weekends in the city. She wanted to ask whether the redhead was happy to have him all to herself again. She wanted to confess that she missed his companionship, she missed *him*. "Things are great. Busy, with the wedding planning and all. How are you? Are you holding up all right? Are you eating?"

"Why wouldn't I eat?"

Now Peggy unfurled the "Going Out of Business" banner she'd ordered for the front window and searched for tape in the drawer under the register. "I should never have done something so insane, staying married to a stranger for money." She could barely look Bex in the eye. "I should have known it wouldn't work."

"Cut it out. You took a chance and it didn't pay off. So we'll all do something different. I'll stay at home with the babies awhile, until we figure out what to do next. And you can enjoy just being Mrs. Clovis."

"True," Peggy said as the doorbells jingled. She didn't bother to look up; what was the point of being friendly to customers when the store would be gone in a matter of weeks? Besides, the clerks at Bath were downright cold, and their business was thriving.

With a little moan, Bex lifted one swollen foot and tried to prop it on the opposite knee but got stuck halfway to her goal and gave up. "Unless," she went on, "you're having second thoughts."

About Brock, Bex meant. It was the only time since the engagement Bex had said anything negative. Peggy had known her friend would, sooner or later. "I'm not having second thoughts," she declared. She wasn't, after all. Hadn't she just booked the honeymoon? She and Brock would be spending a week in Mexico. A whole week together, before he had to go back on the road for baseball season.

"Second thoughts about what?" a voice asked.

Bex and Peggy both looked up for the first time at their customer.

"Please tell me you're getting back together with Luke," said Tiffany Ver Planck.

The day after the rain ended, Luke put on his Wellingtons and squelched downtown to go to the library. The picketing had started up again and grown in numbers. Where there had once been a handful of protesters, now there were dozens, treading a muddy circle in the still dormant grass. Luke noted they'd replaced the "STOP the Sedgwicks" signs with "STOP the Budget Club"—Angelo and Annette's doing, he assumed, and certainly a step up from having his own name plastered all over the town green. He nodded at Annette, who smiled, but a number of people refused to acknowledge him. On the spot, Luke gave himself until the end of June to leave New Nineveh.

"Save our town! Save our town!" the marchers chanted.

Seeing Luke, Angelo lowered his sign and the two moved away from the demonstration. "Real sorry about Peggy. I heard it from the guys down at Seymour's, and Annette heard from Debby." He gestured toward the owner of the Cheese Shoppe. "We're all real sad for you. First your great-aunt and now this."

"I'm all right." Luke shrugged and continued before Angelo could be any more supportive, "I need help patching up the place, though, before I move out in two months. I'd pay whatever you'd like. Interested?"

"Move out?" From under the brim of his Red Sox cap, Angelo appeared confused. "Where are you going?"

"Back to Hartford. Just until I decide what to do with myself."

"You mean you're not going to live in the house?"

Luke answered lightly, "It seems Abby had other plans. But I would like to leave it in decent shape. Will you help?"

"Absolutely. We'll figure out the details later." Angelo nodded back toward the group. "You sure you won't rethink your decision, Luke? Stop the Budget Club? It would mean a lot to a lot of people."

Luke scanned the green—the boarded-up shop windows he'd pelted with eggs as a teenager, the abandoned Nutmeg Coffee Shop, the antiques dealers and Realtors who trafficked in the remains of the dead: centuries-old farmhouses built by doughty settlers, firearms used to win the country's freedom, fine furniture imported from England—possibly by Silas Ebenezer Sedgwick himself—on which generations had worked and dined and slept. It was as if the entire state were being sold off, piece by piece.

"I wish I could stop it," Luke told Angelo, "but it's too late."

"It's *never* too late." Curvy, bouncy, glossy, sparkly, Tiffany was a vision in monogrammed sandals, a divine being who had arrived in Peggy and Bex's shop by way of Palm Beach. "You love Luke, he loves you, I could drive you up to New Nineveh right now and you could be Mrs. Sedgwick again in no time. So what if you got married the first time under odd circumstances? Plenty of couples get together for far weirder reasons. In a way, every marriage is a financial transaction. Don't you think, Bex?"

Bex's face was incredulous. "You love Luke?"

"No." Peggy slapped her hand down on the counter. "Let's talk about something else. Tiffany, how's Tom?"

Tiffany examined her shoes. "We're fighting."

Of all the responses Peggy had been expecting, this had not crossed her mind.

"It's this Budget Club deal he got Luke involved in—the one you were protesting on the New Nineveh green. Oh, I'm on your side," Tiffany interjected as Peggy started to invoke her "I have a right to free speech" speech. "While we were in Palm Beach I happened to call that nice, crunchy-granola couple from your reception. I wanted to ask them to help me put in an organic garden at the Greenwich house, and Annette filled me in on the protest. I had no idea people were so upset! Why does New Nineveh need a superstore, Peggy? Don't they know it only encourages mass consumption of the cheap, petroleum-based plastic products that are destroying our planet?"

"But you drive an Escalade." Peggy pointed out the window. The giant black SUV was parked at the curb—with a driver today, she noted.

"And you own how many homes, all using up energy when you're not there?" Bex chimed in.

"Just three." Tiffany looked almost hurt. "But this isn't about me. It's about you, Peggy. You do too love Luke." She turned to Bex. "She does. And vice versa."

"She's marrying another guy," Bex said.

"Are you crazy?" Tiffany yelled.

"A sports cameraman. He travels all the time. He cheats on her."

"Once, Bex! It was a onetime mistake!" Peggy yelled in return.

Tiffany took Peggy's hand. "What are you doing?" Her voice was a cashmere twinset, her words a string of perfect, gleaming pearls. "Please don't throw your life away on the wrong man when the right one is yours for the taking."

Peggy could feel the anxiety twisting up around her throat. *Damn you,* she told it silently. *Why can't you leave me alone?*

She swallowed it down. "I'm marrying Brock the first Saturday in June. There's no more discussion. My decision is made, and it's final."

Topher Eaton, who lived in Katonah, across the New York State line, hosted poker that evening. Luke was surprised the wives were there as well.

"Carrie and Liddy are having a committee meeting for one of their charities. The Daughters of New England Night of Something or Other." Hubbard, bored as always, stood near the doorway with a drink. *He's been putting on the same act since he was thirteen,* Luke thought. *Doesn't he get tired of it?*

"Night of *Hope.*" Carrie came over to take Luke's coat, a hungry gleam in her pterodactylian eyes, Liddy at her elbow, giving Hubbard the opportunity to head to the bar. "It's in the fall. You'll come, won't you, Luke? Even without..." Carrie let the absent name speak for itself.

"Peggy," Luke said. "You mean 'without Peggy.' "

Liddy took his arm. "There will be other single girls there. I personally know three who would die to meet you. Have you met Kiki Spencer? You'd like her, Luke. She's one of us, you know?"

Something hot and dangerous ignited inside Luke's chest. "No. I don't know. I've never understood 'us.' You'd do me a great service to explain it."

Liddy and Carrie exchanged glances. Liddy picked at a hangnail.

"*Us,*" Carrie took over. "One of us. People like us."

The hot, dangerous thing burned hotter, an enraged insect buzzing inside him. A hornet—no, a wasp. *I'm one mean, angry WASP,* Luke thought giddily. He said, "As opposed to somebody not like 'us.' Tiffany Ver Planck, for example."

"Exactly!" Liddy looked shocked to hear the consensus coming out of her own mouth, as if she'd not ever verbalized this observation—that Tiffany Ver Planck was decidedly Not Our Kind, Dear—to anyone.

"Who isn't here tonight, I notice."

"Well, naturally!" Carrie flashed a malignant smile. "She's not in Daughters of New England. And Tom isn't in town tonight anyway, so we thought, why not take advantage of the opportunity and have the committee meeting?"

"That way nobody feels left out." Liddy was clearly satisfied with her own explanation and looked as if, having made herself clear, she would like to escape to the safety of the Eatons' kitchen. The time-honored rules of etiquette dictated that Luke should now allow her to do just that, but Luke had played by the rules his entire life. He was tired of the rules.

"Tell me, Liddy. Was Peggy like us?"

The two women glanced at each other again.

"Truth?" Liddy wavered.

"Absolutely," Luke assured her.

"She marched against you on the town green. She showed too much leg at your great-aunt's reception. She was a spoilsport at the tailgate—"

"She was cold," Luke tried to cut in.

"—and she was entirely too chummy with Tiffany." There was no stopping Liddy. "We even tried to invite her into Daughters of New England, and she didn't seem the least bit interested. As if she didn't have the slightest idea what an honor it is. Not just anyone can be a Daughter of New England."

"No," Luke mused. "I don't suppose just anyone can."

Carrie slipped her arm through his. "Really, Luke. You're better off without her."

"Committee time!" Creighton Simmons called from the kitchen.

"Poker time!" Hubbard mimicked in a falsetto from his place at the Eatons' dining room table. Simmons and Eaton, too, were seated. There was one empty chair, Luke's.

Luke hesitated.

Eaton began to deal. "You in or out, Sedgwick?"

The eyes of the room—the friends he'd known his entire life; their wives, whom he'd known half his life—were on him.

"Out," Luke declared.

He was unclear exactly why he had chosen to leave, but he drove back to New Nineveh with a heady sense of freedom he hadn't experienced since the first time he'd driven this car alone as a newly licensed teenager and realized he could have taken it anywhere, gone anywhere, without anyone having a say in it. Now he had the audacious notion of having outgrown his friends. He could, if he chose to, simply not see them again. He wouldn't miss them. He'd remain friends with Ver Planck—the only one he genuinely liked. The rest, well, perhaps he'd gotten from them what he'd needed to.

When his cell phone rang, he picked it up absently. It would be Hubbard, scolding him for leaving the game before it had started.

"It's Bex," the caller said. "You need to do something about Peggy."

His foolish heart beat harder at the sound of Peggy's name. He was quiet, forgetting for an instant Bex was on the line.

"Is it true you love her?"

The question shook him. He concentrated on the road, the way it rushed up to meet his headlights, only to be swallowed instantly underneath his wheels. "Where did you hear that?"

"From that friend of hers, Tiffany. Is it true?"

When had Bex spoken to Tiffany? Luke was perplexed at all of it, most especially that Bex would think it appropriate to ask him such a personal question. Did all other people in the world speak this freely about their private thoughts and emotions?

"Because if you love her, you need to tell her right away."

A deer was grazing alongside the road. *Don't jump,* Luke willed it until he was past. "But she's getting married."

"You can stop her. You show up at the store, get down on one knee, plead your undying love, and I swear she'll call it off."

"She's not going to call it off. She wants to marry this guy—Brock."

"Wrong. She only thinks she wants to marry him. I've been telling myself, 'Keep your mouth shut, Bex; she'll come to her senses on her own.' But she's so damn dense, she needs a shove, a big, dramatic gesture, or she won't see the light until it's too late."

Luke laughed at the absurdity of expecting him to stage a scene. "If you want drama, you've got the wrong person. I don't like drama, not in private and definitely not in public. Peggy knows that."

"What do you call those preppy pants, the kind where the right front leg is, like, yellow, and the left front leg is pink, and the right back leg is, I don't know, green, and the left back leg—"

"Go-to-hell pants," Luke interrupted. "What's your point?"

"You people are lunatics," Bex scoffed. "You can wear pants like that, but you won't say one little 'I love you'? Don't be such a WASP, Luke. You've got five weeks before you lose Peggy forever. If that doesn't call for drama, nothing does."

TWENTY-FOUR

Late Spring, May

Peggy was at the point in her wedding planning where she was no longer the slightest bit interested in the wedding. She was only looking forward to not having to do any more planning.

The chores were infinite. There were registries to be decided upon and fittings to be booked and missing RSVPs to be tracked down (why couldn't people just commit to a yes or a no?) and seating arrangements to be reshuffled. She'd spent hours on the phone as Sharon Clovis questioned her reception decor choices. She'd fielded call after call from her parents, questioning her entire life.

"But you and Luke loved each other," her mother argued one night two weeks before the ceremony, as Peggy sat at Bex's coffee table cataloging wedding presents in a special binder she'd bought to keep track of everything, just as she did at the store. Just as she had done, she corrected herself: The store would close for good that Friday. Peggy had barely been able to keep up with the bargain hunters who came to the going-out-of-business sale to buy not just products, but the display shelves and light fixtures—expensively dressed buzzards picking gleefully at a carcass.

She wondered if Luke had returned all of their wedding presents or if they were still up in the vacant room on the third floor. She should call him, she thought, to make sure he had. No, she shouldn't. He had manners. He'd do it on his own.

"See you at the wedding, Mom. Drive carefully." Peggy was tired of other people telling her whom she loved. She was heartbroken over closing the shop, exhausted from working sixteen hours at a stretch. She envied Brock. His documentary wouldn't wrap up for another week, and by the time he returned to New York, the wedding would be a few days away. His only responsibility would be to show up and say He Did.

He would show up, wouldn't he?

Peggy opened the apartment door, peeked into the hall to make sure the coast was clear of neighbors who might catch her in her bathrobe, and knocked on Josh's apartment door. It was nine o'clock, Bex's bedtime, but when Josh let her in, Peggy could see her friend on Josh's new sofa with her feet propped on a pillow.

"I'm trying to muster the energy to get up and go to sleep," Bex said. "Is everything all right?"

What if Brock changes his mind? Peggy was about to ask, when the notion came to her: Bex's answer would be of no comfort. If Peggy kept her worries to herself, she wouldn't have to get upset when Bex inevitably wisecracked, *We can only hope.*

Bex struggled to get her feet from the couch onto the floor. "Sweetie, I have news, and you're not going to like it. I have to go on bed rest, starting tomorrow, doctor's orders. I've got the okay to be in your wedding, but I'll have to sit the entire time. I can't so much as walk down the aisle. I'll have to lie down for the reception. I hope that's okay."

Peggy had thought Bex was about to say she didn't want to be in the wedding. This seemed like nothing in comparison.

"But wait, there's more," Josh added in a television announcer's voice.

"I'm no longer allowed to climb any stairs, so I'll be staying with my parents in their elevator building until the babies are born. And I'm not allowed to come down to the store. You'll have to close it on your own."

Josh squeezed Peggy's shoulders sympathetically. "Those Cohen twins. Not even born yet and already causing all kinds of trouble."

Peggy waited for Bex to correct him with "*Sabes*-Cohen twins." But Bex's lips were trembling. "Please don't fall apart, Peggy. I feel so bad about this. You shouldn't have to close up our business by yourself." A tear slid down her cheek, followed by another.

It took Peggy aback. She had no intention of falling apart. She could handle a seated bridesmaid. She and Padma could close up the shop. "You don't need to cry. I'm fine, truly. You just focus on having healthy babies. Nothing else matters, Bex."

Bex's tears were gone nearly as quickly as they'd begun. "You aren't anxious?"

"What's the point? Worrying won't solve anything."

Josh and Bex looked at her as if she were a stranger.

The last day at ACME Cleaning Supply passed in a haze. Peggy and Padma boxed up the remains of the unsold merchandise and swept out the dust from the corners, stopping only when Bex's mother made a surprise appearance with takeout Chinese food, saying, "I thought you could use lunch." Sue Sabes spread out the white cartons and paper napkins on the front display counter and fixed Peggy a heaping plate. "Bex is at home, beside herself, the poor thing. I guess you're taking this just as badly?"

"It feels like someone died," Peggy admitted. *So much loss,* she thought. First Miss Abigail gone, and now the store.

"You two will be just fine. Bex's dad and I lost our first store. Disco Duds, it was called. Turned out it was a just plain dud. It seemed like the end of the world at the time, but we learned from it, and Sabes Shoes came out of it, and we all survived."

Peggy picked at her beef with broccoli and waved forlornly at Jorge, the UPS man, who was passing by the propped-open door in the sunshine with a hand truck laden with boxes. He made a sad face and waved back.

"Eat, sweetie." Sue waved her hands over the food. "Problems are worse on an empty stomach."

Perhaps Sue was right. "You sound just like Bex."

"Where do you think she got it from?" Sue replied. "Will you be okay, Padma?"

"Oh, it's all good." Padma grinned at Peggy through a mouthful of fried rice. "I forgot to tell you, Peggy. I got accepted into pre-med."

"Excuse me," said a male voice.

Padma and Sue looked idly toward the doorway.

Peggy nearly choked on her lunch.

Luke was here in her shop. Luke Sedgwick.

"I need to talk to you." He picked his way between the stacked boxes. "May we speak privately?"

Something went wrong with the annulment. It was Peggy's first coherent thought. She surveyed the wreck of her business in desperation and pointed toward the sidewalk, but Luke asked, "Do you have a back room?"

Padma and Sue, who Peggy realized hadn't the faintest notion who this person was, were observing with growing curiosity. Sue set down her chopsticks. "Should we leave?"

"Not at all. Finish your lunch." Peggy grabbed Luke by the arm, marched him into the now empty supply closet, flicked on the light, and shut the door. "Make it quick."

Luke inhaled deeply.

Peggy waited. There was barely enough room inside for the two of them. She pressed herself against the bare shelves on the back wall. Was it warm in here, or was it that Luke was so near to her, as close as he'd been the night they'd made love? *Don't think about it.* "What do you want?" Her brusque question filled the close space. "In case you hadn't noticed, we've gone out of business. I'm pretty busy out there."

"I'm so sorry, Peggy." Luke's eyes were grave behind his glasses. "I can't imagine how hard this is for you."

She wouldn't cry. If she cried, he might try to comfort her, and once he did, her tears might never stop.

He breathed in again. It was as if he were drinking his fill of the closet air, as if there hadn't been enough air to breathe in Connecticut. She felt a sneeze coming on and rubbed her nose furiously. There wasn't a thing left in this closet, yet it still reeked. She wouldn't miss all the smells, that was for sure. "Please," she said, "just tell me why you're here."

At length, he breathed out. "You can't get married."

It was the same phrase he'd used when he'd called her at the store back in September. Panic squeezed her so tightly, she thought she'd burst. She refused to give in. There was no way she was going to swoon in this closet in front of Luke Sedgwick. "Don't tell me you and I are still married."

He laughed—nervously, Peggy thought. "That's not it. Don't worry."

His hand was inches from her hip. She thought of the way he'd undressed her in front of the fire, his warm fingers sliding off her Fair Isle sweater, his warm mouth on her bare skin.

She had to get out of this closet.

"You can't marry him because..." He hesitated.

A balloon of anticipation began to expand inside her.

"Because..." He couldn't seem to get the words out.

She understood. He was about to tell her he loved her, just as she loved him, just as she'd loved him for months, maybe since the night she'd met him. She felt ready to lift her feet from the closet floor and float gently up to meet the tin ceiling.

"Because why?" she urged. *Tell me.* She had to stop herself from throwing her arms around him.

"Because you don't love him."

The balloon began to deflate. "I don't understand." She was trying to give him a chance to redeem himself. There was still the possibility he might redeem himself. *Because I love you, Peggy. Say it.*

"You don't love him. Bex told me."

The balloon deflated, and she fell back to earth. "Did Bex put you up to this?" Peggy jerked open the closet door. Padma appeared busy taping up a packing box, and Sue had started peeling the "Lost Our Lease" banner from the window, but neither, Peggy was sure, had missed the last line.

Sue waited for as long as it took to crumple up the banner and toss it in the garbage. "What has my daughter done now?"

"You're Bex's mother?" Luke stumbled a little over his own deck shoes as he exited the closet and stood silhouetted ethereally against the cloud mural on the back wall: an otherworldly visitor with a popped collar. "I'm Luke Sedgwick, a friend. How is she?"

"Driving me nuts," Sue said, "but fine."

"*You're* Luke Sedgwick?" Padma's jaw dropped.

Just what Peggy needed—for Padma to tell Sue who Luke was. She threw the salesgirl a glare as intense, she hoped, as one of Miss Abigail's. It must have been a decent facsimile; Padma stopped talking, though she did wink and give Peggy a thumbs-up sign.

Peggy dragged Luke out onto the sidewalk and down half a block until there was no chance Padma and Sue could overhear. "Let me set the record straight. Bex is my best friend, but she doesn't know what she's talking about." She moved to the side as a taxi stopped at the curb directly in front of her and a couple climbed out. "I love Brock, and he loves me, and we're getting married the way we were always supposed to, and that's the end of it." She moved to the other side as a father with a baby on his shoulders passed between them. "So you tell Bex she'd better get used to it. And as for you… What's this?"

Luke had taken a folded piece of paper from the pocket of his shirt—the pink button-down again, the one he'd worn under his sweater the day they'd met in Lowell Mayhew's office. He offered the paper to her.

She didn't take it. "What is it?"

"Read it."

"What is it?" She refused to give him the satisfaction of following his orders.

"Oh, for heaven's sake." He unfolded the paper and glanced around, as if to make sure no one was observing them. "An aphrodisiac will disappear—" His voice cracked, and he started again:

"An aphrodisiac will disappear,
delusional, like permanence or wealth—
a shimmering, as if love were a ghost—
and yet my passion for you seethes and sears
without an end. Late April leaves can't crave
caress of dew, sunlight's sweet splash, more than
I pine for your embrace, us turned to one;
when harsh reversals scar, the thought of you will salve
like summer wind in autumn; deep red blood
surging along with mine, staid genes worked hot
from your electric charms, as all my moods
succumb to your sweet fire, and perfect wit.
Now you are all I live for—loving you—
in fleeting world of lies, you are the truth.

People were listening. Here were a restaurant deliveryman chaining his bicycle to a parking meter, a kid carrying a violin case, a woman sliding a letter into a mailbox—poised, attentive. Luke raised his eyes from the paper, and Peggy stared at him, stupefied, not knowing what to say, so that the first thing out of her mouth was the first thought to surface: "But this is for Nicki."

"Nicki? I broke it off with her in November."

"But I saw this poem before that, when I..." She was so embarrassed, she thought she might melt. "Snooped."

Luke stepped back into the unmarked doorway of Rubicon, a women's clothing store. The face of the boutique's security guard appeared behind a small porthole. Luke jumped. *He really is nervous,* Peggy marveled.

"That's why you shouldn't snoop." Luke refolded the paper and again held it out to her. "It was never for anyone but you."

All over again, Peggy and Luke were the only two people on earth. Peggy heard, from another universe, the faraway sound of her name; she heard a siren, an idling truck, passing conversations; she ignored it all. Luke loved her. His feelings, which his upbringing wouldn't allow him to express directly, were in this poem, clear as day.

"Peggeee!" There it was again, a voice calling her, a high, faraway cry as if from deep inside Peggy's brain. A call to action. *What's it going to be, Peggy? We're all waiting, Peggy. Make your choice.*

But there was no choice.

She had made it in December, in the garden of the Colonial Inn. She had chosen Brock. The guests were on their way, the dress was waiting in her closet, she was getting married in a matter of days, and the time for choices was over.

How could Luke show up now?

She crossed her arms over her chest and blinked back the

tears in her eyes. She would not cry. She would stay strong, the way Miss Abigail would.

"Peggy Adams!" The shout came again, and it was Padma who'd been calling her—calling to get Peggy's attention, because Brock was striding toward her up the sidewalk, a beaming grin on his dimpled, chiseled face.

"You're too late," she told Luke, and turned hurriedly toward her fiancé, who was half a block away, utterly oblivious to what was happening, to the fact that the tears flowing down Peggy's cheeks were for anyone but him.

"This is it," Peggy heard Luke say from behind her. "If you walk away, I won't go after you. I won't burst into the church yelling, 'Stop the wedding!' "

She turned back around. "I know," she said. "You don't like scenes."

And then she hurried to meet Brock, leaving Luke alone with his poem, her heart aching as it never had, wondering if, were she to look back, she would see Luke suffering in the same way she was. *Pain builds character.* It was one of the Sedgwick family slogans, and Peggy understood that if she was somehow able to live through this, she would be stronger. She'd have to be.

"Hey, Pegs!" Brock tackled her and engulfed her in a hug. When he let go, Peggy glanced over her shoulder one last time.

Luke was gone. In the space of a few seconds, it was as if he hadn't been there at all.

So that was that.

Luke had had a moment on the way into the city, navigating the Volvo through the thick of Manhattan, in which he'd thought, *We'll live here,* and the image had popped full-blown into his head: he and Peggy, happy ever after in a cramped but charming apartment filled with books and sunlight; a baby's crib; trips to the park and the museums; the city noise a lullaby to rock them all to sleep at night. He'd been struck with the sure knowledge that this was how things were meant to turn out, and his only job had been to convince Peggy of the same. Hadn't he planned his appeal to Peggy, thought of nothing else for days? Hadn't he neglected his investment portfolio, ignored repeated phone messages from Ver Planck, daydreamed through the repairs he'd embarked on with Angelo, to write and rewrite and edit and re-edit the grand gesture, the poem that would make Peggy his and bring with her a life he'd only recently come to understand was the life he'd always wanted? He'd not considered this a gamble he could lose.

Peggy had chosen her future, and it didn't include him. Hidden in a shop doorway, he'd watched her after she'd turned her back, watched her run into the arms of that muscled lug on the sidewalk, considered running after her and...and what could he have done? Challenged the guy to a duel? Stung him with his wit, WASP versus Goliath? The contest was over, the match lost. Maybe Peggy had never felt anything more for him than friendship. And now that was gone as well.

Luke dropped his worthless sonnet into the nearest trash basket. He wished only for one thing: that in that closet, he'd inhaled more deeply the lingering fragrance he'd come to associate with Peggy and held it in his lungs as long as he could.

He drove home as if anesthetized. The Hudson River was alive with sailboats, the trees lining the parkways lush with leaves, the farms of Litchfield County overrun with spring calves and foals on spindly legs. Luke saw all of it and absorbed none of it. He thought of his ancestral home, soon to be barred to him. He passed Pilgrim Plaza, its parking lot a lustrous slab of asphalt, and thought about the Widow in the Woods. He came to the Sedgwick land, the last bit of his heritage. The ground breaking had begun the previous week. Luke had watched in silence as an excavator had taken the first grab of land with its greedy steel arm. In just a few days, this single machine had reduced the grassy meadow to dirt. Now Luke parked on the shoulder and watched it work, and something inside him, something he hadn't known was there, ripped open—a gaping wound out of which poured sorrow and anguish and self-reproach. He was a Sedgwick, like it or not. Maybe it was impossible to truly break away from one's heritage. He saw Abigail Agatha Sarah Sedgwick saying, *Nobody but Sedgwicks shall ever live under the Sedgwick roof.* He wasn't angry with her for leaving the house to the cat. In her own off-kilter way, she'd been trying to save what was theirs when her last living relative was hell-bent on destroying it.

It had been months since Peggy had been to Brattie's Sports Pub, but nothing had changed. The TV screens were still broadcasting a hodgepodge of events, from track and field to golf—the U.S. Open; a pantheon of New York sports saints including Patrick Ewing, Joe Namath, and Babe Ruth watched over the proceedings from their photos on the walls. The sameness was comforting after a day of changes and endings. "In fleeting world of lies, you are the truth," Peggy whispered to her grubby reflection in the ladies' room mirror. Now that a few hours had passed since her scene with Luke, she was sorry for her ungracious exit. She might have said a proper good-bye, told Luke how much she'd liked his poem.

Enough. She made a face at herself and rubbed dirt from her cheek. She was a mess. How about regretting not having gone home to shower and change before agreeing to come here with Brock?

Her fiancé was entertaining the crowd at the bar with

stories of his work on the documentary. Somebody started an off-key chorus of "Here Comes the Bride" as Peggy reappeared, and hands reached out to pat her on the back.

"Come over here, Pegs." Brock slid his arm around her and tugged her to his side.

The Commissioner poured Brock a beer. "Why the hell'd you wait so long to pop the question, Clovis?"

Everyone looked at Brock—including Peggy. It was the question she'd wanted answered for months. Had he proposed because she'd followed through on her ultimatum? Because he'd been jealous she'd started dating? Because he'd realized there wasn't anything better out there? Now she wasn't sure she wanted to hear the reason. She held her breath.

"Commish, gentlemen, I've thought a lot on this very subject." Brock was enjoying himself. "And you know what I say?"

"Tell us what you say, brother!" the Commissioner shouted, and the crowd laughed.

"There comes a time in life when you need to take a good, long look at things and ask, 'What do I have, and what do I want?' That's what happened to me last fall. I said to myself, 'Clovis, you jackass, here you had this great thing, and you went and lost it. If you want it back, better do something about it.' So I did something about it." Brock clutched Peggy more tightly around the waist. "Vince Lombardi said it best: 'The measure of who we are is what we do with what we have.' "

"Lombardi," said a guy to Brock's left. "The man was a poet."

"Good for you, Clovis," the bartender said. "Way to go, Peggy."

Peggy couldn't believe it. The Commissioner was looking her in the eye. "I'll be back," she said, and slipped out of Brock's grasp and onto the sidewalk, taking her phone from her purse.

If Bex's mother was worn out from spending all afternoon shutting down the store, she didn't sound it when she answered the phone. Bex was asleep, Sue reported apologetically. Did Peggy have a message to relay?

It was better this way. Peggy was sad and emotional and tired. It would be too easy, were Bex to get on the phone, to pick a fight with her about Luke. Peggy didn't want to fight. Bex had many faults. She was a know-it-all and a busybody, but she was Peggy's best friend, and Peggy loved her. Bex would never come to terms with Brock. But it was all right. The friendship had survived this long, despite Bex and Peggy's differences. It wasn't going anywhere.

"Just please tell her I'll come by tomorrow," Peggy told Sue.

"See you then," Sue said. "And I can't wait for the wedding."

"I can't either." Peggy meant it. It would be liberating to put the past behind her and step into the future.

She went back inside Brattie's. "It's midnight—our wedding is exactly a week away," Brock said. He planted a definitive kiss on her lips and ground himself against her pelvis. "Come home with me. I can't take it anymore."

She couldn't sleep with him—not yet. She didn't know why, but she couldn't until after they were married. Feeling like a prude, she separated herself from him, her hands against his chest. "It's just one more week."

On Saturday morning, Luke was up at dawn in spite of (or perhaps because of) having played umpteen games of mental tennis most of the night. As he came through the grand parlor, he spotted Quibble, who, exactly as in Luke's collapsing-house daydream, was perched on the mantel. The house remained standing. "Look at you, acting like you own the place." Luke scratched the cat fondly under the chin. "Too bad you're legally obligated to live here, or I'd take you with me." To where, beyond Hartford, Luke still didn't know, but Quibble didn't press him for an answer.

By nine, Luke and Angelo were up on the roof with a bucket of roofing tar, enveloped in the heavy odor of hot asphalt. It was the next step after the blue tarp to stave off leaks and a temporary fix at best; in six months or a year, the leaks would be back. As he had many times since reading Abby's will, Luke wondered how the meager Sedgwick Family Trust could possibly cover the cost of maintaining the Silas Sedgwick House in perpetuity. Mayhew was right: Luke should contest the will. He mulled over the idea briefly and rejected it. Taking on this house would be a terrible decision made in an irrational moment. Even with his Budget Club windfall, he couldn't afford the place.

Luke set down his tar-spreading broom and leaned out over the widow's walk balustrade and looked through the treetops to the town green. The protesters were gathering already, their numbers fortified by the weekenders from New York, who had flocked back for the summer. Their chants carried faintly. Luke waited until Angelo looked up, then gestured with a tarry hand toward the green. "Did you want to go? I can finish up here myself."

Angelo's boots left gummy black footprints as he came over to peer through the trees. "Nah. Looks like they've got it covered."

"Listen, about Budget Club..." Luke had an unaccountable need to explain himself. "You and Annette aren't originally from New Nineveh. Neither are most of the people down there on the green. I respect that you all came here because New Nineveh was a picturesque little town, and that you'd like to keep it that way. And I know it's hard for you to understand why we locals seem so keen on selling it out."

Angelo tilted his head upward—just enough of a nod to verify he agreed with what Luke was saying, but not so much that it might provoke an argument.

"It's hard for me, too. My family built this town. We built the Congregational Meeting House, and the courthouse, and the clock tower, all in the name of progress. If my great-great-great-grandfather were alive today, I suspect he'd call this progress, too. All I can tell you is that land is the only thing I have left. My decision was purely financial. If I could support myself and still write some other way, I would."

"No worries, Luke," Angelo said. "You gotta do what you gotta do."

Luke was no less burdened for his confession. "One more thing. Mayhew will be looking for a caretaker for the house once I've moved out. Someone to come in and feed the cat, keep an eye on the place, and make repairs. The salary's pretty good. I'm sure the job would be yours if you're interested."

Angelo wiped his forehead with the back of his sleeve. It was going to be a hot day. "I'm interested," he said.

It was one thing to relax about. The Fiorentinos would take good care of the house. Abby would be pleased if she knew. Luke excused himself and went down into the cool, dim library, over which Silas presided, as ever, from his portrait.

"What would you have done?" Luke addressed his ancestor. "You're all for progress, aren't you?"

It was laughable, his seeking counsel from a painting. This was how it must have started for Abby—first talking to herself out loud as an antidote to the loneliness, eventually conversing with unseen companions. After that, it was only a short hop to believing in ghosts.

Luke locked eyes with the portrait and waited for a sign.

Silas glowered.

"I thought so," Luke said. He had the answer at last.

TWENTY-FIVE

Wedding Day, June

It was as if every good deed Peggy had ever done, every ounce of worry she'd ever expended, every bit of luck she had coming to her, had all converged on this single day. She'd slept like a baby and awoken to the most beautiful June weather imaginable: a benevolent sun against a limitless blue sky. Her mother had checked her anxieties at the door, and her father, waiting with Peggy in the foyer of the Unitarian church on Amsterdam Avenue as sunlight streamed in from the street outside, hadn't complained once about wearing long pants.

It was a perfect day to get married.

Peggy knew she looked every inch the bride. Her makeup was dewy. Her nails were pristine. Each meticulously blonded hair—no dark roots would mar her photos—had fallen into place with military precision. Even Bex had gasped when Peggy had arrived at the church.

"Oh, sweetie. You're getting married!" And for once, there had been nothing behind her words but wonderment.

Peggy had twirled in front of Bex's chair, her dress floating around her like a white silk cloud. "Do you approve?"

She'd meant *of the dress,* but Bex had laid a swollen hand on Peggy's arm. "From this day forward, whatever choices you've made, whatever choices you will make, I'll support you."

Now, through a crack in the church door, Peggy could see

Bex was seated at the altar, round and serene in a dove gray dress. Brock's brother, Brent, stood next to her. Brock was there, too, in a suit, as handsome as any groom in a magazine. The first notes of the bridal processional filled the room. The guests stirred.

It was Peggy's moment.

"You ready?" Her father offered his arm.

Peggy took it. "I'm ready."

I hope, she added silently.

She would remember little of her trip down the aisle, only the indistinct faces of the guests as she passed, the weight of the white rose bouquet in her hand, Brock's dimple. She would recall the minister's thinning hair and rimless glasses, and portions of the ceremony, but other thoughts floated in, too, as she stood with Brock at the altar. She thought of the store on the first day she and Bex had opened for business, of the candle-flame flicker of the twins' heartbeats. Of a dream she must have had once, forgotten and just now rematerialized, with colored lights and bells and a man who made her happy....

A rustle of motion brought Peggy back to the present, and before she could help it, her heart leaped—could it be Luke, coming in to stop the wedding after all?

But the rustle was Bex, gesturing that Peggy should pass over the bridal bouquet. Peggy blushed under her makeup and took a long, last look at the roses as she gave them to Bex to hold. Perfect. The flowers were perfect. Creamy white with the gentlest wash of pink, as if they, too, were blushing.

The minister turned to Brock. "Do you take Peggy to be your wife? Do you vow to celebrate with her in times of joy and give her strength in times of sorrow, to walk beside her into the future, to be her partner as long as you both shall live?"

Brock boomed out his "I do" as if he'd been waiting to say it all his life. He glided the wedding band, a full circle of diamonds, onto Peggy's finger. It glittered alongside her engagement ring. Flawless. Just like the day, her dress, the white rose bouquet Bex was keeping for her.

"Do you, Peggy, take Brock to be your husband?"

Peggy hesitated, immobile, a bride-statue in a wedding tableau.

All she'd ever wanted was to be married. For seven years, she'd waited for Brock to put a ring on her finger. For almost seven months, she'd played the role of Luke's wife. Now she could see a third choice. She could marry no one. She could stand on her own. She could leave the church and have the strength to survive—to thrive—without any man. She was a whole person. If she chose to marry, it would be because she wanted to, not because she needed to. She took a tentative breath; there was no fear. She could breathe clearly.

She was no longer anxious.

"I do." She slipped the ring onto Brock's finger. She looked at Bex, who nodded. She looked out into the audience, at the faces glowing back at her.

"Wait, stop," she stammered. "I don't think I do."

She'd half expected a collective gasp, but the room was suspended in silence. The guests, the minister, Brock—they appeared, all of them, afraid to move. Their uncertainty was galvanizing. Peggy stepped forward to the edge of the altar. She picked out faces in the room: Her mother. Josh. Sharon Clovis, one lacquered hand to her mouth.

The minister leaned toward her, his breath minty against her cheek. He whispered, "Would it help to take a minute?"

"I don't think so," she whispered back, feeling nearly as bad for ruining his performance as she did for Brock—who was gawking at her, his mouth slack.

She turned to him, wishing she knew what to say, wishing she'd not let things come this far. "I'm sorry, Brock. I care about you, but something isn't right. I'm not sure it's ever been right. Maybe someday you'll forgive me. I wouldn't blame you if you didn't." She took off her wedding ring, then her engagement ring, and dropped them into his hand. "Please know I never meant to hurt you." Out of the corner of her eye, she saw Bex give her the tiniest smile.

Peggy turned to address her guests. "I'm sorry, everybody. I intend to explain this to each one of you individually. But right now"—she took a deep breath—"right now I have to go."

And before she could have second thoughts, she retrieved her bouquet from Bex, gathered her skirt with her free hand, and ran with her veil streaming behind her, down the aisle toward the doors through which she'd come in, out into the sunshine, into her future.

"I can't believe you waited this long to tell me," Ver Planck said.

"It wasn't intentional." Luke kicked at a clod of soil upended by the excavator, marveling that there were still wildflowers—buttercups—growing out of it. Nature didn't accept defeat easily. "I thought I might change my mind. But it's been a week, and I still feel the same way. This land wasn't meant to be paved over and developed. It isn't right."

They were standing in the shade of the sleeping excavator. It was Saturday, and a parade of cars with out-of-state license plates crawled past them on Route 202, heading to the New Nineveh Home Tour, the town's biggest day of the year.

Ver Planck shook his head. "Those picketers really got to you, didn't they?"

And it's Peggy's wedding day, Luke noted with a twinge of pain. He knew the subtext behind Ver Planck's question. His friend was using "picketers" to mean just one picketer, Peggy.

"Budget Club won't be happy about you yanking away their lease," Ver Planck said. "There will be legal fees and breach-of-contract fines. It'll cost you a big chunk of change."

"I'll cover it. I don't care about the money. I'll go back to Hartford Mutual. I'll be the first Sedgwick to go into bankruptcy, if that's what it takes." The thought of being penniless, truly ruined, pained Luke as well, but nowhere near as much as the loss of Peggy. He checked his watch: It was close to eleven. The wedding was at one. Bex had told him.

"In case you try again," she'd said when he'd called to tell her the news—that he'd decided to follow her advice and failed.

"She's made up her mind." With any luck, Bex had understood. He would not be trying again.

"You have no idea," Ver Planck said, "how glad I am to hear you say this."

For a split second, Luke thought his friend was talking about Luke's decision to let Peggy go. But that couldn't be it. Ver Planck was referring to the land deal.

"I don't understand," Luke said.

"Tiffany is threatening to leave me. She says you're destroying the planet and contributing to sprawl, and I'm the one who talked you into it. Seems the picketers got to her, too." His mouth twisted into a shape halfway between a grin and a grimace.

"Ah, well." Luke knelt and pressed the dirt clod back into the ground so the buttercups would have a fighting chance. "As Uncle Bink used to say, what's money for but to lose?"

Ver Planck laughed. "That, my friend, is what separates the Sedgwicks from the Ver Plancks. I don't plan on you losing a penny."

Peggy's heart and mind were racing. She felt as though she'd just jumped from an airplane: terrified, breathless, energized.

Nothing underneath her but air. She realized she was still clutching her bouquet and set it gently on the black leather limousine seat, not sure why she'd brought it in the first place. Out the back window, eight blocks behind her, the crowd that had followed her out of the church—everyone, it looked like, except Bex, who'd be stuck in her chair—stood helplessly on the sidewalk. The worried, confused, angry faces shrank smaller and smaller as the limousine sped up Amsterdam. Peggy hoped they'd all at least go to the reception. They might as well—it had already been paid for, by Brock and his family. *Oh, lord,* Peggy thought. *I'll have to pay them back.*

"Where to?" The driver stopped at a red light and caught Peggy's eye in the rearview mirror. He seemed unsurprised by the abrupt change of plans. Perhaps brides pulled this sort of stunt all the time.

Peggy fidgeted with the edge of her veil. She'd been absolutely sure of her decision moments ago. Now, with limitless choices before her, she wondered if she'd been rash. If nothing else, she was being terribly cruel to Brock. Hadn't he done all she'd asked of him? Was she being foolish, giving up on a life that, while perhaps not perfect, was perfectly acceptable?

She picked up her roses, feeling like crying, and buried her face in their soft petals.

The light turned green. Behind the limo, impatient drivers were leaning on their horns.

Peggy barely heard. She tested the roses once, twice, a third time. Nothing. They were beautiful but smelled like nothing.

The limousine driver said gently, "How about I drop you home?"

Peggy began to smile.

"That's exactly what I was thinking." She set down the bouquet and settled back into the soft, comfortable seat. "I'd like to go home."

It took ten minutes in the apocalyptic traffic for Luke and Ver Planck to drive the mile from the Sedgwick land to the town green. It took five minutes for them to announce their decision to the assembled protesters. It took no time for the protesters to put down their signs with hugs and shouts and accompany Luke and Ver Planck in a triumphant march to the Sedgwick House, where Luke threw open the front door and invited everyone inside for an impromptu celebration. Debby Doff from the Cheese Shoppe supplied cheese and crackers, and Luigi brought beer, and Luke dug out his twenty-five-year-old boom box, the one from the Anne Marie Scoggs era, and the party grew and spilled out onto the front lawn under the shade of the Sedgwick maple and into the back garden, where bees engaged in their own festivities around the peony bushes. Luke admired a fragrant white bloom, then looked out across the garden toward Market Road and the Rigas' home. Tourists flowed in and out of the former Sedgwick carriage house. Many of those leaving the property carried bouquets of peonies from Ernestine's flower stand.

It was a pity. Were Luke not moving out at the end of the month, he might have reopened Abby's stand. Keeping Ernestine on her toes was a Sedgwick tradition.

Well, he was a Sedgwick, no matter where he lived. He'd make new traditions.

He came back around to the front lawn in time to see a silver SUV swing into the driveway. Tiffany climbed out of the driver's seat and walked around to the back to hoist Milo from his car seat. The boy spotted his father and went running to him across the lawn, weaving through the former protesters. Tiffany, meanwhile, threw her arms around Luke. "My hero!"

"You're welcome," Luke said into her hair.

She pulled away, her face pink with excitement. "Did Tom tell you his plan for your twenty acres? We'll grow pick-your-own mizuna and amaranth and kohlrabi—organic, of course."

"I don't know what any of those are." Luke nodded to Mike and Norma Garrison as they passed, raising their beers.

"Trendy salad greens. Restaurants pay through the nose for them. It's all about locally grown produce these days—the more obscure, the better." Tiffany beamed. "What do you think of my new car? It's a hybrid. We got rid of that gas-guzzling Escalade. We're all stewards of the earth, Luke. Every one of us."

Cars inched up Main Street. It was midday, peak time for the home tour. The drivers and passengers slowed in front of the Sedgwick House, pointing.

"They want to join the party," Tiffany suggested.

"They want to see the house," Luke corrected her, and as if to illustrate his point, a young couple turned into the driveway behind Tiffany's car.

"Dude. Is this part of the tour?" The driver had a Vermont license plate and a hopeful expression on his goateed face.

"Sorry. It's a private home." Luke started to turn away, then changed his mind. "Go on in."

The couple scrambled out of the car and disappeared into the house. Tiffany looked surprised. "It's so cool you did that." She walked with Luke toward the north corner of the house, away from the crowd. "I'm sorry about Peggy. I was positive you two were perfect for each other. But even if it didn't work out, you're better off for having known her—more sociable, more open to people. That has to be good for you."

She was right. Luke was better off for having known Peggy. He was better off for knowing Tiffany, too. He didn't know how to tell her so, so he asked, "What do you say I get you a drink?"

She smiled at him. “I say, it’s about time—” She cut herself off and stared.

An outlandishly long black limousine had driven into the gravel driveway.

As Luke watched, the driver got out, but before the man could walk around to the back door, it opened from the inside and a woman emerged.

Not any woman. A bride in a swirling white dress and a veil that cascaded over her bare shoulders and framed her sweet, familiar face.

“No way,” Tiffany breathed.

Peggy hesitated at the front gate, looking nearly as stunned as Luke was, no doubt wondering why half the town of New Nineveh was here at the Sedgwick House, laughing and celebrating to Luke’s old Rolling Stones tape.

But what was *she* doing here? Luke found he was squeezing his hands into fists, anticipating the imminent appearance of Peggy’s new husband. Luke might abhor scenes, but if that hulking lummox got out of that limousine, Luke was going to deck him—in front of the entire party, propriety be damned.

Nothing happened. There was no sign of Brock. The driver closed Peggy’s door and stood impassively, awaiting further instructions.

Silence swept over the party like a tide. Annette and Angelo, the downtown shopkeepers, the summer people from New York—one by one, they all stopped talking, until there was no sound but the Rolling Stones, and then somebody turned off the boom box and there was nothing left but a summer breeze whispering through the trees and stirring the bottom of Peggy’s bridal veil.

It was little Milo who broke the spell.

“Pretty!” He ran across the lawn and tugged at Peggy’s skirt hem, and Peggy relaxed and laughed weakly, and everyone else but Luke went running up to Peggy and crowded around her with cries of, "We missed you!" and, "Why did you go?" and, "Did you hear?" A picketer told Peggy of Luke's change of heart, and the crowd broke out in yet another glorious whoop, and there was hugging and exclaiming all around.

"But why do you wear a wedding gown?" Luigi called out.

"It's a long story."

It was the first thing Luke had heard Peggy say. From his position away from the group, he caught her eye.

She stepped out from the crowd around her and made her way over to Luke. She glanced up, above his head, and he realized he was standing directly underneath the placard on the house, the one with Silas Ebenezer Sedgwick's name and the date the house was built, 1796.

He fought the desire to take Peggy in his arms. "What are you doing here?" He was exposed, awkward, in front of all of these spectators. "I thought you were supposed to be getting married."

"I changed my mind," she said quietly.

His heart crowded into his throat.

"Luke." She sounded choked up. "I know you and I only got married because we were drunk. And I know we only stayed that way for the money, but—"

"Peggy—" He couldn't let her continue.

"—but our marriage turned out to be the one I'd always dreamed about. For the first time, I felt part of something. I had a family who cared about me, and a home, and a husband who was the kindest man in the world." The breeze blew her veil against her face. She swatted at it. "And I know you hate scenes, and you're probably wishing I had even a fraction of your WASP restraint and decorum, and I'm sorry to show up in my stupid wedding dress and interrupt your party, but I had to come here and tell you myself, because it turns out…" Tears were spilling down her cheeks. She wiped them away with her fingers. "It turns out," she said, sniffling, "I love you, too."

The crowd—half the town of New Nineveh—sighed in unison.

Luke knew the next move was his.

He ran into the foyer. He sprinted up the front staircase, the squeak of the third step like a child's hysterical giggle, turned the corner at the second floor, and continued running up to the third floor. He ran past his study and into his room, where he collected something from the top drawer of his bureau and then flew down the new staircase, past Charity's Porch, around through the grand parlor and past the library, where the Vermont couple stood in front of the portrait of his great-great-great-grandfather, back through the foyer, and out onto the front lawn again, where the party guests were conferring in fretful whispers and Peggy stood where he'd left her, dry-eyed but dazed.

He stopped before her, out of breath. "Sorry."

Her hands were shaking. "It's okay," she said in a small voice.

"I needed this." He held out the thing he'd retrieved from his bureau drawer—the black box from Star Jewelers—opened the lid, and took out Abigail's engagement ring. "I love you, Peggy." He took her hand in his. "Will you marry me?"

She was crying again. Crying and smiling. So was every woman watching. The men turned away and rubbed imaginary sand from their eyes.

"Yes," Peggy said through a sob and laughed. "When?"

"Tonight." Luke wrapped her in his arms. "I know a great little chapel in Las Vegas."

TWENTY-SIX

Luke's cell phone woke them up.

Woke Luke up, Peggy corrected herself. She'd been awake forever. The hotel pillow was spongy and the mattress too soft. It seemed some of her eccentricities were here to stay, happily married or not.

Luke groaned and turned his back to the sound. "If it's important, they'll call back." The phone stopped ringing. He reached for her and kissed her neck. "Good morning, Mrs. Sedgwick."

"Good morning, Mr. Sedgwick." She turned to face him and kissed him back. They'd been married six hours, and she planned to start the honeymoon right up where they'd left off last night.

The phone rang again. Luke groaned for a second time, got up in defeat, and took the phone from the glass cocktail table, where he'd abandoned it next to a cardboard-framed photo stamped "The Little White Wedding Chapel." "Hello?" he answered politely. "Yes, this is Luke."

Peggy couldn't love him more. Even standing in his boxer shorts, rudely awakened on the first morning of his honeymoon, he was a gentleman. And gorgeous. She didn't ever want to stop looking at him.

"What?" Luke was saying. "Where?" His eyes grew wide.

Peggy's breath caught in her chest. Anxiety, the nemesis she'd thought she might be leaving behind permanently, crept back into her body.

"No, no." Luke's voice shook. "It's all right. I would have done the same thing."

Peggy could hardly breathe.

Luke clapped the phone shut and came to sit shakily on the edge of the bed. "That was Angelo."

"Tell me," she pleaded.

He retrieved his glasses from the nightstand and put them on. "I never wanted to live in the Sedgwick House. You knew that, right? I used to fantasize about it collapsing."

Oh, no. Angelo and Annette had agreed to close up the house after the party. *Someone accidentally burned it down.* "Right." She strove to keep her tone light. "You made that pretty clear."

"I always thought I would move to Key West or somewhere if given the chance, but lately I'd been thinking about challenging Abby's will. Fighting to stay there. It seems I can't imagine living anywhere else. I suppose that makes me exactly the kind of stuck-in-a-rut Yankee I desperately didn't want to be."

He seemed to be waiting for her to respond.

"Well, it's a good rut." Did this mean the house hadn't gone up in flames last night? She felt slightly better. "There's nothing wrong with staying in a place that makes you happy."

He seemed heartened. "So you wouldn't miss New York, then?"

The anxiety was fading quickly. She laughed. "I love New Nineveh, and I love the Sedgwick House. Is that what the call was about? Challenging Miss Abigail's will?"

"Not exactly." Luke slid all the way into bed and folded his arms around her again. "You know that squeaky step in the front staircase?"

She was thoroughly bewildered but nodded anyway.

"Angelo decided this morning to fix it. He thought maybe the top board was warped, so he pried it off to get a better look. You won't believe what he found in the hollow space underneath." Luke was talking faster now, not waiting for an answer. "He found the amended will. The one giving the house to you and me."

"That's wonderful! Now we don't have to contest it!"

"That's not all. Angelo also found a box. A wooden box with a star carved on the lid. Charles made it for Abigail long ago. It was something Abby had always wanted me to have. I didn't think it existed."

Peggy's eyes filled with tears at the thought of Miss Abigail. "She hid that box for you. It must have been very important to her."

"I don't think it was the box she thought was so important," Luke said quietly. "It was what was inside."

Time seemed to stand still.

"A bankbook. A stock certificate. And a note. It seems Abby pinched pennies and sold autumn leaves for a reason. She'd been squirreling away every last cent, first under her mattress, later at the Bank of New Nineveh, for more than eighty years. Angelo was just apologizing for opening the bankbook and seeing the balance."

Luke repeated the sum. Five figures. Peggy was impressed. "I'll never throw away a teabag again," she said. Still, she couldn't quite understand what had Luke so agitated.

"Actually," Luke continued, his voice still shaking, "what's really added up are the hundred shares of Berkshire Hathaway it seems my uncle Bink persuaded her to buy in 1965. I don't suppose you know how much more those hundred shares of Berkshire Hathaway are worth today, do you?" His face looked drained of blood. As if someone were listening, he whispered the staggering sum in Peggy's ear.

Had Peggy been ordered to move at this moment, she would have been physically incapable of doing so.

Even without knowing the specifics of home repair, she understood it was enough—much, much more than enough—to maintain the Silas Sedgwick House for another hundred years.

They could keep the house.

Luke kissed her. It was a kiss infused with all the passion and love and hope and happiness in the world.

"Come on, my love," he said. "Let's go home."

EPILOGUE

Fifteen Months Later, September

I can't believe you have this many extra chairs, Peggy," Josh called up from the basement stairs. "Seriously, Bex. There's a whole room down there the size of my old apartment, just for chairs." He emerged from the basement with a folding chair under each arm—the last of a dozen he'd brought up. He handed them off to Peggy, who was alternating between wiping dust from the other chairs and helping Bex keep an eye on two toddlers.

"I can't believe we have this many children." Bex dropped her dust rag and scooped up a twin, who was trying to pull Quibble's tail—"No, no, Ben"—and kissed the boy's soft, curly-haired head. A wail rose up from his sister, Alexandra, Embryo A, who marched across the worn kitchen floor from where she'd been banging pot and pan lids.

She grabbed Benjamin's sleeve, trying to drag him from Bex's lap.

"Gentle, sweetie. You'll get a turn next." Bex kissed Alexandra's head, too.

"She's exactly like you," Peggy said, laughing. She got to her feet and went to the library. Luke was arranging the already cleaned chairs into two semicircular rows facing the fireplace.

"Guess what Alex just did?" Peggy put her arms around

her husband and relayed the scene she'd just witnessed in the kitchen. Now that the Sabes-Cohen family had moved permanently into the east addition—Josh was helping Luke and Angelo add on a bathroom—Peggy and Luke had come to regard the twins almost as their own. The two would have babies someday, but for now, watching Ben and Alex grow was joyous in itself.

Besides, Peggy and Bex had their hands full at the new store. Home Grown was a showcase for products made locally—fine art by area painters, bread from a nearby baking company, vegetables from the Sedgwick/Ver Planck Cooperative Farm, dahlias from the back garden—and *Sweet Fire,* Luke's first book of poems. The store had been open six months, and business, though nowhere as steady as it might be in New York, was promising. Meanwhile, Josh had recently passed the Connecticut bar and had hung out his shingle downtown—he'd taken the second office at the Law Offices of Lowell C. Mayhew. He was currently representing a group of environmentalists in Bethlehem.

But Luke seemed distracted as Peggy told him her story, and she could see he wasn't in the mood to listen. She touched his arm. "You're nervous."

"A little." Peggy knew in WASP-speak "a little" meant he was petrified. "I've never read one of my poems in public before."

Peggy smiled at him. "What do you call the streets of New York?"

Luke nodded but didn't smile back. "This is probably how you felt walking over the Brooklyn Bridge—nothing underneath you but air."

"If you fall, I'll catch you," Peggy said. "You don't have to be afraid."

A few hours later, as the grandfather clock struck eight,

Peggy answered the door knocker to find that all of their two dozen guests—including the Ver Plancks, the Fiorentinos, the Rigas, the Mayhews, Geri, a reporter from the *County Times*—had arrived precisely on time. Peggy led them to the library, where Bex and Josh offered them peanut-butter-and-bacon crackers and showed them to their chairs. Everyone waited in respectful silence for Luke to appear. Peggy watched the portrait of Silas Sedgwick. The great man's expression seemed more stern than usual, as if he disapproved of his descendant's every action: allowing non-Sedgwicks to live under the Sedgwick roof, letting in the press, writing poetry and reading it to the public. Some things didn't change.

Luke didn't emerge. Peggy and Bex looked at each other, concerned. Had he changed his mind? "Maybe you should go get him," Bex whispered, but just then, Luke entered and made his way to the front of the room.

He stood tall and confident. Unafraid.

"I do plan to read from my book," he said, his eyes on Peggy, taking a folded scrap of paper from the tweedy pocket of his blazer. "But I thought I'd start with a poem I wrote this afternoon. It's called 'Roses in the Snow,' and I'd like to dedicate it to my bride, Peggy Adams Sedgwick."

And Luke Silas Sedgwick IV began to read.

ABOUT THE AUTHOR

We're still disappointed about the chestnut. We were going to quit corporate America off that chestnut. I'd write in the studio my husband would build for me when he wasn't reading the newspaper and drinking coffee on our front porch.

Once again, the house got the last laugh.

We hadn't been living in New York City for long when, like many New Yorkers, we decided our lives weren't complete without a second home. Specifically, a Connecticut farmhouse, circa 1780, with a red barn, sloping hardwood floors, and ancient apple trees that still bear fruit.

The house is charming but challenging, like a crazy lover who won't set you free. It takes two hours to get there on the weekends, and when we arrive, something has always happened. The apple trees have dumped a dozen bushels of rotting fruit into the yard. There's a bat upstairs. A pane of glass has popped out of a window, the driveway needs to be regraveled, the paint is peeling. We've come to call the place the Great Big Hole in Connecticut We Throw Money Into.

A few years ago, the barn started leaking. ("That's what happens when you leave an antique out in the rain," my husband said.) Long story, but we decided, instead of just slapping on new shingles, to replace the whole roof, down to the rafters.

Along with the rest of the barn, the original roof was built from great wide boards you simply don't see anymore. New Englanders pay a fortune for old wood like this to use as replacement flooring in their period homes. So when our contractor mentioned he thought our roof planks might be chestnut, we had a brilliant inspiration: We'd sell them to help pay for the new roof!

We looked up vintage-lumber dealers on the Internet, figuring we'd make two or three thousand dollars. But as our research began, the figure crept up in our heads, from a few grand to ten thousand to twenty-five. Soon it became clear just how rare two-hundred-year-old chestnut planks are. Suddenly we were fantasizing wildly, *three hundred and fifty thousand dollars*, mentally paying off our mortgages and quitting our respective jobs to live the simple life.

The day arrived, and the vintage-lumber dealer came to our house. My husband invited him out to the barn, at which point the dealer explained that the wood was not chestnut, it was oak, and offered us six hundred dollars for it.

As our dream died, I thought I heard the house laughing—a faraway, lunatic cackle. It might have been the apple trees creaking or the floor settling. I'll never know.

But if anyone wants some nice antique oak, we've got a stack of it to sell you out in the barn.

Visit me on the Web at www.laurenlipton.com.

Lauren Lipton

FIVE SIGNS YOU'RE IN SMALL-TOWN CONNECTICUT

1 Your neighbors have a tag sale. (That's "tag sale," not "yard sale" or "garage sale.") You buy their old kitchen table for fifteen dollars. In ten years, when you tire of the table, you sell it to another neighbor. In time, he sells it to yet another neighbor. Repeat for a hundred years.

2 A couple shows up at the town's favorite breakfast spot in the summer. She's got a flashy handbag and high-heeled sandals. He, a sports car and a huge, shiny watch. The other patrons exchange sidelong glances with a meaning only those in the know can decipher: "This isn't the Hamptons."

3 Firemen are summoned to work by a siren mounted on a pole in the center of town, where its air-raid wail can be heard for miles. By everyone. In the middle of the night.

4 The fox that lives under your barn enjoys a possum dinner on your lawn. Mice stash seeds in your underwear drawer. Each spring, your living room is mysteriously infested with ladybugs. Eventually you stop noticing.

5 You moved there a decade ago and the locals still call you "the new people."

If you liked

MATING RITUALS OF THE NORTH AMERICAN WASP,

here are two more books that are sure to hit the **SPOT**

5 SPOT

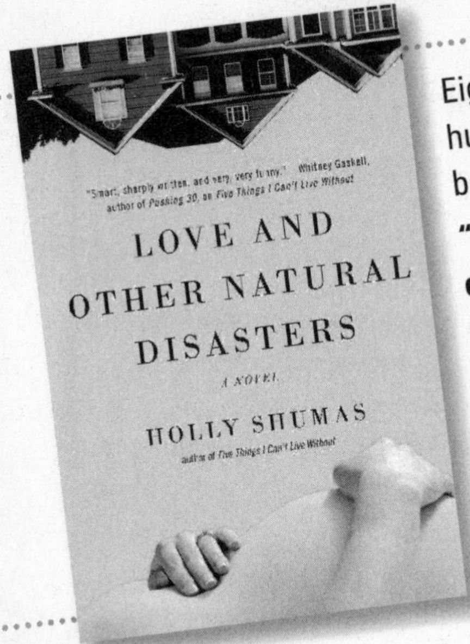

Eight months pregnant + cheating husband = an emotional mother-to-be with a tough decision to make.

"Anyone who believes that an emotional affair is harmless is in for a shock. Holly Shumas parses that tangled web of deceit with dramatic and heart-wrenching impact."

—Victoria Zackheim, editor of *The Other Women*

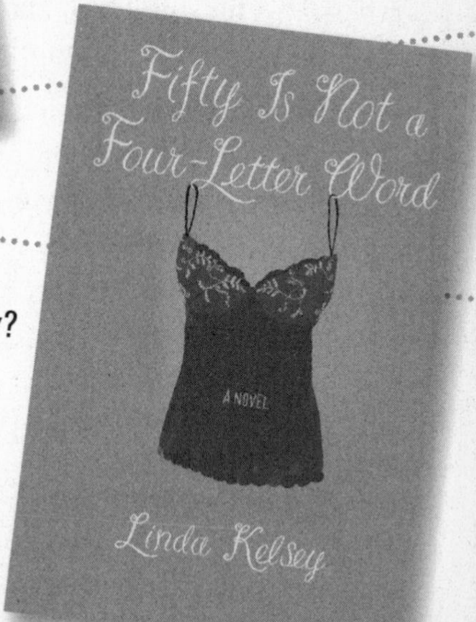

Can a woman who "has it all" at thirty manage to *keep* it all at fifty? Hope Lyndhurst-Steele is about to find out...

"Funny, wise, true."

—Wendy Holden, author of *The School for Husbands*